GIVER *of* WONDERS

ROSEANNA
M. WHITE

WhiteFire
Publishing

This is a work of fiction. All characters and events portrayed in this novel are either fictitious or used fictitiously.

GIVER OF WONDERS

WhiteFire Publishing
13607 Bedford Rd NE
Cumberland, MD 21502

ISBN: 978-1-939023-84-1 (digital)
978-1-939023-83-4 (print)

To my precious children, Xoë and Rowyn,
who inspired me to dig deep for the real meaning
rather than give up on the wonder.

ONE

Patara, Lycia

She would die today, one way or another. Cyprus Visibullis risked one glance over her shoulder without slowing her feet. They still pursued, those lecherous sailors, shouting words at her that would make Mater's face flush scarlet if she could hear.

Abbas, though—Abbas's flush would not just be over the sailors chasing her. It would be over his youngest daughter having ventured to the port to begin with. Never mind she had been waiting for *him*. He would see only the disobedience.

"Get back here, girl! We only want to talk!"

A shiver spurred her onward, faster. Abbas would kill her if the sailors did not. Or worse, sit her down and lecture her about how fleeting was a woman's virtue. Threaten to keep her from worshipping with Mater and the twins, since it apparently did her no good. Ask for the millionth time why she could not be more like her sisters.

"We intend you no harm!" one of the sailors shouted, though it ended with a laugh that knotted her belly. "Come, pretty one, stop running! We will give you the life of a queen!"

She darted around a corner and prayed to the Lord of heaven

and earth that the sailors were not from Patara. That they would not know the streets and alleys as she did. And that God himself would strike her dead before he allowed those men to put hands on her.

How many times had her father warned her never to venture to this part of town on her own? How many times had he lifted a lock of her red hair and called it a curse? Strangers would steal her away, he had always warned her. Steal her and sell her into slavery at Rome—because no one the empire over was worth more as a slave in Rome than a redhead.

Tears burned the backs of her eyes. She would not cry, not now. But oh, when it was all over and she had escaped them—*please, Lord God!*—she may just curl up in a corner of her bedchamber at home and give in to that urge. Let the shaking come. Even let Alexandria and Rhoda fuss and croon and call her their little honey pot.

The thundering footsteps behind her held up, and harsh whispers slicked over her. She could not make them out, but she did not have to. The alley ahead forked, went around a building, joined together again. The sailors must know that, must be planning to split up and surround her. They obviously *did* know Patara as well as she.

Her throat went tight with all the things she could not afford to feel yet. She should bang on a door. Beg help from someone.

But no one in this section of town would help her. Everyone here knew her by sight, and none would give her aid—not being Abbas's daughter as she was. Perhaps if he were here to invoke fear...but alone? No. They would say it served the merchant right to lose a daughter when he had shown no mercy to any of them in their times of need. That it was high time the stone-hearted Dorus Visibullis lose something precious to him.

Perhaps, just perhaps there were a few Christians among the

poor in this neighborhood. They may help. But they did not know her either and always viewed her family with suspicion. Because why, if they were believers as they claimed, did they not gather with the brethren in fellowship?

No, no help would lay behind any of these doors.

She sniffed back the tears and latched her gaze upon a stack of wooden crates just ahead. Her family would not lose her. Not today, not to a bunch of seafaring slavers. Perhaps their legs were longer, their arms stronger, but she had youth and agility on her side. Rhoda kept warning that when her womanly curves began to develop, she would slow. But not today.

Cyprus scrabbled up the crates, latched hold of the roof, and kicked the stack over as she hauled herself up. If the curse from behind her were any indication, the sailor was not so good at scaling walls. And restacking the crates would take time. Time she would use to speed away. Pausing only long enough to stick out her tongue at him, she flew over the flat rooftop.

At least the houses around here were close together, their walls all but touching. At the edge of one roof she could simply jump to the next. And the next, and the next. The fourth one was higher than the others, but she managed that too. A crisscrossing alley loomed ahead though. Narrow, but still. If she jumped, could she make it? Did she dare?

"You think you can get away from us so easily?" The second sailor had run alongside the houses, and a glance downward showed a countenance dark with evil. "He will be behind you in a moment, and what will you do? Grow wings and fly away?"

Part of her wanted to stomp a foot and fold her arms over her chest, as she would have done a year ago. But she was not a child of eleven anymore. She was twelve—almost a woman. Beyond such petulance. And she had no time for it, regardless. She would not even pause to shout down, "Do you not know who I am?

I am Cyprus Visibullis, daughter of Dorus Visibullis, wealthiest merchant in all Patara!"

Her father's name would not help her today. No, the only thing that could possibly help her was a miracle from Almighty God.

Perhaps he would lend her those wings. "Please, Father. Please help me. I know I am not always a good girl, but I will be. I will be, I promise you. Please just save me." She jumped over one last small division between the houses and sped over the final roof.

She had no choice. It was risk a jump or be caught by the men who would sell her so quickly into a life not worth living. Not daring to stop and think it through, she pumped her legs all the harder. Sucked in a breath. Held it.

And flew.

For an eternal moment there was only wind around her, beneath her. For a moment, she could imagine the earth falling away and the sun growing close. Soaring over the sea, the hilltop, the whole world.

Then her foot struck the top of the roof across the alley, her other followed, and she was safe. Her heart soared on, though, so swiftly that she nearly laughed.

Curses stained the air behind, below. But she dared not look back again. No, there was only onward now, and on still more. Running, leaping, scarcely even noting when one roof gave way to another, when the wider spaces loomed. She was a bird, a hart leaping over the hills, a dolphin cresting the waves. And she rode them until the rooftops beneath her feet changed in structure, until the dome of the church loomed ahead.

The harbor and its cheap houses were behind her now. Once she was past the church, the neighborhoods improved, and then she would have to come down. The houses would get farther apart. Then, home.

Her would-be captors were nowhere in sight. She had to stop. Find a way down. As soon as she crossed one more chasm, she would.

The air caught her again, and she spread her arms wide to embrace it. Tilted her face up to receive the kiss of the sun on her cheeks. Arced up, up, stretched out her legs.

No rooftop touched her extended toes. Just air, and it rushed past her too fast. Gravity pulled too hard. She was not…she could not be—*falling*!

A scream tore from her throat, but too late. The ground struck, the sky wavered. Pain shafted through her, so fast and hot it would surely kill her.

Then nothing. The pain, yes, an echo that made everything gray. But behind it, the strangest feeling of *nothing*. Eyes open, she still stared at the blue of the sky above her. The white clouds scuttled overhead. She tried to breathe, but her chest felt too heavy. Tried to move, but her arms and legs would not respond. She could blink, could cry, but could do nothing to wipe away the tears. "Father God…"

Did he hear her, up in his heaven? She stared up at where he should be but saw nothing except the endless blue and wispy white. No loving face peering down at her. No gentle hand there to catch her. Nothing but emptiness, mocking and cruel.

Why had he given her wings only to let her fall now, when home was within reach? Why deliver her from the sailors only to kill her here?

Her eyes slid shut. Perhaps death was better than the life they would have given her. Perhaps this was the Lord's mercy. His kindness. Perhaps—

Footsteps, loud and hurried. Two sets of them.

Tears choked her, pain blazed again. *Get up, get up!* But she could not. Could not move her arms, could not move her legs.

They would come, they would laugh, they would grab her and... what? What would they do to her? See her broken form and deem her not worth it? Or take her and break her still more?

"There she is!"

A sob tore out before she realized it was not the rough voice of one of the sailors. Masculine, yes, but younger. Its accents more familiar, more like this place that had been home for the last few years. The footfalls grew louder, closer, shook the ground beneath her, and then two faces blocked out the sun.

Did she know them? They looked familiar, almost. Maybe. Older than she, but by no means grown men. Were they among the boys who tripped and teased? Who stared with moon-eyes at Alexandria and Rhoda?

"She is alive." Relief saturated the tone of the boy on her right. He reached for something, lifted something. She saw her own hand in his.

But...but she could not feel it. No warm fingers gripping hers, no pressure, no gravity pulling on her arm. Nothing, she felt *nothing*. Her tears came hotter, faster. "I...I cannot...I cannot move! I cannot *feel*!"

Something shifted in the boy's face, moved from relief to pity. He glanced over her, to his companion. "Paralyzed?"

Paralyzed? No. No, she could not be paralyzed. She could not. What would she do? Burden her mother with such a child for the rest of her life?

But it would be short. Abbas may dote on her, may call her his little darling, but he would never suffer being the father of a paralytic. He would toss her to the streets, leave her to die. Set her out on the hill to be killed by the weather...or the hungry dogs. Ripped to pieces, snarled over...

She squeezed her eyes shut. Perhaps it was a blessing that she could feel nothing beyond the tickle of her tears down her neck.

"No." The second voice was so soft, so warm that her eyes came open again. She turned her head a degree to better look at him. No pity in his eyes. No sorrow. They shone a deep brown, steady as they locked on her face. "What is your name, little girl?"

Her lips trembled, the tears still clogged her throat. But she managed a whispered, "Cyprus."

"Cyprus." He smiled, touched his fingertips to her forehead, and her pain peeled back. Still there, but somehow no longer a veil between her eyes and them. "Get up and walk."

He gripped her hand, tugged on it…and she was on her feet, the stones of the alley hot beneath her soles. The linen of her garment brushed her legs. The wind caressed her arms.

Tears surged to her eyes, and she threw her arms around the stranger. "I can feel!"

He chuckled in her ear and held her tight for a moment before setting her away. "Of course you can. Yours is not to live the life of an invalid, Cyprus, not today. Yours is to know the power of God."

To know the power of God. She stared for a long moment at the stranger-boy and knew without asking who he must be. Not one of the adoring throng trying to win the hearts of Alexandria and Rhoda. Not one of the gang of boys who delighted in taunts and jests as harmless as they were frustrating.

Nay. She must be looking into the eyes of…of… "Wonder worker." The words came out in a whisper.

The boy took a step back. "Just Nikolaos. Please. God is the wonder worker, not I."

The second boy bumped a companionable shoulder into Nikolaos and stole her attention with a grin. "And his greatest claim to fame is, of course, that he is my cousin. I am Petros."

"Petros." Cyprus smiled up into his eyes, as clear as a gem, and then looked over to Nikolaos. He was the better dressed of the two, his tunic simpler yet of higher quality linen. His eyes were the same color as Petros's, but different. Absent the sparkle of good humor. Filled instead with something she could not name. Something that at once made her want to be better and despair of failing in that. She swallowed and lowered her gaze. "I cannot thank you enough."

"You need not thank us at all. Give your gratitude to the Lord." Nikolaos angled away.

Petros moved into her line of vision. "May we see you home, young Cyprus? The streets are not safe for a girl on her own."

She shivered, wrapped her arms around herself. That was a truth she knew now—and one she would never forget. "Yes, please." She fell in between the two boys, taking comfort in how tall they towered, how confidently they strode. How normal they sounded as they jested and teased each other over her head.

They did not say how they found her. If they saw her running across the roofs or heard her scream. They did not ask how she came to be doing so, or how she fell, if they had not seen it for themselves. They did not ask what had brought her out on her own that day or who her family was. They merely turned where she turned, their words a buzz in her head as they mentioned uncles and parents and bishops and something about Ephesus and the sea.

Cyprus could not convince her hands to let go her opposite elbows. Her stomach hurt. Her eyes begged for the release of tears. She wanted to curl into her mother's side and let the twins fuss over her. And yet...she also wanted to climb back onto that roof and shout to the world that God had healed her. That her nerves still sang with his glory. That her very blood felt charged with a song her ears had never heard.

She would get in trouble with Abbas if she told what happened today—but could she keep it to herself? Would that be a sin?

Darting a glance up to her left, to her right, she nearly asked her saviors what to do. They would probably be happy to tell her—men always were, were they not? But she could no more speak than she could let go of her arms.

Whatever consequences came, they would be hers.

TWO

It had been years since the heat had filled him quite like that. Years since he had felt that surge of Spirit in his veins. Nikolaos put one foot in front of the other along with his cousin and the girl, but his mind was still in that alleyway. On the knowledge that had filled him. The certainty that this girl was not meant to be paralyzed. That her purpose was to be well, that she believed she could be well—whether she understood already from Whom that gift came or not. That it was for the Father's glory she be well.

He had wondered, those years in Ephesus, if God would ever ask him to do something like that again. If something in Nikolaos had changed, to make it impossible for him to reach out and let the Spirit heal through his hands. If his faith had weakened as he grew up and learned how rare miracles were.

But they need not be. If ever he had doubted that, he would no more.

He looked at the road beneath his feet while Petros kept Cyprus entertained, and he sent silent, uncountable praises heavenward.

He followed his companions around a corner and looked up

into the afternoon sun with narrowed eyes. The girl led them down the most prosperous street in Patara—the very street his parents had lived on. The one *he* had lived on before their deaths six years ago, when he had moved in with Uncle. There, on the corner, was his old house. His step faltered for just a moment as he looked at it, as the memories swept through him. Mother, with her luminous eyes and ready smile. Father, with his deep laugh and gentle lessons.

He was nearly a man now—had gone away for his schooling, had just come back, was already a reader for Uncle in the church. He knew who he was, what the Lord was calling him to. But sometimes...sometimes he still awoke in the night and thought he was in that bed he'd spent his first eleven years in. Sometimes he thought the voices he heard in the hallway to be Mother and Father, laughing together. Sometimes he thought the missing of them would break him in two.

Sometimes he still remembered looking at their feverish forms, trying to heal them, and the cry that had wrenched him apart when he realized he could not. That it was not the will of God that day.

He flexed the fingers he had touched them with. No Spirit had warmed them then. And it had not since. Not until now.

Forgive me, Father.

God had spoken to him in other ways during those long years. He had heard his Lord calling him into service and had not doubted it. But the grief had been there all that time, a wall between them, and Nikolaos had not even known it.

Only now, with it in crumbles at his feet, did he realize he had drifted one crucial step away from his God.

Forgive me, Father.

When the girl between him and Petros came to a stop and tightened her arms still more around her middle, Nikolaos focused on the here and now again. Her current troubles were not something he could help. So he sent his cousin a glance that said, *Work your wonders.* No one could make people relax as quickly as Petros, with his quick wit and quicker smile.

And now Petros grinned and touched a hand to the girl's arm to draw her attention. "Your name is Cyprus, you say? After the island?"

She nodded, and the sunlight caught on her extraordinary red hair. When they had heard the shouts of the sailors and had seen the white-clad figure flying overhead as they passed through the alley, it had taken only a moment to realize what was happening. The sailors spoke with the accent of Rome—and they were probably all too happy to steal a girl from her homeland and sell her for a tidy profit in Italy.

"I..." She paused, cleared the catch from her throat. "We lived there when I was born. My father is a merchant, and we have moved throughout the empire. They had just moved from Alexandria to Rhodes when my sisters were born—twins. So one is Alexandria and the other Rhoda. I am Cyprus. Mater jests that she was about to insist they move only to places whose names she could live with saying day in and day out, but..." Her fair cheeks flushed. "Sorry. You did not want my family history."

Petros chuckled. "It sounds worlds more interesting than mine—I have lived in Patara all my life, as did my father, and his father before him. But for the years I escaped for school, I have never left it, and their stories are the same. We are Greek to the core. Where did your father grow up?"

One of her hands released her arm, though only so she could take a lock of hair in her fingers and worry it between them. "Philippi. Though his family came first from Rome. They scattered, if the stories are true, when the persecution of the church struck under Caesar Nero, and they have spread throughout the empire in the two centuries since."

"You believe." Nikolaos had not been sure her faith was already in the Lord. Sometimes God sent healing upon one of his children, a testament to their faith...and sometimes he touched a heathen, to draw him to Christ and redirect to him their existing faith in the dead gods of Rome. But a family that could trace its Christianity back two hundred years, to virtually the beginning of the Way—Nikolaos stood taller, smiled, and opened his mouth to ask if she knew any of their stories.

Petros burst into laughter. "Nik, you should see your face! Look at him, Cyprus—you mention Christian history, and he all but salivates. You have no doubt heard the tales of my cousin. How he was so pious from the time he was a babe that he fasted even from his mother's milk on Wednesdays and Fridays, and that—"

"Petros—"

"—when he was baptized, he stood upright—"

"I will hurt you if I must." Grinning the grin that only his cousin could elicit, Nikolaos dispensed the obligatory shove to Petros's arm.

His cousin laughed and turned his sparkling gaze upon the girl. "He no doubt finds it enthralling that a family with a long history of faith has settled in a town that had some of the earliest conversions to Christianity. And yet he is also probably wondering why we have not seen your family in church."

"Oh." She twisted her hair around her finger and drew her lip between her teeth, looking first at Petros and then at Nikolaos. "My father will not allow it." Here she frowned and glanced at the house across the street from where they stood. "He is not a Christian, though his family was. He says he will follow the faith of the Augustus Diocletian. Though he never worships Jupiter in our home, he just...he just will not worship God. But he does not stop us from doing so at home. So long as we do not do it publicly."

"Nikolaos's uncle is Bishop of Patara. His parents, when they lived, did so right there." Petros pointed down the street, to that beacon of memory on the corner. "Had they not caught the fever, you and Nik would have been neighbors."

Amusement lit her eyes, and her hesitation melted away in the face of a grin. "Lucky for you, Nikolaos, you left the street before my sisters descended upon it. Their life's work is to claim every young man in the empire as suitors."

His cousin chuckled again. "He would have proven himself a challenge—if his uncle has his way, Nikolaos will dedicate his life solely to the church."

It was not just Uncle's way. He could still remember the first time he had heard the whisper of the Lord in his ear, when he was just a boy too young to realize everyone else did not hear God so clearly. When his faith was so pure and true that it never once occurred to him to doubt that the Lord could and would do whatever his children asked of him.

The years in Ephesus, learning all the great philosophy both of his Christian family and his Hellenist neighbors, might have called Petros to the law, but it had only made firm what Nikolaos had already known. This was his calling. His purpose. He would serve the church. Follow in the footsteps of the apostle and live a life unfettered by a wife and the concerns of a home. To go wherever the Lord led him, whenever he beckoned.

To be a conduit of the Spirit, whatever he asked him to do.

"The church is my home." Nikolaos smiled and waved a hand toward the house their young friend seemed reluctant to approach. "But this, little Cyprus, is yours. Your mother and sisters will be worried for you."

And her father, if that was who the hulking shadow in the

doorway belonged to. A man stepped through, out onto the street, glowering just as Uncle did when Nikolaos spent too long poring over a manuscript and neglected his other duties. That distinct scowl that bespoke worry and love, not just displeasure.

"Cyprus!"

She jolted, apparently not having seen him, and a smile warred with fear on her countenance. But after a moment's hesitation, she crossed the street. "You are home, Abbas! We missed you dearly."

With a glance at his cousin, Nikolaos followed Cyprus across the stone street, Petros now beside him. No whisper came to warn him that harm would befall the girl if he left, but still. He would see with his own eyes that she received no more punishment than was due a girl who had disobeyed her father's order. She had been injured enough for one day.

Her father's eyes smiled at her, though his lips did not. Then he looked to Petros and to Nikolaos. They were keen eyes, so dark a brown as to appear black—a far cry from the startling blue of his daughter. Keen eyes that noted Nikolaos's fine linen and went calculating. "You can imagine my surprise, daughter, when I got home and we discovered you were not spinning in your room as you told your mother you would be."

Red hair cascaded over her shoulder when she ducked her head. "I am sorry, Abbas. I only wanted to meet your ship."

He would have words for her on that—he must. Nikolaos would have, and he had only known her for a few minutes. But her father rolled back his shoulders and produced a smile that he aimed at Nikolaos. "I have a feeling I have you fine young men to thank for seeing my daughter safely home. I am Dorus Visibullis."

He held out a hand to Nikolaos. *Visibullis*...it sounded familiar. Nikolaos chewed on the name as he clasped the man's thick wrist. He would ask Uncle where he had heard it. "It was our honor. I am Nikolaos, son of Epiphanius. This is my cousin Petros, son of Theophanes, who was my mother's brother."

"Epiphanius." The glance Dorus sent down the street proved he knew the name, and to what house it belonged. "I met your father when business brought me to Patara, before we moved here. He was a good man."

Warmth swelled in Nikolaos's chest. "The best of them, yes."

"I was sorry to hear of his passing when I brought my family. I had hoped—but never mind that." Dorus renewed his smile and motioned them toward the door. "Come, let me repay your kindness with refreshment, and you can tell me how you found my wandering darling where she ought not to have been."

It was on the tip of Nikolaos's tongue to beg off—Uncle was expecting him back, and he wanted some time in the quiet of his chamber to pray and let this afternoon sink in—but he made the mistake of looking down into Cyprus's face. She had her hands clasped in front of her, her blue eyes wide and pleading. No doubt she would want the buffer of guests between her and her father's anger as long as possible.

Beside him, Petros's lips twitched into a grin. No doubt at her silent begging. Nikolaos drew in a breath and nodded. "It would be our delight." Except that, as he followed the two into their home, he had the distinct impression that something had just shifted in the fabric of his life, something other than realizing the Spirit would still move through him.

He very nearly spun and ran out again.

"Cyprus. Come."

Cyprus looked up from the cloth on her bed that she had been studying with far more attention than it really needed. Mater stood in the doorway to the room Cyprus shared with the twins. She wore a smile that said, *Do not be afraid.* She held out a hand that said, *Trust me.*

But Cyprus still trembled at the thought of what Abbas might say now that their guests had left.

She slid off the mattress though and eased her way across the floor. Put her trembling fingers into her mother's.

Calm settled over her, starting at Mater's fingers and working its way through Cyprus until it stilled the quaking. She looked up the few inches that remained between her own height and her mother's.

Mater smiled at her and squeezed her fingers. She was so beautiful—the twins had inherited her looks. The lovely dark hair, the gleaming brown eyes, the flawless olive skin and almond-shaped eyes rimmed with blackest lashes. But mostly when Cyprus looked at her mother, she saw not the beauty but the love.

It shone now, radiating off her as she slid her arm around Cyprus's shoulders. "You took a risk today, my sweet, that you ought not to have taken."

The quiet words pierced more than Abbas's ranting and roaring possibly could. "I am sorry, Mater. I am. I do not know why I did such a thing."

She did—of course she did. She hated being confined always to these walls, unable to step outside but for into their courtyard garden. She had seen Aella go out, skipping along to the markets on some errand for Helena, no doubt, and she had thought, *The slaves can do what they want—Aella is no older than I am, and she goes about freely. Why should she enjoy what I cannot?*

But she had been a fool. She had envied her slave and had nearly ended up one herself. *Sorry* did not begin to cover the shame that surged through her. Her impulsive actions had very nearly been her destruction. First with those sailors...and then the fall.

She shuddered.

Mater rubbed a hand up and down her arm. "Your father is not that angry, Cyprus. He would have been, no doubt, had you not come home with that particular guest. But you will get off easy this time." She halted them, leaned over until their noses nearly touched. "Do not take advantage of the leniency. Do not think it permission to repeat this foolishness. Do you understand? This is a very serious thing you did."

Cyprus nodded, tears gathering in her eyes. "I know, Mater. I am so, so sorry. I will never do anything like that again."

Mater kissed her forehead and pulled her in for a tight embrace. "I cannot lose you, my sweet girl. It would tear me apart."

Cyprus clung to the familiar arms, breathing in the familiar scent of jasmine and love and Mater.

"Artemis!"

At Abbas's voice, Cyprus pulled away. Mater smiled when she heard him calling her name. Cyprus cringed. The twins always said she was his favorite, the apple of his eye...but she had her doubts. *They* never did such foolish things. *They* never conjured up his temper like this. Which was why he would no doubt ask her, for the hundred millionth time, why she could not be more like *them.*

The old rivalry chafed now. It did not fit, somehow, alongside this new song in her veins. *Forgive me, Abba God, for those thoughts.*

"Come, sweet one. His mood will not improve with the waiting." Mater took her hand again and pulled her down the corridor, into the main room with its familiar furnishings of the best woods, softened with plush cushions in bright colors.

Abbas, of course, was not sitting. He was pacing before the

hearth, his face in hard lines, his dark hair mussed as if he had run his fingers through it one too many times. When he faced them, his eyes snapped.

Not with anger. With calculation. Which was so much worse. He held out a hand and pointed at one of the couches.

Cyprus slunk to it, grateful when Mater kept hold of her hand and lowered herself to a graceful seat at her side.

"You are lucky. *Very* lucky, Cyprus, that the great Jupiter was smiling on you today."

Mater bristled. "*Dorus*."

Abbas rolled his eyes. Within a day or two, Mater would have reminded him that the gods of the Hellenists would have no place in their house—but when fresh from a voyage, his lips always spoke as his sailors did.

"Forgive me, my love." But his tone asked for indulgence, not forgiveness. He clasped his hands behind his back, eyes still doing whatever mathematics he had devised this time. "I have been hoping the son of Epiphanius would return from Ephesus. He is the single richest young man in the region."

Mater dragged in a long breath through her nose. "He is the nephew of the bishop, under his tutelage. From what I have heard, his uncle has had him give away all his inheritance."

"Bah." Abbas waved that off. "Nonsense. His fortune was too great to just give it all away in one fell swoop. The boy is rich. And just of an age where his uncle should be making marriage arrangements for him. How fortuitous that we have three eligible daughters."

"His uncle means for him to dedicate his life to the church." Mater sounded weary.

Cyprus's brows tugged down. Mater knew an awful lot about Nikolaos, for him having not even been in Patara since they moved here. And for the brethren keeping them always at arm's length.

Abbas scowled. "You insist on *Christian* husbands for our daughters, Artemis—why do you argue with me trying to find them?"

"I am not arguing about Christian husbands. It is the hope of my heart." As always, Mater kept her spine straight in the face of Abbas's tempers. "And that is why I have been asking quietly around ever since we moved here, trying to find suitable matches. Hence why I know that this particular young man is not one. His uncle will never agree to a union with *anyone*." Her gaze darted to Cyprus. "And I believe we have more important issues to discuss just now."

Cyprus pressed her lips together. Mater could have just let it go. Let Abbas focus on marrying off the twins. Why must she draw his temper down on Cyprus's head?

Because you deserve it. Because Mater is more interested in you learning to be good than in you being comforted.

She curled her fingers into her palms. Sometimes she wished her mother would be just a bit lazier about shaping her daughters' characters. Just a bit. Now and then. Or that she would at least let go of Cyprus's hand when she said such things, so Cyprus could just be *angry* with her instead of being too aware of the love behind her actions.

That strange song pulsed, stretched itself out inside her. Her fingertips tingled where they dug into her palm.

Abbas's brows drew down, too heavy, over his eyes. "Indeed. Tell me what you were doing out without escort, young lady."

Cyprus turned her eyes down to focus on her hand. On the perfect little crescent moons she had made in her palm with her fingernails. "I...I only wanted to see you, Abbas. I thought to meet you on the way from the port."

Stupid, stupid, stupid. Of all the places she could have run off to, that was definitely the stupidest.

"Of all the places you could have...Cyprus, how many times must I say it?" His shadow fell over her. Then he crouched, so that he appeared in her downcast vision. He reached out and lifted a strand of her cursed hair. "You are a beacon to those sailors. A treasure to be stolen. Worth far more than they make in a year. In *two* years, or even three. You would be a coup for them, if they got their hands on you."

She shuddered, the slimy voices of those sailors still echoing in her ears. "I know. I *know.* I was a fool, Abbas, and they nearly—"

"They? Who?" He stood again.

She tucked her chin closer to her chest. "I do not know. Two sailors. They saw me, and I ran. They chased me for a while, but I got away."

Curses blistered the air in two different languages, and a few dialects she had never heard.

Mater slipped an arm around Cyprus's shoulders. And reached up to cover her ears, as if she were still a baby who had never heard foul language. As if she could not hear perfectly well through her mother's fingers.

"Dorus, please! Watch your tongue around the children. I beg you."

"She could have been stolen away from us, Artemis!"

"But I was not!" Cyprus pulled her mother's hands away and surged to her feet. Fully aware of the miracle that allowed her to do so. Feeling, more than she had ever felt before, the way her weight balanced through her legs, onto the balls of her feet. The way the floor, the earth beneath it, pressed back against her to hold her up. "It was a miracle, Abbas! A true miracle of God. I was running and I climbed up onto a roof to get away from them and I jumped to another, and all was well and then I lost them. I did! I lost them, and I was just thinking I needed to come down but then I fell. And it hurt so much, and then…then it still hurt, but it was even worse because I could not move. I was paralyzed, Abbas. But Nikolaos—he came and he touched me and he said I should rise and walk and I *did*, Abbas! Just like the stories Mater tells of the Scriptures. I rose and walked and I…"

Mater stared at her with wide eyes, fingers pressed to her lips.

Abbas scowled. "What have I told you about lying to me, Cyprus?"

"But it is not a lie! It is the truth, I swear it!"

"Do not swear, sweet one. Your yes is yes, which is enough." Mater had stood too and rested a hand on Cyprus's shoulder again. She closed her eyes. And her face went…joyous. "I believe you. I believe you, sweet girl, that you felt the power of God this day. I can feel it in you."

Abbas made a scoffing noise. "She was obviously just stunned, Artemis. Nikolaos helped her up is all."

It was *not* all. She knew it was not. She had not felt—and now she did, so very much. And this song pulsing through her veins with her blood…she had never felt anything like it.

It was a miracle. It was God, the one true God, reaching down and touching her through that boy's fingers.

Abbas waved it away and turned back to the hearth. "Why would your God do such a thing? Much as I love you, Cyprus, you are just a little girl. The stories your mother tells you of such miracles are only ever about boys, or girls whose families are important and who need to be won over. And as *I* am not about to be won over…there would be no point."

No point. No point in saving her?

The song faltered. Disappeared behind…*noise*. Cyprus sank down to the couch. "But…" She had been healed.

Mater sat with her, arm still around her. Into her ear she whispered, "I believe you, sweet one."

Cyprus leaned into Mater's side and closed her eyes when Abbas started talking about marriages and matches again. And she tried, she did, to hear those beautiful notes of heaven through his words.

But his voice drowned it out. And all she could hear was that question, pulsing with every beat of her heart.

Why. Why. Why.

THREE

Two Years Later

Petros rounded the corner, somehow not surprised to hear the Visibullis door slam. And somehow even less surprised to see a flash of red before it was obliterated by a sapphire-blue veil. A smile twitched at his lips. Where there were slamming doors, there was inevitably Cyprus—though often with the slaves hurrying to catch up and the twins scurrying behind her, trying to soothe. Well, Rhoda trying to soothe. Alexandria preferred lectures and insisting upon reason.

Reason was not always Cyprus's strength.

But no sisters chased her today. His friend stomped her way down the street alone, not so much as glancing over her shoulder. Nor, it seemed, awaiting a servant to accompany her to wherever she intended to go. Were Nikolaos with him, he would sigh and shake his head and say yet again that she would find herself in trouble from which she could not be saved if she did not invest in an ounce of sense.

Petros jogged to catch up. "Cyprus!"

She paused, turned, and even smiled. Fleetingly. "There you are. You nearly made a liar of me—I swore to my mother that you were waiting outside."

And *his* mother would frown and tell him he made a fool of himself, always hanging about the Visibullis door waiting for Cyprus to emerge when Dorus had made it more than clear that it was Nikolaos he wanted as a son, not Petros.

There were worse things to be than a fool. He grinned and fell in beside her. "Well, we cannot have you being made a liar. What has you ruffled today? No, no, let me guess." He screwed up his mouth, squinted his eyes. "Alexandria called you 'honey pot' again."

"As a matter of fact—but I have given up getting angry over it."

"Ha! Since when?"

There was something inexplicably captivating about the way amusement sparkled in her blue eyes. "Since Mater threatened to take me with her to Philippi if I did not stop arguing with Xandria every moment."

A thought that did not bear thinking. Being a year or more apart from her? Petros shook his head. "But it is *how* she says it—as though you are a pet. Not like when Rhoda does it so absently."

Her very complaint, word for word, which she sputtered no fewer than a dozen times a month. His serious delivery earned him a throaty chuckle and her fingers tucking themselves into the crook of his elbow.

He loved her laugh. Loved the way it lit her whole face. Loved how, when it stilled, contemplation entered her eyes. He had not just watched her grow into a woman these last two years—he had watched her struggle to find her meaning. To discover why the Lord had done a miracle in her life only to have most of her family doubt her and her father declare it nothing but a way to introduce her to the richest young man in Lycia.

Not that Petros was supposed to have heard about that conversation.

And oh, the times he had wished she had not fumed to him about it. But then, she had still been a child at the time. He had come to visit, not to try to woo her but to see if the tale of her healing had perhaps softened her father to the faith. It was only later, more recently, that he had wished to un-hear about Dorus's matchmaking schemes.

She turned them at the corner, toward the main street of Patara. If they headed north, it would take them to the acropolis with its towering white columns and bustling agora. That was where the court building was, where Petros went now every day, with Father. He would argue before the judge for the first time next week. It was Father's case, of course, but he said Petros was ready. And the man in whose favor he would be advocating had agreed to let him try.

Cyprus pressed him southward instead, toward the sea, and lifted her face to the sunshine, which would no doubt tease freckles onto her nose and cheeks. He never tired of trying to count them, of wondering at the pale ivory of the skin beneath. Her sigh sounded happy. "I still cannot believe the twins are betrothed. That as soon as Mater returns from Philippi, they will be wed. For so long they have thought of nothing but who they will marry, which of them would secure the better match...what in the world will they talk of now?"

"Whose husband is the most doting, whose house the bigger, who has the laziest servants. And then, of course, whose children are the cleverest, the loveliest, the best tempered." His gaze tracked to the right. From here, he could just make out the start of the agora. And the school where the children of the region learned Greek and Latin, rhetoric, and the art of public speaking. Petros had excelled in the classroom, had excelled even in the higher schools in Ephesus. Studying the law had been a natural choice. More, one he already loved. And an advocate in the courts could earn more than any other profession in the empire, once he made a name for himself.

But it would not give him means enough now to make Dorus Visibullis look twice at him for his favorite daughter. It would not give him the reserves of gold that Nikolaos, son of Epiphanius, had inherited...and likely given away, though his cousin never, *never* spoke of such things. Petros knew of nothing that would provide him that much. And did not, as his mother warned him against, intend to spend his life in the pursuit of gold at the cost of his soul.

He wanted to spend it in the pursuit of family. He wanted to spend his days pleading for justice before a judge. He wanted to retire in the evening to a wife who greeted him with a kiss, to children who tackled him and wrapped their arms around his legs. He wanted to pore over a manuscript that Nikolaos had transcribed and talk over the fine points with his wife, with his cousin, with his father.

He wanted to do it all knowing that Cyprus's smile would greet him each morning, each eve.

But she would not want to talk of such things—she never did. Probably because her sisters spoke of nothing else and spoiled the topic for her. He nodded instead toward the theater on the hill. "A new play opens tonight, written by a fellow I went to school with. Shall I go and then reenact it for you tomorrow, line by line?"

Most of the brethren frowned on such things. They frowned on anything that the Hellenists did. But he had gone to a see a few of the plays over the years anyway, claiming he could not speak to his neighbors and try to win them to Christ if he was ignorant of the things filling their conversations.

It had not earned a smile from the bishop. But his parents had given in.

Cyprus laughed again, the sound of sunshine and birdsong. "Please, no more recitations. Last time I nearly died of laughter."

And he had nearly kissed her as she clutched her sides, her veil fell to her shoulders, and...best not to think of it. He settled for a grin. "Where are we off to today, since I am apparently cast in the role of your conspirator yet again?"

"Nowhere in particular." She looked up and down the street they trod, as if it were not perfectly clear where they were going. As if she actually considered angling them toward the shops with their colorful awnings and their multitude of merchants shouting their wares. "Perhaps the beach?"

She was the only young lady he knew who liked to leave the stones of the roads and let the sand get in her shoes. The only one, for that matter, who would remove her shoes so she could feel said sand between her toes. The shore was where the rabble went, hunting for sea creatures or useful debris that had washed up. Where sailors lurked. A place that decent folk, his mother said, avoided.

Petros had taken Cyprus to where the Mediterranean lapped against the sand at least once a week for the past two years. Better with him than alone.

They passed through the southern gate along with a few farmers and their carts. But where the others followed the road toward their farms, Petros and Cyprus struck out into the grass that would eventually give way to the sea.

Once alone, he looked down again on her beautiful, familiar profile. "So if it was not Xandria and her infernal 'honey pot' that drove you out in anger today, what was it?"

She was silent for so long that he began to think she would answer nothing at all. But no, once they passed a gaggle of children on their way to town with their harried mother, she drew in a long breath and tilted her face toward the sun again. "Father was talking yet again this morning about how a betrothal must be arranged for me before the year is out. How shameful it is for a family as great as ours to have a daughter with no husband promised."

Perhaps he ought not to have asked. "You are only fourteen. And your sisters' betrothals have only just been finalized—"

"But you know as well as I that daughters' betrothals are usually arranged long before my age. Had we not moved to Patara when we did, when he would usually have been finding husbands for the twins...they would have been married by now, and my future would have been decided long ago." She sighed and scrunched up her face. "Is it wrong of me to want more than a husband and family, Petros? To wonder if the Lord would have bothered saving me if that were all that was in my future?"

"All?" He heard the disbelief in his own tone too late to temper it. "I know you question your purpose, Cyprus, and you wonder at the Lord's workings—I know you tire of hearing your sisters go ever on about such things. But building a family, teaching your children of the Lord...is there any nobler pursuit?"

Another sigh, and with this one she took her hand from his arm. "Is there not? What of dedicating oneself fully to God, to the church, as your cousin is doing? I have heard of places where women do the same, where men and women alike vow to chastity and make the Lord's work their own. Where they feed the poor and care for the widows and orphans, where they study out his word. Would that not be nobler?"

The wind whipped, salt-tinged, the sun beat down, but he just stared at her precious, familiar face that he memorized over and again. "You have never mentioned this. All the times we have spoken on this subject, but..."

But he would lose her to Nikolaos even if his cousin refused to wed her? Was that what she was now saying? Was it love of him that made her want to follow him into his life's choice of work, or love of the Lord? Or simple distaste for all the expectations her father had put upon her?

Her blue eyes sought the ground, her hands fisted around the blue silk she wore. "I do not...I cannot...how does one know, Petros? How does one know what one is to do? If one should marry, *who* one should marry? Nikolaos speaks of hearing the Lord call to him—you talk of the happiness the law brings you, as nothing else could. The twins have never once doubted the path they were on, but I...I look at the future and see only the sea." She paused and gazed out at where the Mediterranean stretched before them, the shoreline still two minutes' walk away but the water sparkling in the sun. "Vast. Endless. Mysterious."

"And full. You cannot forget how full it is, and how life follows wherever it touches." He took her elbow, wishing himself bold enough to take her hand again, raise it to his lips. Pour out his heart. But he would only scare her away. "I cannot know what your future holds, or is meant to hold. But my friend, I *do* know that if you chase a noble thing for the wrong reasons, you will find no joy in it, and no purpose. You must seek God and do what he wants, not what you think he *must* want."

The ocean's breeze snatched at her groan but not before it made it to his ears. "But then, again—how do I *know*?" When she shook her head, a wisp of scarlet hair escaped its covering and blew into her face, and she was too distracted to notice and smooth it back again.

Petros tucked his hands behind his back to keep from doing it for her.

She kept her gaze on the water. "There is so little I can do for the Lord from my father's house. Sneaking out those couple times to help you and Nik distribute food to the poor is all I have ever managed. I have no allowance to give. No time that is not measured out by my father like a miser. I cannot even attend the church!"

"The church is the people. Not the building where we meet—and I daresay we will all be reminded of that if we continue to fall out of the emperor's graces and must revert to practicing our faith in secret."

She sent him an exasperated look, as she always did when he dared say something Nikolaos would have. Though heaven knew when his cousin spoke, she paid rapt attention.

Petros turned his face into the wind. It was not Nikolaos's fault that everyone hung on his every word. For that matter, Petros himself hung on his cousin's every word, so why did he expect anything different from Cyprus? Still. Was it so much to ask that she take him seriously too?

"The Hellenists in Patara hate me because I am my father's daughter. The Christians distrust me because we cannot join the fellowship. I have no money of my own to give for alms, or even to their businesses. I am not allowed to become their friend..." She finally caught the lock now blowing across her mouth and jabbed it behind her ear. "Or maybe they just do not like *me*. But leaving seems...it sounds so...promising."

It promised to tie his guts into knots, if that was what she meant. He scrubbed a hand over his face. "I cannot think why you persist in this notion that the town hates you. For the hundredth time, they do *not*." They greeted her with a bit of wariness, it was true. But for good reason. "It is only that you always act as though you do not belong here."

"So it *is* me." She turned wide eyes on him, glistening with sudden tears.

Petros turned his gaze heavenward. "No. Not *you*, just...listen, please. That day we met, when the sailors were chasing you. Why did you not bang on a door and ask for help? Why did you appeal to no one?"

He had asked her before. Then, as now, she greeted the question with a sorrowful exhalation. "No one would have helped."

"You gave no one the chance. And *that* is why the town holds you at arm's length—because you do the same to them. You do not give them the chance to meet your needs. More, you act as though you have no needs for them to help with, even when you do. Your sisters—they bustle about the marketplace, they trade what they have for what they want. They gossip, they laugh, they bounce babies on their knees."

Now she stared at him with mouth agape. "You want me to *gossip*?"

He lifted a hand, let the wind slice its way around his fingers. "To be involved, Cyprus! To give of yourself, of your heart, to open up—even if it means opening yourself up to the possibility of pain, of rejection. Unless you give them the chance to hurt you, you are never giving them the chance to love you."

Had Nikolaos said it, her eyes would have gone contemplative, she would have tilted her head to the side as if to let the words better trickle into her ear. She greeted the words from Petros with a glower and folded her arms across her chest. "No need to mince words, Pet. Tell me what you really think."

Not for the first time in their friendship, frustration boiled up, heated his blood. He loved her—but oh, how she could infuriate him like none other. "I shall." He stepped closer, close enough that he had to tilt his head down to look at her, close enough that she had to crane her head back to scowl. She hated it when he towered over her. Good. "You are not judged for your father. You are not judged for your sisters. You are judged only for yourself. Before God, certainly, but also before the city. If you but showed them what you show me..."

Then the world would love her as he did.

He spun away and marched the last few feet into the sand.

Night wrapped around her, soft and cool, but it did nothing to soothe. Cyprus rolled onto her other side again and heaved out a quiet breath.

It was not quiet enough. Rustling came from the bed nearest hers, and Rhoda's voice whispered through the darkness. "What is the matter, honey pot?"

Cyprus smiled into the darkness. Not at the name that drove her mad, not at the sister who at least did not use it as a way to make her feel like a child. But at the memory of Petros imitating her complaint in that way he had. "Nothing. Sorry if I woke you, Rhoda."

Rhoda—the younger of the twins—slid from her bed and padded across the tiles between them. Nudging Cyprus to the side, she slipped onto the mattress and snuggled down into the blankets with her. Were the darkness not so heavy, Cyprus knew she would be seeing her sister's mass of deep brown hair curling beautifully down her shoulders, her almond eyes shuttered by a sweep of black lashes in a perfect fan.

They were so beautiful, her sisters. Both of them with that perfect face, the ideal figure, the rich, deep coloring that never marked them as different, as other, as outcast. Why could she not have been born to look like them? A third set to their twindom. Another matching face. Abbas had told a tale once of three identical children that he had seen in a market in some far-off city. The twins had scarcely believed him—Cyprus had wished it were them.

Rhoda's fingers slid through Cyprus's hair in the same way they had done ever since she could remember. A gentle, methodical stroke that had been putting Cyprus to sleep all her life. She sighed. "I imagine you were over there dreaming of Hero."

"Is that what bothers you? Our betrothals?"

Did it? Perhaps a bit. Her sisters would be leaving, making their own homes. Their dowries had gained them the attention of the finest young men in the region...which meant that Rhoda would be moving a few streets over but Alexandria ten miles out into the countryside, to the largest villa between Patara and Myra. Perhaps it was nearby, but not near enough. Even that nearby house to which Rhoda would go was not near enough. "I will miss you." The admission whispered out to disappear into the darkness. "But I am pleased for you both."

Rhoda crossed a sigh with a hum. "It is practically next door. And Hero will give me more freedom than Abbas ever has—I can visit whenever I like, he promised as much. And Kosmas has promised to bring Xandria to town whenever she wishes. Certainly for church on Sundays. We will see her then." She levered up onto her elbow, her hand falling to the pillow. "But I do not like that Mater is leaving. Perhaps it is selfish of me, wanting her here to plan the weddings. Or perhaps it is simply the fact that we have never been parted, and though I know *I* will go soon, this is somehow different. That *she* is."

The same insecurity had been plaguing Cyprus. But Mater's father was ill and wanted to see her again before he passed. Who were they to complain about it when their reasons were solely selfish? "I know. What surprises me, though, is that Abbas is allowing it. It seems different from him going, too."

"Mm." Rhoda repositioned herself, and the moonlight seeping through the window showed that her eyes had slid closed. "At least he promised to stay while she was gone. We will not be alone."

By the last, her words had faded. Cyprus held still until her sister's breaths had evened out, then she slid from the opposite side of the bed. Abbas would probably still be up, reading. Mater would probably be in her room, humming a hymn and stroking her hair with a brush. She would not mind if Cyprus stole in for a few minutes just to be with her. She never did.

Those moments with her mother were the closest thing she knew to church. Even more than when the four of them gathered together each morning—Mater, Cyprus, Alexandria, and Rhoda—this was where she really learned of God. Snuggled against her mother's side, just listening to her stories. Listening to her musings. Not reading from the Holy Scriptures or the Didache, by discussing Clement or Polycarp or Ignatius. Just *being*. Together with the Lord.

Her bare feet made no sound on the tiles of the hallway, but still she kept to the shadows as she neared the entrance to their main living area, where Abbas would be. She saw no shadow from his chair, though. Heard no breathing. Had he retired already? She nearly scurried back to her room, but no. He had probably merely gone to the kitchen to sweet-talk a snack from old Helena or one of her daughters.

Except that, as she neared her parents' bedchamber, voices came from within. Hushed, but bright with feeling.

Alexandria would hiss that she ought to hurry away, not listen. Rhoda would say their parents had a right to a private conversation. But hearing her own name come from the room drew her feet closer instead of away.

"But Cyprus is younger than her years in some ways, Dorus, you know this. Please, just promise me you will do nothing while I am gone. She is not ready for a husband. Nor even for the promise of one."

Abbas grunted. "I can make no promises. If the bishop relents while you are away and a betrothal can be arranged, then I would be a fool not to act on it."

Cyprus's stomach went tight. Two years now he had been talking of marrying her to Nikolaos, but she could never wrap her mind around it. She liked him, certainly. He would be a kind husband, a good one. But Nik's thoughts were always on higher things than a mere girl. He did not want a wife. And if by some miracle her father *did* wheedle them into a marriage, Nikolaos would resent her all the rest of his life for demanding attention he wanted to keep focused on the Lord.

But Abbas never cared about that. Once Mater had convinced him to find them Christian husbands rather than Hellenist ones, he had set out to find the most prosperous Christians in Lycia, and nothing less would do.

Mater's sigh sounded ripe with frustration. "You will not convince him. Surely you know this by now. And I wish..."

Rustling came from within. "You wish what, my love?"

Another long exhale from her mother. "Dorus...you tread a precarious line, you know this. What if my father does not give me the inheritance? What will we do?"

"He will." Her father's tone was pure confidence...and a great deal of bluster. "He *must*."

A shiver raced up Cyprus's spine. She eased closer to the door, resting a hand on the wall for support.

"But..." She knew that tone from her mother too, but she had never heard it directed at Abbas before. Usually it was Cyprus she spoke to like that—begging, pleading for her to just do what she ought. "But my darling, you have made such promises. And if my father has not relented in his distaste for you, then what? What will we do? We cannot afford even *one* dowry such as you have agreed to, much less three—"

"Hush, Artemis. Leave the finances to me."

Money? All the air seemed to vanish from the hallway. Try as she might, Cyprus could not breathe. Could not move. She was paralyzed as surely as she had been when she fell from that roof, only now there was no Nikolaos there to touch her and make her well.

She had always half expected problems to rise in the family. Surely they were inevitable when husband and wife had such different views on faith and religion.

But *money*? She had always assumed...the way Abbas spoke, spent...but then, the signs were there, were they not? It had been years since he had slipped a coin to her or the twins. They had no allowance, nor did Mater. He said it was to keep them from frittering it all away to the church, but...

And he had been gone more and more over the years, off on new business ventures. She had thought. But perhaps he had been trying to salvage failing ones?

A dull *thud* came from within the chamber, along with Mater's muted, feverish voice. "I can*not* leave it to you any longer, Dorus! That is the whole point. You have made a mess of everything, have lived for years beyond our means, have borrowed from half the empire, and now you send me home to my father to beg!"

"Artemis—"

"How am I supposed to look him in the eye again? When he will see in a heartbeat all of your lies? Do you think it will appease him that you let me raise the girls as Christians when you forbid us all from the fellowship?"

"This again?" Abbas did not sound weary. He did not sound frustrated. He sounded disappointed, when by rights Mater was the one who deserved to feel so about that topic.

"You say that as if we ever even talk about it anymore. Has it not been years since I have *bothered* you with the topic?"

"After badgering me about how any husbands for the girls must be of your precious faith, you mean?"

A soft sound, like Mater setting something down. "Is it so ridiculous to want them to avoid the pitfalls of our early years? How many times did we fight over it? How much strain could they avoid by having that as a foundation?"

The ropes under the mattress squeaked. "I saved you. Do not forget that. While all your family and friends were running for cover when Valerian struck out against Christians, you were safe because of *me*. Because I was not afraid to bow my knee to the emperor and his gods."

"Oh no, you were never afraid. Never afraid to say whatever you needed to say, true or not. You were not afraid to lie to my father. To tell him you would never need anything from him. You were not afraid to go to my uncle and beg the use of this house from him."

"You think I *want* you to have to do this? By all means, if you know of another way to provide for our daughters—"

"It is for them I go."

Silence took over for a moment, so that Cyprus debated whether to stay or sneak away. She had eased a few inches back down the corridor when Mater spoke again.

"Dorus, you know I love you. But I am so tired of the lies. I am so tired of fearing it will grow worse, and worse again with every day. I will go to my father, and I will pray he does not see the truth, and I will assure him, if he does, that these matches are with fine Christian men. But I need to know that while I am gone, you will not be digging us even deeper into debt. We cannot afford a match with Nikolaos. You must relent. I want your word."

Cyprus squeezed her eyes shut. She had no memory of her grandfather, and Mater spoke of him so rarely...she had assumed it only distance between them. She had thought...was he even ill? Had he sent for her mother at all, or was this trip solely her parents' idea? To...to *beg*?

Silence hummed from within the room. Then the sound of Abbas dragging in a long breath. "It is a father's responsibility to see his daughters well placed. I cannot do that without promising good dowries. If I limited our offers to what we could afford, then they would be fishermen's wives. How am I to do that to them, after raising them to think the Visibullis name one of wealth and power?"

Mater must have sunk down onto the bed too. The wooden frame squeaked, and a quiet *whoosh* came from the feather-filled mattress. "He said your hubris would be our undoing. I fear he was right, Dorus. I fear—"

"Do not fear. Just do as we have discussed. Tell your father I made a daring investment, but the ship went down. Tell him your daughters are promised to some of the leading Christian men of Lycia, and that once they are wed, all will be well. We will never ask him for another piece of silver. And be assured that while you are securing their futures, I am securing ours. We will move to a smaller house so we can return this one to your uncle, like you have long wanted. Just us and Gaia and Linus—the other slaves will go with the girls. We will live simply. All will be well, beloved. Once the girls are married, all will be well."

Cyprus pressed her fist to her mouth to suppress a cry. Pressed, squeezed her eyes shut, and spun. Her feet were still silent on the tiles, but the hallway did not feel so familiar anymore. The house they had lived in for so many years suddenly seemed a rather austere prison, trapping them in a lie.

And why? Why had Abbas lied all this time? Spent more than he could afford, borrowed? How much debt did they have? How would they ever repay it?

Her hands shook as she stole back into the bedroom she shared with her sisters. She had known forever about the argument over God. Had learned years ago that Abbas had lied to Mater about it in order to convince her to marry him. Why had she never wondered if he lied about other things too?

Perhaps they had counted on having a son to help support the family. A son to earn, rather than daughters who must be given dowries. Cyprus slid back into bed beside Rhoda and let the tears burn her eyes. How must it have hurt her parents all these years to hear her sisters go ever on about marriage, knowing that the fine matches they strove for would just push them further into debt? How must they have felt at all Cyprus's arguments, fearing they would be saddled with her forever, unable to relinquish this too-large house lest she ask questions?

What foolish pride. Hubris, as Mater had said—or apparently, as Mater's father had accused. And her poor mother, having to face him again. To *beg*.

Cyprus curled up around her pillow and stared into the darkness. *Father God...give her strength to do what she must. Soften her father's heart. Let my sisters, somehow, be able to marry these men they so love. And...and help me to help. Somehow. Someway. Help me to be a help and not a burden.*

No peace filled her heart as Nikolaos always spoke of. But she could have sworn she heard the hair-raising cackle of an enemy out to steal and destroy.

FOUR

One Year Later

Nikolaos could feel the soft arms of a dream folding around him. He watched the earth rush away, the waters crash and wave. Enjoying the feel of the wind whipping over him, he tipped his face up and watched the stars wink and twinkle, noted that the moon was at three-quarters wax. His speed increased, salt from the sea stinging his nose and eyes. Nikolaos smiled and wondered if he could dive beneath the waves and then come back up to fly again. Wondered if, here in the dream, he could even breathe under water.

A chuckle rumbled above him. Pleasant, familiar thunder that shook the earth just as his father's laugh had used to shake Nikolaos when he sat on his lap as a boy. He smiled up at the sky and decided the swimming could wait for another night, another dream. Now he focused on flying faster and faster, following the bidding of the flash of light in the distance. *Come*, it said. *Hurry.*

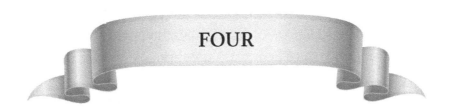

Beneath him, a sea creature surfaced and spouted, bathing Nikolaos's face with moisture. He laughed and called down a greeting to the enormous beast. Was it a fish like that one who had swallowed Jonah? Perhaps. It was monstrously large as it rolled up over a wave and back down into the deep, making him shake his head in awe.

What marvels the Lord had done in his creation.

Another glance showed him that the stars had vanished behind a black curtain, the rumbling laughter had turned fierce. The beckoning flash of light was now forked and vicious.

Still the same maker, the same creator. Still the same God, both in the gentle and the strong. And still that storm song drew him. Closer and closer to where the clouds churned. Farther and farther from his warm little bed in his safe little town. How many miles had he flown through? Endless numbers, it seemed. A day's journey, two. Perhaps a week.

Thunder and lightning tripped over themselves now, the waves crashing in a crescendo to echo the heavens. Salty spray soaked him from below, rain from above, but still he could skim the tops of the churning waves without faltering, without falling. Was this what the storm had been like on the Sea of Galilee when their Lord had slept in the boat? When his disciples had feared for their lives and awakened him? Was this how Peter had felt when he stepped foot on those waters another night, this joy at being able to do the impossible? Was this—

"Help! Lord God in heaven, help us—*help us*!"

Nikolaos pulled up, hovering over the water as it dove low, rolled upward again. There—a ship. He could barely make it out in the darkness. Barely see the outline of hull, of mast, of rail. He floated closer, until he could see the terrified face of the sailor who had called out. The man was lashed to the mast, his screams joining hands with the storm.

"Save us! Please God, save us!"

The ship rolled, a wave crashed, water washed over the deck. For a moment Nikolaos lost sight of the man. "No!" He lurched forward, ready to...what? How could he help?

Then the water washed away again, and the man sputtered. Wiped his face...and looked straight into Nikolaos's eyes. His went wide. "Holy saint—beloved of God! Save us! *Save us*!"

Save them? Nikolaos stretched out a hand, but the waves did not obey him. Why should they? He was not Jesus, nor Peter, nor Paul. He had no power here. Perhaps he could touch the injured and bring them healing, but that was not so big. Not so strange. That was faith joining with faith to affect a body. But this? The very forces of nature, of God?

He sighed. "I am sorry, friend. I am but a man."

The sailor's scream still echoed in Nikolaos's ears when he jerked awake. Anxiety rolled in his stomach. He was no stranger to the world of odd dreams, but this one...was the Lord trying to tell him something? It could not...it could not be *real*, could it?

Of course not. Yet still he rubbed a hand over his face, his hair, his tunic. Damp, but only from perspiration, not soaked through with sea and rain. *Father God...I feel uneasy in my spirit. Why? Please Father, give me your peace.*

It did not come. Instead, his churning stomach propelled him to his feet, and he moved to the banked fire in the hearth, stirred it, and borrowed some of the heat to light a lamp.

Was there a fault in his faith? Another wall between him and God, like his grief had been? He set the lamp down on his table, crammed to overflowing, a scroll tumbling over a codex and into another scroll. His eyes brushed over the Latin visible on one, but he felt no desire to read. No, he wanted only to figure this out. Slumping into his chair, he rested his elbows on the table and his head in his hands. *Lord?*

The chair was hard. The table simple. He had given up all the trappings of his wealth when he moved here to Uncle's home, attached to the church. "Not," Uncle had said, "because money is itself bad. But it is distracting, Nikolaos. And if we rely too much on it, we are relying not enough on God."

He had thought himself well focused on God. But why, then, even in his dreams did his faith fall short of the mark? He should have been able to calm the sea. Well, not *him*, but the Spirit could have, through him. Why bring him there, if there was nothing he could do?

"It was only a dream, blockhead." But still. Nikolaos rubbed at his tired eyes. Everyone knew dreams spoke from the depths of one's mind, of one's soul. This one must have been meant to shed light on some lack of faith. Why had he thought himself incapable of one feat of the Spirit when he was so quick to grasp hold of others? Did he really think that God could heal through him but nothing more?

But why? As he had observed in the face of the mounting storm, it was the same God, the same Spirit. Just as Paul said. The same Spirit both healed and produced miracles. Taught and discerned. The same Spirit welcomed strangers and spread the Good News. When filled with him, a child of God could do whatever the Lord asked of him. Anything. So long as one believed and kept one's eyes on him.

Nikolaos's gaze drifted over a codex and landed on a piece of torn parchment he had used to take a few notes on a text. His throat went tight. Words were not the only thing his hand had produced as he thought through the triune baptism. He had drawn the curve of a shoulder, the graceful fall of hair that was—in his mind if not his ink—red. Eyes staring from the parchment into his soul, lips just beginning to curve up in a smile.

He reached for the scrap and balled it up. It would never do to let Petros come in here and see such a drawing. His cousin already struggled daily with his love for Cyprus, with her father's disdain, with the fact that it was all Nikolaos's fault, however inadvertently. The last thing he needed to think was that Nik had any amorous intentions toward her.

Even if it was somewhat, occasionally, true.

No. He knew his calling. He knew what the Lord asked of him. He had known it since he was a boy, and he refused to question it just because a pretty girl lit a flame in his heart with her laugh. Just because his stomach went tight whenever she smiled at him. Just because he could pass hours in her company, talking of everything from the tides to the blasphemy of those whisperers who tried to claim Jesus was Christ yet not divine nor eternal. Just because he spent far too much time wondering what it would be like to touch his lips to hers, to pull her close and breathe in the scent of jasmine she most loved, to...

No. Cyprus was a dear friend, and that was all she ever could be. If ever he gave in to the desire to kiss her, it would change everything. Everything. It would hurt Uncle. It would hurt Petros. It would hurt her...because it could change nothing, even as it changed everything. He could not give up on the path he had long ago set his foot on. If he did...

If he did, he would never be happy. How could he be, if he turned his back on what he knew the Lord wanted him to do?

Perhaps that was all the dream had been about. His fear. His fear of falling out of communion with God, of putting his foot to the wrong path. Of not being able to act in the Spirit, if he were not walking in him. That must be it. No more, no less.

Still no peace came.

Perhaps the dream was just showing him his own distraction. Because he could not give God the full measure of his heart, of his attention, when he wasted so much time thinking of Cyprus. He had to align his thoughts. Keep them on track. Extinguish those errant feelings like the flame of a candle.

It should not be too difficult. He did not love her as Petros did.

Unfortunately, telling himself it was easy did not make it so easily done.

Sighing, he pulled forward a codex. He read for a while, prayed for a while longer, and finally blew out the lamp and fell back to sleep for the remaining hour or two before daylight. Then it was back up, prayers with Uncle, and...

He stood on the street outside their modest home, in the shadow of the church, and stared down the street. Petros would be before the courts today, pleading for a potter accused of theft. Their old friend Antipas was still in Ephesus at school. He could follow his uncle about church business, of course, and would no doubt end up there, but...

But his feet were already pulling him toward the Visibullis house. Not just to see Cyprus. But Hero would no doubt be there, and perhaps even Kosmas, if he were visiting town, as he often did. With only weeks left before they wed the twins, they could be found at Dorus's table more often than their own.

Kosmas he liked only marginally well, Nikolaos had to admit. Uncle had been muttering of his frustrations with the family of Gallus for years, but Nikolaos had made his own judgments...and found they largely agreed with the bishop's.

But Hero—Hero had long been a friend and become a dear one since Nikolaos and Petros returned from Ephesus. A smile tugged at his lips as he wondered what the young man—only two years his elder—may have found in the week since he last saw him. He was always unearthing some new scroll or another, engaged in some new study of Holy Scripture or the writings of the great fathers of faith from the previous centuries. He had obtained a pamphlet of some of Ignatius's writings last year that Nikolaos had never seen before.

Soon the familiar house appeared before him, and he was knocking upon the door. Dorus himself answered, and with a grin so wide Nikolaos wondered if perhaps Artemis had returned from her voyage with yesterday's tide.

"There you are!" The older man clapped a hand to his shoulder and ushered him in. "It is a good thing you showed up, Nikolaos, or Hero would have made off with them."

Nikolaos's brows tugged down. "Made off with whom?"

"You mean 'what.' Manuscripts! Come." A bounce in his step, Dorus led the way to the main living space and its long, solid table. Or at least, there was usually a table. At the moment the surface was invisible beneath the stacks and stacks of scrolls and codices. Hero and Rhoda bent over it, Alexandria sitting in a chair with her arm over her eyes, as if she had given up on the conversation—or perhaps on the hope that Kosmas would come today.

Nikolaos stared at it all in wonder. "What is all this?"

Cyprus stepped from the hallway, her hair gleaming scarlet and her eyes twinkling blue. "Father's Christian heritage—not that he cares to actually read any of it himself." She moved to Rhoda's side and picked up a roll of parchment.

Dorus rolled his eyes. "A ship made port last night from Philippi. Apparently my uncle has passed away, and he left all this with Artemis's father for us. She sent it ahead, though she says she will be but a week behind."

When Hero looked up, his eyes were blazing with discovery. "Look at all this, Nik. You will not believe it." He held up a scroll, opened about halfway. "A copy of Paul's letter to the Roman church."

Nikolaos sidestepped Alexandria and her chair and moved to his friend's side. His eyes widened when he noted the fading of the ink, the wear of the parchment. "It looks old."

Hero breathed a laugh and moved the scroll back up to the top. "Not just *looks*, my friend."

In the top corner, a date had been scratched. Nikolaos's breath fisted in his chest. "But that...so early? It must be..."

"I told you my father's family were among the first Christians." Cyprus gave him a cheeky smile and handed him the parchment she held. "You will find answers in this one. It is written by Benjamin Visibullis, who was born the very day our Christ rose from the grave. His mother was an eye-witness to the crucifixion, and he tells her story here, and how they came to Rome. How the church flourished, and how they fell out of favor with Nero."

Maybe he *would* kiss her—at least had they not been surrounded by family that would think it more than the exuberance that came of such a find. Which it would not be...much. But he settled for a laugh and clearing space on the table. Then feasted his eyes on the writing rather than the young woman who had given him the scroll.

I, Benjamin Visibullis, a bondservant of Christ, do write this for my beloved children. Fear not, dear ones. For though our future is uncertain and our church sure to scatter and hide, our Lord and our God will await us wherever we go. And we go with the sure knowledge of who we are and what he has given. Never forget the truths my mother and Titus witnessed at the cross that day...

A shiver coursed up his spine. The handwriting remained the same, but the tone of the words changed as this Benjamin told his mother's story, as if she were there dictating it to him. Word for word. "The words of an eye-witness..." He shook his head, awed. "It agrees perfectly with the accounts recorded by Matthew, John-Mark, Luke, and John the Apostle. Either this woman was indeed there, or she memorized every account put down by those other men."

"Impossible, given the dates." Hero edged closer. "They would not, in Rome, have had all the accounts by that time, only the one of John-Mark. But some of her details…they were seen in the other accounts, but not in his. And his was the first, correct? The others added their own memories and observations to it."

"Very true." Nikolaos read until his side grew warm, until the nerves tingled. And then he looked down onto Cyprus's profile. She studied the parchment too, from beside him. Just as intently as he did.

She was a woman of faith, strong if still not certain of all the *whys* of her own life. If he *were* to take a wife, there could be no one better suited for him. They could study together, serve together. She would not mind living simply, would she? She never seemed to care for the trappings her father gave her. But then, she had never had to do without.

And—no. No. She would study with him only when she could, but how long would that be? Marriage led to household troubles, to children. And while little ones delighted him like nothing else—such unbridled joy!—he knew well that being a parent was far more than patting a head and touching a hand to a broken bone so that it knit back into place. Parenting was every moment, every day. It was dedication.

He could not be dedicated both to a family and to the Lord. Not fully. Perhaps some men could, but he knew himself. He did not do well with a divided focus. He gave himself fully to whatever he did, and that left nothing for others. Cyprus deserved a husband who could love her completely, who could focus upon her. She deserved…she deserved Petros. They would be far better suited.

If only repeating it often enough did away with these errant thoughts. But how could it, when she went and did something so foolish as to tip her face up to his and grin? "Is it not amazing? I was hoping you would come, I wanted to ask you…" She read down the scroll but then tapped one of those first lines. "This

Titus he mentions. Could it be the one to whom Paul wrote the letter of instruction?"

"Hmm." Excitement pulsed at the possibility—could there be more original manuscripts in this collection? But as he read further down, he shook his head. "It does not appear to be. That Titus traveled with Paul, and we know from our history that he was then left on Crete to found the church there, where he became their bishop. This Titus appears to have lived in Rome during those same years."

She sighed. "Well, that is a disappointment."

A laugh slipped out, and Nikolaos very nearly reached for her hand. He settled for bumping his shoulder into hers and motioning toward the table with his head. "There is no room for disappointment amidst all this, Cyprus."

She titled her head as if debating his words before another brilliant smile bloomed. "You have a point."

Dorus chuckled from his seat by Alexandria. "If you ask me, the best letter in the lot was the one saying your mother will be home within days. That she is en route even now."

A strange feeling seized Nikolaos. Not exactly like the one he got when the Lord was impressing upon him the need to pray. Similar, but...but darker than that. More foreboding.

No. Please, Lord, forbid it. Forbid anything bad from happening to Artemis, I beg you! If it did—it did not bear thinking about. Cyprus had been so muted this year, with her mother gone. Worried for her, he supposed, or missing her. She had said often enough that her mother was the anchor of faith in their house, and this past year had proven it. He had tried a few times to draw Cyprus out, to get her to talk of whatever concerned her, but she would always just smile and assure him she was well, all was well.

Perhaps she had confessed more to Petros. She spoke more to him of her heart than to anyone else. He could hardly blame her for that—he did the same. Still...that uneasiness inside turned to a pang that echoed long within him.

An echoing pang that said everything was *not* as it should be. And that nothing he did now could change that.

FIVE

Another week. Cyprus rolled up the last of the scrolls that the men had been reading and darted a glance at her sisters. They were all but bursting with laughter and smiles, Rhoda playfully slapping Hero in the arm, Alexandria gesturing grandly about something or another to Kosmas, who had just arrived an hour ago—though he did not so much as look over at her.

Cyprus's stomach ached every time she watched those two. Though Rhoda seemed blissful with her betrothed, affection between Alexandria and Kosmas had shrunken rather than grown this last year. She thought. Or perhaps she simply did not understand such things. Perhaps this cool detachment was normal for some and spoke not of lack of affection but of...comfort. Security.

"Much happier than the letter that just arrived at my house." Kosmas directed his words to Alexandria but barely glanced at her. "My *brother* sends his felicitations on our betrothal. As if we need his approval."

Alexandria sent her gaze to the ceiling. "It is good of him to do, Kosmas. Expected. I daresay there was nothing condescending in the wishes."

"You do not know him. He is the personification of condescension, always lording over me all that his mother's family has left him."

Alexandria did not look inclined to comfort him. Should she not have been, if she loved him? Should she not have taken his side by default?

Had Mater been here, she surely would have known. And if something *were* amiss in the relationship of her eldest daughter, she would know how to put it to rights. A soft word, a guiding hand. All would be well for her sisters, and Cyprus would not have been fighting off this heavy feeling of doom for the past few months.

Or perhaps the feeling had been linked more directly to her mother's absence. Perhaps it was the fear that Mater's father would refuse to provide the dowries the twins needed. That she would come back empty-handed, see that Abbas had done nothing to control his spending while she was gone—had indeed spent a fortune on items for the wedding feasts—and...and what? What would they do? Her father would never speak of business matters with Cyprus, but so far as she could tell, nothing had changed for the better there.

If her grandfather did not come through...then they would have nothing. Nothing.

Then it would hardly matter if Alexandria were not happy with her betrothal—the weddings would never happen. Their fathers would forbid it, break the betrothals, and the twins would be the ridiculed everywhere in Lycia. *Please, Lord God. Please guard my sisters' hearts. Provide for them, I beg you.*

A warm hand landed on her shoulder, and Cyprus looked up to find Nikolaos by her side, his brows drawn. "What bothers you, my friend?"

She produced a smile and took a moment to be grateful that her father had not succeeded in convincing the bishop to relent on a match between her and Nikolaos. It would have been but one more thing to worry about. A far bigger concern than the current truth—that she would never find a husband at all if they were poor. She did not even know if she wanted one, so… She nodded toward her sisters. "We shall only have a month together after Mater returns."

Hero turned their way with bright eyes and grinned. "We should make an agreement to join together here for the solstice."

Abbas clapped his hands together. "A fine idea! We can celebrate Saturnalia together—"

"I believe you mean that we will celebrate the birth of Christ." Hero, it seemed, never had trouble arguing with Abbas. Nor would his father, if it came down to calling off the wedding.

Abbas made a scoffing sound and poured himself another glass of wine. "You cannot even be sure of when the man was born."

"We can be sure enough. We know when he was killed."

Her father swallowed and sighed, regarding his future son with impatience. "And what has that to do with anything, Hero?"

Hero motioned to Nikolaos. "Explain it, Nik."

Cyprus reached for another open scroll and carefully rolled it back up. Hero always deferred explanation to Nikolaos, when he was there. Without question, he had the best understanding of matters of the faith, having dedicated his life to them. Without question, he intended to *keep* dedicating his life to them. Why could Abbas not leave it at that? Put a halt to the infernal matchmaking schemes that made her feel a little more awkward around her friend after each attempt to persuade the bishop?

Nikolaos grinned. "It is simple enough, Dorus. Passover, and therefore the execution of the Christ, was on 14 Nisan—the spring equinox. As everyone knows, the most important men in history live a full number of years, with life beginning and ending on the same day so—"

"We know that, do we?" Dorus snorted and set his chalice aside. "Ridiculous."

"It is a well-established tradition. And why not?" Nikolaos, looking confident as could be, slid away from Cyprus and gestured toward the heavens. "A God who ordered the heavens just so, who aligned the stars, who created all we see that bears testament to him, can obviously order it such that there is symmetry and order to the life of men as well."

Her father sent his eyes heavenward but certainly not in awe of the logic. "Fanciful nonsense."

"Then you will dismiss all the claims of the greatest Greeks and Romans who claim that stars appeared to herald their births? Alexander the Great? Julius Caesar?"

Now Abbas pressed his lips together. One thing he never did was argue with an emperor—ever. "Of course not. I simply fail to see what that has to do with this argument."

"Everything, lord. If you will grant that God orders the heavens such that a star appears for great men, why not also grant that those of that level of importance to humanity and history can also be brought into this world and taken from it on the same day? Ours is a God of perfect symmetry, after all. One need only to look at a flower or seashell to see as much." Nikolaos lifted a shell from the mantle, a conch that Cyprus had brought home from one of her walks with Petros a few months ago. Abbas had not wanted it in the house, but she had merely grinned at him and put it there beside his favorite vase.

And remembered, every time she spotted it, the way Petros had held it to her ear for her and, when it failed to speak, had whispered for it. She could not recall now what his jest of the moment had been, but it had sent her into gales of laughter. Rare times, these days, with so little to laugh about and so much worry to keep her up long after her sisters fell happily, obliviously to sleep.

Abbas folded his arms over his middle. "So if I grant your point about them living in whole years—though I still fail to see why you would *want* to make that a requirement of great men—what then? Jesus of Nazareth was killed on 14 Nisan, so he must have therefore been *born* on 14 Nisan—"

"No, no." Nikolaos grinned and perched on the edge of his usual chair. "Life begins not at birth but at conception. Surely you know that too, with how strict Roman law is concerning saving a child at all costs during a birth, even cutting open the mother if necessary. If it were not yet considered alive..."

"Very well then. *Conceived* on 14 Nisan—"

"Which only makes sense," Hero put in, leaning onto the back of Rhoda's chair. "As it is also held as the day God created the world. The first day of spring, of new life. So certainly the day he would create the new Adam."

Abbas blinked, long and lazily, at the two young men. "There is no arguing with you on that, I daresay, so I will not waste my breath. So then he was born nine months later."

"Which is, of course, the winter solstice." Nikolaos grinned and waved a hand. "By the Roman calendar, December 25. Which merely by coincidence is also a festival in other cultures, like the Roman Saturnalia."

Her father hummed. "A happy enough coincidence. You all can do what you will to celebrate your rabbi's birthday, and the rest of us can enjoy our candlelight and gift-giving."

The shadows from the window touched her foot and reminded Cyprus to keep to her task. Petros would be by soon, and though he too would no doubt be eager to go through the scrolls, she hoped to convince him to take her for a walk first. No one else had been willing to leave the house all day, but if she did not get some fresh air soon, all the thoughts and worries swirling through her head might just smother her. She blocked her ears against the conversation still underway and set about stacking the scrolls in earnest.

To think that all these had been in her father's family for two centuries. Two centuries! Sometimes, when Cyprus listened to Nikolaos talk of the discussions the bishop had on matters of the church, it seemed it had all gotten so…official. Their parents' generation remembered what it was to worship in hiding, to fear for their lives if they clung to their faith, but in the intervening years it had become…easy. And with ease came rules. Religion. But had that not been what Jesus spoke against so often?

Faith was not easy here, though. The Augustus may not keep his foot upon the church, but Abbas certainly did.

There. Nice, neat stacks. They would have to find a permanent place for them eventually, but there was no point yet. The men were by no means done looking through them. She glanced back over just in time to see Petros through the window.

Slipping quietly along the rim of the room, she opened the door before he could knock and slipped out with a grin. "There you are."

He lifted his brows. They were dark, like his hair, but the eyes sparkling with humor could not rightly be called brown. Sometimes they looked it, flecks of them were…but sometimes they looked more green. Sometimes amber. And always ready to fill with laughter or warmth, as they did now. "Waiting for me?"

Because he offered his arm, she tucked hers through it and used it to tug him away from her door. "Indeed. You will want to go inside this evening—there are scrolls that Mater sent ahead of her, from Abbas's uncle. Hero and Kosmas and Nik have been poring over them all day. But I need an escape first."

Nikolaos would have had to think long and hard about whether to grant it to her or to follow his longing to delve into the scrolls. Hero and Kosmas had simply ignored the twins' pleas for a break from it all. Petros though—he did not even look over his shoulder with an astounded gaze. Nay, he merely patted her hand and grinned down at her, his feet following along without hesitation. "You know I am always happy to assist in that. Nik is there?"

"Mm. Though I imagine he will be running from the door in a moment when he realizes what time it is." He was always the first at the church in the evening for prayers. He said he liked those first quiet moments when only he and God were present, filling the room with sweet communion.

Cyprus tilted her face up to receive the sunshine. These were her vaulted ceilings, the world around her the only paintings she had to remind her of the stories from the Scriptures. And here, she could feel the Lord. Sometimes.

"So you had word from your mother today?"

"Yes." Joy tugged her lips up...and worry pulled them back down. "She said she is but a week behind this ship that delivered the trunks of scrolls. Though of course it depends on weather. Still, within a fortnight, for certain, she will be home."

Petros pulled her to a halt at the corner and looked down into her face in that way of his. The one that seemed to read her heart as adeptly as he did a Latin text. "Why is there shadow in you when you talk of her return, sweet one? I know you miss her."

"Yes. But..." She pressed her lips together, as she had done for the last year. Every time she wanted to speak of it all to someone, anyone. She could not. She knew she could not. And what was the point? Whatever was coming was already on its way. It was decided. Their fates, though still a mystery to them, were sealed. There was no point in speaking of it all now, when she could just wait a week and see the answers.

And yet now, stronger than ever before, the words came gurgling up. She had to speak. *Had to.* Now, before Mater returned, before whatever fate she had secured for them became known. She had to share with one other person this burden that had weighed her down so heavily all these many months. And there was no one in the world she would trust with it but Petros, whom she knew would make her smile, somehow, no matter what came of it all.

She leaned in close, glanced around to make sure no one was near, and pitched her voice as low as she could. "Things are not well in our family, Pet."

He did not look surprised by the pronouncement. "You mean with Alexandria and Kosmas?"

He had noticed the tension there too? Of course he had. Petros could make people laugh so well only because he saw them so clearly. "That is only part of it." She cast another furtive glance over her shoulder. "There is more. Mater…Mater's father was not ill. She went to him to try to convince him to give her an inheritance. Otherwise, Abbas cannot pay the dowries he has promised."

Petros's feet came to a halt, and his eyes went wide. "How can that be? Everyone knows Dorus Visibullis is one of the wealthiest merchants in Lycia."

"*Was.* Or maybe never was, I cannot be sure. Maybe it has always been a lie." She motioned toward the large house, wondering for the hundredth time how they had convinced Mater's uncle to give them use of it. Wondering how much Abbas had spent on all the items within. "He obviously had enough to create the image he so loves. But perhaps that is why we have moved so often. Perhaps his debts keep catching up with him."

"Cyprus." His arm loosed hers, but only so he could grip her hand. "This is a serious accusation you make against your father. Can you be sure?"

"I overheard them before Mater left." She tugged him onward, toward the edge of town and the insulating silence of the countryside. "And have done some poking around since. He has only the one ship left, Pet. The one Mater is on. And while a man can make a decent living from one ship—"

"He cannot make the kind your father demonstrates." Nodding, Petros looked straight ahead, and the muscle of his jaw ticked. He said no more as they turned onto the main road that came down the hill from the acropolis, barely managing a smile for all the people who called out a greeting.

To him. They made no effort to greet *her*, though she had tried, as Petros told her she must, to befriend the people of her hometown. She had asked after aging mothers and new babies. She had lent a hand when someone looked ready to drop an armful of goods. She had smiled until her cheeks ached. The only thing she had not done was spend money in the shops.

And that was not a choice so much as a necessity—one her sisters did not know. Perhaps beside them she looked like the stingy sister. Perhaps her neighbors saw only the expensive clothing her father insisted she wear and the contrast to the empty purse she carried and thought it a reflection on her, thought her a miser.

Or maybe she was simply not as likable as her sisters. Why else would she have no friends beyond Petros and Nikolaos while the twins had scads of them? Why had she never bonded with the other girls her own age? Maybe there was something wrong with her personality. Maybe that was why the only two people beyond her family to ever like her were the cousins who had saved her life.

She dragged in a long breath and let her gaze find the ground. It would not matter for long anyway. Either Mater got the money she needed and Abbas would soon pawn her off to some rich young man, or...or she failed, and they would likely scurry away from Patara and find some other city to call home, where no one knew of their slide from wealth.

Not until sand enveloped her feet did she realize Petros had led her to the shore. Sighing, she sank down into it and let it sift through her fingers. "What will I do, Pet? If there is no more money? My sisters will be devastated."

He acknowledged that with a tilt of his head. "Both Hero and Kosmas are well enough off that they do not need the dowry to set up house, they—"

"They are both well enough off that their fathers would consider it an insult and madness to *not* receive a dowry. You know how these things work as well as I. The only families who would accept them with nothing are those with nothing to offer themselves. And my father is far too proud to ever let his daughters marry into such a situation." She dug her fingers into the sand until she felt the cool touch of it beneath the sun-warmed surface. "I wish there was something I could do. Something to make it all work out."

Petros lifted her hand from the ground and wove their fingers together, not seeming to mind the damp grit that clung to her skin. "Because you are selfless of heart, Cyprus, and want only the best for them. But it is not yours to accomplish. It is in the hands of God, and you can achieve most by lifting it in prayer before him."

She tried. Oh, how she tried. But she did not seem to have the bent toward prayer that Nikolaos had, or these long-gone ancestors whose words she had spent the day reading. Her prayers never seemed to be anything more than a few words slapped together and directed upward. She knew not how to pray beyond that. She tried talking to the Father as these friends of hers did, but her thoughts always interrupted her. Or a sister would giggle. Or a dog would bark outside and distract her, and then she would find herself five minutes later wondering, worrying, working out a problem from the day on her own rather than waiting on the Lord's silent voice to fill her spirit.

She was no good at this. This living out faith, this making one's whole life defined by Christ. She failed at it every day. And then had to ask, every day, *Why did you save me, God? Why did you heal me? What good am I?*

"They could surprise you, you know." His palm warming hers, Petros bumped their arms together and kept his face turned toward the sea. "Hero and Kosmas. They could ignore their fathers and wed them anyway, even if the worst happens."

She could almost, almost imagine Hero doing so. But Kosmas? "They would not. Not at the risk of being cut off by their families. No one would."

Petros leaned back onto his elbows and tilted his face up to catch the rays from the low winter sun. "I would."

She jerked her hand free. "You would marry one of my sisters?"

His laugh was so quick, so robust that she knew before he spoke that she had misunderstood his claim. "*Them*? No." The laugh rumbled out into a chuckle. "But if I were in love with a woman, I mean. I would follow my heart, not my purse."

"Ah." Sometimes, when sleep would not come and her prayers clanged around in her head, she let herself wonder if he would ever look at *her* that way—but it would not matter, even if he did. Abbas would not approve, not as things stood now. Petros was not wealthy enough. And if Mater had failed, if *they* were not rich enough to secure the match he would prefer...then he would be too proud to admit it.

She took Petros's hand again. Alexandria had asked her last month if she had fallen in love with him. Cyprus had been able only to shrug. She could imagine herself at his side for the rest of her life. Laughing with him, walking with him through their days. But was that love? She had dreamed, a few times, of his lips on hers, had awoken with a pleasant heat in her stomach. But was that love?

She had certainly not liked, just now, the idea of him with one of her sisters. "And when will that be, Petros? When will you settle down and take a wife?"

"Soon, I hope." He did not look at her when he said it. Did not smile. Did not squeeze her hand. Proof that she was not the bride he dreamed of? Perhaps. She could never tell with him. Sometimes, when he looked long into her eyes or knew just what to say to make her laugh, she was sure he felt more for her than he would a friend. Other times…he seemed an ocean away.

He sat up straight. "Let us assume your mother succeeded in her reasons for going. She is on her way home now, and with all your family needs. What then? Rhoda will be happy with Hero, but what of Xandria and Kosmas? And what of you? Your father cannot hold out hope for Nikolaos forever, and we all know the bishop will not relent. What then? What is your father's plan?"

"I…do not know. Mater asked him not to make any move on my betrothal until she returned. I suppose we shall soon see."

"Yes." His tone, so very serious, lit a hope that maybe he *did* care. "I suppose we shall."

SIX

Unease had been gripping her stomach for weeks, and it did not let up any as Cyprus trailed the twins, a basket looped over her arm, into the market. Her sisters were laughing, joking, and inspiring smiles on all the shopkeepers' faces.

Most of their smiles faded when they caught sight of Cyprus.

What had she done to them? Why, *why* did they dislike her so?

It required all her focus to keep her lips turned up, or at least in a pleasant, neutral expression, as the twins laughed and bartered for fresh fruit, vegetables, and nuts. Helena or Aella or Enyo usually did the shopping, but the servants were all about other tasks today, preparing the house for Mater's return. The twins had been happy to volunteer for the task of marketing, and Cyprus happy enough to join them and get out of the house.

Perhaps she ought to have stayed home instead.

"Alexandria!" One of the younger shopkeepers waved a hand. "Come here! I found a headdress I know you will love. It will be perfect for your wedding ceremony."

Alexandria squealed and darted to the girl's table, Rhoda but a step behind.

Seeing the headdress presented with a flourish, Cyprus nearly groaned. It was heavy with gold, costly. Too costly, surely, even if Mater had managed to convince her father to fund their dowries.

The old olive oil peddler beside her let out a disgruntled snort that drew Cyprus's gaze back to her wizened face. But the old woman was not scowling her disapproval of the expensive headdress—she was aiming it at Cyprus and added the shake of a gnarled finger to her rebuke. "What is wrong with you, girl, that you cannot be pleased for your sisters?"

Cyprus took a step back, eyes going wide. "I know not what you mean. I am very pleased for my sisters—"

"Then a strange way you have of showing it. Always frowning at them, always looking about to snatch from their hands whatever they try to buy—they are good girls, about to become wives, and just because your father cannot find a man willing to take *you* is no reason to hate them for their good fortune."

The arm holding the basket fell to Cyprus's side. For a long moment she could only stare at the woman. Take in the maze of wrinkles, the dark eyes sparking with knowledge—and rebuke. The wisps of gray-white hair slipping from her head covering. Was that what *everyone* thought? Did Patara hate her *because* they loved her sisters and thought she did not?

She shook her head so hard her veil slipped off. "You are mistaken, old mother. So very mistaken. I would do anything for them."

The woman snorted again. "You think no one has eyes to see the truth? You are jealous of them, have always been. Why else would you try so hard to outdo them with your own match, to catch the wonder worker? But he is not for you, girl. If ever he marries rather than dedicating himself fully to the things of God, he would not choose *you*—a redheaded she-devil shamelessly dangling his cousin even while trying to steal his heart."

The basket clattered to the ground, but Cyprus did not bend down to reclaim it. She could not. Her stomach hurt, her vision blurred with tears, and her limbs went weak and shaky. "Eyes to see the truth?" Her words shook too as she stumbled backward a step. "No. No, you have no eyes to see the truth or you would—you would—" A sob tore its way up, and Cyprus spun, ran. Down the familiar street, around the corner, toward that big house that proclaimed them better, richer, more respectable. The big house that was such a lie, such a deception.

She slammed through the front door and wished Mater were home *now*, right this minute, so she could toss herself into her familiar arms and weep, knowing she would be comforted.

"Saints be blessed, child, what has gotten into you?"

She came to a sudden halt, though her eyes were too filled with tears to see the figure belonging to the voice. She did not have to see her, though. "Helena." The slave had been with them as long as Cyprus could remember, cooking and cleaning. Helena and her husband, her sister, their children. A family within their family. "Do you hate me too? As my neighbors do? Do you think me jealous of my sisters? Selfish?"

Helena's cluck sounded more frustrated than dismissive. "Where is this nonsense coming from? You are a loving enough sister, no more selfish than any other pampered young lady. Now clean yourself up before your father sees you—you know how he hates having a house full of female emotions."

Loving *enough*? *No more* selfish? Cyprus trudged toward her room, her head too heavy to hold upright. Her heart too heavy to let any more tears surge up and cleanse her.

It was not possible that their own slaves misread her as the oil peddler. Not Helena, who had been with them all her life. So then...what? What was she doing wrong? Was her heart not good enough? Did she simply fail at expressing herself? Or...or was she something other than what she thought herself? Perhaps all her striving these years to be worthy of the miracle Nikolaos had performed on her had managed only to stifle her, not to make her any better. Perhaps...perhaps she had missed the mark somehow.

Shuffling into her room, she closed the door and then slid down it so that she was staring at the wooden frame of Alexandria's bed. Her fingers caught up a lock of hair, tangled with it. Maybe she had thought herself special where she was not. Maybe she had thought too highly of her affection for her sisters—maybe what she thought was so big was really but a pittance compared to how *other* people loved. Maybe her heart was not capable of the depths of feelings others felt.

Otherwise, would she not be shouting from those fateful rooftops that she was in love with Petros?

Maybe God meant her to be alone. To give her heart solely to him.

If so, she failed there too. She never heard him speak. She never felt his nudge upon her spirit. She never saw her prayers answered or felt that calm assurance that they would be. She was no Nikolaos.

Her limbs sagged, so very heavy she could not bear their weight. She told herself not to wallow, not to pout, but the silent words did no good. She could not move. She could not convince herself to get up, clear the way for the twins, who would no doubt follow her back when they noticed her departure. She could...she could not move.

Laughter trickled out, weak and small. How many nights had she woken up in a panic, convinced the paralysis had returned, that God had retracted his healing? Sometimes she would lie there for what felt like hours, not moving. Afraid that if she tried and could not, then it would be proof that the Lord did not love her. That he had moved then only for Nikolaos, but that she was unworthy to keep the healing.

From behind her door came the slam of the one at the front of the house. "Helena! Helena, come quick." Mellos's voice—and her father's manservant sounded panicked. "Master, sit now. Just sit. It will—"

"It will *what*?" Abbas's curses stained the walls, punctuated by the crash of something large and heavy.

Cyprus jolted to her feet and pulled her door open a crack. She could see nothing down the hall but a shadow, slumped.

"Will sitting bring her back? Will it raise her from the dead? Put the ship beneath her feet again?" Another curse, violent and harsh, but no more crashes. The shadow slumped further.

Cyprus eased into the hallway, stomach churning. One step, two, more, until the shadow attached itself to the broken figure of Dorus Visibullis, hunched on the floor. He did not look up to notice her arrival. He did not glance at Mellos, who was picking up the shards of a vase, his lips tight and nostrils flared. He scarcely seemed to breathe, just stared at a spot on the floor, motionless now.

Everything within her screamed. Wanted her to turn and hide, close her eyes against the truth that her father's posture shouted. Instead, she gripped the corner of the wall. "Abbas?"

He did not look up. "There was a storm, Cyprus. The ship sank. Your mother is gone. Everything is gone."

Her fingers dug into the wall. Questions swirled before her eyes, making her dizzy. "But…she…are you certain? Perhaps they wrecked somewhere, perhaps—"

"No." Where had the fire gone from a minute before? Now he sounded wooden. Lifeless. "One man survived and was picked up by another ship. They found no one else."

"No." It could not be. It could *not*. Mater could not be gone. Through all her worry over whether she would get the money they needed, she had never questioned that her mother would return. She had assumed, *trusted* that they would always have each other, even if they had nothing else. "No."

Laughter punctured the pain, coming from the door still swinging open to the street. Cyprus looked that way, her vision foggy. The twins. Their good mood quieted as they paused at the open doorway, probably wondering why no one had closed it. Their smiles faded entirely when they stepped inside and spotted Abbas on the floor.

Alexandria gripped the basket Cyprus had dropped. Rhoda sucked in a breath. "Abbas, are you unwell?"

He did not look up. "We are ruined."

Cyprus swallowed when her sister looked to her. But how was she to put words to the unthinkable? She had to shake her head, swallow again. "The ship...the ship went down. With Mater. With everything."

The words seemed to echo, to grow louder, to bash her about the head until, in self-defense, she slid to the floor and covered her head with her arms.

Candlelight flickered, sending shadows dancing over the walls. Creating a golden glow that did nothing to lighten the darkness. Cyprus sat on her bed, legs crossed, knees touching her sisters'.

Alexandria held the tablet they had pilfered from Abbas's room. Rhoda a scrap of parchment and a reed pen, the ink sitting on their bedside table. "What about this house?"

Alexandria ran a finger down the tablet, went to another. Shook her head. "I do not see it anywhere, but his records are only for the last three years."

"It is surely worth enough to cancel the debts. If we can convince him to sell it..."

Cyprus squeezed her eyes shut. The debts—the debts were nearly as suffocating as the grief. In the three days since word came to Patara about the loss of their ship, creditors had been knocking incessantly at the door, convinced that Abbas had wealth hidden somewhere, and he ought to pay them with it before his resources shrank any more. They would not believe that there was simply nothing left.

And Abbas would not even rise to answer them. Mellos had gotten him to bed, and he had not budged from it since.

"He does not own the house." She reached a shaking hand to a lock of hair, wound it around her finger. "It is Mater's uncle's. He only gave us use of it until we marry, then Abbas and Mater were to move to a smaller place and return it."

They did not ask how she knew. Her eavesdropping had already been well established, and given the distressing truth, they had not even chided her for it.

Rhoda gripped the pen so hard she probably damaged the shaft. "We can sell what we brought with us from Cyprus, surely. The furniture. The vases."

It would not be enough. Not nearly enough. Cyprus drew in a slow, careful breath. "Perhaps contact this uncle? If he owns this house, he must be well off. Perhaps he will help us."

"Why do I doubt that?" Alexandria pinched the bridge of her nose. "I will find his name, where he lives. Write to him. But we had better prepare ourselves for reality—we will have to sell everything, including the jewelry we have been collecting for our dowries."

Silence overtook them, soon drowned out by the pounding of Cyprus's pulse in her own ears. "If you do that..."

"What does it matter?" Rhoda tossed the pen to the table, the parchment to the floor. "We do not have the amount agreed upon anyway. A handful of jewelry each, the promise of two of the slaves. Hero's father will never accept such a paltry offering. And so, if it is not enough, why keep it?"

Alexandria nodded. "We will get what we can from the sale. Settle what debts we may and ask the other creditors to give us time. Surely Abbas has other business investments somewhere. Surely, once he rises, he will help us solve this."

"And we will speak with Kosmas and Hero." Rhoda gripped one of Alexandria's hands and one of Cyprus's. "Perhaps…perhaps they will agree to wait for us to rebound from this. Or marry us anyway." Hope, fervent and fevered, dripped from her voice. And yet seemed to sizzle away upon the hot coals of reality.

Alexandria's gaze drifted away. "Why would they? Kosmas does not love me."

Rhoda breathed an aching laugh. "Of course he does! How could he not?"

"It hardly matters." Taking Cyprus's hand, completing the circle, Alexandria shook her head. "Their fathers will say ours lied, that the betrothal contracts are null. Perhaps…perhaps we should just do what Abbas apparently always did before—leave. Find a new city, one that does not know our story."

"It requires funds to leave, though." Cyprus squeezed their hands, holding on while the world surged and swayed beneath them. While the storm clouds growled overhead.

"And I will not leave Hero. He will yet marry me. He will, I know it."

Alexandria looked far less convinced of her own future, but no less determined as she said, "You are right, both of you. Leaving is no option, especially if money is as low as it seems. We will just have to stay here and deal with the consequences."

Words clawed their way to Cyprus's tongue, though she had been biting them back for three days now. This time, she could not. "What if there really is no more? If Abbas has nothing else to draw on? What do we do?"

Her sisters' hands tightened around hers. They exchanged a glance with each other, then looked back to her. Rhoda forced a smile. "He will come up with some plan. Abbas never lacks for a plan."

"He has managed this long with virtually no resources," Alexandria added. "He will find a way to do so again."

If they could stir him enough to get up. If he cared enough to try. If he did not consider life too bleak to bother with now that Mater was gone. Having seen that terrifying emptiness in his eyes as she tried to force him to eat a few hours ago, Cyprus was none too sure he would be any help.

She moistened her lips. "What if he does not?"

"Then... *we* will. We will find a way."

Alexandria nodded her agreement with Rhoda's pronouncement. Their matching faces wearing matching expressions of determination, they both squeezed her hand. Then Rhoda leaned over and kissed her forehead. "Do not worry, honey pot. We are in this together, and we will not give up."

"And so, if you learn anything else in all your sneaking about that affects us, you let us know. Right away. Do you understand?" Alexandria narrowed her eyes at her, though with all the sorrow filling them, she did not look very menacing. "No more hiding things."

Cyprus's throat felt too dry to swallow. "There was no point in all of us worrying, not when Mater was doing what she could to fix it."

"Was there not?" Alexandria straightened her spine. "We were spending this last year as we never had before, as Abbas had never before allowed. Had we known—"

"She tried to check us." Letting go her hand, Rhoda then

reached to tuck back the lock of hair Cyprus had been toying with a minute earlier. "We should have asked why. Instead, we ignored you. Now we will have to sell everything and probably take a loss on much of it. Everyone will know we are desperate. They will take advantage."

"No." Cyprus knew not where the faith in their neighbors came from, but she said it firmly. "Everyone likes you. They will want to help."

"Perhaps." Rhoda's smile was none too convinced. She let go their hands and slid off the edge of Cyprus's bed. "Regardless, tomorrow will be another long day. We had better get to sleep."

Sleep. It had evaded Cyprus, evaded them all the last few nights. As soon as she closed her eyes, the images battered her. Their mother, on the merciless sea in the grip of a storm. How frightened had she been? Or perhaps the Lord had granted her peace. Perhaps as the winds raged, as the waters roared, she had closed her eyes and sung a song, as she used to do for Cyprus when a thunderstorm sent her seeking solace.

Alexandria moved to her own bed too. "Good night, honey pot. Good night, Rho."

Rhoda murmured her response and blew out the candle.

The darkness came, quick and complete. *That* must have been what actually surrounded Mater in the belly of Abbas's ship. The lanterns would have gone out as the vessel tossed and rolled. Darkness would have closed over her. She would have heard only the pounding of certain death against the hull. She would have huddled in a corner, the two servants who had traveled with her no doubt there too. Sweet Gaia would have held her tight. Mighty Linus would have fumed at the threat he could do nothing to hold back.

A shudder overtook Cyprus. Pulling the blanket up, nestling under it did nothing to banish the cold. Linus had been Mellos's dearest friend, Gaia's husband. Gaia was Helena's sister. *Their* family had been ripped apart just as much as Cyprus's had been—but when she had tried to pull Helena into their circle the other day, the cook had rebuffed her. Pushed her away and hurried to the kitchen, wiping at her eyes. Hurried to the two daughters who had said scarcely a word to Cyprus or the twins in the days since. Mellos had greeted anything they said with silence as well, unless it pertained to caring for Abbas.

They blamed them. Of course they blamed them. Why would they *not* blame them? It was because of the Visibullis family that theirs had been fractured. And if they knew the real reason for their mistress's journey...

Then they would likely hate them. If not this moment, then when they found out. And they would find out. Everyone, everywhere would discover the truth of their situation soon enough.

Cyprus pulled her blanket over her head. In another fortnight, Patara would celebrate. Candles would be placed in every window, gifts would be given, laughter would ring through the streets.

But it would not touch them. Could not. Darkness lay too heavy over the Visibullis house for any Saturnalia celebration to pierce.

SEVEN

"Petros."

He paused and looked over his shoulder at his parents. Father sat at the table, his midday meal before him, while mother stood behind and to the side of his chair with a hand resting on his shoulder. Both wore a look he knew all too well. The one that meant a lecture was coming, and given that he had just announced that he was headed over to check on the Visibullises...

He sighed. "They are suffering. Would you keep me from giving what comfort I can?"

Mother looked down into Father's eyes briefly, as if for fortification. Pain shivered over her face. "We have said before that you need to guard your heart against what is sure to come concerning this girl, Pet. The things people are saying in the markets..."

"What things?" He turned to fully face them, to face the gossip, to face it all. "What things will people say of a family that has lost what matters most?"

"That is the thing." Father toyed with his glass, running his finger along its rim. He did not look up. "They are saying that Dorus Visibullis lost more than his wife when that ship went down. They are saying he lost *everything*. That it was his last vessel. That all the wealth he had in the world was on it. They say...they say the family is now destitute."

For once "they" had the right of it. Petros sighed again and lifted a hand to rub at the sore spot in his neck. He had spent too many hours working on his next defense last night. And too many hours after that begging God to show the Visibullises mercy. "That is all the more reason to support them. To help them."

"Help them? That selfish, arrogant man?" Father surged to his feet. Rare indeed it was to see anger on his face, but his jaw was clenched, as was his fist. "Dorus Visibullis arrived in this town ten years ago lording his wealth over us all. Forbidding his family from worshipping with the brethren, though they claim to be believers. Never lifting a finger to help anyone else, never—"

"They *are* believers. And they do what they can, when they can." Petros spread his hands wide. "Why should anyone judge them for their father?"

His father looked at him as though his sense had flown away with the birds. "Why should they *not*, when they can do nothing on their own? When it is in their name that Dorus acts as he does? When he has made it clear he considers none of us to be their equals? He is the father—he speaks for them all. Heaven knows none of his household ever speak against him. They dote on him."

"They love him, as daughters should. That does not mean they are blind to his faults and failings, and it certainly does not mean they share all his views."

Mother's fingers tangled in her garment. Her eyes were bright, the color of rich wood, and glassy with emotion. "How many more years of your life will you give to her, Petros, when she will not have you? When you should not want her to? She has nothing now. Nothing but her heart, and she has never given you that. Please, my son. Save yourself the heartache she will bring you. Better things await you in life than *her*."

His lips turned up. "There *is* nothing better than her. The greatest heartache would be not having her in my life. I love her, Mother. Even if she will never be my wife, my heart is hers. If it is a friend she needs, a brother, a comic to remind her that light burns on even in these dark times, then that is what I will be."

Exchanging a look whose meaning he did not know, his parents both pressed their lips together. No doubt they would un-press them soon, find more words to say, but Petros did not linger to give them the chance to speak. He nodded his farewell and pivoted back to the door.

It was time to find a house of his own. Given that he was still young and with no wife, no one had mentioned it. Were he betrothed, though...he would be preparing his own home, relying on his bride's dowry to fill it. He had been thinking for months that he ought to anyway, and this was his proof. He would operate in faith that his bride would come, as Nik always said one should when one prayed. His bride would come—even if she came empty-handed. He knew with everything within him that these prayers were aligned with the will of God.

His parents would question that. He had certainly wondered it himself over the years. But just now, all doubts fled. He would prove his love to her, now when she needed it most. And if still she would not have him, could not love him...then it would be many long years before his heart would be ready for another—years he would not be happy spending in his parents' home. No, the time had come to begin his own life.

And oh, how he prayed Cyprus would want to begin it beside him.

He had put aside his earnings since he took to the courts,

spending little. He had a bit over two thousand denarii saved. Not enough for a house befitting the Visibullises, but perhaps for a small place. If he purchased one on the outskirts of town, near her beloved seashore, there would be room to add on as his reputation as an advocate grew and his fees increased. He was making a decent name for himself, he thought. Crowds had begun to throng to the courts when he spoke, though the cases rarely warranted the attention. In part, granted, because nothing was so intriguing to his countrymen as a new word to hear... but hopefully it would turn to genuine respect. Hopefully, God willing, he could make a decent life for a family.

The sun warmed him as he traveled the familiar streets to the Visibullis home, even as a cool breeze reminded him that the solstice was just around the corner. The solstice, Saturnalia, the birth of Christ.... Petros frowned as he turned a corner. He should give Cyprus a gift this year. In seasons past he had dared only to offer a trinket, something to make her laugh—a small clay figure of a child standing on its head, a string of beads so long she had to wrap it five times around her neck to wear it. This year, he would give her something *real.* Something meaningful. Something to show her his heart. Something, perhaps, to make a difference in her life.

A chiseled-faced man was exiting her house as he drew near it, which gave Petros pause. He did not know the man well, but he recognized the fearsome Timon—the man always happy to lend money to those down on their luck...and who was known to charge so much interest that the bishop always mumbled about special eternal punishment waiting for the man's ilk.

Surely the girls were not dealing with Timon. Surely. He rushed forward, catching the door before it fell shut behind the monster.

The sisters all sat within, pale and wide-eyed, on the single crude bench left in the room. What had happened to the rest of their furnishings in the day since he had last visited? Brows tugging down, Petros closed the door quietly behind him and took a step into the room. "What has happened?"

Alexandria sniffed. Rhoda turned her face away.

Cyprus turned hers to him, her eyes gleaming with tears as she clutched her hands in her lap. "We have sold all we could. It is not enough. It is not—he had borrowed so much. So much, Petros."

His feet carried him to her without needing a command from his head. Kneeling, he took her hand in his and held it tight. Held it until her fingers curled around his, until she held on with all the strength she could likely muster, given the deep circles of exhaustion under her eyes. How long since she had slept? Really slept? "But Timon? Tell me you are not turning to him. Not him. He will—"

A frantic laugh from Alexandria cut him off. Her lips quavered, as did the fingers she pressed to them to try to still the panicked sound. "*We* are not."

"No." His eyes slid shut. Their father must have gone to the monster already. "How much?"

"Eight thousand sestertii." Cyprus's whisper barely feathered over his ears, but still it struck fear into his heart like a hammer would a peg.

Rhoda stifled a sob. "We will have to do as he suggests. We have nothing else."

"No." Cyprus gripped Petros's hand even tighter. "We cannot sell the servants to that man, he will—no."

Eight thousand sestertii. That equaled… Petros drew in a long breath. Two thousand denarii. He could cover this debt for them. It would leave him with only a few hundred—certainly not enough for a house, not of any size. But if his goal was really to prepare a home for Cyprus, then he had to consider her first. And she would never agree to marry *anyone* with such debts hanging over her head, threatening to consume her. That he well knew.

"No, do not sell your servants. We will pray. We will trust." He rubbed his thumb over her knuckle and dredged up a smile. "I promise you, you will not long be at that man's mercy." When he left here, he would go to the various merchant bankers with whom he kept his coins. It may take him a day or two to collect it all, but surely Timon had granted them a day or two.

And he would talk to Nikolaos. Though Petros's parents would object to his using all his income on them, Nik would surely understand. He would advise him in how best to pay off Timon, having more experience in handling money. It had been on his suggestion that Petros had placed all his coinage with the bankers, so that interest could be gained. He had wondered at the time if Nikolaos kept his own coins there…or if he had simply collected them from the bankers when his father died, to then give it all away. Petros did not know. And it did not matter.

With her free hand, Cyprus rubbed at her temple. Perhaps a headache formed there—or perhaps her thoughts merely bludgeoned. "I know not how we will escape this rising tide, Pet. Even if this debt is somehow wiped out, there are probably more. Every day new creditors show up, and Abbas…" She shook her head, and the pooling brine in her eyes overflowed and dripped a gleaming diamond onto her cheek. "We cannot convince him to stir. He will not eat, he will not speak. He will not offer any solutions."

"There *are* no solutions!"

They all jumped at the raspy, explosive voice. The girls wheeled around, but Petros had only to lift his gaze from Cyprus's face to see the haggard form of Dorus emerging from the hall. He had braced a hand against the wall, but somehow he did not look weak or worn as he supported himself. He looked furious, ready to shove the whole house down with one push of Samson-like proportions.

"Abbas!" Rhoda was the first to her feet.

Dorus held out a hand to stop her from advancing. Needlessly—his glare surely would have brought his daughter to a halt all on its own. "What have you done with all our things?"

Rhoda lifted her chin. Bolstered, perhaps, by the sisters who rose to flank her. "The only thing we *could* do to keep the wolves from the door. We sold it all."

In order to keep ahold of Cyprus's hand—which was paramount—Petros had to stand half-behind Rhoda. And so he noticed the slight tremor that possessed her, though he doubted Dorus would be able to see it from across the room.

The flare of their father's nostrils was his only reaction for a long moment. "You sold it. All of it. The only things we had left of her, and you—you—"

Alexandria did not quake as she planted her hands on her hips. "We had no money in the house. *None.* And you refused to so much as acknowledge our existence. There were men banging at the doors demanding to be paid what was owed them. What would you have had us do?"

Dorus opened his mouth, looking ready to rain fire down upon them.

Alexandria held up a hand much like he had done a moment before. "No. It hardly matters what you would have had us do. You were not here. You were too deep in your own pain to let us share it, and so you left us to flounder about on our own. If you are not pleased by our decisions, then you have only yourself to blame."

Hand pressing even harder against the wall, Dorus's face went red. "How dare you speak to me that way."

She raised her chin. "If you want the respect due our father, then perhaps you should act like him."

He pulled his hand from the wall only to slam it back. None of the girls jumped, though they pressed a little closer together and raised their chins. Dorus growled. "Is it not enough I lost my wife? Will I now lose everything else too? Will the vultures swoop down and feast on my carcass?"

"Only if you leave yourself for dead. Please, Abbas." Cyprus squeezed Petros's hand but then released it and stepped around the crude bench. "We need you. We are doing all we can, but we *need* you. We need you to mourn with us. We need you to help us figure out how we will survive now."

But rather than step forward, rather than grow angry again, Dorus's eyes went blank. His face lax. "I have nothing left." He leaned into the wall, his other hand gripping his soiled tunic above his heart. "Nothing."

Cyprus took another step toward him and stretched out her hands. "You have *us*." Her voice caught. And when Petros moved to the side he saw the tears making tracks down her cheeks.

Silence stretched until it pulsed and ached—until it wept along with her. Petros thought that terrible quiet might rip him apart… and then wished for its return when a heavy knock at the door shattered it.

Few knocks had been blessings these last days, and that made him ache too. Where was the kindness the town was known for? The Christian charity of the brethren that he had never doubted until now? He had truly believed that it was Cyprus's perception of her neighbors that was faulty. Apparently *his* had been. She was right—they had all been crowing and laughing about reaping what one sowed since news spread of the family's hardships. Not just the Hellenists, from whom he had expected it—even in the church.

Alexandria turned toward the door, more weight looking to settle on her shoulders with every step, until she all but stooped as she tugged the iron ring.

Petros winced when he saw the fathers of Hero and Kosmas standing there. Together. The two men were not exactly friends—one must have sought out the other to come with him.

This could not be good.

Hero's father, Mydon, was the taller, the broader, and he stepped inside with sorrowful eyes and a dim smile for Alexandria—the kind of dim smile that said he had no idea whether he gave it to his son's betrothed or to her sister. "Good morning. Is your father within?"

Alexandria moved to the side and motioned them in, closing the door softly behind them.

Dorus looked up, but his eyes remained hollow, lifeless. He made no move to fully enter the room. "It is all gone. Is that why you are here, to see if the promised dowries are still intact?" He shook his head, showcasing the matted, scraggly hair he usually kept so well-tended. "They went down with my wife. There is nothing left. Nothing."

The two visitors exchanged a glance, Mydon still looking so very sad, Kosmas's father frustrated. This time it was Gallus who spoke. "You understand, of course, that this changes everything. We accept that we are responsible for seeing our sons set up in a house befitting them, but it is you who are responsible for your daughters coming to that home with enough means to equip it and slaves to run it. If you cannot—"

"Would you pick the very sinew from my bones?" Dorus scrubbed a hand over his face. "There is no gold. None. We have nothing left but the four slaves."

The smaller man's chest puffed out. "You have this house—"

"I have not. It is my wife's uncle's. I daresay now that she is gone, he..." Shoulders slumping, Dorus sagged into the wall again. "Nothing. We have nothing."

Hero's father stepped in front of his companion and lifted a hand toward their broken host. "We understand how terrible is this blow. But I know you, Dorus Visibullis. You will recover. You will find a way to regain your stature. My son..." The man paused, smiled. "He spoke with me earnestly last night. He loves Rhoda deeply. He says he will wait however long it takes you to regain your feet."

Gallus grunted and folded his arms over his chest. "Foolishness, if you ask me. Kosmas will not be budged either, but I tell you this—he will *not* marry your daughter when your family is in this state. It would be the ruination of ours. The original agreement will be met or the wedding is off. Two slaves each, whatever goods and jewelry you see fit, and twenty-five hundred sestertii. No less."

"Gallus." Hero's father shook his head at the other man. "I will happily renegotiate the terms, so long as any new ones are fair to our children and sufficient for their needs. Hero is doing well for himself, but we all know how difficult it is to begin a life and a family of one's own. I will see them well situated. However long it takes to achieve that."

"And if it is never achieved?" Dorus pushed himself upright, a bit of that angry fire overtaking his eyes again. "You do not understand—you with your happy homes and burgeoning coffers. We have *nothing*! Less than nothing—I owe more than I can ever now repay. I have no other ships with which to earn more, and I have borrowed from every relative willing to acknowledge me. I have *nothing*!" He sliced a hand through the air stained by his shout.

Petros clenched his hands at his side. Cyprus didn't reply this time, but he could still hear her words echoing from before. He had *them*—he had his daughters. They were still a family. But if Dorus did not see that...

Even Kosmas's father shifted his feet, his expression softening a bit. "Perhaps we have come too soon—you are yet in the height of your grief. Mydon thought it would be helpful to know that our sons will wait for your daughters."

"As if anything can help us now." Dorus's eyes slid shut, his shoulders slumped. "We are naught. I may as well do the honorable thing and fall on my sword to spare my daughters the shame of such a father."

"No!"

So many shouted it at once that the word echoed in the empty chamber. Still, Dorus did not open his eyes to see what love—or in the case of the men, what moral compunction—prompted such an outcry. He did not even open his eyes when Cyprus surged through the space between them and wrapped her arms around him.

Petros edged closer so he could hear her whispers.

"You must not, Abbas," she said with shaking voice, holding tight to him. "It would break Mater's heart, surely you know that. Her greatest hope was that you would come to believe before you die, so that you may spend eternity in heaven with her."

Her father did not lift a hand to smooth away the hair that brushed his cheek. He did not hold close the daughter who loved him so well. He did not twitch a muscle at the mention of his wife. "There *is* no heaven, girl. Your mother is gone. A puff of smoke, vanished. In death there is only death. From dust we come, as your own book says, and to dust we return."

"There is more than that, Abbas." Cyprus squeezed him tighter. "Mater knew it, and so do I."

Now he moved, lifting his hands to settle on her shoulders. But he did not pull her closer. He pushed her away, his eyes opening to reveal those lifeless depths again. "You are deceived. You are all deceived if you believe such nonsense. What more proof do you need that your God is nothing? She believed, she was devout, she worshiped him with all reverence—and this is the reward he gives? He snatches her away and leaves her daughters with nothing?" Dorus shook his head. "If that is your God, I want none of him."

Gallus snorted. "Perhaps *you* are why he took her away. Have you considered that? She knows no pain now, but you—no doubt you are being punished for your pride, Dorus Visibullis, and for your lies."

Petros had to stifle the urge to give the man a helpful shove out the door.

"Enough!" Dorus pushed Cyprus away with enough force that she stumbled. Stumbled backward himself. "Get out of my house, you whitewashed tombs! I do not need you intruding on my grief and pointing your hypocritical fingers at me, as if I do not know where I have failed and when. But while I yet breathe, my family will obey me, and this is where I take my stand. No more mention of your cruel God in my house. Do you understand?" His cold gaze moved from Cyprus to Alexandria to Rhoda. "No more of your insipid songs, no more prayers, no more...no more!"

Rhoda brushed tears from her cheek. "Abbas—"

"No more." Pivoting on an unsteady heel, Dorus lurched back out of sight, no doubt to return to his cave of a chamber. A moment later the door slammed shut.

Cyprus shivered with the sound.

Mydon cleared his throat. "We will not intrude further upon you. Our condolences, girls. Truly."

Gallus stared at his companion as if he had taken leave of his senses. "How can you stand there so calmly, when that man has just declared his house must turn their backs on the Lord?"

"Do cease being such a fool, Gallus." Mydon turned toward the door. "He is angry and has no one to blame but God. And had no faith in him to begin with. But his daughters will not stop worshipping the Almighty Lord simply because their father said they must. Is that not so, girls?"

The twins gripped each other's hand, Rhoda putting on a shaky smile and Alexandria lifting her chin as she proclaimed, "Never. He can stop our lips, but he cannot silence the cries of our hearts, and they will beseech the Lord God without ceasing."

Petros drew in a deep breath, though it caught when warm fingers slipped into his. He looked down on the top of Cyprus's head as she leaned into his side, and he gave those precious fingers a squeeze. He wanted to assure her everything would be all right. He wanted to slip an arm around her and hold her tight until it all went away.

But all was not right. All was terribly, terribly wrong. And while he knew the Lord would not loose them from his hand... that did not mean he would not allow them to spiral downward until his will was realized, whatever it might be.

Gallus snarled. "Hear me, whichever one of you intends to marry my son. I will bring no heretic into my family—and the sins of the father are visited on the child. I was willing to overlook Dorus's lack of belief so long as he allowed his family's faith, but now? No. He cannot curse God without consequence, and that consequence will *not* be visited upon my house. Do you understand?" He looked from one twin to the next, obviously not knowing which was which, much less the one his son had fastened his heart upon.

Alexandria stood rigid and tall. "You are very clear, lord." Her chin remained lifted, her hands steady while Gallus turned and strode from the house.

Mydon, his face lined with apology, gave them a weak nod

and followed Gallus out, closing the door softly behind him.

Then Alexandria seemed to crack and crumble, slumping down to the floor and leaning her back against the splintered bench. Cyprus let go of his hand and joined Rhoda in crouching down to wrap her arms around her sister.

"He will never accept me. Glad as I want to be that Kosmas has not abandoned me already, it is useless. His father will never allow it, not unless ours repents and the dowry miraculously appears." A sob slipped out, then a sniff. She turned her face into the crook of Rhoda's neck. "But at least you will be happy. You will yet marry Hero, Rho. He will wait for you, and his father is kind at heart. He will take whatever offer we manage to put together."

"No." Rhoda smoothed her sister's hair and then left her hand on her neck. "We were betrothed together, we will marry together. Both of us, or neither."

"Do not be stupid. You will not forgo your happiness if mine is withheld—I will not allow it."

"Since when do I obey you?" Rhoda pressed a kiss to Alexandria's head. "Tell her, honey pot. Tell her we act together or not at all, all of us."

"No, tell her she will not suffer just because I do. She must take what happiness can be found, for both of us."

Cyprus settled her other hand over Petros's too, holding on as she never had before. When he looked down again, he saw her smile was far too brave to be honest. "You will both be happy. We will find our way out of this mire. We will. The Lord will deliver us."

He would. And Petros would do his part. First a trip to the markets to make sure they had enough food. Then he would find Nikolaos—and from there, he would begin the process of collecting his money. It would not solve all their problems, certainly. He had not enough to supply dowries for them, not on top of this debt. But that was the more pressing concern. He must keep the most bloodthirsty of the wolves at bay...*then* they could negotiate with Gallus and Mydon.

EIGHT

Nikolaos slid the codex back onto the shelf with a nod for his cousin. "Of course I will come with you." He should have gone before. Not to the bankers, but to Cyprus and her family. He knew he should have...but every time he tried, his feet ground to a halt and his palms went damp.

What could he say to them? *I am so sorry, my friends. I knew. God showed me in a dream what was happening, and I should have commanded the waves to calm, but my faith was not great enough.*

His fingers dug into his palms as his cousin turned toward the door. But then Petros stopped and pivoted back to face him, his brows pulled into a scowl. Rare, and all the more troubling for it. "What is the matter, Nik? Aside from the obvious, I mean. You seem..."

Dejected? Guilty? Unworthy of the call with which the Lord had filled his ears? Nikolaos gave his gaze the respite of studying the ground rather than his cousin's earnest face. Necessary, if he were going to confess his failing. And just now he needed to do so. He needed someone else to hear his sin and advise him in how to deal with its consequences. "I should have prayed for her. I should have...I should have saved her."

Petros's hand landed on his shoulder. "Nik—you were not there. There was nothing you could have done."

Nikolaos stepped away from the comfort he did not deserve. "I dreamed, Petros. I dreamed of a ship tossing about in the waves, going down. And I did nothing."

"A dream. My friend, you are not responsible for anything you did or did not do in a dream."

"But I *am*." Nikolaos passed a hand over his close-cropped hair, wishing he could wipe away the shame with the action. "It was not a normal dream. It was…it was something else. The Lord was showing me something, and I failed to see it."

Petros's sigh gusted through the room like a spring breeze, quick and cool. "Even so. Even if you saw a ship, you do not know it was hers."

That brought Nikolaos's gaze up—and a bit of angry life to his blood too. "Who else's would it have been? Who else would the Lord have shown me?"

His cousin gave a sorrowful version of his normal smile. "You think he loves others less than he did Artemis? If indeed he gave you this dream so you could save someone, it could have as easily been another someone. Another ship. Did you see her on it?"

No. But when he heard the news…it only made sense.

Petros stepped near again and rested his hand, again, on Nikolaos's shoulder. "Maybe you are right, and you could have calmed the waves. Maybe it *was* her ship. But maybe…maybe it was not, Nik. Maybe, little as we can comprehend it, it was her time. Maybe the Lord just wanted to show this to you, knowing you would not act, to teach you that you *could*."

Not could—*must*. If ever the Lord showed him something again, even in a dream, he *must* act. He could not bear this suffocating thought that someone—many someones—died because of him.

"Cousin..." Petros's hand fell away. "I am no theologian, as you are. But I know this. A man whose first response to a tragedy is to wonder if he should have prayed and could have changed it... he is a man after God's own heart. And God does not want you to wallow, does he? He wants you to go out and minister in his name. All the more for the times you fear you did not when you should have."

That much was beyond debate, at any rate. The Lord would not want him, even in failure, to hole himself up in his room and bemoan his lack of faith. He would want him out on the streets all the more, willing to learn and act and touch in the name of the Almighty God. Willing to exercise that strength until it grew anew.

Nikolaos sucked in a long breath and nodded. "You are right, cousin. I will tuck the lesson away and go forth ready to do better."

One corner of Petros's mouth pulled up. "If you were not my cousin, my dearest friend..." He shook his head. "I may have to despise you on principle. It is disheartening, spending all one's time with someone so much better than one can ever hope to be."

"You say as I stand here wallowing in my failure." But no more. Nikolaos took another moment to straighten the scrolls on his table and led the way out the door. "Come. To the bankers. How much will you withdraw from their hands?"

Petros made no reply as they stepped out into the weak sunshine. A silence odd enough that Nikolaos shot a look at him over his shoulder.

Petros swallowed. "All of it."

He could not help it. He halted, tilted his head, and knew the frown pulling at his brows wasn't nearly so rare, nor so striking, as the one Petros had put on a few minutes before. "*All* of it? Pet—"

"I do not need a lecture." Indeed, he stood straight, shoulders back, chin up. Challenge ready to be fanned to life in his eyes. "I need to help. My parents would not understand, but you must. The Visibullises need the exact amount I have saved. The exact amount, Nikolaos."

Logic he himself would have been quick to point out, were it anyone but his cousin ready to give up his life's savings. What could he do but exhale, nod? "Then it is for you to do, if the Lord stirred your heart. I will not try to talk you out of it."

He would instead be glad his cousin had an ear to listen, even if Nikolaos had not.

Petros strode past him, bumping their shoulders together as he did. "You are wallowing again."

"I am not." Nikolaos moved to catch up as his cousin continued along the street.

"And now pouting too."

Despite himself, his lips started to curve. They did not quite manage a full smile, but they had a start. It was more than he could say for the last few days. "I am reflecting. It is different."

Petros shook his head and clucked his tongue. "Making excuses now too? Next thing I know you will be cloistering yourself away altogether, and I shall have to make an appointment just to see you."

"Not I." A bit of peace, too long absent, breathed over his spirit. "That is not the life I am called to. Mine is to serve."

Petros sent him what might have been a grin, had it not looked so serious. "I know."

Neither said more while they walked to the nearest money house, nor while Petros waited to collect his coins from the banker who held them for him. They said nothing beyond reasoning which was the next nearest banker after that. Nor between their second stop and their last.

But once Petros had all of his gold in hand—one little bag, that was all—Nikolaos paused in the weak December sunshine to examine his cousin. "Will you give it to Cyprus or take it directly to Timon?"

"Timon. Cyprus would refuse it. Or worse, feel indebted to me." He gave the bag a little bounce in his palm, his gaze locked upon it. "If I can, I will keep her from knowing altogether. I do not want to gain her love with gold."

It should not make him ache. *Would* not make him ache. Nikolaos pressed his lips into a sympathetic curve and spoke the simple truth. "She will love you, Petros, because you are you. And because you love her as no one else ever could. It will have nothing to do with gold, whether she knows of it or not."

The uncertain smile that overtook his cousin was worth the ache. "I pray you are right. That she can love me. And yet I so fear you are wrong."

"I am not. Not about this." He nodded toward the street that led to the least expensive of the shops. It was above one of these that Timon worked. More than once Nikolaos had paused in the entrance to this alley, stopped by the sound of broken men muffling their pain. More than once he had approached them, seeing fractured arms and hands, wanting to touch. To heal.

But those men—the men who turned to Timon rather than God—they never had the faith. No, more. They never *wanted* to be healed. They would rather beg, borrow, and steal. And then hate the world for its cruelties. For those men, Nikolaos prayed for a change of heart. Prayed they would see other miracles and believe.

But those men usually chose blindness instead, closing their eyes to the movement of the Lord.

How Nikolaos feared that Dorus Visibullis was one of them. How he feared that he would sooner sacrifice himself and his family to his pride than ever humble himself before the Lord. How he feared what that would mean for his friends.

"Down here?" Petros shifted from one foot to the other. "Are you certain?"

"I visited the shopkeeper who works in his storefront, when she was ailing last winter. She mentioned that he works in the rooms above." Nikolaos motioned toward a basket weaver who sat with her wares.

"Right. Well then. Best to get this over with." Petros squared his shoulders and adjusted the light cloak he wore today, given the cool air.

Nikolaos motioned him toward the narrow side street. "The one on the end. Shall I go in with you?"

"If you refuse, I will hide garlic in your tunics again."

A laugh reminded him of how much he needed his cousin around him, day after day. "Well, with incentive like that, you can be sure I will stay at your side."

"I thought so." Petros gripped the little bag of gold and set off toward the stone stairs attached to the last building in the row of them.

There were no whimpering men outside it today, no one cradling broken fingers. Somehow that did nothing to put him at ease.

He murmured a prayer as Petros led the way up the unforgiving steps. Then put a hand on his cousin's arm to make him pause once they reached the slab of wood standing sentry at the top. He nodded out, across the low roof of the building on the other side of them. At the market stalls.

That was where they had been standing four years ago, when they had looked up and seen a streak of white, of red, flying overhead as Cyprus jumped from rooftop to rooftop.

Petros's exhale was long. "God led us there that day. At that moment. He led us to her. So you could heal her."

"And so you could come to love her and save her again now. Her and her whole family." The bigger gift, arguably. It had required no sacrifice for Nikolaos to touch her, believing. Just faith. Something that had always come easy to him, even if muffled by grief for those few years. Until that dream.

Petros grunted. "I should have reserved the garlic threat for your sulking. Do not put it past me, Nik."

Chuckling again, Nikolaos turned away from the street and motioned to the door. "Knock."

"I am." Though it took him another moment, another breath before his fist echoed his words.

Silence enveloped them, then came the sound of footsteps, of a bar being raised, and the door opened to a slender man in the garb of a slave. His wispy brows lifted. "Yes?"

Petros looked every inch the advocate before the courts as he raised his chin and looked past the servant. "Petros, son of Theophanes. I am here to see Timon."

"Let him in!" The voice boomed from the interior of the building.

The slave swung wide the door. Timon appeared to have been taking some wine at a low table, but he was on his feet when they stepped through, moving to greet them. "Petros, son of Theophanes! I have heard you argue before the courts. You have a brilliant career ahead of you. Tell me, what can I do for you?"

Nikolaos snuck a glance at his cousin, half expecting to see a flush on Petros's cheeks. But no—if the words flattered him, he gave no indication of it. His jaw was just as tight as it had been before, his spine just as straight, his shoulders just as even.

"It is not my own business I come for." He lifted his hand, held out the bag. "I am here on behalf of the daughters of Dorus Visibullis. To pay you what their father owes."

"Dorus Visibullis." Timon did not reach for the bag of coins. His face, usually set in hard lines that bespoke a life spent finding pleasure in others' pain, held its smile. He motioned toward the couches, the wine, flicking a gaze to Nikolaos as well...and scowling. "You. You are that Christian bishop's boy, are you not? What are you doing here?"

Nearly, nearly he stepped back. Not from fear, not even repulsion exactly. But much as he disliked the reputation of this man, he had not expected to feel such forceful darkness in his gaze. It took all his willpower to keep from grabbing Petros's arm and pulling him back out that door. *Protect us, Lord God.*

Petros stepped between them. "He is my cousin—we were out together, that is all."

The curl of Timon's lip looked like the snarl of a wild dog... one that had gone too long without a meal. "Well. I certainly never expected to host *him*. But you, young Petros. You I have been hoping to meet. Such a way you have with words! A true orator."

"While I thank you," Petros said, edging a bit more in front of Nikolaos, "I am short on time just now and must see to this business for the Visibullises. Two thousand denarii."

Timon turned back to his couch. "I do not conduct business with a man I know so little. Sit. Have a glass of wine. And you can tell me how you come to be here instead of Dorus Visibullis or his...very lovely daughters."

Petros craned his head around, met Nikolaos's eye. Questions marked his.

Nikolaos gave a miniscule nod. "Do what must be done. For them." The sooner they humored Timon, the sooner they would be free of him.

His cousin's tension was discernible in his gaze solely because Nikolaos knew the light that usually sparked there instead. He returned the small nod and moved toward one of the couches.

"It is not I with whom you are doing business," Petros said as he sat. "As I said, I am merely here on their behalf. I have long been a friend of the family."

Timon snorted a grating laugh and lowered himself to his cushions. To Nikolaos's eye, the man's swarthy complexion and nearly-black hair looked even darker, given what lurked within. "Friend, he says. I can just imagine. Which of the girls is your especial *friend*, young man?"

Petros kept his face in neutral lines, looking neither offended nor amused. "The girls were understandably distressed when they realized their father owed you money. Dorus is still unwell after the shock of losing his wife, and we all agreed it was best if the young ladies not venture here." He leaned forward and set the bag of gold upon the table. "I trust you will have to count it."

Timon motioned to the slave, who appeared with a second chalice. Nikolaos, apparently, was not invited to partake.

Shame.

He contented himself with leaning into the corner, where he could watch both their faces.

Petros accepted the cup after Timon had filled it but did not lift it to his lips. Timon took a long draught of his, studying Petros all the while. "They are beautiful girls. I confess I am rather disappointed they gathered the funds so quickly—I had plans for those girls. Twins—and such beautiful ones!" His lips curled into a smirk. "Oh yes, I had plans for them. They would have earned back those denarii within a half-year."

Nikolaos winced. Petros did not. He merely quirked the corners of his mouth up and said, "I am afraid they have their own plans and will be happily married within that half-year."

Timon held his chalice before him, looking at Petros over its rim. "And what of the younger one? The redhead?"

Nikolaos hid his fist in the folds of his garment. Petros must be fighting to avoid the same telling gesture. His only movement was his lips, which said, "She is also spoken for."

Not officially perhaps, but it was an accurate enough statement if one considered intents. Nikolaos certainly had no urge to correct him.

Timon clucked his tongue and shook his head. "I could have gotten five thousand sestertii for her. I have a buyer in Rome who has long been looking for a young, vivacious redhead."

Had it been Nikolaos on the couch, those words would have brought him to his feet. His cousin merely put on a smile. "I would say I am sorry to disappoint you...but I am not. Not in the least."

Timon boomed out a laugh. "I like you, young Petros. Indeed I do. I will be keeping an eye on your career, to be sure." Settling again, he watched his guest for a long moment before nodding, leaning toward the table, and exchanging cup for bag of coins. He loosened the drawstring and shook out the gold. "Very well, then. Tell those lovely girls that if their father is true to form and gets them in trouble again, I would be glad to assist them."

"Forgive me if I say I hope that is never a consideration for them again." Petros stood, wearing a charming grin. "Good day to you, Timon."

"And to you, Petros, son of Theophanes. I will be watching next time you are before the courts."

Nikolaos turned toward the door, happy to find the servant already there, lifting the bar again—and repressing a chill at the realization that they had been locked in. But it was soon open to him, and he stepped out into the fresh air, his cousin a step behind.

Once they were back in the alley, Petros made a shuddering sound. "I have never been so glad to leave a place."

"You handled yourself perfectly though. I would not have."

Petros laughed. "You give yourself too little credit. You are all the time facing men of authority, and you do so with dignity and grace."

"Not men like him."

"Indeed. Well, that is, I believe, your uncle frowning at us at the end of the alley. If you do not mind, I shall part ways there and go home so I can wash away the feeling that place gave me."

Nikolaos chuckled again. "Go ahead. I shall see you at prayers tonight."

Petros nodded, nodded again to Uncle as they drew near him. "Good day, Bishop."

"Petros." Uncle's scowl did not lessen and soon focused itself on Nikolaos. "Nephew. What were you doing down there?"

Nikolaos had no trouble smiling into his uncle's concern. They shared a name, he and the bishop, and more than a few personality traits. He understood the concern of his guardian, and certainly did not wish to add more white to the hair already fading from gray, more lines to his aging face.

But if his uncle had taught him anything, it was that one never apologized for doing the right thing. "I went with Petros to settle a loan Dorus had drawn from Timon."

Uncle's wrinkles turned to seams. "Timon? That man is evil."

"And now he has no claim to the Visibullis daughters. Petros..." He watched his cousin's form retreat around the corner and pitched his voice low. He would never tell anyone else what Petros had just done, but this was Uncle. The bishop. "Petros settled the debt. He gave all he had saved to save them."

Uncle's seams relaxed again and worked their way into a small smile. "He is a good boy. And he loves young Cyprus very much. Dorus would have done well to seek an alliance with *him* all these years, rather than you."

"I know." But he still saw that bag of gold. So large, when one considered its meaning. But so small when one considered the gold just sitting in Nikolaos's coffers. *God will tell you when to spend it, and how,* his uncle had said when his parents died. That was all he had ever said on the matter.

God had not told him to use it here. Had he? Had Nikolaos's ears been stopped? "I could have done it, and it would have barely put a dent in my holdings. I could have saved them without sacrifice. Without my cousin—"

"Nikolaos." Uncle's wizened hand settled, warm and comfortable, on his shoulder. "You cannot save the world. You cannot give to all who have need. If ever you begin doling out your gold, you will soon find the whole countryside clamoring at your door, claiming desperation."

"But they are not the world—they are my friends."

"All the more reason to stay out of their affairs. It is one thing to help a friend in need, but to obliterate their debts, to take from them the consequences they have rightly earned..." Uncle shook his head, and a wisp of silver hair drifted across his cheek. "Give without reason and you will take from them a reason to improve. Dorus Visibullis has a lesson to learn here. One he will not learn if he does not taste the fruits of his behavior."

Uncle led him down a bustling street, too busy for anyone to pay them any heed. Still, he leaned his head close. "Petros...Petros was trying to save the woman he hopes to marry from a terrible fate. That is to be applauded. He gave all he had, and it was, I pray, enough—and may finally convince Dorus to hold him in the regard he deserves. He will be forced to reevaluate his judgment upon the boy, which will in turn force him to rethink other judgments. But you, Nikolaos. You have too much. You could give more than they could ever need, and it would be their ruin, and yours. No. Start down that path, and you will be trapped into thinking of your coffers more than your calling. You will think of nothing but how much gold to give, and when. Focus on the

Lord, my son. And if ever he means you to help another in such a way, he will whisper it in your ear."

Exactly what he had said years ago. And no doubt he was right—the bishop was *always* right. Petros had just fulfilled the need right now, had saved them from the streets.

So why did the talons of foreboding still dig their way into Nikolaos's chest?

NINE

Cyprus blinked into the gray light of dawn, trying to untangle nightmare from reality and determine what had woken her. Her sisters still slept, their breathing even and soothing. She listened for a noise from the window but heard nothing.

Her stomach growled into the stillness. She had eaten only one meal yesterday, and she did not anticipate much more today. There were only a few coins left. Their debts were still staggering, and they had nothing else to sell. The shopkeepers would not let them buy on a promise anymore.

Her stomach was going to have to get used to this hollow feeling.

She flipped her legs over the edge of her bed. Water, at least, was free. She could get a drink, and perhaps trick her spoiled belly into thinking itself full for a time.

Halfway down the hall, she heard what must have woken her—her father, calling for Mellos. His throat sounded dry and scratchy, and apparently Mellos did not hear him. And if he did not, she did not much relish waking him. Abbas's last mutterings the evening before had been a threat to sell the slaves, and he had said it right there before them all.

They would not be happy today.

Slipping silently into the kitchen, she drew a cupful of water and carried it carefully toward her father's room. A knock upon the door brought no answer.

She sighed. "Abbas, it is Cyprus. I have a drink for you. May I come in?"

She decided to take his grunt as permission and pushed the door open with her hip.

She would never, never get used to entering this room and seeing no mark of Mater there. No hairbrush, no cosmetics and perfumes. No sheer fabric draping, its golden embroidery gleaming in whatever light was handy.

No more.

Cyprus drew in a careful breath and padded her way into the dim chamber. "Here you are, Abbas. You sounded thirsty."

Her father lay on the bed, making no move for the cup. Making not so much as a slit with his eyes through which to peer at her. "Where is Mellos?"

"Asleep, I assume. You were so quiet, no doubt he did not hear you call for him."

"Wake him."

"But—"

"Do as I say, Cyprus, or it will be *you* on the auction block rather than him."

She stumbled backward, sloshing water all down her tunic. It was drier than her eyes, which burned with brine as if it were fire. How could he say such a thing? And so calmly, without even a token of regret in his tone?

Her limbs felt heavy as she stumbled out the door. Cumbersome. Uncooperative. She made it only a few steps into the dark hallway before she had to stop and lean into the wall for support. Her feet would not move another inch. Her hands hung limp at her sides, the cup somewhere on the floor.

Had he ever loved them? He said he did, she and her sisters claimed he did. But it had always been a love tempered with fear. She had known, that day she fell from the rooftop, that he would not love her any longer if she were a paralytic. The years had done nothing to change that deep-set terror. No, they had only shown her a new truth.

If Abbas had ever loved anybody, Mater was the only one who could rightfully claim it. And without her...it was as if his heart had been replaced with a stone. Or carved from his chest altogether.

She squeezed her eyes against the tears. He was all they had left, and he did not care whether they lived or died. He would have indeed left her out for the wild dogs had Nikolaos not healed her. And he might just deliver them into the hands of slavers now, if they were liability rather than aid.

She rested her head against the cool stone wall. She would just have to be aid, that was all. She and the twins would figure out some way to support one another, and him too. *Please, Lord God. Show us what we can do. How we can survive. I will beg if I must, I will scavenge along the shore...I will do anything, just show me your will. Please.*

Her hands lifted, brushed at the wet spot on her tunic. It was cooling, and the air in the house was bordering on uncomfortable. Soon they would have to start setting fires in the evenings—which begged the question of what they would use for fuel, now that they could not buy any. Driftwood from the beach? Dried animal dung, picked up from the street?

Or they could just use heavier blankets. Those had not been worth selling, so they had plenty. It would not get *that* cold.

She pushed off the wall and continued toward the kitchen and the servant quarters beyond it. Perhaps Helena and Mellos and their two daughters could help them come up with a plan for survival—they must, if they did not want to be sold and separated. They must all work together.

"Helena? Mellos?" She paused to stir the fire in the kitchen, needing its light. The one window here faced west, and the chamber was still shrouded in shadows. Should Helena not have already been up and about though? She was always up at the first breath of dawn. "Aella? Enyo?"

The girls were usually up with their mother, ready to assist with the household chores.

No noises came from their rooms.

She felt odd, tiptoeing to their doors. Abbas had always discouraged them from being overly friendly with the servants, so she had been permitted only rarely in the kitchen, and never in their quarters. Rapping her knuckles against the door, she sucked in a ridiculously anxious breath and waited.

Nothing.

She knocked again, louder.

Nothing.

The anxiety multiplied. "Mellos? Helena?" An ear against the door picked up no noises of pain or illness, to account for their absence from the kitchen. "I am coming in."

No objections. She gripped the latch and eased the door open. The scant light from the wakened fire barely reached inside...but it was enough. Enough to see that the room was empty.

Not just unoccupied—*empty.* No clothing, no shoes, no belongings scattered on the tabletop. Nothing remained inside but the furniture.

"No. Dear Lord, no." She spun to the next door, opened it too without bothering with the knock. The girls' space was just as empty.

Like her chest, where her vital organs ought to have been.

Slumping for a moment against the doorframe, Cyprus willed the image to change.

It did not. They were gone. They had taken everything and... *everything.*

She dashed back across the kitchen, to the shelf by the doorway to the main house and the little clay jar in which they kept the household money. Where she and the twins had put the last of their coins, knowing they would need it for food—it was not enough for anything else. Not enough to take them to another city, where they still would have no skills but might at least outpace their father's reputation. But it would feed them for a week or so.

No jar occupied the shelves. "No!" She wanted to scream it again, to throw something, to rage until all of Patara could hear her. But her arms would not work and her legs would not move and all she could do was sink to the cold tile floor and sob like a child. A child who desperately wanted her mother and could find her nowhere.

The floor was cold and hard. The air was cold and empty. The world was cold and unwelcoming.

Footsteps pounded, two familiar sets of them, and equally familiar hands gripped her shoulders, smoothed back her hair. "Honey pot! What is it? What is wrong? Are you hurt?"

Cyprus could not move, but she did. She lifted a hand that felt wooden and unconnected to her body and gripped Alexandria's wrist. Rhoda's hand. "They have gone. Mellos and Helena and the girls. They have gone, and they took everything we had left with them."

"No. They would not. They would not do that to us." Alexandria shook free and stood, ran to the bedrooms to see the truth for herself.

Rhoda sank to the floor beside Cyprus. "Heaven help us. Of

course they would—why would they not? Abbas threatened to sell them."

A sharp invective came from behind them, and Alexandria punctuated it with the tossing of a wooden bowl against the wall. The sound fed that hungry place inside Cyprus, the place that had made her want to do the same thing.

"What is all the commotion in here?"

Cyprus shrank into Rhoda at the intrusion of their father's voice. It grated against the hunger, made it yawn open into a black nothingness. He had no slaves left to sell now—only daughters.

Heaven help them indeed.

"The slaves have run away," Alexandria spat. "We should set out now to find them, they cannot be that far ahead—"

Abbas's hard bark of laughter cut her off. "Not far? No doubt they left last night and found a boat to sail on with the tide. They will be out of our reach by now."

"You do not know that! How would they have purchased passage? Even with the coins they stole, they would not have had enough."

Rhoda sighed and rested her head against Cyprus's. "They had money. Helena had sold some bread over the years, here and there, and had a small stash—I saw it last winter when she was ill."

Abbas's shadow covered them, cut off the meager warmth from the kitchen fire. "My slaves had money of their own—money earned with things *I* bought—and you did not see fit to tell me?"

Rhoda winced. "It seemed harmless at the time, Abbas."

"If you thought so, then you are a fool. You are all fools, every last one of you."

"We?" Alexandria matched her volume to his. "*We* are the

fools? If *you* had treated them better all these years, if you had not threatened to sell them, then they would not have run away with all we had left!"

Silence spoke into the seconds to follow, clanging and harsh. Cyprus gripped Rhoda's hand and risked a glance up at Abbas.

His hands were in fists at his side, his eyes blazing with the hearth's fire. "I would have sold them to save *you*. But if you will be ungrateful, then so be it. There is nothing left. Nothing. You want to eat, you will have to earn it yourselves."

Rhoda sucked in a breath threatening tears. "Abbas...we have no skills. No one will take us in and teach us, not after the way you have lorded over them all."

They would find someone to help, though. They could try the church. They could beg with the rest of the blind and lame and widows. And at least for now they had a home to return to.

Though Cyprus suddenly regretted that letter the twins had sent to Mater's uncle, who owned the house. He lived only twenty miles away—he could arrive any day to take even that from them.

"Do not act even more the fool, Rhoda." Abbas released his fingers from their fist. "We all know what option you have as unskilled women—prostitution. You and Xandria can take to the streets. Or we can sell Cyprus to someone in Rome. Those are your choices."

"No!" Rhoda pulled Cyprus close and wrapped her arms around her. Alexandria draped herself overtop, shielding her from their father's words.

Still they penetrated. But with them, through them, surrounding them was the realization that even if Abbas did not love her, her sisters did.

"We will never let that happen to you, honey pot," Alexandria whispered fiercely into her ear. "Never. Do not fear. We will protect you at all costs."

All the times she had raged at Alexandria for calling her that. All the meaningless arguments. All the times she had brushed away Rhoda's fussing hands.

She squeezed her eyes shut and held on to them both. "You will not sacrifice yourselves for me. You will not. I will not let you. I love you too much."

"We love *you* too much—and we outnumber you." Tears laced Rhoda's voice as she stroked Cyprus's hair.

We outnumber you. So they did—and that made it all the worse. The both of them could not suffer just to save *her*. She could never let that happen.

"We will find another way." Alexandria pressed a kiss to her head as Mater used to do. "We will appeal again to Hero and Kosmas. We will go to the church. We will—"

"You will *not*!" Abbas tore Alexandria away. His grip on her arm must have been painful, given her wince. Or perhaps it was the look on his face—pure hatred—that elicited the response. "You step foot in that church and I will kill you, daughter, I swear I will. Your *God* took from us the only thing that matters. I would sooner my daughters be whores or slaves than appeal to a being so cruel."

Alexandria pulled away from him. "Is that what Mater would want? For you to send her daughters to the streets or the slave docks rather than let go of your mighty pride?"

"Your mother is gone. Your God, if he exists, delights in our hardship."

Rhoda hugged Cyprus tighter. "And what of our father? Where is *he*? The man who is supposed to care for us, to provide for us?"

Abbas turned away, the slump of his shoulders the only hint of feeling. "He died with your mother. And this body will join hers soon enough—but while I yet breathe, you will honor my commands, so help me. You will grant me that."

They said nothing while he trudged away. But the silence had no time to strangle them in his wake. Once his door slammed, Alexandria sat beside them, their arms all a tangle. "He cannot claim to be dead in one breath and demand obedience in the next—and as he is not acting like our father, I will not honor his ridiculous words as such. I will go today to the church, straight to the bishop. Perhaps they will give us a little food and help us find someone who can teach us a trade."

Rhoda nodded. "And we will go to Hero. His father is reasonable...perhaps he can be swayed."

Cyprus squeezed her eyes shut. "Timon said he would come back today. We have not so much as a copper to give him."

The silence bludgeoned its way back in for a painful, unending moment. She wished, on the one hand, that she had held her tongue. But it would not have changed the impending. So if she were going to spend time wishing, she would wish instead for a way to change it.

"I say we not be here when he comes. Let him deal with Abbas, if he even rises to answer the door."

"We must deal first with food, at any rate." Rhoda nodded. "As soon as the hour is acceptable, we go to the church."

Cyprus wrapped the end of her hair around her finger and stared, unseeing, into the fire. If only Nikolaos could lift his hand and make this all vanish. But there was no miracle to perform now, nothing he could do. All the faith in the world could not mitigate the consequences of twenty years of her father's actions.

You believe, he had said to her that terrible, amazing day, after Petros had held her hand and she had felt nothing. After Nikolaos had delivered that impossible command and she had obeyed. *Get up and walk.*

How could a handful of words have changed her life so completely? *Get up and walk.* A simple command. Followed minutes later by that simple statement. *You believe.*

I believe, Father God. She felt the texture of her hair between her fingers. Felt the cold tiles warming beneath her. Felt the stir of life inside, under the layers of fear and grief. She *felt*—though by rights she should not have. Had she lived this long, she should have been unaware of anything touching her below her shoulders. But she could feel. *I believe. I believe this is all in your hands. I believe that you have us in your palm even now. I believe that somehow, someway you will deliver us. That you spared me for a reason. Show me, Father God, what that reason is.* "Take care of us this day, Lord, please."

"Yes." Alexandria's fingers wove through hers. "Show us the path to safety."

"Give us what we need to survive today, Father."

Cyprus's lashes still felt wet against her cheeks. "Protect Mellos and Helena and the girls, wherever they are. Keep them safe and well."

Both of her sisters leaned closer. "Yes," Rhoda breathed, "help us to forgive them for taking all we had left."

"And Abbas. I am so angry with him, Lord. Help me love him, even now." Alexandria sniffed and rested her head against Cyprus's shoulder.

This time the silence tasted sweet and light. They let it hold as the sunlight crept upward and lit the world beyond the window. At length, they breathed their amens and stood, each heading toward a different corner of the kitchen.

Cyprus checked the grain bin. There had been flour left yesterday—not much, but enough for a little cake each, perhaps. She lifted the lid and peered inside, willing the tears to stay away. Empty. Of course. Helena must have taken it.

"The oil is gone." Rhoda's tone was even, controlled.

Just like Alexandria's sigh. "As are the dried figs."

"And the flour. They took every morsel." Cyprus breathed in slowly, through her nose. *Help me to forgive them, Lord. I do not want to. I would not even think to pray it, if not for Rhoda reminding me I should.*

A tap at the door startled her out of her prayer. Being the closest to it, she stepped over and lifted the bar, ignoring the squeaks of protest from her sisters. Timon, she had to think, would not come to the rear entrance and scratch like a servant.

Though she would not have thought Petros would either, yet there he stood, looking every bit as surprised to see her as she was to see him.

"Cyprus." He blinked, brows drawn. "Why are you answering the kitchen door?"

He held a basket in his arms—a large one—and she could smell fresh bread even from two steps away. It was enough to bring the tears up again. Grateful ones this time. "The servants have run away. They took everything we had left. The food, the money."

He muttered something she could not quite hear and stepped inside, sliding the basket onto the table. "I cannot believe they would abandon you." He folded her into his embrace.

He smelled of cedar and citrus—and fresh bread. Cyprus buried her face into the soft cloth of his cloak and breathed it in. "Abbas threatened to sell them."

His arms tightened around her. "I cannot say as that surprises me. Nor, in that case, does their reaction. Even so."

The twins drew near, Rhoda lifting the cloth from the basket. Her eyes went wide. "Petros! There is enough here to keep us for weeks!"

His arms loosened, and he cleared his throat. His cheeks, in the scant light, looked flushed. "I did not mean for you to know it was from me. Us, really. Nikolaos and I, and my mother baked the bread. She said…I did not think you would need the offer, but you may. She said she would teach you, all of you, to bake. And cook. If Helena is gone…"

"Oh." Alexandria covered her mouth with a hand, but it did little to hide the sudden sob. "Forgive me. The Lord answers some prayers so quickly."

And this one he answered years ago, when he gave them such good friends in Petros and Nikolaos.

Cyprus wiped the moisture from her eyes. "Indeed. And we do need those lessons, Pet. When would she like us to come? Or will she come here?"

"I will check with her. Right now, I must go—I will be before the courts today." He stepped away, nothing but a hand lingering on her back. And his gaze lingering on her face. "Try to rest easy today. And eat. You know I speak with the utmost concern when I say you all look horrible."

Rhoda snorted a laugh and wiped at her eyes too. "You are flattering as always, Petros."

"There is a time for flattery, and now is not it." He leaned over to press a kiss to Cyprus's head, set a hand on Rhoda's shoulder and squeezed, nodded at Alexandria. "I will check on you later and have an answer from my mother. Try not to worry today. The Lord will take care of you."

The Lord and his faithful servants. Cyprus stepped back to the door with him and held it as he moved out into the misty morning. "Petros…thank you. And again, thank you."

His smile might not have been as carefree as normal, but it was every bit as warm…and warming. She felt it all the way down to her bones. "It is what friends do. Good-bye, Cyprus."

"God be with you before the court today." She watched him disappear into the mist and then shut the cool air out of the house. It seemed warmer in the kitchen than it had before, being no longer empty where it ought to have been full.

Alexandria was pouring grain into the bin, Rhoda was filling a flask with oil. Cyprus moved to the basket, still bursting with supplies.

They had thought of everything. Dried fruits, fresh vegetables, the grain and oil. Fish and salt and spices and even a jar of honey.

It would not be as sweet as him. Cyprus picked up the spices and moved toward the shelf that held them. For now, the wolf of hunger was held at bay. Perhaps with a full stomach, she could think of how they would answer Timon when he came knocking on their door in a few hours.

TEN

Nikolaos nearly dropped the stack of scrolls he carried when he stepped into the room and spotted, not just Uncle at his usual table, but Alexandria and Rhoda before him, kneeling as supplicants in search of sanctuary. Uncle glanced up at the sound of his footsteps, but his eyes gave nothing away—no hint as to why the Visibullis twins were here, in the church their father had long ago forbade them from entering.

Had Dorus tossed them from the house? But if so, where was Cyprus?

He slid inside and went about silently stacking the scrolls. Uncle would have given him a discreet motion if he were to leave. But perhaps the girls would find his presence comforting.

"Please, Bishop." Rhoda kept her head inclined with respect, her back bowed in perfect deference. "We are not asking for alms. We are asking to be taught. Surely there is someone in your flock who would teach us a trade that a respectable woman might ply."

"We are quick learners, all of us." Alexandria's posture matched her sister's, though her tone was more eager than humble. "We are good with a needle, at the least. And my sister Rhoda has made a tapestry grand enough for the emperor himself."

"Alexandria is a wonder at embroidery. And Cyprus—Cyprus sings like an angel."

Uncle sighed. "Girls, I appreciate your situation and your desire to support yourselves. But surely you realize that these skills are shared by every lady—and of no use to humbler families. They are not tradeable."

Nikolaos glanced at the scrolls he was stacking but then back over at the girls in time to see Rhoda swipe at her eyes. Alexandria leaned forward. "Please, Bishop. We will do anything respectable. Please, ask those women in your congregation who earn livings if they could use an apprentice. Please."

"Please," Rhoda echoed. "The only other option is the streets, and surely a man of the church would not wish us to end up living a life of such sin."

If not for the dire implications of their words, Nikolaos may have smiled at the clever manipulation—but he could not, not given those implications.

How could it possibly have become as bad as all that, in so short a time?

His uncle sighed again and waved at the girls to stand up. "I will ask. I can promise no more—most of those women already have daughters to teach and will not want to raise up competition. Have you food enough for now?"

Nikolaos's shoulders relaxed, hearing his uncle ask the question. He had not mentioned last evening that he went out with Petros to purchase them supplies—he had not known how the bishop would respond. But hearing him now, no doubt he would have at the very least invited them to receive of the bread and fish soup they distributed to the poor.

Rhoda darted a quick glance his way that proved Petros had been unsuccessful in delivering their basket without being seen. She nodded. "Friends have seen to that."

"Good. My nephew will walk you out, will you not, Nikolaos?"

"Of course." He pushed the last of the scrolls into place and offered the twins a tight smile. He said nothing, though, until they had left the chamber and made their way to the high-ceilinged meeting room of the church. "Trades?"

Alexandria drew in a long breath. "Abbas has given up. He told us—he told us to sell ourselves to put food on the table."

Nikolaos's feet came to a halt of their own will. He had thought it dramatics before his uncle. An exaggeration. He had thought that, surely, Dorus would rouse himself and provide for his family. *He* ought to be the one out pounding on doors for some job that could earn him money for food. Not his daughters. "You must not."

"We will not. Not so long as there is any other option." Rhoda met her sister's gaze, their matching eyes lit with matching sparks. "But if no one will help us, and it is the only way to keep him from selling Cyprus to the slavers—"

"*What?*"

"That was our father's other brilliant option." Alexandria looked ready to stomp home and pummel the man for the suggestion.

Nikolaos was tempted to join her. "Where is she now?"

"Home, trying to convince Abbas to eat. He refuses, saying he will starve himself so he can join Mater."

She would take such care, after he said such a thing? Nikolaos shook his head. "I will be praying for him. All of you. And I will do all I can to help you get back on your feet. Know that."

"We know. And thank the Lord for a few good friends." Rhoda tucked her arm through her sister's. "Our next stop is to find Hero. Perhaps..."

"Yes. Perhaps." He walked toward the door again, going mentally over any women among the congregation who could teach them...anything. Anything that would help them survive. Otherwise, their father was right—there were no other options for women. “I will talk to people too. Anyone I can think of.”

“Thank you, Nik. For everything.” Alexandria nodded to him as he held open the heavy wooden door that let them out into the street. She stood tall, her shoulders back, her chin up. He could admire the strength it showed, the determination.

But he wondered if, to those from whom they would seek training, it might come off instead as pride.

Nikolaos turned back into the church, but he did not go in search of Uncle again. He instead settled onto a hard seat—meant to be so, because faith was not a matter of comfort, nor was prayer supposed to be restful. He turned his eyes past the paintings that adorned the walls with those stories from Scripture he could recite in his sleep. To the wooden cross that dominated the front of the room.

His eyes slid shut. His heart opened.

Wonder worker, they called him. They would not, if they knew how at a loss he felt just now. How he wondered, wondered what wonder could possibly be worked to put this to right. If he had acted that night, in the dream, perhaps...perhaps he could have changed things for them. But now?

They need a miracle, Lord. And I know not how to provide it and be still in accordance with your will. I can give gold...but then it is me, not you. And that is not what you ask of me. I know this. I know that my uncle is right about the dangers of acting as a man rather than a servant of your will. So show me, I beg you. Show me what you want me to do.

The silence echoed to the beams.

Cyprus set the plate down on the table, wishing she could set aside the desire to cry as easily. It was still filled with the offerings she had taken to Abbas—bread, fruit, cheese. He had refused so much as a taste, even after an hour of cajoling and begging. It was as though he had stopped his ears to her voice altogether.

She covered the plate with a towel and moved it to the cool pantry so the food would stay fresh for when the twins returned. They could not waste even a morsel, not when the supplies Petros had brought must stretch indefinitely.

Cleaning up took only a few minutes. Wandering the house took no longer. It was so empty—the only furniture left beyond Abbas's chamber was that crude bench in the main room and their beds. The only decorations remaining were that seashell Petros had picked up for her and two clay figures the twins had made as children.

Once, it had been a home. Now it felt like an unoccupied house.

Longing for sunshine, even if it were cool and wintry, Cyprus slipped out the kitchen door and turned her face up to receive heaven's light. She leaned against the house and soaked it up, praying that the twins found favor with the bishop. Praying that Hero would say he would marry Rhoda this very day and that Kosmas had sworn the same with Alexandria. If they could both be happy, then Cyprus hardly cared what became of her. She would—

"Hey, get back here! That is not yours!"

Cyprus started at the sound of her neighbor's voice. Sapphira had not a kind thing to say to them lately, but the woman was far too old to be chasing a thief through the streets, and Cyprus could hear pounding steps fleeing the matron's house. Before she could think, she ran around the corner of the house, into the street.

It was a boy barreling down on her, no more than eight by her estimation. And grinning like a fiend as he clutched a wriggling puppy to his chest. Cyprus sighed. Sapphira's husband raised mastiffs for the army, and this was not the first time some daring young scamp had tried to liberate one for his own pleasure. Luckily, the boy was paying more attention to pup and woman than to what lay before him.

Cyprus merely reached out, caught the child, and lifted the puppy from his arms. "I believe if you want one of these, young lord, you will have to pay the same price as the emperor."

The puppy whimpered. The boy kicked at her shins. She tightened her grip rather than loosening it, even as pain shot up her leg. Held the boy tight against her.

He bit her arm—not the puppy, which she may have expected, but the child. And he obviously had no qualms about making it hurt. A gasp of pain escaped her lips, and her arm disobeyed her command to hold tight. The boy pulled away, grinding his shoes into her bare toes, and took off at a sprint.

Old Sapphira hobbled up, glaring at Cyprus as if *she* had been the one to liberate the dog. "You let him get away!" She snatched the puppy.

Cyprus used the newly freed hand to rub at her arm. The little monster had broken skin in two places. "My apologies, lady. I tried to hold him. At least I recovered the pup, yes?"

"For all the good it will do if the thief returns again. You should have put down the dog to better hold the boy. The pup would have run right back to me."

A fine thought *now*. Cyprus curled her toes against the street—they protested and thumped in pain. "Again, my apologies."

"I believe," a masculine voice said from behind her, "that the proper response when someone tries to help you, lady, is to say thank you."

Sapphira's eyes went round, and she edged back a step. "Yes, of course. Thank you, Cyprus."

Cyprus's stomach twisted into a knot. She had only heard that voice once before, but she knew it. As much by the fear in her neighbor's eyes as its familiarity to her ears. *Father, help me.* Her sisters would be furious with her, if she were still here to be angry with when they got home. She turned slowly, until she faced Timon and the two slaves who shadowed him today just as they had the first time he came to call—one hulking, one thin as a myth.

Could she run from them, like a boy with a stolen puppy? Somehow she doubted that biting their arms and stomping on their toes would achieve freedom if they caught her. Would Sapphira tell her sisters what became of her if they returned to a house devoid of all but their empty shell of a father?

Timon was chuckling. At her fear? Sapphira's? She could not say. But the sound made her flesh crawl.

Knowing fleeing would achieve nothing, she opted for dignity instead and squared her shoulders. Lifted her chin. "Master Timon, we—"

"Do not fear, fair one." He bent a bit at the waist—a bow surely meant to mock her. "*I* know how to thank people for doing what they ought. That is why I came by, to assure your esteemed father that our accounts are settled and that if he needs another loan, I am happy to grant it. Never let it be said Dorus Visibullis does not pay what he owes!"

Cyprus's brows knotted. She should not question it. She knew that. If Timon wanted to clear the slate of their debt, how could she possibly argue? And yet he obviously noted the question on her face before she could clear it. The best she could do was cover it with the clearing of her throat and a quick dip of her knees.

Her arm still pulsed in pain, and her toes begged for relief from her weight. She forced a smile. "Forgive me, lord—I was unaware my father had left the house."

He had not. She knew with absolute certainty he had not. She or one of the twins had been with him nearly every moment, and he could not have gone out and come back without them noting his absence.

More, if a man could not be put upon to eat, he certainly would not go trekking across town to pay his debts.

Even more than that, he had no money with which to pay them, even if he stirred himself to rise.

Timon laughed. "When has that ever stopped a fellow such as your father? I always knew he was a man I could appreciate—one with friends to accomplish tasks in his name. And quite a friend he has in that young man." He looked nearly friendly, jovial, as he leaned close. "He said you were all spoken for. One of you by him I suspect, hmm? And a fine husband he is sure to make—that boy has a future ahead of him! I was just listening to him, advocating for a fisherman of all things, and his words were so beautiful I could have wept."

"Petros?" Her blood went cold, then warm as the summer sun. He had gone to Timon? Had…had paid off their debt? But how? With what?

"Petros indeed! Is your father within, my lovely? I would like to congratulate him on his future son's success."

His future… Cyprus shook her head, but it did not help Timon's words make more sense. Where would Petros have gotten that kind of money? And why would he have given it for them? It was one thing to bring them a basket of food. Quite another to pay off a debt so staggering. "He…he is asleep, lord."

"Another time, then." Still chuckling, he lifted a hand and quirked a finger. "A fine day to you, young lady."

"And to you." The words came out by rote. But she stood there, still as a statue, for a long minute after Timon and his slaves passed by.

Sapphira had disappeared, and there was no one else around to assure Cyprus that she had not dreamed that exchange—that Timon really had just walked away, after saying their debt was settled.

Father God... What words could she even pray? Ones of thanksgiving? Of incredulity? Or horror, even, that her friend would give up so much for them?

Petros. She had to see Petros.

A few steps on aching toes reminded her that she wore no shoes, so she darted inside to put some on and grab a covering for her hair. This she put on as she flew out the door, ignoring the pain in her foot as she sped toward the acropolis, to where the courts reigned supreme with their towering white columns and blindfolded statue of Justice, the scales in her hand.

He would be here still. He must. Cyprus had never even come near the courts to hear him—Abbas would never have permitted it without accompanying them, and he never had any interest in doing so—but she did not pause to wonder where she was going. She simply scanned the throngs of citizens in the agora until she spotted a familiar head, familiar shoulders. "Petros!"

He turned, question heavy in his brows, and said something to whomever he had been conversing with. Then hurried her way through the crowds.

Concern pierced her. What had she just drawn him away from? Something important? She had not even paused to consider that he could be about business far more crucial than this. Likely was, given that they were right before the courts. And even if not, was it not rude of her to assume, to interrupt?

But he had come, without hesitation, without a hand raised to tell her to wait. He had come at the first moment she called and approached her now with eyes filled with the deepest concern.

With something more?

"Cyprus—what is wrong? Are you well? Your father, your sisters?" He drew near, reached for her hands—and his eyes went wide. "You are bleeding! It looks like—bite marks?"

She should have taken the time to wrap the wound, if for no other reason than to avoid alarming him. "It is nothing."

"Of course it is something. Come, sit. Do you need a drink? A meal?"

"No." But she let him lead her by the hand out of the crowded space before the court, around the side of the building, into a quiet yard at the rear with a peaceful garden. "It really is nothing—a boy was trying to steal a dog from Sapphira, and he bit me when I stopped him."

Petros frowned. "The dog?"

"No. The boy." It brought a hint of a grin to her lips, quickly faded. "Timon found me in the street while I was helping with the dog."

Petros stiffened, going taller somehow. His hazel eyes glinted hard, his dark hair waved in the cool breeze. "Why? What did he do?" He motioned to a bench.

She did not sit. "He wanted to thank my father for paying his debt and offer him another loan—and to tell him how fortunate he is to have you as a friend. Petros. What have you done?"

He looked away quickly, but not quickly enough. Not if he meant to hide the acknowledgment in his eyes. "I know not what you mean. What *he* means."

"Petros." So often she had said his name—but today it sounded like music. Rock, it meant. And that was what he had become to her these past four years. Especially now. Her rock, always there for her to lean on. To bolster her. To provide a firm foundation. She reached up and rested her hand against his cheek. "Why?

Why did you pay it? It must have taken every last bit you had saved."

His eyes slid closed. "It was only money. I can earn more."

Tears—too familiar a companion these days—clogged her throat. But this time they were not sorrowful. "You had to have had plans for that money."

"They meant nothing. Not if I lost you." He turned his face toward her again, and his hands lifted, framed her face, fingers burying themselves in her hair.

Never in her life had she been so aware of each curve of her cheek, her jaw. Of each strand of hair. But then, never in her life had Petros studied them so intently. She rested her hands on his wrists, anchoring him there. "Petros."

"You have to know how I feel for you, Cyprus. How I…how I love you." His nostrils flared, his eyes shimmering gold and green as he leaned closer. "I know I am unworthy of you—"

"You are not!" She gripped his arms tighter. "If anything, the reverse. Especially now. I am nothing, less than nothing—"

"You are everything. Everything that matters in the world." He leaned close, making her lips tingle by mere proximity. But he did not kiss her. He stopped a breath away, sighed, closed his eyes. "I did not want you to know. I did not want you to feel…to feel *obligated* to me because of it."

She did not speak the language of romance. She knew not what to say, what names to call him beyond his own. The endearments her parents had used all fought for a place on her tongue, but none of them felt right there. *Beloved. Darling. Dear one.* "Petros." She had thought before that she could imagine growing old with him. In this moment, she realized she could not imagine growing old without him. There was no question remaining of *if* she loved him. Only the question of how it had overtaken her so completely and left her unawares. "I loved you long before this. I will love you forever after. I would love you if you had not lifted a finger, had not offered a sestertius."

And his smile was worth a million sestertii, and more besides. So small, yet so full. As if his heart could not hold all he felt, and a bit of it slipped out onto his lips. Lips that drew near again and did not retreat this time. No, they found hers in a soft caress.

How could a touch so light, so gentle, make her whole being thrum? She leaned into him, her hands abandoning his wrists in favor of sliding around his waist. One of his stayed buried in her hair while the other settled on her back and pulled her closer.

She could spend a thousand years just like this and count it time well spent. His lips moved over hers like a song, filling her with music and light and pushing away all the darkness. Because Petros loved her. And she loved him. And surely that was all that mattered.

Except it was not. As he put a breath between them, his sigh said that he knew it as well as she. He loved her. But he could not marry her. She would be his ruin—she may already be his ruin.

He rested his forehead on hers. "It matters not to me. You know that. I do not care that you come empty-handed, so long as you come. Be my wife."

"Do you read my mind now?"

She felt his grin more than saw it. "Have I not always?"

Hers eyes slid shut. Not to block him out, but to savor the feel. "I love you, Petros. I want nothing more than to be your wife. But my sisters…I cannot abandon my sisters."

"I know." He pulled her into a tight embrace and tucked his head in beside hers. "I know. We will figure this out. We will. It may take some time, but we will see them happy and provided for. And your father too. And then, my little honey pot—"

She dug her fingers into his side, full to bursting at his laugh. At being able to move from serious to jest. At finding joy here, now, when she had no right to it.

He gripped her hands and pulled away enough to smile down at her. "We will see to them. Then we will make it official. If you will still have me then."

She prayed he saw her heart in her returning smile. "Keep calling me 'honey pot,' and I may just change my mind."

His eyes shimmered as he lifted her hands and kissed them each in turn. "But you are all things sweet in my life."

A shouted laugh from somewhere in the distance drew her attention back to where they were, and the fact that someone else could come upon them at any moment. "I pulled you away from your tasks. I am sorry."

"Apologize for telling me you love me, and I will never forgive it. You can interrupt me so anytime."

Laughter felt like a luxury she could ill afford, but she could not help investing it in him. "Very well then. Next time you are before the judges, I shall burst in and shout it to all."

He grinned and tucked her hand into the crook of his arm. "And I shall be the envy of every man there. But for now, I had better see you home. You ought not to have come here alone."

"Can you leave? Are you finished?"

"For today, yes. I will have to go soon to write my next defense, but I have time to take you home and help you tend that bite mark."

She scarcely felt it anymore. They kept a slow, leisurely pace on the walk back. Talking of little, and happily so. Cyprus soaked up the feel of him at her side, the wonder that he wanted to remain there always. That he wanted her for a wife.

A wife. So long she had railed against the idea of being married off for her father's gain. Had she actually said to Petros that she felt God would not have saved her life if he wanted her only to be a wife and mother?

She tightened her grip on his arm and leaned close, wishing she could take back those words. Even so, the questions persisted, drumming in her mind. She loved him. She wanted to be his wife. Mother to his children. But was that purpose enough, or did the Lord have something else in store for her—for them?

The old worry rattled about, but this time new possibilities joined the noise. Perhaps...perhaps she was meant to mother a child who would be important. Or perhaps she was to support Petros, who was apparently winning far more fame than he had ever told her. She looked up at him, studying the strong jaw she knew so well. The dusky skin. The dark hair. Those beautiful hazel eyes.

Those eyes looked down at her now and grinned along with his lips. "Why do you look at me like that, my love?"

She shook her head. "Just thinking. Why did you never tell me how your reputation is growing? To think that I was proud of your skill in oratory without having a clue that all of Patara shared my affinity for your words."

He chuckled and looked ahead again in time to steer them around a rut in the road. "What is there to tell? I talk. Some cases I win, some I lose. Some people admire me, others think I am nothing but clever words with no thought behind them."

They turned onto her street. And barely stepped foot upon it before the door to her house flew open and matching dark heads sped out. With matching expressions of panic and frustration on their faces.

Petros cleared his throat. "Let me guess—you did not tell them you were coming to see me."

"They were not at home." And she had not thought to take time enough to write a note. Her cheeks burned, and she tugged him along faster. "I am sorry!" she said as soon as she could be sure they would hear her without shouting. "I thought I would get home before you."

Her cheeks burned hotter. She had not thought about it at all, in truth.

Alexandria looked fit to smack her for her oversight. Rhoda flew directly to her and gathered her into a fierce embrace, pulling her from Petros's arm. "You foolish, foolish girl. Sapphira said Timon came by. We thought he had taken you."

"He had no reason to. Petros paid our debt."

The girls' exclamations were a cacophony in her ears. Odd how she could hear Petros's sigh so clearly over it. She met his scowl with a grin.

He shook his head. "So much for my grand secret."

The twins both threw their arms around him, apparently all but squeezing the life out of him, if his exaggerated choking sounds were anything but for effect.

When Alexandria pulled away, she was dashing at her eyes. "We owe you everything."

"And this is why I wished it to be a secret—you owe me nothing." He held out his hands, palms up. "You are my friends."

Rhoda sniffed and sent Cyprus a familiar look. Familiar, but one she had never bothered to interpret. One she did not *need* to interpret now—she knew its meaning. That look that said she knew well Petros was—or wanted to be, which was what it had meant before—more than a friend to Cyprus.

Her cheeks may stay hot for a year. And she was happy to have the warmth.

"This goes well beyond the call of friendship, Petros." Rhoda smiled, though sorrow dimmed it in her eyes. "Kosmas has not even come to see us. Hero's mother would not let us in the house. And then you..."

Cyprus wanted to cling to him again, thank him again. Kiss him again. But her sisters turned toward each other, shoulders with matching hunches and, she knew, hearts with matching fractures.

A glance at Petros told her he was thinking the same thing she was—now was not the time to talk of love. Not while her sisters were in such pain.

ELEVEN

"A woman should always know how to bake bread." Petros's mother, Korinna, kneaded the dough with ease and a smile, flour decorating her wrists. "My mother taught me when I was just a girl, as her mother taught her. She said that even if one has servants, one still should know—otherwise, what do you do that day when your kitchen slave is ill but important guests are coming? You cannot always count on being able to buy it—or on it being good enough to serve, even if you do."

Cyprus nodded along and pressed her knuckles to her round of dough again. It squished rather pleasantly under her fingers, its yeasty smell rising to tease her nose. On one side of her, Alexandria pounded upon her lump as if applying exactly the right force and direction could save the world. On the other side, Rhoda hummed as she pushed at hers like it was a toy and she a toddler.

Cyprus's lips hovered in a smile. Love for her sisters remained close to the surface of her heart these days. How could Hero and Kosmas not be knocking down their door to get to them?

No, that was unfair. They were honoring their parents. She ought not to wish they would disobey.

She wished they would disobey.

"I cannot remember Mater ever cooking." Alexandria shook her head but did not take her eyes off her bread. Perhaps she thought it would turn to stone if she glanced away for so much as a second. "But I wish she had. Or that Abbas had let us learn from Helena. Your point is an excellent one."

Korinna smiled. She was a woman who aged with beauty. The few strands of silver in her hair gave her dignity, and the light in her eyes—hazel, like her son's—made the warm room feel like home. "I enjoy working in the kitchen. My father tried to dissuade me too, saying it was unbefitting his daughter. But my mother, thankfully, prevailed. It has saved our reputation for hospitality a time or two, when there was too much work for poor Xanthe to handle on her own."

Rhoda looked up with a smile. "And you will teach us to cook meals too? We will be in your debt."

"Nonsense." Korinna gave her lump a final pat and transferred it back to a bowl. "It is no sacrifice—though Xanthe will handle that part of the instruction. I *can* cook a meal, but she has turned it into an art. If anyone ought to be the teacher, it is she."

From the hearth and its simmering pot, the white-haired Xanthe smiled. "It will be my pleasure to have three such avid pupils."

Korinna leaned in to check their dough. "Rhoda, another minute ought to suffice. Alexandria, just a touch more flour, I think. Yours looks ready, Cyprus, which means you can be the one to go outside with me to bring in the herbs Xanthe will need for the next lesson."

It was not exactly praise, that her dough was ready. But it felt like it. Cyprus laid the ball carefully into the clean bowl Korinna had provided for her and set it beside her hostess's in a warm corner.

Her hostess—soon to be her mother? Her heart quickened at

the thought. Despite four years of friendship between her and Petros, she had rarely interacted with his parents. She knew not what they thought of her, if they approved of their son choosing her.

But they were here now, in Korinna's kitchen. Learning from her hand. That surely spoke to her heart, and how similar it must be to Petros's.

Still, her pulse quickened even more as she followed Korinna out the kitchen door and into the little plot of ground they had turned into a garden.

Korinna sent her a soft smile. "We have already harvested and dried most of the herbs, of course, to get us through the winter. They do not thrive this time of year, but Xanthe always prefers fresh when she can use it, and I think there will be enough. Will you grab that basket please, Cyprus?"

She followed Korinna's pointing finger to a small basket hanging on a hook on the side of the house. A moment later she settled beside the woman before a row of leafy green plants.

"Basil," Korinna said, reaching into the basket for a pair of scissors. "My husband and son are both very fond of basil."

Cyprus nodded. Her heart, already so fast, thudded. Petros liked basil. His mother was making sure she knew this. Though of course, she already knew that. Still.

Korinna leaned over the plants. "My son told me that you went to see him yesterday, after he went before the courts. He came home happier than I have seen him in years."

Her cheeks would definitely never be cool again. Cyprus cleared her throat and watched the woman's hands with more care than required. What was she to say?

Korinna did not look up, nor did she wait overlong for a response. "I confess I was never certain of your heart. But you do care for him, do you not?"

Now too many words tumbled to her lips. She settled for simple ones. "More than I can say."

This time it was Korinna who nodded. She trimmed a few leaves off the plant and placed them into the basket. "I am glad of it. And I am happy to teach you and your sisters how to run a household. I have no desire for you to suffer, Cyprus—any of you."

The pace of her heart slowed. Something in her voice...

Korinna glanced up. "I am going to ask you to do something—for Petros. If you love him as he loves you, then you will hopefully see the wisdom in my request."

The heat in her cheeks chilled. Her arms grew heavy. "What is it?"

Korinna drew in a long breath and reached for another basil plant. "He is special. We have long known it, but recently...everyone knows it now. People are beginning to come from other towns to hear him present a case before the judge. Even the governor—did you know that?"

Cyprus had to rest the basket on her legs. Her hands felt like lead upon the handle. "He did not mention it."

"No. He would not." Korinna's lips curved up. "He is ever humble, our Petros. But it is so—the Vicarious himself. And then, just last week, he came to Patara again, to speak with Theophanes."

Much as she wanted to swallow, her throat would not work. She could not possibly ask why the governor of Lycia had returned to speak with Petros's father.

Korinna met her gaze and would not release it. "He came seeking a betrothal. He has a niece in his charge, just turned twelve."

Her blood cooled, slowed. "Betrothal."

Korinna's eyes showed pain. Or perhaps Cyprus just saw her own reflected there, because why would it cause *her* any sorrow at all? The woman sighed. "I know it is not what he wants. And if we were to ask him, he would refuse—because of you. So I come to you, not just as a mother seeking a favorable union for her son, but as someone who sees his value as you surely can too."

Favorable union. A union her father had never entertained before because Petros was not rich enough. A union *his* parents would now refuse because *she* was worth nothing.

Korinna set down the scissors. "You have surely heard of Augustus Diocletian's growing impatience with our brethren. I have not forgotten what life was like for the Christians after the last persecution. And I have long felt that we will have to go into hiding again. All our little churches, our orders, our bishops and priests and...it could be gone in a moment. It would mean nothing—*nothing*—if the Augustus decides we must be crushed. But someone like Petros...with his gift...he could change things. He could win favor for us all. You can see that, can you not? If he were to marry the ward of the Vicarious..."

He could change the world. Cyprus's eyes slid shut.

"I know he will not be easy to convince. And he will mourn you. But he has years to prepare his heart for her, before they could wed. It would be time enough."

Her feet had gone numb. And her legs. And her abdomen. Her arms were useless weights. She could feel nothing but the trickle of a tear down her cheek, but she could not stir herself to reach up and wipe it away. For four years they had grown close, had come to love each other. How long would it take him to purge his heart of that love?

Warm fingers touched her wrist, making her feel all the colder in comparison. "Cyprus, I do not ask this of you because I do not like you, or because I think you would be a bad match for my son. On the contrary, had this not come up...but it has. My only concern before was whether you could possibly love him like he loves you. And that is what I ask you now. He loves you enough to sacrifice for your better good. Do you love him enough to sacrifice for his? For all the church?"

Was it selfish now to want to be with the one she loved? Her heart twisted. She had already lost her mother, her home, every tangible thing that had ever meant anything to her. Her father could not remember he still lived. Other than her sisters, Petros was the one good, solid thing in her life, the one shining hope. And his mother asked her to give him up too? Willingly?

The warm fingers retreated. "I bid you to think about this. To pray about it. My son told us last night that he intends to ask you soon to be his wife. We have not yet told him about the possible arrangement with the governor. He would not hear us now. But if you refuse him, he will listen. I pray you, seek the Lord on this, as I have done. See what he tells you."

Cyprus's nod felt wooden, nothing but a conditioned response to a question from an elder. But inside, she was screaming rather than agreeing to Korinna's request. Inside, she was begging God not to ask this of her. Inside, she was none too sure she had the strength to lose someone else and keep living.

Was this what Abbas was feeling, even now?

Korinna stood, lifting the basket from Cyprus's lap. "I will tell your sisters you are taking a moment to see to a personal need. And Cyprus—I know it does not seem it to you, but I *am* sorry to ask this of you. Especially now. I just…I see no other way. My son has a great purpose. I have known it from the moment he was born. He has a great purpose, and it is my duty as his mother to do all in my power to help him fulfill it."

A great purpose. How many times had she asked God what hers was, since that fateful day? Would it not have been better if she had died then, or soon after from her injuries? Petros never would have loved her. His parents could have arranged this betrothal without any complaint from him.

She would not now be feeling such agony.

For a long moment she sat frozen in the winter sunshine, letting the tears slide unchecked down her cheeks as that old refrain pulsed.

Why. Why. Why.

Then a strain of Alexandria's laughter floated out to reach her, and she pushed to her feet. Her sisters still had a hope of happiness, however small it may be. All that stood between them and their men was money. Just money. Money could be gotten, though Cyprus knew not how to acquire it. It was not like *purpose* or *better good.* Not insurmountable.

Her fingers sought and found the edge of the green silk she wore. Ridiculous, this garment, in light of how little they now had—but all she possessed. She used it to wipe away the tears. Squared her shoulders. Walked back into Petros's house. With any luck, she could avoid her sisters' eyes until hers cleared.

Xanthe was already giving her lesson, demonstrating how to pluck a fowl. The twins watched with fascination, horror, and the occasional laugh as feathers flew. Cyprus slipped in behind them but hardly heard the words of the old servant.

"There now. Once that is done, it is time to remove the innards."

Her stomach barely turned. What if she just refused to refuse him? Would Petros marry her anyway, above his parents' objections? For they would surely tell him not to if he came home saying she had agreed. They would tell him of this other opportunity. He would shake his head and claim love was all that mattered.

He would, she knew he would. He would say he cared nothing for the governor's niece, nor for advancing his career. He would say all that was in God's hand, and that God had also led him to Cyprus, had given him this love for her.

"These we cook separately." Xanthe set aside the dark organs and wiped her hands. "Now we prepare the oils. Rhoda, could you hand me the flask?"

Rhoda reached for a tall container of deep olive oil, the same green-gold as Petros's eyes.

Cyprus slid the cellar of salt closer to them when Xanthe motioned toward it. He would never agree to this. Never. Love was more important to Petros than career. More important than politics.

More important than the whole church? What if his mother was right? What if the Augustus's impatience turned more biting? Could Petros influence those who could influence him?

And was it so certain that he would succeed at that only with the governor's niece at his side? Would Cyprus hinder him?

"The basil, please."

The basket was at her elbow. She gathered the leaves from within it and handed those over too. Xanthe slid the leaves between the skin and the meat and then poured the oil overtop the whole bird, rubbing it in.

Of course she would hinder him. All of Patara laughed, now, at her father's misfortune. All would think less of Petros if he married her.

And surely all of Lycia hated Dorus Visibullis just as much—he had no doubt found occasion to lord over too many. An association with her—with Abbas—could indeed bar doors to him that he deserved to have open.

"There. Now we put it in the oven and turn to the rest of the meal." Xanthe stepped over to the hearth and slid the prepared bird into the oven built into the bricks.

Rhoda leaned close to Cyprus. "Are you all right, honey pot?"

No. Just now, she was unsure if she would ever really feel right again. But she forced a smile. "Of course."

They remained in the warm kitchen for another interminable

two hours, while the meat roasted and then the bread was baked. Korinna had disappeared, for which Cyprus was glad. But her absence did nothing to purge her mind of those words she had spoken. They clanged around like the pots Xanthe got out, mixing together along with the spices and vegetables and grains.

By the time they set out for home, carrying baskets filled with food they had cooked, the words had stilled and settled into a pervasive sorrow, as heavy as night. Every footstep felt like a mile, but Cyprus trudged along in time with her sisters, who laughed and joked and beamed with pride at what they had accomplished that day.

Cyprus could not have repeated a single instruction Xanthe had given.

"Ho there, ladies. If you could help a weary traveler?"

Cyprus nearly ran into Rhoda's back—the twins stopped at the corner that would take them to their street, their gazes latched upon the traveler...who looked none too weary, sitting as he was upon a litter draped in silk and decorated with silver. The servants carrying him looked weary enough, though, to justify the greeting.

Alexandria dipped her knees in respect. "Greetings, traveler. How can we assist you?"

The man was young, no more than thirty years of age, surely. Hair dark and shining under his turban, eyes deep, and his teeth gleamed white and even when he smiled. "I am looking for the home of Dorus Visibullis and his daughters. Do you happen to know where I can find it?"

Her sisters stood straighter. Cyprus would have preferred, for a reason she could not quite pinpoint, to run the other way. But Rhoda was already dipping her knees as Alexandria had done. "You are in luck, good lord. Not only can we show you the way, but we are in fact the daughters of Dorus Visibullis."

"Are you now?" The man's smile grew, and his gaze sharpened. "Fortuitous indeed."

Alexandria lifted her chin. "If I may be so bold, lord—who are you, that you seek our father?"

Apparently boldness was no offense to this man. He snapped a finger, and a servant who had been walking beside the litter appeared to help him down. Whoever he was, he stood more than a foot above Cyprus, and his garments were as fine as any the Vicarious could have chosen.

He bowed. "I am Yiannis, adopted son of Stelios—your mother's uncle, who I regret to inform you passed away some two years ago." He straightened, his smile just as bright. His eyes just as sharp. "Your cousin, it would seem."

The twins exchanged a look that Cyprus could not quite interpret—though it may well be that it simply had no translation. That it was more question than conclusion.

Questions she shared aplenty.

"Our cousin," Alexandria echoed. "You received the letter we sent to Mater's uncle."

"Quite right, and why I came. I am heir, you see, to all that was his. Including..."

Cyprus's eyes slid shut.

The twins sighed. And said, as one, "Our house."

TWELVE

Petros tried to push away the worry gnawing at his stomach, but each footstep made it worry him all the more. "What if she changes her mind?"

Nikolaos rolled his eyes and glanced behind them, to where Hero had paused to retie his sandal. "Why would she? She loves you—she will not just *stop* loving you."

No, but his cousin had not seen the sorrow in her eyes when she beheld her sisters'. "If we cannot convince Hero and Kosmas though... She will never abandon her sisters to such fates. You know she will not."

"And she would not be the woman *you* love if she did." Clapping a hand to Petros's shoulder, Nikolaos gave him a shake. "Stop this. I beg of you. Give it to the Lord and focus on today's worries before you drive me to absolute madness."

It was enough to make him grin, if not to make the fearful voice inside still. "But a mad Nikolaos sounds quite entertaining. Just think of it. You can stumble around shouting Scripture in Ancient Hebrew and scare the health into people before they can even ask for a healing."

Nikolaos snorted and gave him a playful push in the arm.

Hero rejoined them, weariness in his eyes. "How much farther, do you think? I have never walked there."

"Another half hour." Petros motioned to the sea lapping against the beach at the bottom of the hill. "We have a bit more to travel along the coast, then we turn inland." At least they would reach the villa before the treacherous mountains standing between Patara and Myra could do more than loom.

"Where no doubt Kosmas will simply tell us he cannot go against his father." Hero watched a gull swoop down and then directed his gaze ahead again. "A position I well understand. Mine is at least trying to be understanding, but my mother..."

Mentions of mothers made Petros's pulse kick up. The girls were at his house right now, learning at his mother's hand. He wished he were there too, spying on them. Rarely had he seen Mother interact with Cyprus, and the need to observe how they fared together made him itchy inside.

"Well, let us pick up the pace, my friends, or we will not have a hope of getting back to Patara before nightfall." Nikolaos lengthened his gait, leaving Petros and Hero little choice but to keep up.

"Easy, cousin. We are walking to Kosmas's villa, not to Jerusalem."

"I groan at the very thought of walking to Jerusalem." Hero hurried to Nikolaos's side. "Do you not agree, Nik?"

His cousin's smile looked soft...and faraway. "I have been contemplating a pilgrimage, actually. Not, of course, that you have to walk the whole way, Hero. A ship to Caesarea, and then a five days' journey on foot. It would be...amazing."

"It would be blister-inducing." But Hero grinned. "Of course *you* must go, if you mean to join the church. And then you will return with countless stories for all your old friends."

Petros ran a few steps to put himself on Nikolaos's other side. He knew he was frowning, but he could not smooth it out. "Since when are you contemplating a pilgrimage?"

Nikolaos cast him a quick glance, there and then gone. "It has only recently become more than a passing fancy. The last few days, really."

"The last few days." While Petros was dragging him around Patara in search of Timon? The timing seemed odd. "You have mentioned nothing."

"I just did." Nikolaos shook off the faraway look, his smile turning brighter. More...*normal.* "It is not something I would do on a whim, Pet. It would require careful planning. Certainly not a task to tackle before all these weddings I am determined to see to fruition."

"I pray you do." But Hero's face had sobered, and his pace slowed again for a moment. "I cannot explain how strange this all feels to me. I had thought...I had thought this would be a month of festivities and planning. That I would soon be married and that these final weeks would be a whirl of preparations. We would celebrate the birth of Christ, and then go straight into weddings. Relatives arriving, gifts to sort, final plans for our own house, filling it with all we would need to live comfortably."

Nikolaos made a face and motioned for Hero to keep up. "It makes me glad to realize I will not have these worries. I do not intend to lead a life free of complications or emotion, but happy I am to swear off those particular trials."

Petros was only too happy to embrace them. And more besides, if it meant having Cyprus as his wife.

Gulls cried out their greetings as they continued on their path along the narrow road through the hills. Another few minutes, and the track angled inland, toward the mountains that stood sentinel. Here, it was just large, rocky outcroppings that only hinted at the difficulty the path would take on a few miles past the villa.

Hero leaned around Nikolaos to catch Petros's gaze. "Speaking of weddings that will hopefully, eventually take place...have you yet convinced Cyprus to view you as anything but a friend?"

His cheeks warmed. "I know not of what you speak, my friend."

"Ha!" Hero followed the bark of laughter with a longer strain of it. "That is the way you will play it, is it? When we all know very well how you feel about her."

If he was so transparent to everyone else, how had Cyprus remained oblivious for so long?

Not that it mattered. She knew now—knew and returned the affection. When he closed his eyes, he could still feel her in his arms, her hand on his cheek. He could still see the pure, unbridled love swelling in her blue eyes.

He had despaired of ever seeing it. But the moment he had...

He wanted to be at his house now, spying on her and his mother...and drawing her aside for another kiss. Perhaps if they made it home before dark tonight, he would slip over to her house and sit with her for a while in the courtyard. The air would be cool, but he could put an arm around her, draw her close. Touch his lips to hers again.

"He is dreaming of her even now," Hero said in a mock-whisper to Nikolaos. "Look at him—walking around as if asleep."

Nikolaos chuckled and nudged Petros. "Wake up, Pet, or you will wander off the road into a ditch, sprain your ankle, and we will be stuck at Gallus's home until you heal."

Petros shook off the wistful thoughts even as Hero loosed a gusty sigh. "Will your parents not object if you seek a union? Mine...there is no way they would even entertain such notions now, had we not already sworn our promise to Dorus. And they are quite adamant about acceptable terms being met."

To that, Petros lifted a shoulder. "Under normal circumstances, I imagine they would object as yours do. But they know how I..."

"How you love her," Nikolaos finished for him. "There is no point in denying it now, cousin." He turned to Hero. "Just yesterday he confessed his love to her, and she returns it."

If she did not change her mind. Or think herself undeserving of happiness if her sisters failed to gain theirs. So many things yet stood in their way, and he had no easy way to scale them.

"Well, that is wonderful! Petros, why did you say nothing?"

"I did." He fastened a wry smile onto his lips. "I told you it was of the utmost importance that you and Kosmas find a way to marry her sisters."

For a moment, his friend looked at him in bemusement. Then understanding struck, and he let out a breath ripe with enlightenment. "Ah. She will not marry you until we marry them."

"You see, this is a purely selfish trip on my part. I—"

A cry from the road ahead cut him off. They barely exchanged a glance before they all took off at a run, rounding the bend and the hillock that separated them from whoever had called out.

A man in black stood over a figure cowering off the side of the road, the sunlight glinting off a blade raised above his head.

"Halt!" Nikolaos's voice rang with authority that a young man of one and twenty ought not to have had, and he charged forward as though he weighed a full hundred pounds more than he did and could just tackle the attacker to the ground. "In the name of Christ Jesus, stop!"

Ice whispered over Petros's neck when the black-clad figure spun toward Nikolaos. "Lord God..." It was all the prayer he could manage aloud as he sprinted in an effort to keep up with his cousin, whose feet seemed to have sprouted wings.

The dread in his stomach foretold a confrontation, a fight, possible tragedy. So much so that he could scarcely make sense of it when the attacker staggered back a step at Nikolaos's thrusting hand—Nik was still ten strides away. He could not comprehend it when the man in black spun and ran off into the hills.

The figure on the ground moaned.

Nikolaos skidded to a halt at the victim's side. "Petros, Hero, hurry! We must get him to Kosmas's house right away!"

Petros's feet obeyed, his hands reached to help lift the man to his feet. But his gaze still traced the retreating figure that was even now melting into the scrub. "We should catch him. He will only attack another, later."

"We cannot. We must see this young man to safety. Kosmas's house will have bandages and a place for him to rest." Nikolaos's words still rang with that authority.

It had never grated on Petros before. But just now it chafed against what he knew in *his* gut. "But—"

The young man looked up, his eyes cloudy with pain. His hand was clutched to his side. "You know my brother?"

Brother? Petros finally pulled his eyes away from the figure he could scarcely see anymore, to the profile that did, indeed, look vaguely familiar. "He is a friend of ours. Are you...?" What was the name of the brother Kosmas complained about so ardently? He rarely used a name—just spat out *my brother* as if it were a curse.

He had been in school at Rome. That was all Petros could recall.

"Felix," Hero said with a nod. "I did not know you were due home."

Felix winced and pulled his hand away, bloody. He quickly pressed it again to his side. "My brother did not mention it? Apparently the years have changed little then."

Nikolaos had covered Felix's wound with his own hand as well and was murmuring something Petros could not quite catch.

After a moment he nodded. "You will be well, but the wound ought to be bound, and a salve with honey applied."

Felix's brows knit. "The pain has—what did you do? Who are you?"

Hero smirked. "You have never met the won—"

"Nikolaos." He shot a glare at Hero. "Son of Epiphanius, of Patara. Can you walk?"

Felix nodded. "I am sure it is barely a scratch. But it hurt terribly just a moment ago, and now I scarcely feel it. What did you do?"

"It did not hurt much until you saw the blood, did it? It was only your reaction to that sight. I merely prayed it back into proportion. Come." Now Nikolaos scanned the hills. "We should hurry. Hopefully the bandit has no friends hiding in the hills."

Petros bit back the urge to point out that they would know whether he had or not if they had pursued him. Nikolaos would only argue that they could well have been running into an ambush, if he had.

Sometimes it was annoying to know his cousin so well. And even more annoying to realize he could well be right.

"Have you anything with you?" Hero looked around, brows knit. "Did they make off with anything?"

"No." Felix motioned them onward, but though his face was clear of pain, it was by no means clear. "All my things will follow as soon as a cart is available, but I did not want to wait. I thought to just walk home."

Petros fell in on Felix's side, his eyes still scanning the distant scrub, looking for any movement to indicate the fiend had friends who could jump out and attack them all. "How long were you in Rome?"

"Eight years." His lips curved up, making him at once look more like Kosmas—they had similar smiles—and less like him—

Kosmas rarely smiled. "I confess part of me wondered if I would even remember the way home from the port."

"Apparently you did," Hero said.

"But I do not remember it being so dangerous."

Petros shook his head. "I come this way at least once a month and have never heard of any ruffians. They must be newly arrived in the area. Perhaps your father will know more about them."

"Are you all from Patara, as Nikolaos is?"

Petros and Hero nodded. "We know your brother through the church, of course, but more through his betrothed," Petros said. "Hero is engaged to her sister."

"And Petros soon will be to her *other* sister." Hero grinned and elbowed Petros in the ribs. "Eh?"

He nudged him back and kept his gaze ahead. "And Nikolaos is my cousin."

Nikolaos turned somber eyes on them from a step ahead. "If you have been en route from Rome, you would certainly not have heard what just befell the Visibullises—the family of Kosmas's betrothed."

He told the tale during the last few minutes of the trip, and by the time he fell silent, the bustle of the busy villa—animals lowing, shepherds calling to them, field hands lifting voices high to make lighter the work of their hands—covered any need for a response. Soon enough the imposing structure that Kosmas called home rose into view. It sprawled out across the countryside as no house could ever do in the city. Larger than it probably needed to be, Petros had always thought, and grander. He had heard the bishop mutter more than once that Gallus put money into the upkeep of needless finery that he could have been spending on feeding the hungry and clothing the poor. But the villa saw to the livelihood of countless peasants, so the bishop always bit his tongue.

Their knock was answered by a servant, whose usual emotionless greeting of him and Nikolaos melted away when he spotted their new companion. "Master Felix! Come, come—what happened? You are bleeding!"

"I was waylaid on the road—but it is nothing. A bandage and a salve and I shall be well." He peered over the servant's head as he stepped inside. "Are they home?"

"Yes, yes, come." The servant gripped Felix's shoulder. He glanced at the rest of them only long enough to wave them toward the usual room in which Kosmas received them. "I will tell Master Kosmas you are here. But of course, his brother's homecoming takes precedence."

"Of course." Petros inclined his head, smiled, but let it fade as he turned into the room with his cousin and friend. "Kosmas will not be happy to see his brother. Felix is younger?"

"Older, by a year. His mother died birthing him, and Gallus quickly remarried." Hero sank into one of the cushions arranged for their comfort, looking as though he had walked a hundred miles rather than ten. "Kosmas's mother never much cared for Felix. She was, I understand, all too happy to send him to Rome when his mother's family asked for him to come and finish his education there."

From the back of the house, Gallus's shout came, loud and boisterous and obviously far happier to see his eldest son than his wife might be. Laughter ran out, filling the house.

A sound Petros had never heard here before, aside from what they brought with them.

Nikolaos took a seat too. "Well, Petros. We have time. Tell us about your next case."

He did so, but got no more than a few minutes into the explanation before stomping steps preceded Kosmas's entrance into the room. "Greetings. I hear you saved my brother's life."

Nikolaos lifted a brow. "You say that as though we should apologize for it."

"Of course not. I am sorry." Rubbing a hand over his face, Kosmas folded himself onto a cushion. "The servants are fussing over his wound, Father hovering at his elbow. They have no need of me. What brings you here? Is Xandria well?"

"I imagine so. They were all with my mother today, learning the fine art of bread baking." Petros smiled.

Kosmas did not. "Why? My wife will have no need of such knowledge. That is what servants are for."

Servants she would no longer be bringing with her to her marriage. Petros slid a glance to Hero, who cleared his throat. "And if she cannot bring them? If they cannot muster the gold? What will you do, Kosmas?"

Kosmas's frown only deepened. There were emotions there, Petros was sure. But they were so tangled up that he could not be certain which one dominated. "It will not be an issue. Dorus has spent a lifetime conniving and plotting and turning a bunch of nothing into gold. He will do it again. The wedding may be delayed, but not for long."

Hero firmed his lips. "Dorus will not get out of bed. He has declared them all lost. He has…he has told the girls they will have to turn to the streets if they wish to eat." He surged to his feet. "I will not let that befall Rhoda. I cannot do that and still live with myself. I would sooner wed a pauper than watch the woman I love stoop to prostitution."

"Romantic nonsense." It sounded like an echo—probably of Gallus's words. Kosmas kneaded his temples. "You say it now, you feel it, and so do I. But reality will paint a different tale, and your parents will never permit it. You know they will not. *Mine* certainly never will."

"You cannot just abandon her!" Hero stepped forward, his

cheeks flushed. "You cannot. If not because of what it will do to the woman you swore to protect, then for her entire *family.* One of them will not choose happiness at the cost of her sister, you know this. If you abandon Xandria, you are consigning her *and* Rhoda *and* Cyprus to the streets." He stood taller, sucked in a breath. "I *will* keep this promise. It is one I made with my heart, not my purse, and I will honor it."

Petros looked from one to the other. "Kosmas, I have watched you this last year, not sure if your heart was even involved. I worried, I prayed...and I was beyond relieved when I heard your father say you still wished to marry her. You love her. You must."

"Of course. But what am I to *do*?" Kosmas splayed his hands wide, his eyes a confusion of feeling.

Petros stood, smiled. "You are to keep your word—your...let us call it your *smaller* word. You swore that you would celebrate the birth of Christ with us, at the Visibullis house. We promised we would all be together. Come on the solstice. Come and celebrate." *And see her again.* Surely, when faced with Alexandria's imploring eyes, he would care more for her than Gallus's dictates.

Kosmas narrowed his eyes. "You were not even there."

"I added my promise later." And now he grinned. "Come, Kosmas. You can stay the week in Patara with one of us."

"Kosmas!" Gallus's bellow echoed through the halls. "Where did you disappear to, with your brother so newly arrived?"

A shadow overtook Kosmas's face.

"Or..." Petros turned his grin into a smirk. "You could always stay home with your brother."

Kosmas pushed himself to his feet, his expression now determined. "You may have to give me an hour to pry myself free."

With a laugh, Hero leaned against the wall. "Take all the time you need, my friend. So long as you come."

THIRTEEN

"Praise God that Xanthe and Korinna sent us home with food."

Cyprus nodded and handed the platter over, into Rhoda's shaking hands. She could only imagine the sneer that would have overtaken Yiannis's too-white teeth had they offered him nothing but a crust of bread and some cheese.

Not that he had thus far sneered. Exactly. Though he had come rather close when they led him inside and he saw the empty state of the house. And then had come even closer when, rather than come out to greet him, Abbas had insisted their guest come to *him*. Yiannis sat on the single chair in Abbas's chamber now, listening to their woeful tale.

They could be homeless by nightfall.

"He will be kind." Alexandria measured wine into a serving carafe, her voice less hopeful than insistent. "He surely did not come all this way to be cruel. He could have sent a steward to do it if he meant only to kick us out."

Unless he were the type who took pleasure in doing such things himself. Cypress reached into their baskets for the roasted vegetables, still warm, and arranged them around the fowl that

Rhoda had just positioned on the old, scarred wooden platter.

Rhoda hefted the tray with the food, Alexandria carried the wine and glasses, and Cyprus gathered plates and bowls. The men would have to eat in Abbas's room—it was the only one they had not stripped of furnishings. Still inside were the table and cushions that he and Mater used to recline at.

They moved quietly through the hall and slipped into the chamber, sliding their goods onto the low table without interrupting Abbas's tale of the heartless neighbors that would not pay full price for any of their belongings.

As if he had been the one haggling with them.

Cyprus clamped down on the uncharitable thoughts toward her father and focused on helping the twins arrange the food on the table.

A shadow fell over them. "My dear cousins—I appreciate the effort you have gone to, but please. Do not think you must serve me yourselves. Leave that to the slaves, I beg of you, so that you may join us in our meal."

Alexandria was the first to stand, her chin lifted. "I beg your pardon, cousin. We would, but our slaves have run away."

"They saw the weakness of an old man and seized it. Vile creatures." Abbas *looked* old, weak as he said it. How could so few days effect such an enormous change in him?

Yiannis's brows knit. "Vile indeed. But then, one can never trust a slave to behave nobly. They have inferior natures, after all."

Cyprus rose along with Rhoda, not sure why she wanted to defend Helena and Mellos and their girls when they had done them such harm. Yet opening her mouth to do just that.

Rhoda beat her to it. "Their natures are simply human, nothing less or more. When Abbas threatened to sell them, separating their family, they reacted as any family would, preserving themselves above all." She shot a look at Abbas.

Cyprus pressed her lips together against a smile. She ought to have said "as any family *should*." For Abbas certainly had not acted to preserve *them*.

Yiannis smiled, but it looked...tight. Unconvinced. "Even so. I do beg you to join us. The older of you anyway. The youngest can serve—that will do, will it not?"

Cyprus, standing on the opposite side of the small table as her sisters, watched both their backs straighten, matching defiance in their shoulders. They would refuse, she knew, to leave such tasks to her alone.

Alexandria went so far as to raise her chin. "You came with a full retinue of servants, lord. Surely one of them can serve you."

Yiannis smiled at her. "My servants are currently busy turning the empty chamber you lent me into one suitable for sleeping in this night. So unless you would prefer to send your sister to help there and call one of my men in here..."

They would argue more, Cyprus knew. Before they could, she smiled and dipped her knees. "I would be pleased to serve my family. Do sit, sisters, and rest."

"But—"

"Come." Yiannis touched Rhoda's elbow and gave her a warm smile. "You can sit on my right side, your sister on my left. Please. I wish to hear how such lovely young women have survived such a trying situation. I can only imagine the hardships you two have endured since that terrible news reached you."

"We *three*." Alexandria moved with their guest, but she looked none too relaxed as she sank down beside him. "Cyprus—"

"Can begin serving now." Yiannis positioned himself on his cushions like a king and flicked a cold look Cyprus's way.

Perhaps it felt colder than it was. Harder. Perhaps he was not *trying* to degrade her, much as it felt like it. Perhaps her heart was just still raw from that conversation with Korinna.

Or perhaps he simply saw in a glance that apparent truth—she was not what her sisters were.

She dished up hearty portions of each dish and delivered the first plate to their guest. He did not acknowledge her. He had launched into some explanation or another of how Mater's uncle had come to adopt him when it became obvious he would sire no heir of his own before his death.

She portioned out a plate for Abbas next—smaller, since he had eaten nothing in days and would likely not be able to stomach much, but still generous. He would surely eat in the presence of a guest. She must take advantage of that.

Abbas did not look at her either. His gaze was riveted on Yiannis.

Then two matching plates for the twins, who not only met her gaze but managed to convey two lectures within them. Cyprus sent them muted smiles as she handed over the food and turned to hand out glasses.

She felt a bit outside herself as she circled the room, pouring wine from the amphora into each chalice. In her mind's eye she saw Petros reclining on a cushion lush with gold and silver thread. He wore the best clothing, deep and colorful, looking so handsome as he smiled and gripped a cup edged in gold.

Beside him she imagined a woman, petite and beautiful. What would this governor's niece look like? Perhaps she would have that rare golden beauty, with fair hair and eyes. She would be wearing silk in purple or blue. Gold adornments for her hair. She would hang on Petros's every word, look at him with complete adoration. And he would look at her with that same love with which he had gazed at Cyprus yesterday.

"You foolish girl! Take care!"

She jerked back to the present, but even so could not immediately discern what she had done wrong. Why Yiannis held out his arm like that, with disgust on his face.

"Fetch a towel, girl. Quickly."

For what? She had to stare for a long moment before she spotted the single drop of wine she had splashed onto his arm. Not even onto his expensive garment, but simply onto his wrist.

Alexandria rolled her eyes. "It is nothing, cousin. Please, allow me to—"

"The girl did it, she will clean it up." He sent her a scathing glare.

Cyprus dipped her knees again and set the bottle of wine down on the table. "Of course. Pardon me."

They had not brought a towel in with the tray of food—Helena would have, but Cyprus was new to this. She hurried from the room, back to the kitchen, and snatched one up. Then had to squelch the urge to linger there in the quiet, just to spite him.

"Stop behaving like a child, Cyprus," she whispered to herself.

Chiding delivered, she forced her feet to carry her back to Abbas's bedchamber and padded over to Yiannis. He still held his arm out, aloft, as though it were a snake that might bite him. One gentle daub with her towel, and the offending drop of red was gone.

Not that he so much as thanked her. Apparently, having decided she would serve, he also determined to treat her with no more respect than he apparently did any servant. Perhaps he thought *her* of an inferior nature too.

Were Petros here, he would have some jest ready about how apparently that nature was tied to the towel, so that whoever held the thing immediately possessed it.

Of course, were Petros here, he would tell her with a glance that she was all she needed to be—the woman he loved.

Her gaze darted to the window. What were the chances that

he would stop by tonight? Rarely did a day pass that he did not visit...but then, his mother had said he had to travel out into the countryside today. In which case, he might not get back until late. And might be too tired to come here.

Or perhaps his parents would intercept him at home and begin the campaign to convince him to marry the Vicarius's niece instead.

No—they would wait for Cyprus to break his heart first. Trusting that she would. That she loved him enough to push him away. Her own heart broke at the very thought.

"What is the matter, honey pot?" Rhoda touched Cyprus's wrist, her words in an undertone, sneaking in below Yiannis's strong voice.

She shook her head, hopefully clearing her face in the process. Now was not the time to spill out these woes. There may never be a time. She had not told her sisters of Petros's confession of love—it had seemed too cruel, when their own beloveds were out of reach. How could she do so now, just to follow it up with the realization that she must relinquish him?

They would tell her she need not. They would tell her she deserved happiness, that she deserved love, and that his mother could keep her ambitions to herself. They would tell her everything she longed to hear, stroke her hair, assure her she should hope in a bright future.

But that would only cloud her judgment. No. She would tell them of all this after she had prayed and reached a decision. But just now...just now she needed to seek guidance from the Lord alone.

And pray that, for once, she heard his answer clearly.

Jerusalem. With every footfall, Nikolaos heard the call of that far-off land. He had gone to sleep last night wrestling with his own heart, praying for an answer. He had woken with that crystalline echo in his mind.

He had smiled and laughed with Petros yesterday evening, after his cousin had rushed in and fallen on Nikolaos's hard little bunk with a happy whoop. He had congratulated him on finally being sure of Cyprus's heart. He had wished his cousin all the best things in life—and he had meant it. He wanted them both to be happy. He knew they would be happiest together. He knew that they were suited to marriage and family.

He knew he was not.

But knowledge was never enough to curb feelings. Not without work.

His eyes scanned the seashore now, as they topped one of the many sandy hills between the mountains and Patara. He ought to praise the Lord for this experience—for how was he to serve a flock of heartbroken people if he had never felt such sorrow himself? He had lost his parents, it was true, but that was a different kind of ache.

He ought to praise the Lord for this experience...but again, the knowledge was not enough to make him do so with any feeling.

He could act, though, without feeling it. He could say the words. He could do what he knew—*knew*—was right. And when he saw them happy, together, it would be worth it. It would help the ache.

As would then taking some time away from them. *Jerusalem.* He had long ago suggested to Uncle that a pilgrimage was appealing to him. But the bishop had dismissed it when Nikolaos first brought it up, insisting he was too young to travel alone, and that he could not join him.

He was old enough now though. He could go. Follow whatever path the Lord set him on. Sleep where the Spirit whispered to sleep. Eat where the Spirit told him to eat. Take a few months or even years to focus on nothing but the sound of his voice. Purge himself of all inclinations that were not of God. Ready himself to take on whatever role the Father asked of him.

"So. When did you decide you wanted to go to Israel?"

Had his thoughts been painted on his face? Nikolaos summoned a smile and squinted into the setting sun so he could look over at Petros, who had fallen in beside him. "You know I have long wanted to do so."

"As a vague 'someday' idea, certainly. But you sounded a bit firmer than that earlier."

"The idea was bright and clear when I woke up this morning." He spared his eyes the glare, looking forward again. Toward home. But how long would it be home? "The timing makes sense. You will all be marrying soon, starting your families. When better to dedicate myself fully to God than when all my friends are dedicating themselves to wives?"

Petros grunted. "I suppose my reaction is purely selfish—when we left Patara before, it was together. Always together. I cannot imagine a life where I cannot just knock upon your door and find you there. Where I cannot seek you out."

To share stories of his bliss with Cyprus...about their children...to ask advice on how to surprise her with a grand gift.

Thought of Cyprus and Petros brought merely a pang, not a stab of pain. It was an infatuation, not love. Nothing like what Petros would have felt, had their situations been reversed. Nikolaos glanced behind them, to where Hero and Kosmas trudged, arguing about something or another. "It is not that I want to leave my friends—you know that."

"Indeed I do. But we answer to a higher One than each other." Petros's gait hitched, his shoulders knotting. "Did you hear...?"

His cousin had been on edge the whole way home thus far, relaxing only a degree after they passed the spot where Felix had been attacked earlier in the day. Nikolaos opened his mouth to assure him that all was as it should be.

He got nothing out. Not before a soul-crawling scream pierced the air, the kind that came from multiple throats but in one accord.

Then they were everywhere, jumping out from behind the scrub and rocks. Nikolaos could get no count of them. He saw only the flash of the setting sun on gleaming blades. Heard only those blood-curdling cries.

A scuffle. A *thunk* that reverberated through his skull. The world lost its color. It swayed, the sky dipped down to meet him, the earth reached up to cradle him. He blinked but saw only blurs edged in darkness. He could hear only a rushing.

Then black.

Jostling brought awareness back, and pain with it. He winced and reached a sluggish hand up, toward his head.

"Nik!" A hand, familiar and warm, gripped his shoulder. "Nik, are you all right?"

Petros. Nikolaos blinked his eyes open, expecting to wince at the light. But there was precious little of that, just the dusky shadow of twilight. He tried to speak, but a groan slipped out instead.

His cousin helped him to sit, his eyes darting this way and that. "Hurry, if you can stand. They are gone for now, but I do not trust them to stay that way for long. Here." Petros reached for the skin of water they had brought with them, held it up for him.

Nikolaos took a quick drink, though his head pounded too much for him to want to tilt his head back for a longer pull. "What happened?"

"Bandits—a considerable pack of them, though one looked

much like the fellow who attacked Felix earlier. They were lying in wait." Petros tugged on Nikolaos's arm. "They knocked you out first, took the few coins Hero and I had with us."

"And Kosmas?"

Petros looked to his right, brows drawn. "His leg has been injured. We lost the light too quickly for me to see how bad it is—I am not even certain if one of them cut it or if he perhaps hit a rock when he fell. But he will need to be supported back to Patara. We are only a mile or so out of town. Can you walk?"

"Yes, of course." To prove it, he let go of his cousin's arm and tested his balance. Aside from the crashing pain in his head, he was well enough. "At least they wanted only our coins and not our lives as recompense for interrupting them earlier."

"Praise God for that."

Nikolaos reached up to probe at the place on his head that seemed to be the wellspring of all the pain. A knot greeted him, though no blood slicked his fingers.

Kosmas certainly did not seem to be faring as well. His groan drew Nikolaos toward where Hero knelt over him.

"Nik." Hero's face, though cloaked in the gathering darkness, was drawn. "Perhaps you can help."

Perhaps he should have stopped them. Should have heeded Petros's warning, listened to his cousin's concerns. He had scared the bandit off earlier—if he had but seen them this time...

The thoughts joined the cloud of pain over his eyes. Nikolaos pushed them away with a whispered, "Take them, Lord," and picked his way carefully over the rocks to his two friends. His head still throbbed, but at least his vision had cleared. Though he had not realized it had been literally clouded.

"Can you heal him?" Hero edged out of the way, seeming at a loss as to what to do with his bloodied hands. The hem of his robes had been rent, leaving six inches of ankle and leg visible.

Nikolaos crouched down and reached toward the injured leg, bound in the missing length of Hero's garment. Still, Nikolaos could see that the once-light linen had been stained dark.

"Do not touch me!" Kosmas jerked away before Nikolaos got too close, his voice drenched with pain. "It hurts too much."

"I know. I will not injure you more, I promise you." He stretched out his hand over the bound wound, careful to hover a few inches above it.

His head pounded. Perhaps that was why he felt no rush of the Spirit as he opened his heart toward God. Perhaps that was why no heat gathered in his hand as it so often did when the Lord bade him reach out and touch, heal. Perhaps that was why he heard no whisper to reach out at all.

"Just leave me alone. Take me home." Kosmas turned his head to the right then the left, his breathing hard.

"Patara is closer. We can treat you there and send for your family." Petros rested a hand on Nikolaos's shoulder. "And you as well, cousin. We must see to your head."

"I will be fine." He was confident of that. What baffled him was why he felt the same impotence with Kosmas as he did with the broken men in Timon's alley. "We should hurry."

Petros and Hero lifted a groaning, shouting Kosmas between them. A few steps told Nikolaos he would do best to concentrate on putting one foot in front of the other rather than trying to find some other way to help them. The mile between them and help seemed to stretch on forever into the night, but at last a few twinkling lights from the outmost houses of town came into view.

They headed for Hero's home, as it was closer than any other. Nikolaos hurried ahead when they got to the right street, raising his fist to the door.

A servant answered it with a lamp in hand, recognition instant on his face. "Master Nikolaos. Hero is not—"

"He is coming behind me with Kosmas, who is injured. Please, we need a bed for him at once, and whoever in the house is most skilled at tending wounds."

The manservant's eyes went wide. "Of course! Come in, come in! I will prepare the room next to Hero's."

"I will stay here to tell him so." He stepped out of the doorway, holding the solid slab of wood open for Hero and Petros, who panted their way over the threshold.

The light struck their faces, carving lines of exhaustion and discomfort that the darkness had hidden.

"The room beside yours," he said to Hero, who nodded and led the way.

Nikolaos closed the door behind them and followed. The throb in his head had eased a bit during the walk. Still there, but better. Enough that he could give more focused attention to prayer for Kosmas and whoever would be called to tend him.

Within a few minutes, Kosmas was settled on a bed, a servant had been dispatched with a message for his father, and an aging woman had settled beside him with a basket of herbs and balms and a warm smile on her face.

The rest of them stood against the wall while she unwound the fabric stolen from Hero's garment and examined the wound. Worry did not pucker her brow. She smiled, in fact. "There now, young man. It is not so bad a cut. Deep, but I will stitch it after I cleanse it. You will be well."

"I will not be well." Kosmas turned his face away, his jaw tense. "My betrothed is destitute, my father is without any compassion, my *brother* is home to lord over me, and now this. I am not *well* at all."

Nikolaos pressed his lips together. It was not just that he had felt the same way he did when facing the broken men in Timon's alley—Kosmas sounded like them too. Which meant he was right, oddly—he was definitely not well.

FOURTEEN

Everything was burning. No, only half of it was burning—the other half was still raw. Cyprus pulled the toasted bread away from the fire, shoved the meat closer, burned her hand mildly, and blamed the tears on the discomfort, rather than her complete failure to do something as simple as make breakfast.

If only she had paid more attention to Xanthe's lesson yesterday, rather than mourning the loss of all her dreams. Then they would be able to eat now—and she could mourn later.

A light knock sounded on the door. It opened before she could do more than spin that direction, and Petros stepped in, his cloak rain-spattered. She flew at him, wrapping her arms around him even as she suspected she was consigning the meat to destruction in doing so. "Petros! I am the worst cook in the history of kitchens."

He chuckled, cradled her head, and leaned down to touch his lips to hers. For that moment, the world was all as it should be. Right. Perfect. Beautiful. She heard only the song of promise in her ears, saw behind her closed eyes only sunshine.

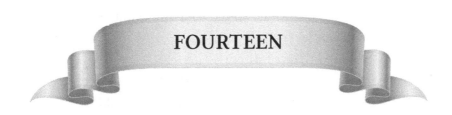

Then he pulled away to take off his damp cloak, and even his grin could not help her ignore all the different tragedies poised to destroy them. He kissed the tip of her nose. "Why are the twins not helping, if you are so terrible? Xanthe said they learned her lessons quickly."

The tears were still hovering in her eyes. He would see, but he would also see if she turned her face away and tried to wipe at them. "He will not let them."

Petros frowned. "Your father?"

"No." She cast a glance over her shoulder, as if their guest might appear at her mention. But no, Yiannis would never lower himself to appearing in a kitchen. Though his servants might. She was rather surprised he had not sent one of his slaves to make sure she was creating food fit for his exulted mouth. "Our cousin has come—the one who owns this house."

Petros winced...and then stepped around her to tend her raw meat. "What is he like?"

A dozen uncomplimentary descriptions sprang to her tongue, but she bit them all back. She would not whine about him. She would not speak ill. She would remember that he held their futures in his hands, and she would pray he leaned toward mercy.

So she shrugged. "He seems quite taken with the twins. He insists they sit on his right and left and tells me to serve. And, apparently, prepare the food. Which is not a problem," she rushed to add.

"Except you cannot cook." Petros grinned at her over his shoulder.

Her heart stuttered. How would she survive seeing him walk about town with a pretty little wife in a few years? She could not. There was no way. She would have to find the means to leave after she turned him down. It hardly even mattered where she went, so long as she did not have to see him and love him and miss him and...

She did not want to turn him down. Was not sure she was

strong enough, selfless enough to do so.

Apparently satisfied with the meat now, Petros stood, his smile fading. "I came by to tell you what happened yesterday. We were waylaid on our way back from Gallus's villa. Nikolaos was struck over the head and passed out for a few minutes—he seems better this morning. But Kosmas's leg was cut somehow. Fever has set in already, and the wound is..." He shook his head. "I thought perhaps if Alexandria came to see him and reminded him of why he was on that road to begin with, it would help. At the moment his thoughts seem to be festering more than his leg."

A feeling she knew well. "Poor Kosmas. Of course. I will go and tell them, if you would keep an eye on the food."

Petros waved that away. "It will be fine for a few minutes."

She blinked. "It will turn to ruin." Just look at the toast, and she had scarcely glanced away for half a moment.

Her beloved smiled and took her hand in his. "It will be quite a while before that lamb is ready. We will toast a few new slices of bread for your guest and father when it is finished. Unless you prefer to hide me in the kitchen?"

Cyprus rolled her eyes and tugged him forward. He had bought the meat—it was his prerogative to ruin it if he wanted. "They are all in the main chamber. Yiannis apparently sent his servants out at first light to purchase furnishings fit for his..." She swallowed down the mocking adjective that had wanted to slip out. "For him."

"Mm." His fingers wove through hers. They were longer, his palm wider. So how did they fit together so perfectly? "And how is your father doing, now that he has an esteemed guest under his roof?"

"I cannot say." Keeping their pace slow, she turned her face up to his. "Even with the company, he ate only four bites last night. And only when Yiannis commented on a dish, so that he could answer him. Then later, after our cousin retired, I heard Abbas retching. It made no one else sick, but perhaps his stomach could not handle the food after going without? I planned to make some broth. Once I figure out how. Sapphira may be willing to teach me. Perhaps."

"Or perhaps he forced himself to lose those bites." His face shadowed with concern, Petros gave a slow shake of his head. "I am so sorry you must watch him behave this way."

"I just want..." She closed her eyes, knowing Petros would never permit her to walk into a wall or trip. Not while he was there, their fingers woven together. "I just want him to want to *live*. To realize that even without Mater, there is still love in the world."

As there would be without Petros. Abbas still had her and Alexandria and Rhoda. She would still have *them*.

And even if that too were stripped away... God would still be there. It may not *feel* like it, but faith could not rely on feeling. If it did, then Nikolaos would not have been able to heal her that day when she had lost all feeling, when despair had flooded her spirit.

But she had believed. She *had*, and she walked now as proof of it.

She would walk still no matter what life brought her. Even if she walked it alone.

Her fingers tightened around Petros's, then relaxed as they reached the open archway that led into the main room.

He did not let her go as they came within sight of the others. She watched him take in the scene in one thoughtful gaze, though. The way Yiannis had positioned himself on a lush cushion, the way his four slaves fawned and hovered and responded to the slightest twitch of his finger. The way the twins sat stiff on either side of him. The way Abbas perched on a chair as if he were folded in on himself. There but not there. Even now.

Yiannis was the first to note their arrival, evidenced by the thunder in his brow. "I thought you were tending the meal, girl. And who is this who comes into my house at such an hour?"

Alexandria looked as though she were gritting her teeth together. "Her name, dearest cousin, is *Cyprus*."

"And that is our dear friend Petros, son of Theophanes." Rhoda smiled but it was small and tight.

"The advocate?" Yiannis's face cleared, even went bright. He rose. "In that case, welcome to my home, Petros, son of Theophanes. Tales of your arguments before the courts have gone throughout the whole region."

Petros inclined his head. "I am humbled that you know my name, lord. I assure you, I am but an avid student of my father, who is a better advocate than I can ever hope to be."

"Nonsense. And you are friends of these cousins of mine?" Yiannis's gaze narrowed onto their joined hands.

"For years." He smiled in that way that always put everyone at ease. But his fingers gripped hers.

He liked Yiannis no more than she did, she could tell.

"A friend who does not usually come at such an hour." Abbas glared at him, apparently not impressed by the fact that Yiannis was.

"Forgive me for intruding so early." Petros bowed slightly, aiming it at her father. "I would not have had it not been important." Now he turned toward the twins. "It is Kosmas. He came back with us yesterday, and we were attacked along the road. He is injured. I thought if Alexandria—"

"Of course! I am coming." She sprang to her feet, panic in her eyes. "How bad is it?"

He spread his free hand in a gesture of helplessness. "I cannot rightly say. It should not have been too terrible, but infection seems to be setting in."

Yiannis folded his arms over his chest. "Who is this Kosmas, that he takes my lovely cousins away from my side?"

Rhoda had stood too, linking her arm through Alexandria's. They would go together, as they went most places.

But neither had actually seen her betrothed since the tragedy. Would things have changed?

Alexandria lifted her chin. "My betrothed."

Abbas snorted. "He *was*, anyway, before our misfortune. We all know he will not marry you now. His father will not relent."

"He is my betrothed, he is injured, and he needs me." Alexandria, exuding pure stubbornness, dipped her knees. "Excuse us, cousin. Abbas. We will return once we are assured of his well-being. He is at Hero's home?"

Petros nodded, obviously trying to tamp down a grin at her sisters' defiance. "They are expecting you."

"Then we must hasten. Rhoda, Cyprus, hurry."

"Cyprus must stay." Abbas spoke the dictate with a ring of authority, but with nothing else coloring his tone. "Yiannis needs his meal."

She could disobey. Ignore him. See if he stirred himself enough to actually care and come after her. She wanted to go with them and see how things stood with the men on whom they had hinged their hearts. She wanted to leave Yiannis to his own devices.

But something stayed her tongue, and her intentions. She was unsure what it was...until a familiar refrain filtered into her mind. *Honor your father and your mother.*

Her nostrils flared. When God had given that command, when Paul had expounded on the charges of honoring and respecting and loving and staying beside one's family, they obviously knew that sometimes those people would be undeserving of such respect.

They commanded it anyway. Not to the point of disobeying

God in other ways—she would never, never obey Abbas's command to stop praying. But honor was not just obedience, was it? It was something more. Something deeper. Something, perhaps, that sought the best thing *for* that person, not just *from* him.

And the best thing for Abbas right now was to show him she loved him. To show him, somehow, that even through all of this *God* loved him.

She nodded. "Of course, Abbas. I will go and check on it now."

The twins were already rushing for their room and, no doubt, head pieces and heavier robes to defend against the rain pattering down outside. Cyprus and Petros headed back toward the kitchen.

He looked none too pleased. "I do not like the way he spoke to you—or rather, *of* you."

"It hardly matters. He will make whatever decision he will make about the house, and I will never see him again." She could stand to be belittled for a few days.

"Hmm." Petros steered her back over to the fire, where the lamb was beginning to waft a pleasant smell. He crouched down and turned each cutlet over. "I suppose so. We will hopefully have your sisters safely wed by the end of the festival of lights, or soon after. Then *we* can be—and your father can go with whichever of us he desires. No one will need this house anyway."

She could not bring herself to disagree. How could she, when his thoughts were all for her family, for taking care of them? For loving her?

How could she, when *her* thoughts were all for loving him, and them? There was no place for denial in the middle of such love. "I know not what I would do without you, Petros."

He rose, his eyes as smoldering as the fire, and drew her close again. Fingers on her cheek, gaze locked on hers. "Nor I you. And I pray to God that neither of us will have to figure it out for many years to come."

"To God's ear."

He kissed her again, still so tentative and sweet but enough to make her wish for a longer moment alone, without the noise of her sisters even now intruding. Though even then, it would all come crashing back down as soon as he pulled away. His mother's words and expectations would still intrude. There would be no escaping it.

The twins bustled in, pulling head coverings over their hair as they walked. "We are ready," Alexandria declared.

Petros nodded. His fingers had left her face, of course, but sought her hand again for another squeeze of her fingers. "I will return later, after I have finished my work for the day."

Cyprus nodded, said farewell to her sisters, and shut the door behind them. It was too quiet in their wake. Nothing but the patter of rain and the pop and sizzle of the meat. For a long moment, she just rested her head against the door and listened to the near-silence.

Dear God... She pressed her palm to the door. *Show me how to help them. How to honor my father. Please, help me to show him your love, not just my own. Make yourself manifest to him, Lord Almighty. Awe him with your truth and goodness.*

How many times had she prayed and yet felt her prayers just hovered in the room with her? And it felt that way still. But then she drew in a breath and the realization came. It was not her own words hovering there, clanging against each other and her expectations. It was the Spirit hovering, the loving hand of her loving God, assuring her that he heard. That he always heard. And that his arm was not too short.

Thank you, Father.

She turned back to the food, adding to her prayer that she somehow manage to present an edible meal. Praying that their guest show them mercy. Praying that the twins would find their places beside the men they loved. That Kosmas would recover. That a way would be made for all of them.

That he would tell her what she was to do about Petros and his mother's request.

The room filled as she prayed. With the scent of the cooking meat, with the music of the rain, and with the certainty that her Lord was right there, at her side. She had only to listen for him, and she would hear his voice.

Never had that certainty settled so fully into her heart as it did then, when there was no one to intone the Scriptures, no sisters to assure her of their truth, no mother to promise her a bright future. No father willing to indulge.

She had only him to depend on. And it was more than she could ever need.

The smell of the meat bade her return to the fire, and a quick slice of the cutlets told her they were done. She took a quick bite to see if it was edible, smiling at the flavor. Petros must have added a few spices when she was not looking, though she could not imagine when he had done so. Or what he had added.

It took only a minute to toast a few new slices of bread over the coals, and then she added everything to the tray, along with some cheese and dried fruit. She prayed for steady hands as she carried it out.

Her feet paused at the entrance to the main room. Abbas had vanished, leaving only Yiannis and his slaves within.

She forced a small smile and carried her tray toward him, sliding it onto the low table his men had brought in this morning. "Here you are, cousin. Will my father be back out, do you know?"

He did not answer. Merely lifted a hand. Raised one finger, then another, and motioned.

One of his slaves leapt forward and began filling a plate. A second one said, "Master Dorus indicated he needed to rest again, good lady."

Good lady. Strange how the slave could call her such while his master ignored her very existence.

She summoned the smile back to her lips. "I thank you. I will take him a plate then, if there is nothing else I can get for you, cousin."

Again it was the slave who said, "Of course. See to your father and we will see to our master."

Not knowing what else to say—and to whom she should even address another comment, were she to come up with anything—she dipped her knees and turned to put small portions of everything on a plate for Abbas. She chose each piece carefully, in the hopes that it would tempt him to taste and be filled.

Then she took plate and a chalice of spiced wine down the hall and to his closed door. She had to balance the plate on top of the cup to have hand enough to knock, and then to enter despite the silence from the other side.

Abbas was curled on his bed like a child, knees tucked up to his chest. It chiseled away at the hurt inside to see it—strange, since it made new hurt bloom. A different kind of hurt, though. One that pulsed *for* him instead of *because of* him.

She slid the plate onto the table beside his bed. "Abbas? I brought you some food."

He made no reply.

Sighing, she sank down onto the side of the bed. "I know you miss her—we all miss her. I know you mourn the loss of all you held dear. But Abbas…it was never the things that mattered to us. It was never the wealth or the appearance of it. All that mattered to us was you and Mater. And now that she is gone…we have only you. Do not leave us, Abbas. We love you, even if we have nothing to our name. We love you, and so does God."

His every muscle went tense. "You would speak to me of your God, after I have forbidden it?"

Given the venom in his tone, she ought to have recoiled. Instead, she found a strange little smile taking possession of her mouth. "Yes. I will. Because I love you. I will speak of him because he is the only way out of this mess. Because he is the only way to Mater. And I will pray that he is made manifest to you in this terrible season in a way you cannot deny."

Abbas snorted. "Unless he makes gold rain down from the heavens, I will not ever bend my knee to a deity who would do this to us."

"We did it to ourselves, Abbas." She studied the angry knot of his shoulders, the way his fingers dug into the mattress. "I think you know that. I think you blame yourself, not God—I think that is why you have given up."

"You know nothing."

She scooted up until she could lean back against the wall at the head of the bed. "That day I first met Nikolaos and Petros, when I had gone down to the docks to meet your ship…you know what happened. How the sailors were chasing me, how Nikolaos and Petros saved me. You never had ears to hear what really happened that day."

"You fell- but you were not paralyzed, Cyprus. You could not have been, because this God you claim cannot undo something so final. You were only stunned, out of breath."

She tilted her head back to look up at the ceiling with its elaborate plasterwork. "I stared up at the sky, and I felt *nothing*. Just the echo of excruciating pain. Petros picked up my hand, and I could not even tell." She could feel his fingers now though, around hers. Giving her warmth. Giving her promise. Not there, yet she could feel them.

Swallowing, she whispered, "Sometimes that is what I feel

now, thinking of Mater. The echo of the most excruciating pain, and then nothing. As if the world has ceased to be. As if *I* have ceased to be."

Abbas said nothing. But he turned his face into the mattress.

"When I am afraid, when I am consumed by uncertainty or my own misery...I feel again as though I am lying in that alley. My arms and legs get so heavy I cannot move them. I cannot feel anything but the despair of that moment. And I wonder why God spared me. Why he saved me. Why he allowed Nik to heal me. What can I possibly do to be deserving of this life?"

She turned her head to him, where he lay so broken. So lifeless. Yet alive. "Then I realize we are none of us deserving. But he loves us. He loves us enough that he gave up the one most precious to him...for *us*. When we are so unwilling to give up anything for him."

"So if we do not sacrifice willingly, he takes by force? How is that a loving God?"

"Was it God who took from us, Abbas? God did not spend all our money. God did not decide to lie about our wealth. God did not dictate that Mater must go to her father to seek her inheritance." She shook her head, but strangely she felt no anger now at what could have been accusations. Just a strange, pervasive calm. "These are decisions we all make, every day. Decisions we often make without him—so why do we then blame him when things go wrong?"

"He sent the storm that *killed* her!"

At least he admitted God had power over the storms. "That storm would have raged whether Mater was on the sea or not. They were our decisions that put her there."

Abbas shook his head, his shoulders angry again. "He could have spared her, if he is the God she always claimed. He could have saved her."

"He could interfere in our lives every day—and then we would complain that he does not allow us to choose freely what path we will take. Tell me, Abbas—are you one to obey out of compulsion?"

A beat of silence, during which Abbas's muscles stayed loudly bunched. "You weary me, child. Go away."

"I will, once you eat, and once I am sure you will not make yourself toss it up again. And as long as I am here, I will happily continue this conversation. So perhaps you ought to sample that lamb and toast, hmm?" She gave a cheeky smile that he did not turn around to see. "I made it myself, after all. Well, not the cheese. I still have less than a clue how people manage to create cheese from milk."

Abbas did not look at her. But he sat up. He reached for the plate. And he tried a bite of lamb. Today, that counted as a victory.

FIFTEEN

Petros hovered in the doorway, not wanting to intrude upon Alexandria's visit with Kosmas but a bit curious as to what exchange passed between them. It was not as though they were alone anyway—that would hardly be appropriate, him still laid out upon a spare bed in Hero's home as he was. No, Hero's mother sat in a corner, bone needles clacking away as she knit something or another. Her gaze kept moving from Alexandria to Rhoda, who stood in the hallway as well.

Perhaps she was sorry she had barred them from the house the other day when they came seeking help. Or perhaps she was wishing she could have barred them now. Petros did not know her well enough to say.

Alexandria sat on a stool beside the bed, Kosmas's hand between both of hers. He had greeted her, but without much enthusiasm. Petros could only imagine how *he* would have felt had Cyprus received him so coolly in such a situation. But Alexandria smiled and spoke to him in hushed tones too quiet for Petros to hear over the other conversation behind him.

Rhoda and Hero edged away, toward an alcove in the hallway. Their conversation was louder, brighter, filled with laughter. And with conspicuous silences. Petros did not look to see if they were sharing a kiss, or if they were just staring at each other with affection after their days apart. Either way, he felt more than a little out of place here between the two couples as the minutes dragged on.

Finally, Nikolaos emerged from the room where he had been with Hero's father. Petros breathed a sigh of relief at his entrance. One that turned to concern when he saw the look upon his cousin's face. Either his head was paining him…or the conversation had. "Is everything well?" Petros asked in an undertone once Nikolaos was near enough.

His cousin cast a glance over his shoulder. Mydon did not emerge from the room. His son did not look away from Rhoda's smiling face.

Nikolaos swallowed. "It is all very complicated. You know the laws about betrothals better than most of us, probably—and Dorus had the agreements drawn up legally. Mydon is willing to make changes, but so long as Gallus is not, he feels stymied. At least knowing, as he does, that Rhoda will not agree to anything if her sister is left without."

Petros pressed his lips together. "More, a change to a legal agreement would require Dorus's consent as well."

Nikolaos studied his face for a long moment. "What is it? Did something happen while you were there?"

Unwilling for the twins to overhear him, he motioned Nikolaos to follow him away from the bedchamber, toward the main receiving room. Empty now, but for the impeccable decorations and all his unspoken fears. The rain let only dreary, dim light into the house, and it did nothing to lend him hope. In a few short words, he told his cousin about the arrival of Yiannis. What he could not quite put into words was the way the man had made his blood feel a few degrees too cool.

But perhaps it was just a reaction to the way he had treated Cyprus.

Nikolaos's brows remained knit all through the telling and had not time to relax again before a loud knock sounded on the front door. The same servant who had answered the night before scurried forward.

"Where is my son?" boomed through the wall separating them from the view of Gallus. He sounded angry. And when he charged past the doorway, he looked it too.

Petros winced, glad the man had not spotted them.

His relief was premature. A second later the man's form filled the doorway, having apparently turned back when he realized they were within. "You." He pointed a finger at Petros, though he came no closer. "It is your fault my son was ever *on* that road! Your fault he is injured now."

"Father." Felix eased into view, standing tall and with no sign of pain from his own travel-born injury. "It was no doubt the same bandits who attacked me, waiting for their revenge. The bandits they *saved* me from."

"And who would not then have been able to also prey upon your brother had Petros not lured him away from his home, where he ought to have been with his family." Gallus slashed a hand through the air. Veins pulsing in his temple, he grunted and spun. "No more. He will have no more to do with the lot of you!"

Gallus spun and stomped off. Felix watched him for a moment and then turned to join them. "My apologies for his behavior. I would say that I am certain he will soften in time, but honestly, I feel I scarcely know him. Or Kosmas. I have been too long away from home."

"And it is Kosmas's reaction we need to worry about." Nikolaos pressed his fingers to his temple.

Petros took a step toward his cousin, reaching out without

knowing quite what he meant to do. Nik was not wavering, to need steadying. He was not distraught, exactly, to need comfort. But he looked...troubled. "Are you all right, Nik?"

His cousin was quick to drop his hand and school his features. "I yet have a bit of a headache. Perhaps that is why..." He shook his head. "I had better head back to the church. I will be praying for everyone here, and I will return later."

"Nik." Petros followed him a step, though still he was unsure what he meant to say. He sighed. "I am sorry. Gallus *is* right that it is my fault we were all on that road. You were injured—"

"Cousin." One corner of Nikolaos's mouth pulled up. "Stop. No one forced me to journey with you. I came willingly, and if I had it to do again, I would still come. Though perhaps I would heed your bad feeling a little more on the way back." He turned again, exiting the room. "But have no fear. I will be well with a little more rest."

Silence whooshed in with the cool air as he opened the door.

It melted away with its closing. Felix turned to him, eyes bright with interest. "How did he do what he did for me yesterday? My wound..." He touched a hand to his side. "It is barely a scratch. It was worse than that, I know it was."

Gallus's voice echoed down the hall, through the stone. Harsh words whose syllables were muffled by the walls but whose meaning wasn't.

Petros looked into the eyes of this eldest son, but he saw none of the father in him. Not like he did in Kosmas. "Nik has always been...special. His faith is unlike that of anyone else I have ever met. Even when we were children..." He sank down onto one of the chairs, letting his mind cast itself back in time. Oh, he liked to tease his cousin about how devout a child he had been, but beneath the jests was truth. Even as a little boy, Nikolaos had always been unlike any other child their age. Sweet, thoughtful. He would give up anything of his own to make someone else smile.

"We were about six, I think, when everyone else realized how different he was. We were playing with a bunch of other boys by the shore, and one waded too deep. The current caught him, sucked him out—he could not swim. And none of us were strong enough to fetch him, not in time. Our shouts brought the adults out, one managed to pull him in. But he was not breathing."

Felix entered his vision again, groping for a chair and planting himself upon it without taking his eyes from Petros. "Did the child die?"

Petros smiled. "I do not know. It was probably not so final, but it could well have been. The boy's father was slapping his back, trying to get the water from him. The usual tricks did nothing. But then Nikolaos broke away from my side and ran up to him. He threw his arms around the boy, as if he were embracing his dearest friend. And the next thing I knew, the boy was sputtering, breathing."

"He healed him?" The words were arranged like a question, but it was not question in Felix's eyes. "Wait…I heard stories of a boy in a neighboring town when I was young. We did not attend the gathering of the brethren often, back then. But I heard stories of one who could work miracles. They called him…"

"Wonder worker." Petros grinned. "I do not recommend you call him such where he can hear you. His pride is as small as his faith is great."

Felix expelled a breath that left a smile on his face. "Would that I had even a portion of it. I have heard all the stories. I believe in the Christ. But today…I see so little evidence of the world they speak of in the Scriptures. I attend church services, and it seems like so much…tradition. Rote. Pray every three hours. Read the Didache. Recite the prayers."

Petros nodded. "Religion. Odd, is it not, how easily religion can push faith aside?"

"Exactly. My aunt in Rome, she said it helps her to focus. But it did not do so to me. It made it too easy to fail to think about it. My hands could perform the actions, my lips could say the words. But my heart was uninvolved. My mind free to wander."

"I know what you mean. Too often I have the same experience in a church service." He would never confess as much to the bishop, but he and Nikolaos had discussed it many times. How easy it was to pay lip service when there was a service to move one's lips along to.

It had not been so in the early days of the church. It had been spontaneous gatherings for prayer and sermons. Even when order began to prevail—because chaos certainly was not desired—it had still been new and fresh and heart-written.

"But it is different for Nik. And for me, when I am around Nik. Everything he does, he does from a heart full of faith. He simply...*believes.* And so, does."

Felix's smile grew. "I think I need to spend some more time with you all and learn how this is done."

Petros chuckled. "You are welcome, always. Though one cannot learn to be like Nik just by watching him—or *I* have not managed it thus far, at least."

But he did believe. He believed his cousin could do whatever miracle God wanted. He had seen the ill made well. The still breathe. The paralyzed walk and run and leap and laugh...and love. He believed a touch of Nikolaos's hands really could work wonders when the Spirit moved through him.

He glanced down at his own hands. It was not lack of faith that made them unable to do the same. He did believe. He believed that if ever God needed him, Petros, to do some miracle, then the Spirit would give him that ability.

But right now, his hands had only the power to move a quill

over parchment. To be stained with ink. His voice had never had cause to bid someone rise and walk or stand up and be healed. Only to plead for justice before the courts, to elicit laughter or tears.

To some were given the working of miracles. The gift of healing. To some like Nikolaos.

To others were given...other gifts. Petros did not know which, exactly, he had received. But he listened. He listened to that whisper from the Lord. He did what he knew he should. He believed. It would never earn him the awe it did Nikolaos, but he did not need awe.

"I do not need to be like the wonder worker exactly." Felix's gaze had gone distant too, fixed on some point beyond Petros. "I just...I need to be like *me*. Does that make sense? I need to live in my own faith."

"Exactly. Day by day. Wherever you are, whatever he calls you to."

Felix nodded. Then his eyes went wide, his gaze sharp.

Petros turned his head just as Alexandria gusted into the room as though a tempest were at her heels. "That man is impossible!" She headed straight for the mantel but then spun again and retraced her own steps. "And if anyone in this world knows impossible men, it is the daughter of Dorus Visibullis."

Petros could not quite decide whether to be concerned or amused. "Which one of them has risen to your father's level of stubbornness? Kosmas or *his* father?"

"Both!" She all but spat the word, pivoted, marched to the mantel again. "All these months. All these months of working to establish a relationship, of trying to build a firm foundation that will see us through life—and what does he do at the first trial? He wallows! It is self-pity burning him up, not infection."

Petros sighed. "I had hoped seeing you would pull him out of it. I had thought for sure it would. He has only been a few hours laid up, after all. He has no reason to bemoan this injury."

She snorted. "To hear him talk, his leg is already lost, and with it his future, and it is all *my* fault."

He tried on a smile, though he suspected it could affect little. "Well you are in excellent company—his father swore it was *mine*."

She did not exactly laugh, but she came to a halt and huffed out a little breath that had at least the essence of amusement in it. "What am I to do, Pet? Rhoda will not wed Hero if I do not wed Kosmas. And while, honestly, I would be perfectly happy to remain at home and just care for Abbas...she will not. You know she will not. Together, or not at all. But she loves Hero so much. So much more than I love Kosmas—perhaps more than I could ever love anyone."

"Do not sell your heart short, Alexandria. Even so—if marriage would not make you happy, your sister would not want it for you."

She shook her head, sending her hair swaying. She must have discarded her head covering when she was with Kosmas. "It is not that it would not make me happy. It is that I could be happy without it, if not marrying were an option. But it is not, not now. Abbas has nothing left with which to support us. Although *marrying* is not an option now either, for the same reason. We have no options. That is what it feels like. Like there is nothing, nothing we can do now to *live*. We can only survive, whatever ugliness that might require."

"There is a way." Petros stood so he could move to her side and put an encouraging hand on her shoulder. "I do not know yet what form it will take. But the Lord is still with you. He is waiting to turn this trial into a blessing, somehow."

She sniffed, her anger turning before his eyes into sorrow. "I know he *can.* But what if he means to teach us something by letting us fall even further? What if it is through even more suffering that he works? I have lost my mother, Petros. My father because of it. I am losing the man I thought I would marry. What have I left but my sisters? What if the Lord asks them of me too?"

He could only lift his hands, palms up. He wanted to insist that the Lord would not ask that, never that. But he had no authority to make such promises. "I do not know, Xan. Except that whatever he asks of us, he gives us the strength to handle. Not on our own, but through him."

She wrapped her arms around her middle. Turned toward where Felix sat in the corner. "Nik, if you would..." Her mouth fell open, and she took a step back, away from Petros's hand. "You are not Nikolaos. My apologies, lord, for...for assuming..." She flushed, looking poised to run back out of the room.

Felix sprang to his feet, one hand outstretched. "Please, do not be embarrassed on my account. I am only Kosmas's brother—not exactly a part of it all, but by no means a stranger to the story."

Today, anyway. No doubt after the explanation they had given him on the road, he had later heard Gallus's side of things. Heaven only knew what sentiments that had entailed.

The introduction did nothing to make her face lose its flush. "His brother. He did not...I did not realize you were coming home."

Which was to say, Kosmas would have complained about it—loudly—if he had known. Perhaps Felix knew it, for he pressed his lips together in that flavor of smile that said he knew the why of a thing, and it pained him. "I thought to surprise everyone. Be home in time for the wedding. It is not every day, after all, that one's baby brother gets married."

"It will not be *any* day, if your father prevails. That he marries me, anyway." Alexandria locked her gaze onto the corner of the room, where walls met floor. The color finally leeched out of her cheeks.

Felix took half a step nearer and then seemed to realize this sort of distance was not bridged so easily. "Forgive me if I sound harsh toward my brother—but if Kosmas lets you go simply because Father tells him to, if he blames you for this injury...then he is too big a fool to deserve the honor of having you for a wife anyway."

"Honor?" The word sounded scoffing as it fell from her lips. But those lips turned up a bit. As did her gaze. Not quite rising to Felix's face, but at least turning his direction. "Forgive *me*, lord—but you do not know me. I appreciate the sentiment, but for all you know, your brother is lucky to be rid of me." A sigh slipped out, and she averted her face again. Toward Petros this time. "Heaven knows Rhoda is the sweeter of us. I no doubt seem a shrew beside her."

It should have smacked of self-pity—would have, had such a thing been said by, say, Kosmas. But somehow Alexandria managed to say it in a way that admitted fact, possibility, without implying she would change a thing. Rhoda was the sweeter of the two, without question. But perhaps not the stronger.

Their family needed both. Needed all—Cyprus's strengths too. Petros touched a hand to her shoulder. "Kosmas does not know quite what he wants right now, I think. Give him time. Bathe it in prayer."

"I am not certain how much time we have. Yiannis..." Alexandria sucked in a breath and then dropped her arms from around her middle, lifted her chin, and met Petros's gaze. "I am keeping you from your work. Are you before the courts today?"

"Not today. But I must go and write my defense." He darted a glance to Felix, back to Alexandria. "Do you want me to see you home first, or...?"

"No." Still in that posture of defiance, she half-turned toward the door. "Rhoda is not ready. And I will try talking to Kosmas again after his father has quit the room. *If* his father quits the room. Hero will see us home, I am certain."

"All right." He still felt a bit odd, leaving her with a stranger, even if for all appearances that stranger was far friendlier than her betrothed.

Felix must have been aware of it. He cleared his throat. "May I keep you company for a while, Alexandria? I have missed much in my brother's life, and I would love to hear you speak of him."

"Of course." She relaxed into her usual posture and turned back to smile at Felix for the first time. "It would be a privilege."

Petros nodded, said a quick farewell...and could not help but note that Felix looked just a little dazzled by Alexandria's smile. Perhaps he could help remind his brother of what a gift these Visibullis girls were, with or without a fortune to their name.

SIXTEEN

Supper was edible. That was all Cyprus could say in its favor. She had not quite ruined anything, though she had come nowhere near doing any of it right, she was sure. Rhoda had sneaked into the kitchen at one point to help her season the meat. And the bread was by far the best thing she had made—good to know that at least she understood dough. The rest...

It would do. It had to. And if their guest found it unsatisfactory, then he could either let someone help her or buy his meals from a place in town.

She loaded the tray. Helena had always put much more on it than this, and her girls would help her carry out the rest so that it took them only one trip. Cyprus had a feeling that if she tried to replicate even Helena's feat, it would end in disaster. Better to make a few trips than to drop it all.

They were in the dining room tonight, now that Yiannis had brought in couches and cushions and low tables. Abbas, shrunken and ragged and looking as lively and soft as a sea urchin, reclined on cushions near the door. He held the chalice of wine she had poured for him fifteen minutes ago.

It was still full.

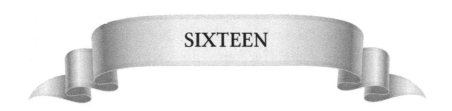

Yiannis's, apparently, was empty. He quirked a finger toward one of his slaves, who leapt into action to remedy this great travesty.

Cyprus had tried to talk to them today. All she could get out of any of the menservants were their names—which was Ennius and which Iovite? And what were the other two?—and that they had been serving Yiannis for four years, ever since Mater's uncle adopted him.

She slid the tray onto the central table and beat a hasty retreat back to the kitchen to fetch the rest of the food. Not exactly a seven-course banquet like their guest was probably accustomed to, like the one he was currently talking about to her father. The kind so extravagant that the guests had to visit the vomitorium between courses to purge themselves of what came before so they could continue indulging.

Thank the Lord Abbas had never extended the pretense of their wealth to that particular Roman custom. To Cyprus's mind, vomiting was something to be avoided whenever possible.

She gathered up the last of the food and traipsed back in her own invisible footprints. When she reentered the dining chamber, she saw that Ennius—or Iovite?—had filled a plate for his master. That the twins had somehow managed to change seats so that they were beside each other, not flanking Yiannis, and their heads were now bent together. They whispered as Yiannis droned on about this meal fit, he was sure, for Augustus Diocletian.

Abbas sat, sea-urchin bristly, with that full cup clutched in his hand.

Iovite...or Ennius...sidled up to Cyprus and leaned close. His breath smelled strangely fragrant, like he had been chewing on herbs. Perhaps Yiannis insisted on it. "You did not bring enough plates," he whispered. "We need another setting for Edesia."

She bristled until she too felt like a sea urchin. "We do not offer food to Roman idols in our house."

Only when Yiannis's droning fell silent did she realize she had spoken too loudly. Only when he set his chalice down with a loud *thunk* did she realize she would have happily shouted it.

He did not rise, not physically. But he seemed to. His anger crouched on his shoulders like a visible thing, making him hulking. "In *my* house, you will offer what I tell you to offer."

"I will not." Her voice was not a shout. Not filled with any of the things she felt. She heard it echo through the still-too-empty room, and it sounded…it sounded like Mater's always had when she butted heads with Abbas over such things.

Warmth spread through her chest, though she had not realized it had been absent before.

Alexandria lifted her chin. "None of us will. We are Christian, cousin—if you did not realize that already, then our sincere apologies for not showing the love of Christ as we should."

Yiannis did not so much as shift his gaze toward Alexandria. He moved it instead toward Abbas. It looked heavy as the night. "Dorus Visibullis is…a *Christian*?" He spat out the word like it was a bite of rotten food.

Abbas did not flinch. He just held tight that cup he would not raise to his lips and stared into nothing. "Artemis was. I told her I was too, at first. It was the only way to convince her to marry me. And she believed it. I had the family history to make her think it true." His eyes had a foggy look to them. His lips hinted at a smile flavored with pain. "My uncle and aunt led the church in Philippi. It is where I met her."

"Ridiculous nonsense." Lips curled away from his teeth, Yiannis gestured toward his servant.

For once, the four did not seem to read his mind. They stood, eyes wide and panicked, looking at one another, until their master snapped, "Take the plate from Dorus, you fools! He will not eat anyway. Use it for Edesia."

Cyprus's stomach went tight. Sick. A kind of sick it had never been before. "No." So few of the old rules were asked of them—to love the Lord their God above all. To love their neighbors as themselves. To abstain from food offered to idols.

That was all. All God asked of the churches that had sprung up among the Gentiles. And now would even that be taken from them in this house?

Rhoda was, somehow, at Cyprus's elbow, whispering into her ear. "It is not our house. Not our authority. We cannot stop him, but we can still obey the Lord. *We* will not eat of anything he offers. Just pay attention. That is all we can do. Make sure no food passes our lips that he has first given to Edesia."

Cyprus nodded because this felt less wrong than any other alternative. But it still did not feel *right*. Nothing, lately, had felt right. Except Petros.

For the first time in her life, she watched as a place was set at her table for a goddess. As the choicest meat and bread was put upon it. She listened as words were spoken dedicating the meal—the whole meal, not just those selections—to Edesia and to the great goddess Artemis under whose protection Patara rested.

The sick in her belly churned and churned.

Rhoda's sigh was a sound of pain...and hunger, perhaps. Had she eaten anything earlier, at Hero's home, or had she been too busy gazing into his eyes and whispering love into his ears to see to such base needs?

Even if she had fasted all the day, she would not touch a bite of this food now, Cyprus knew. Her sisters would both sooner wait until they could sneak into the kitchen and find some cheese and dried fruit later than raise a bit of this to their lips.

Abbas said nothing. His foggy eyes had drifted downward. Perhaps in their clouds he saw Mater as she had used to be. Young and beautiful—looking, no doubt, just like Rhoda and Alexandria. Perhaps he was remembering whatever lies he had told her to convince her he was what she wanted in a husband. Perhaps he was seeing the disappointment that must have been shadowing her deep eyes that night a year ago when he had insisted she must return to Philippi and beg an inheritance from her father, so that their lies could be perpetuated in the eyes of Patara.

Had Mater ever regretted marrying him? When she realized her mistake in believing him, had she wondered at how he had convinced her? It could not have taken her long to realize the truth. Cyprus could remember no father but the one who was so cold toward the faith. So clear on where his indulgences of their "foolishness" ended.

But Mater had always, always loved him.

Yiannis finished his libations and settled back down with a smug little smile. "I am glad to hear that at least *you* have not been seduced by this foolish religion, Dorus. But then, you are filled with strong Roman blood. My own is Greek, of course. Just as strong."

Abbas said nothing. Perhaps he did not even hear.

"I cannot believe how this disease has spread so throughout the empire. In my opinion—and I will offer it to the great Diocletian if ever I meet him—it ought to be stamped out. It is bad enough we tolerate a synagogue in every city." He took a sip of his wine, his expression saying he hoped it would wash the distaste of the word *synagogue* from his mouth. "I noticed Patara's, of course, on my way into town. They are a blight, those Jews. *They* ought to be stamped out as well. If it were up to me, everyone with even a drop of Jewish blood should be expelled from the empire at the least, if not killed—they do nothing but rouse the rabble and sew dissent."

Abbas still said nothing. But perhaps he was seeing, as Cyprus was, those scrolls stacked even now in a crate in the corner of Mater's dressing room. The ones that revealed that there was Jewish blood in the Visibullis line.

Alexandria sat statue-still. Her fingers were pressed so hard to her opposite palm that Cyprus knew the nails would leave little half-moon marks upon her flesh. "What they do, and what the Christians do, is *feed* the rabble, not rouse them."

Yiannis made a scoffing sound. "The rabble should be left to fend for themselves. If they are clever and worth the air they breathe, they will find a way to prosper. If not, then they deserve to die."

A sentiment so diametrically opposed to all Mater had taught them, everything their friends stood for, that Cyprus could only stare. Perhaps Abbas had never been of faith, perhaps he had always spoken of honoring the gods of the emperor, but even he had never said things like *that.* Such utter hatred toward people of faith...

Something soft and cool touched the back of her neck, where fearful fire blazed under her hair. She thought for a moment it was Rhoda's fingers, but her sister had shifted a step away. Far enough that now she could meet Cyprus's eyes and mouth the word *Go.*

Cyprus did not have to ask where, or why. She knew.

The scrolls, the codices. They had to be removed from this house—from *his* house. He would no doubt oversee the removal and dispersal of every item under his roof, and if he found those... he would at best destroy the parchment. At worst, destroy *them* for being the owners of it.

Cyprus hurried back to the kitchen, brought out the rest of the food. She did not look again to Yiannis as she flew back and forth, but to note that Rhoda had settled on the other side of him again. Her sisters, heretofore silent, were chattering at him in that way they had perfected long ago—first one speaking, then the other, him caught between their words, in the melody of their voices.

It would keep him distracted. Long enough that Cyprus would not be missed as she slipped into Abbas and Mater's room.

Darkness had settled here. The bed, the chair, were but bare outlines in the scant light from the moon that snuck through the window. The empty pots still on Mater's dressing table were but bare outlines of the mother who would never sit there again.

She hurried through the room and into the closet that had once housed Mater's finest garments. It was empty now, for she had taken it all with her to Philippi. Empty but for that crate of precious history they had stored here just to get it out of the way.

It was far heavier than the tray she had struggled with earlier, but Cyprus lifted it. She had no choice. She would not have time to make more than one trip. So her arms would burn, and her legs would probably end up shaking, and she may have to stop a few times in the alleyways to catch her breath. But she would do it, because she must.

She stubbed her toe on the way back out of the closet, bit her lip to keep from giving voice to the pain. *Lord, give me strength. Help me get these records to safety.* She paused at the doorway from the bedchamber, listening.

The music of her sisters' voices still wove its way through the air, punctuated by Yiannis's laugh. She wished the servants were louder—if anyone were to leave the assembly, it would be one of them.

She would just have to risk it. Slowly, silently she slid down the hall, away from the central rooms with their lamplight and dancing candles. Toward the kitchen, where the scents from her uninspiring cooking hung heavy. Out the door into the garden that Helena would never tend again.

The rain had turned to a mist that glowed around the windows, where light spilled out of neighboring houses. It touched her skin, chill and damp, everywhere the fabric fell away from her arms. She should have grabbed a cloak. But she had no time for such things.

Hurrying out of the garden entrance, she took every back alley she knew. On the one hand, it was dangerous to keep to shadows. On the other, it was more dangerous to be seen by those who would recognize her.

The church felt a long way away just now. Out of the most prosperous streets, toward where the merchants and shopkeepers lived. Everything was quiet, the residents tucked safely inside their homes as she stumbled her way along. No one else would want to come out in the misting rain, not if they could avoid it. This was a night for a blazing fire in the hearth, for good food, for family and laughter. The Christian families would be planning how to celebrate the birth of Christ in a few days, planning to attend services at the church. The bishop would no doubt speak a special sermon. Nikolaos and Petros and Hero would sit there with all the other Christian families, praying and praising.

How she wished she and the twins had been a part of the community, a true part. This would all look so different if they were surrounded by real friends. Brothers and sisters beyond the ones who shared blood.

Her feet hesitated at the corner that could take her to Theophanes's house. She could take the scrolls to Petros. He would take care of them, she knew that. He would appreciate having them in his house, even.

But that was not the image of safety that had filled her mind when that cool breath had touched her neck, when Rhoda had told her to go. No, she had seen the church. She had known without needing to think about it that these treasures belonged there, where all the brethren could read them and learn and grow together. That, she was sure, was what those long-gone Visibullises would want. They would want their words to be shared with other believers, to strengthen them through whatever trials might come.

Maybe Diocletian *would* grow tired of them again. Maybe trouble would come. Maybe, somehow, it would make a difference to read these words and see so clearly how the Lord used the bad times. It was always easier to see it in the distant past than in the more recent one.

Her feet remained true to her path, even as she sent a silent message down the street to Petros. Maybe God would let the *I love you* sink into his mind. Maybe her beloved would pause, his stylus over his tablet, and think of her and know it was true. Maybe it would bring a smile to his lips. She prayed it would.

The church was not much farther. No one stopped her, no one so much as spotted her as she paused for a moment to regain her breath and to reposition the heavy crate. Her arms screamed, but she promised them rest in just a few minutes and started up again.

Then she spotted the shadow that was the church. It was not as grand as the synagogue Yiannis had just sneered over, certainly not as impressive as the temple to Artemis in the acropolis. No white columns here, no bas-reliefs. The exterior was somewhat humble, though when she stretched her neck up, she saw the mist glowing around the dome and had to smile.

She set the crate down and tried the latch—unlocked. "Thank you, Lord." Pushing it open, creaking door on creaking hinges, Cyprus opted for shoving the crate over the threshold rather than lifting it again.

A candle burned inside, near the front of the room, far from the narthex she had stepped into. It cast a weak circle of light up, out, shedding just a breath of light on the paintings she had never gotten to study as closely as she would like. Daniel, resting easy among golden-haired lions. And on the other wall, Jesus calming an angry sea.

Tears bade leave to well, but she blinked them back. Not every storm was meant to be calmed. Not every tragedy was meant to be averted. Death came. It always came, eventually. For now. But it would not have the victory for long.

The candle was not alone in the front of the church. She saw a figure kneeling beside it, even though it was not one of the designated times of prayer. The head was familiar, as was the curve of the shoulders.

"Nikolaos?"

He started and stood, turning. She could not see his face for the shadows, but she did not need to, to know he would help her. Closing the door behind her, she hefted the crate again.

"Cyprus?" He did not sound quite so sure of her identity as she had been of his. He would not expect to see her in his church. "What are you doing out at this hour?"

She moved forward, by the hard benches. The crate felt heavier than it had before she put it down. "I need you to take these. To protect them."

"Take what?" But he met her halfway down the aisle, and he reached to take the crate. In the darkness, he would not be able to see much, except that they were scrolls and codices.

That was all he would *need* to see. His breath hissed out between his teeth. "Cyprus—I cannot. This is your family's heritage."

All of it they had left—and not the part Abbas *wished* they had. She swallowed and released the box once she was sure he had it. "That is why I need you to take it. To keep it safe. Our cousin, the one who owns our house—did Petros tell you?"

"A bit."

She nodded. "He has brought the Greek gods into our home. He has announced that Christians and Jews are his enemies. Those scrolls are the proof of our Christian faith. Of the Jewish blood somewhere in our veins. If he finds them, he will destroy them, and quite possibly us along with them." She lifted her chin. "I will die for my faith if God asks it of me, but I would preserve its history if I can."

"You will not die for your faith. Not now, anyway. I cannot speak for the distant future." He said it so calmly, as if he knew. Perhaps he did. Turning back toward the front of the sanctuary and the lone candle, he tilted his head to indicate she should follow.

She should not. She should turn and go home and hope no one but her sisters realized she had gone.

Her feet followed his steps up the aisle, drawn by that golden circle of light.

Nikolaos bent once he reached the candle and set the crate down. Cyprus stopped a small distance away, her eyes eating up the church she had never attended. Was that podium where his uncle stood when he was delivering his sermon each Sunday? Did the other believers sit on these benches every day to pray, or did they only manage to make their way here once a week?

She sank down onto one of the pews. It was hard and cold and felt damp under her palms. "I wish Abbas had let us attend here."

"The Lord knows when you worship, Cyprus. Wherever it is. The Word says that where two or three gathered, he is there in their midst. He has always been in your midst, with you and your sisters and your mother." He settled too, on the bench in front of the one she had chosen, turning to her. In the dimness, his face was all angles and planes. "Even so. You will not be long under your father's authority. And with Petros and Hero and Kosmas, you will all be free to worship with the brethren."

With Petros. He knew, then, of Petros's heart for her, and hers for him. His cousin would have told him. She did not mind that, though she had not mentioned it to her sisters. Even so, she had to turn her face away, toward the wall she could only guess existed somewhere in the darkness.

She heard Nikolaos shift, rather than seeing him do so. "What is it?"

She should not confess the sorrow that had not stopped swirling inside her all the past day. She should not...but she had to. "His mother...his parents have other plans for him. Plans that do not include a destitute daughter of a despised merchant. They have not told him yet. He will object. But...but I wonder if it is best for him. Not to be burdened with me."

Nikolaos's breath eased out, slow and contemplative. "I think the burden would be living *without* you, my friend. He has loved you long. He loves you with everything in him. You are second in his affections only to God himself."

The words made the blood go warm in her veins, made the mist-inspired chill flee from her skin. Petros had proven as much. He had given everything—*everything*—to help them. But then, Mater had given up everything to marry Abbas. All for a lie that ended with her destruction. Love did not always mean it was the best thing, did it?

She squeezed her eyes shut. "And I love him. I cannot imagine a future without him. But what if Korinna is right? What if he could use his gift with language to save the Christians further trial?"

She had no idea if Nikolaos had ever heard this theory of his aunt and uncle's. If he had ever thought it himself. But he spoke often enough of his cousin's way with words that it should not be a surprising idea, at any rate.

Nikolaos hummed and tilted his head back to study the ceiling.

It made her wonder what images were painted upon it that she could not make out in the darkness. "I wonder if it is even the will of God that we escape persecution. As a man, of course I do not *want* it. As a shepherd guarding his flock, I would do all in my ability to protect them from it. But when faith is easy, it loses its potency. Do you not think so?"

She tilted her head back too and studied the varying shades of black and gray upon the ceiling. If she squinted just right, she could imagine a garden scene there. Adam and Eve perhaps. "I am not the one to ask. Faith has never been easy in the house of Dorus Visibullis."

"Which is, perhaps, why his daughter can walk when she should by rights have died or worse from that fall." His fingers brushed over her wrist. A silent encouragement. "Perhaps it is the will of God that Petros speak for him. And if so, do you think yourself so powerful that you can stop him from it? You may be second in his affections, Cyprus...but you are *only* second. Marrying you will not foil God's plan for him. Marrying you will give him the strength he needs to stand up in whatever way he is called to do and speak whatever words the Lord gives him. Knowing that no matter whose favor he falls from or attains, he will have *you* at home."

"But what if a different match would aid him in this call, as one with me never could?"

Nikolaos shook his head, his fingers gone, back into the shadows of his lap. "I have been thinking. Perhaps God's plan is not one straight line, from point alpha to point beta. God's plan is a living thing because it deals with living people. People who are imperfect and often deaf to his voice, blind to his movement. How often does he call us to something and we miss it? But his plan does not just falter to a halt. He will call another to do the work. Or call us in a different way. Perhaps...perhaps there is the *best* way. But if we people are too stubborn or frightened to grasp it, then he will find another. And another, and another, until someone says *yes*. Until someone does the work."

By that logic, then even if marrying her were not ideal, it would not necessarily force Petros from the one true path to what God wanted him to do…it may just make it more difficult. But then, by that logic too, *not* marrying her would not hinder him either.

Nikolaos was right. She was not so important. Not so powerful, even though Petros loved her. She was only one person in his life full to brimming with people.

"And Cyprus."

She looked back over to his face of angles and planes, golden light and deepest shadow. He wore a crooked, boyish smile.

"He has never once spoken to me of feeling the Lord call him to such grandiose things. He has spoken only of finding justice for the poor. And of *you*. Do not let his parents' ambitions for him blind you. They are *their* ambitions. Not his."

Because it brought a flood of peace into her heart, she could smile back. And say, "Ah, but did not Christ himself defer to his mother when she told him to help at the wedding feast, even though he had just claimed it was not his time?"

Nikolaos chuckled. And stood. "You had better get home before you are missed, my friend. I daresay no one realized you slipped out."

"My sisters knew." And they would do whatever it took to keep Yiannis distracted. A thought which chased away all that newly found peace and replaced it with a hungry urgency. "And you are right. I had better hurry back. Thank you, Nikolaos."

"I did nothing but agree to take some very interesting reading off your hands for a while." Though she could not see it on the face he had turned toward her, away from the light, she could hear the smile in his voice. Yet somehow she knew as it faded. "Be safe, Cyprus. I will be praying."

"I know you will." She slid off the bench, back into the aisle between the rows of seats. When she turned from the candle, darkness ate up the path, making it impossible to discern safe steps from unsafe ones in the unfamiliar room. She would be able to navigate the aisle easily enough, but she did not quite trust herself not to ram into the wall at the end rather than turn toward the door.

"Cyprus."

She paused halfway down the aisle, frowning. She had never heard that particular note in Nikolaos's voice. Pain? Regret? Guilt? Those were the words she would have used had the tone come from anyone else's throat. It seemed odd to apply them to him. She turned back to face him. "Yes?"

"I...I am sorry. For your mother's death."

Her brow felt tight and knotted. It was an expected sentiment—why did he say it in that strained tone? "Of course. I know you are."

"No. You do not understand." She saw only his silhouette against the candlelight. Hands fisted at his sides. Shoulders slumped. An odd combination that perfectly suited the torment soaking his words. "I had a dream that night. A dream of a ship going down, and I did nothing. Nothing. I could have saved her."

Her feet did not know whether to run toward him or away. Her heart did not know whether to leap or break. She slid cautiously back up the aisle, not quite knowing what to make of this confession. Knowing nothing but that the ache in her chest was as much for him as for her mother. "Nik...do you think yourself so important? So powerful?"

His head snapped up. "What?"

"If God wanted her ship to stay afloat, do you think you were their only hope? Do you think he could not have worked that miracle without you?"

This time, when his shoulders sagged, it looked more like relief than defeat. "Of course he could have. What am I?"

"A willing vessel. A faithful servant. But not his *only* servant." She reached out until she could rest her hand on his arm. "Did you see her in this dream?" The question tripped from her tongue before she could stop it, though it was equal parts hope and fear possessing her as she asked.

But he shook his head. "Just a sailor, lashed to the mainmast. He asked me for help...and I did nothing."

She squeezed his arm, that hope-and-fear fading away. "I am not as educated as you in these things. But in all the stories I have heard about dreams given by God, it is not how we act *in* them that matters—it is how we respond when we are awake." She was unsure exactly what she meant by that, what she expected him to do about such a dream when no longer in its clutches.

But the words made him relax another degree, and he nodded. As if they made perfect sense to him.

Perhaps they did.

She squeezed his arm again and then dropped her hand, turned again. "Sleep well tonight, Nik. And thank you for those prayers."

He shook himself and stepped forward, even with her. "I must walk you home. The streets are not safe at night."

She would not have asked, but she would not argue.

They made the journey in silence, mist-damp and comfortable. She knew Nikolaos as well as she knew anyone in Patara, more than most. She knew all about the years he and Petros had spent in Ephesus, even, having heard all their stories of school. She knew that while Pet had studied the law, Nikolaos had focused on philosophy, so that he could better debate the merits of Christianity with the Greeks in their city. She knew that he loved the Lord above absolutely everything.

What she did not know was why, when he counted all the church here as his brethren, when he viewed the whole city as his mission field, he spent so much time with her and hers.

Perhaps it was just because Petros had wanted to, and he and his cousin were so close.

Whatever the reason, she was glad to have his familiar warmth beside her through the darkened alleys, now that she had no just cause to feel like armor around her. They said nothing even as they came to her street and she led the way to the back of the house, to the garden that would not flower in the spring without Helena's touch...the garden that she would likely not even *see* in the spring.

They said nothing as she slipped to the door and rested her hand on the latch. She turned, but the mist-shrouded night showed her nothing of his face, just the outline of his form. She lifted a hand in farewell.

He lifted his in return and pivoted, making his way silently out of the garden again.

Cyprus tugged on the ring beneath her hand, and the door obligingly opened with a quiet *shush.*

The kitchen was still soft with the light from the hearth and the lamps she had lit while cooking, the air still redolent with the smells of roasting meat and baking bread. As if she had not gone out at all. Hopefully Abbas and Yiannis would think she had merely taken her meal in here while they ate in the dining chamber—surely that would be befitting her new role in the house.

She held still for a few minutes, certain she heard the dual melodies of the twins' voices still chiming from down the hall. In a few minutes she would check on them, see if anyone needed anything. Tell her sisters with her eyes that she had done what she was supposed to do.

For now, she should eat. Or clean up. Something productive. Something to help her shake off the gravity still clinging to her. Something to occupy her hands while her mind turned to prayer.

Either task would require the pot still hanging over the fire, so she spun that way—and loosed a cry of surprise when she saw the towering form in the doorway.

She splayed a hand over her chest and pasted a wavering smile on her lips, though her pulse did not calm upon recognizing the figure. If anything, it thudded harder, so loudly she feared he would hear it as clearly as she did.

Yiannis took one step into the room and stood there, glaring at her as if she were a slug he debated crushing beneath his sandal. "You. Where have you been?"

A dozen answers sprang to her tongue, none of them completely honest or even the least bit respectful. She bit them all back.

Not that he waited for her response anyway. He surged forward, wrapping his fingers around her arm so tightly a whimper crowded her throat.

She bit *that* back too.

He shook her. "Your clothing is wet."

"*Damp.* I was outside."

"Playing the harlot, no doubt. With that advocate?"

Fire burned away any uncertainty, leaving no room for fear. She pulled her arm free. "How dare you? What could I have possibly done to make you think me so low, so deserving of dishonor in the *day* you have been here? Why do you hate me so, when you know me not at all?"

"I do not need to *know* you. You wear your unbridled disposition upon your head."

It took her a moment to sort through the venom in his tone,

look beyond his curled lip, and realize he spoke of her hair. And then it was all she could do not to stomp like a child and proclaim him grossly unfair. She settled for folding her arms over her chest and glaring back. "Is that the famed logic and reason of the Greeks? That because a fluke of nature made my hair red, I must be a creature who has no control over her passions and tempers, must be indiscreet and untrustworthy?"

"Asks the girl who snuck away when she ought to have been serving her father and now bears the dew of her shame upon every strand of that hair."

She tried to remember how Mater used to stand when arguing with Abbas. The way she somehow combined respect with a spine of Damascus steel.

Cyprus probably looked as furious and scornful as she felt. "Forgive me, *cousin*, if I do not display the virtues of a good servant—I have no experience with it. Helena always left us to enjoy our meal without her hovering, so I assumed that was acceptable. Ought I not to have left the room? Is it a crime to seek solace in a garden?"

He advanced on her again, the waves of his anger crashing well before he got any closer, forceful enough to make her stumble back. He backed her into a corner, towering above her, pinning her there without needing to touch her.

It made her want to spit in his eye. Or perhaps stomp on his toes like the puppy thief had done to her. Bite his arm, as well, if he lifted it toward her.

He remained still, hovering there above her. "Let me make something very clear to you, girl. I have no need of you. I have no desire to claim you as a cousin, or an acquaintance, or anything else. I will take your sisters home with me, and they will live a life of luxury and pleasure. I will sell this house that you have cursed with your worship of this ridiculous invisible God you serve. I will leave you and your broken father to do what you must to survive, until he gives up and dies. And then you can scavenge in the streets like the other dogs, and I will never have the displeasure of seeing you again."

No. She would marry Petros, and he would care for her and Abbas. She would...her head went light and hot. "What do you mean, you will take my sisters home with you? You cannot! They are betrothed to—"

"They cannot pay their dowries, therefore the betrothals are naught." He leaned closer. "Which is just as well. It is a shame to separate them, do you not think so? But with me, they can be together. I will not even force them to make offerings to Artemis or my household gods, so long as they promise not to defile my house with *your* God. They will be well cared for."

Perhaps she would have believed him more easily if his eyes were not alive with dark promises, blacker than the shadows of the night. She did not have to wonder at what his intentions toward them were—he certainly could not marry them both, not under Roman law. No doubt he would refuse to anyway, given that they came empty handed. He meant to make them concubines. They would be no better than slaves, at the mercy of a master who did not know the meaning of the word.

No. She could not, *would* not let him take her sisters. Her fingers dug into her arm. "This may be your house. But we are not your slaves, to command about at will."

"You are no better. Orphans, for all purposes, given that your father is determined to die. And if he lives, he will sell you himself. You are of no use to him now, any of you, except for the price you can bring."

The terrible words curled into that hole Abbas had made with the same suggestion. The hole that might never quite be filled again. Mater, Mater with her Christian heart and loving spirit, had always said children were precious. That orphans and widows were to be cared for and protected. That this was the will of God.

Abbas, Abbas with his Roman history and Greek upbringing, had always said that children were possessions. To be used to advantage if they could be and gotten rid of if they could not. Abbas had never so much as lifted a brow at the news that a neighbor had left their newborn babe exposed on the hill outside of town when the little one was born with a hare-lip or a missing finger.

"Now, no need to look so glum." Wicked smile on his lips, he reached out and picked up a lock of the hair he found so distasteful. "You can still do your duty as a daughter and provide for your father. Plenty of rich idiots in Rome would pay a handsome price for you. Plenty of them covet unbridled passion. Or maybe Petros, son of Theophanes, will buy you from him. No doubt he needs a little plaything to come home to after a hard day arguing for justice."

She winced and turned her face away from him, pulling her hair from his fingers. Clenching her teeth together to keep from responding—it would only please him to argue. And he did not need to know that Petros would marry her, not buy her.

But if Abbas tried to sell her...what could her beloved do then? Nothing. Nothing.

His chuckle was slick as oil, heartless as the statues in the center of town. Yiannis took a step back. "We are waiting on our sweet, girl. Bring it, and then clean up this mess."

Cyprus dipped her knees, though Yiannis was not stupid enough to think it anything but mockery. Which was no doubt why he tipped the pot as he walked past the hearth, spilling its contents out on the stones.

The broth sizzled, popped, and quickly blackened into a mess that it would take her hours to scrub off.

Cyprus clenched her teeth even tighter. She had saved their past from him—but she had no idea how to keep their futures out of his hands.

SEVENTEEN

Nikolaos closed his eyes, closed out the world. Asked his ears to stop processing sound, his fingers to forget the feel of the linens beneath them. All his focus, all his attention he put squarely upon the man who lay prostrate, burning with fever, and upon the prayer for him.

He had never had to focus so. Not when it worked. He knew, even as he turned his entire being toward the plea, that healing required more than *his* focus. Otherwise, he would be able to make well every person in the empire merely by thinking of them.

Kosmas groaned on the bed. He was not so feverish as to be incomprehensible. He was not, Nikolaos felt sure, in danger of dying any time in the next few days. If he wanted it, he could be moved. Home, if that were his desire. Or to the Visibullis house for the solstice celebrations tomorrow, as everyone was trying to convince him to do.

Everyone, of course, but Gallus, who had demanded his sons both return home. Kosmas had sworn he would as soon as he felt able. Felix had stood there with tight lips and made no promises.

Nikolaos whispered into the room, words in whatever language wanted to spring from his lips—Greek, Latin, a smattering of Ancient Hebrew. Perhaps a few words in a language that existed only between him and God. He commanded, he prayed, he could feel the heat of the Spirit inside him, ready and willing to touch.

The Spirit was not always willing. But he was today. This should work. Should…but did not.

Sensory details worked their way back into his consciousness. The foot that had gone numb. The floor, hard beneath his knees. The sound of footsteps entering the room. Nikolaos glanced over, up, and nodded to Felix.

The young man frowned. "Have you been here all night?"

"Is it morning?"

Felix motioned to the window. Fabric draped it, but a bit of pearly gray that murmured of morning seeped out beneath the folds.

Nikolaos sighed. "Then I have been here all night." He had come after he saw Cyprus safely home, after he had returned to the church just long enough to store the scrolls and tell his uncle they were there.

Felix settled beside him—not on the chair lush with a cushion, but on the floor where Nikolaos had been kneeling. "Has his sleep been peaceful?"

"Nothing about your brother has been peaceful for many days." Exhaustion settled on him like a beast, heavy and hot. Nikolaos leaned his elbow on the bed frame and propped his head on his hand. Hero's parents had offered him a bed—he might have to accept it.

His face a mosaic of torment, Felix reached out, touched fingertips to his brother's hand, and then retreated. "I wanted to come home and find things different. Find that the bonds of brotherhood had somehow strengthened in my absence. That he would have ceased resenting me. That we could be *friends.* Instead..."

"Instead," Kosmas slurred in a voice still soaked with sleep, "you find a brother broken while you are whole. Like always, you are the favored one."

The muscle in Felix's jaw ticked for a few seconds before he whispered a response. "You are not broken, Kosmas. It is a simple injury—the infection will clear up, and you will be well."

Kosmas snorted and turned his head toward the window.

Felix pressed his fingers to his eyes. "And I am not favored. I cannot think why you would say I am. Your mother—the only one I ever knew—despises me. She has rejected me at every turn. And Father...he would have been happy had I stayed in Rome. His every letter to me encouraged me to stay. You have no idea how that feels, to realize your parents and brother are quite happy to keep you hundreds of miles distant."

And yet no bitterness tinged the words. Just a tired, ancient sorrow. Nikolaos could sense the peace beneath it—the kind that had come of years of struggle and prayer and now needed no sympathy spoken. The kind that had formed a foundation of faith that relied more on the love of his Father in heaven than the one upon earth.

Kosmas's fingers tangled in the sheet beneath him. "I have nothing so long as you are here. Can you not see that? You are the elder. You will get it *all.*"

"I will not." Looking as tired as Nikolaos felt, Felix mirrored his pose—elbow on bed, head on hand. "You surely know that. The moment my mother's father adopted me as his heir in Rome, I sent word home saying all the Lycian estates ought by rights to be yours. Father agreed. He surely, *surely* told you."

"But you have come back again." All the bitterness missing from Felix's words seemed to have gathered in Kosmas's. "You are back, and you will take it."

Perhaps, had he more energy, Nikolaos would slip out and leave this argument to the brothers. But he was too tired. He had not slept a wink since he awoke yesterday at this time. His legs did not want to move. So he stayed, and he prayed that the peace in Felix's soul extend outward until it covered his brother too. Until it existed between them as a palpable thing, knitting together what the night and its darkness would keep torn apart.

"I will not take it!" For all the fervency in his tone, Felix kept his voice hushed. "I do not *want* it—Lycia stopped being my home when everyone I love here told me to leave and not come back. I did so only to be here for your wedding. So stop feeling sorry for yourself, get out of that bed, marry the beautiful woman waiting to be your wife, and I will leave again!"

Nikolaos could feel the ache—it pulsed like the sea, a wave that rolled out of Felix and then *shush*ed its way back in.

Kosmas did not seem touched by it. His fingers twisted the linen he had balled up, and he kept his gaze on the window, as if he could see through the blue fabric and out into the gray morning. "I am not going to marry Alexandria."

Nikolaos's huff melted into Felix's. "Kosmas." He knew not what else to say.

Felix did not suffer the same uncertainty. "Why in the world not? She is everything you could possibly want in a wife!"

"Some of us must remain in Father's good graces, Felix. He has said he will leave everything to you if I marry her, and I do not doubt him."

Felix rose, though apparently only so that he could pace to the window. "A threat that means nothing unless I agree to it, which I do not. He cannot leave me what I do not want—I would only give it all to you anyway. We can sign a contract saying as much. I daresay your friend Petros could draw one up for us."

Kosmas turned his face from his brother, back toward Nikolaos. "My leg may never heal. She will not want a husband who is lame."

"Alexandria would not care about such things," Nikolaos murmured.

Felix paced back toward them, pleading eyes focused on Nikolaos. "And you can heal him. You can, I know it. As you did *my* wound."

Nikolaos did not mean to sigh. It was just how his breath emerged through a tired throat. "I have been trying."

Felix looked far more tormented by the failure implied in the words than his brother did. "Then why is it not working?"

Nikolaos leaned away from the bed, his gaze upon the man who lay upon it. "There are many reasons why people do not receive a healing. Sometimes they simply do not *need* to be healed— they can live quite fully with their injury. Sometimes it is because there is something they need to learn through the infirmity. Sometimes it is because they can serve God better in their weakness than they could in their strength. Sometimes it is simply their time to die—not that I think that the case here. And sometimes...sometimes it is because they refuse to be healed. That is your brother's real ailment, Felix. He does not *want* to be well."

"That is absurd!" Kosmas shoved himself up a few inches, fury making his face look like his father's. "You think I *want* to lie here in agony?"

"Yes." Nikolaos used the bedframe and the chair behind him to haul himself to his feet. "Like a child who wants a stomachache as an excuse to keep from going to school on the day of an exam. You want to remain unwell to have an excuse not to marry Alexandria."

Though sputtering and fuming like a volcano, Kosmas had no

reply.

Felix, again, did not suffer from silence. His gaze had drifted to his brother, and his voice emerged soft and pained. "Is that who we are, brother? Do the sons of Gallus break our promise because of a threat? Because of gold?"

"If the word of the sons of Gallus is so important to you," Kosmas muttered from between clenched teeth, "then *you* marry her. Burden yourself with a wife who has nothing but beauty to her credit. Go ahead."

Felix's laugh was a mockery of the word. "So that you can hate me when you realize your mistake, when you realize you still love her?"

Kosmas did not flinch. "I do not love her. I liked her well enough, when she came with a dowry. But I will not risk Father's wrath for something so insignificant as that affection. I will not be disowned for her. But by all means—*you* risk losing his respect and affection for that pretty face."

Nikolaos did not dare move. Had Kosmas ever really been a friend? Had he ever really known him? Perhaps he had not, for he would have sworn, as Petros had when they made the journey out to his villa two days ago, that love of Alexandria would have won out over fear of Gallus. But he detected no regret in Kosmas now. No uncertainty as he belittled the bond that would have led him to matrimony had that ship not been sucked down into the Mediterranean.

And if this was the true Kosmas, then Alexandria would be better off by far without him.

Felix swallowed audibly and held his hands by his sides, palms facing his brother. A gesture of helplessness. "Is this what I have to do to prove to you that I want your best? Do I have to take our father's wrath on my own shoulders?"

"As if it would be a hardship for you. You do not need his favor, you have all those holdings in Rome. And you would get a pretty wife in the bargain—and get to preserve the name of the sons of Gallus as keepers of their word."

Felix's brow knotted. "You cannot possibly want me to marry her. You cannot. You would regret it and hate me all the more. Not to mention that *she* will have something to say about it."

Kosmas's breath of laughter was much as his brother's had been a moment before—false, mocking. "Oh, yes. She will. And it is no longer my problem *what* she chooses to say. I am finished with her, one way or another. I will tell her so when she comes today."

Felix shook his head, his helpless hands curling into fists that looked more resigned than resentful. "You will break her heart."

"She is too pragmatic to suffer long." As if the conversation were over, Kosmas closed his eyes and sank back onto his pillow. "Go away, Felix. You make my leg hurt."

"And you make my heart hurt, brother—if only I could stir you to care about such things." With a defeated shake of his head, Felix strode from the room.

Nikolaos lifted a hand to the wall to steady himself. Perhaps he should have eaten or drunk when a servant offered him sustenance sometime in the middle hours of the night. "You will regret this, Kosmas. Have you really thought of how you will feel if he does as you ask? If Alexandria agrees? Could you really stand to see her with him and know she is *his* wife?"

The curl of his lips looked small and mean. "Oh, yes. Yes, I will survive quite well knowing it is Felix being cut to pieces by her sharp tongue. Felix receiving the foul words and threats of our father."

No wonder his leg was festering—it was trying to keep pace with his heart. Nikolaos shook his head and eased toward the door. But he had to pause on the threshold and look back to the man he had tried for years to make a friend. "It is in times of trial that our faith is revealed, Kosmas. Whether it withers or whether it stands strong in the winds of tribulation."

"I do not need a sermon from you, priest. Go away."

All he had ever wanted was to be a shepherd. To have the honor and privilege of serving this flock of believers who sought the Way in a land filled with pagans. But perhaps part of that was recognizing when someone was not a sheep among the flock at all. And could not be forced to be.

Nikolaos tapped his fingers on the doorframe. "I will not stop praying for you."

"Whatever makes you feel pious."

His mouth tasted of failure as he stepped out of the sickroom, into the hallway where it was still night. He could not heal Kosmas, not physically and not spiritually. He could not make things right for Felix. He could not make Dorus see how he was hurting the only people he had left in the world. He could not force Yiannis from the house the Visibullises called home. He could not guarantee his cousin's happiness.

He could not school his own heart. Sagging, he leaned against the cool wall. He did not love Cyprus like Petros did. But he loved her. Not enough to give up the life he knew the Lord had called him to...but enough that it *hurt*. Oh, how it hurt. To look at her last night in the candlelight and hear her speak of her love of Petros. To realize that though he was the one she came to when she needed manuscripts guarded, he was not the one she wanted to marry.

Of course he was not. And he did not *want* to be, but...

But some small, petty part of him did not want Petros to be either.

"Father, forgive me. Take this from me." He turned his lips to the wall as he spoke, so that the words—barely even words, more like breath—sank into the plaster and vanished.

He had said the right things to his cousin. He had laughed and rejoiced with him, and he had prayed, never gave hint of that shadow inside him. He had told himself everything he could think of to make this bearable.

But it still hurt. And knowing that God could use the hurt later did very little, frankly, to ease it *now*.

Petros had been hurt, too, when Nik had said he intended to go to Jerusalem without having discussed it with him first. He had seen it, even if he had not had the opportunity since then to address it. And what could he say? *I have to go, Pet. I cannot stand to watch the two of you day in and day out. Not just yet.*

No. Better to claim he needed the experience of the journey. That God was calling him to the land he had once walked as a man. Better to tell his uncle the same, and promise that as soon as he got back, he would speak the vows and accept the mantle of a priest. Officially. Irrevocably.

"Nikolaos? Are you well?"

He started and straightened, blinking against the lamp in front of him. The blurry figure holding it solidified into Mydon. He summoned up a smile for Hero's father. "Exhausted is all. Is that offer of a bed still good?"

"Always." Mydon smiled too, with much more energy. "Come."

He followed his host along the corridor, past the main hall with its beautiful tile work, past the entrance to the garden. Mydon slowed as they gained the hallway that held more bedchambers. "Nikolaos...I have sought the council of your uncle. About Hero and Rhoda."

Nikolaos drifted to a halt. He had not the wherewithal just now to both talk and walk. He would probably run into a wall if he tried. "And what did Uncle say?" He asked, but he already knew. His uncle would say all the right words...but all the right words would not be able to disguise the fact that he distrusted the Visibullis family. They were not part of his community—and his community always came first.

Mydon drew a long breath in through his nose. "He reminded me that he had advised against the betrothal at the start—he had warned me that Dorus Visibullis was a Hellenist through and through. Worse, a Roman. That an alliance with his house would bring trouble upon mine."

Nikolaos pressed his fingers to the wall and told himself it was to support his tired frame. Not to push his frustration out into the stones that were strong enough to bear it. "I did not realize he had told you such things."

A corner of Mydon's lips turned up. "Of course, he also reminded me that when I accepted Christ as my Savior, he had urged and urged me to let go my ties to the things of this world. That he has been urging me so for the last two decades, but that still I place too much value on gold." He flicked a gaze toward one of the doors, and the lamp failed to light his eyes. "Not as much as Gallus, let it be known. But then, I should not compare myself to my neighbors. I know. God will judge me for my own heart, not for anyone else's."

An observation whose truth did not need Nikolaos's voice to agree with it. He waited.

Mydon sighed. "Perhaps this is my failing—that while my heart belongs to Christ, I still live in the world I was born into. I am unwilling to abandon it all and give everything I own to the church. But I can reach people through my businesses—why can your uncle never grant that? I have brought three new families into the church over the years through my contacts. Contacts I would not have had if I had done as he requested. I cannot operate all I do without a home suitable to hosting visitors."

Still Nikolaos said nothing. He trusted the bishop's guidance...

but he also knew well that his uncle had prejudices just as any man. Only the Lord's guidance could be trusted implicitly.

Mydon waved him onward. "All that to say this: All I have worked for, the position I have fought your uncle to keep, will be compromised if I let Hero follow his heart and marry Rhoda when she has no dowry. I cannot support a second household, not without the strain carrying down to all my workers. And it is not right to ask all of them to suffer so that Hero can be happy."

Nikolaos halted again, this time when Mydon opened the door to an unoccupied chamber. But he did not look at the room. He looked at the man. And he found words that matched the ache in his heart in timbre, if not in meaning. "You will forbid their union."

"I do not *want* to do so. I like Rhoda. The Visibullises are good girls, and they will be fine wives. But…I will at least insist they wait. Until Dorus gets back on his feet and can replenish their storehouses. Until Rhoda can come with *something*, even if not as much as we first agreed upon."

Perhaps it would have sounded fair, had this terrible cloud not been hanging over him, warning him that *waiting* would not be enough. Would not be possible. Nikolaos shook his head. "Their circumstances are direr than that, Mydon. If you do not let your son marry her now, she…she may not be here when you have changed your mind."

He knew not, exactly, where she would go. But he had such a terrible feeling. Like a storm brewing far out at sea.

This time, he could not let the ship caught in the tempest go down. Not when the Lord was there, giving him the warning so that he could speak calm into it.

He just had to figure out *how*.

EIGHTEEN

"Abbas?" Cyprus slid into the room, making no attempt to be quiet. The sun was high in the sky—it was time for her father to greet the day, whether he wanted to or not. She needed answers. "Abbas." After sliding his breakfast tray onto the small table, she reached down and shook him. Not exactly gently.

Why. Why. Why.

His eyes creaked open. "I am awake, Cyprus. Thank you. Now you can go."

"I cannot." Into a chalice she poured some spiced wine—once his favorite beverage for beginning a day. Something they only had now because of Petros's generosity and Yiannis's insistence. "Sit up."

He frowned instead. "Is this how you speak to your father?"

"A question that is growing quite old, as my father lies about in his bed determined to die. Sit up. You owe me answers. If you will not rise and be a man, you at *least* can give me answers."

The affront to his pride served to pull him up a few inches, anyway, into a reclining position against his pillows. His scowl did not lessen. "You will regret using such words with me, child."

"I will not have time to regret anything if you do not stir yourself." She thrust the cup at him and, after he reluctantly took it, crossed her arms. "Do you love us? Are we the gifts of God that Mater always claimed, or are we just burdens to you? Possessions, like this table or bed?"

Abbas sipped at the cup. "You weary me."

"Is that your answer?" She pressed her fingers to her arms to anchor herself there, in that stance of defiance. To keep her voice from wavering, the tears from burning. "Because I need to know. I need to know if you would really sell us, as you threatened. I need to know if we mean so little to you."

Abbas took another sip. Perhaps it was torment in his eyes. Or perhaps it was simply grief over Mater, the one person in the world he truly loved.

Cyprus's nostrils flared. "Yiannis means to take the twins with him. Make them his concubines. I cannot fight him on my own, Abbas—I need you to stand up and claim the authority you have as their father."

His eyes slid shut, and his glass tilted. She did not reach out to help him steady it. If it tipped, he would just have to bear the momentary discomfort of a damp tunic. But it did not spill. "I know his intentions."

Her throat ached. "And?"

"And it is a better alternative for them than any other available. Better to be the concubines of one man than whores for hundreds. Surely you see that."

Her eyes were dry, but her vision was still blurry. "What I see is that he has a cruel heart and thinks of no one but himself. He will not treat them well. When he realizes they will not abandon their faith as he commands, he will..." She had to press her lips to hold down the sob. Shake her head.

Abbas leaned down to set the cup on the floor. "They are not so foolish. They will give it up, or at least hide it from him."

A breath slipped out, half laughter. Because he knew them so little. And because she loved them so much. "They have too much of you in them—we all do. We will not any of us relent. We will not cower. And we have too much of Mater in us, too—we will not give up our faith, no matter what man tells us to. We will not hide our faces in shame of our God."

Abba's jaw worked, back and forth. "They must, or he will kill them. He told me as much."

"And you still think this the best course for them?" Her voice screeched, too loud, too raw.

Abbas shut his eyes, squeezed them. "It is the *only* course, can you not see that? They will have a chance at life."

They would not. He must know they would not. Yiannis would try his best to crush them, and when he failed, he would punish them instead. Because he would fail. Her sisters would never crack, never crumble. They would go to the grave defiant for the sake of Christ and count it to his glory to serve him so.

Abbas sniffed. "He said he means to leave you here, with me. I will not burden you long, Cyprus. Then you can marry that Petros boy, if it is what you want. If he will have you."

"If he will have me?" Did her father know *him* so little too?

"You have nothing now, daughter. Nothing."

She had this great ball in her throat, making her want to laugh and cry and curl up beside her father and beg him to stroke her hair as he had done when she was just a little thing. She had this bone-deep need to make things right. "Have you not wondered why Timon has not returned, Abbas, demanding his money?"

Abbas's laugh sounded dry and rusty. "Because he is wise enough to know there is no use demanding wine from a casket long since drained."

"No. Because Petros paid your debt."

"What?" He sat up straight, eyes coming open and filling

with...she had no name for it. Something akin to disbelief, colored with shock, shadowed with shame. "He...he could not. He cannot have made enough in all his life to cover that debt."

"He has—just. It took all he had. But he gave it, Abbas. For us. For you."

"Foolish boy." He bent over the opposite way now, curling toward his stomach. "Why would he do such a thing?"

"Because that is what love asks of us—that we give our all. That we give our very lives, if it will save our brother's."

Or sisters'. Cyprus took a step back, her arms falling to her sides. Her mother's voice echoed in her mind as she read the Scriptures to them. *There is no greater love than this: to lay down one's life for one's friends.*

That was the sacrifice of Jesus. That was the choice that led Mater to a watery grave. That was the call upon all of them, really, the heart of the faith.

It seemed her whole body trembled. Maybe it did. And that question—that loud, furious, quiet, unending question finally went silent. No more *why.*

She knew.

A strange sound came from Abbas's throat. "Then I am doing right. I am giving my life."

"No." She started for the door. "You are not giving it for us—you are giving it for *you.* If you want to serve your daughters, then you must *live.*"

But for all the faith she had in God, what she had once had in Abbas had dried up. It crinkled under her feet like dried grass as she strode from his room.

The twins' voices came from their room, raised in a hymn. She could hear Mater's voice there, too, harmonizing with theirs. For a moment, she paused and savored it. The rich *hallelujahs* and triumphant praises. That familiar words that had never meant before what they did just now.

She had to save her sisters. That was love—the love God had for them, the love he wanted them to emulate. The love that Petros may mourn but would understand, because he had the same burgeoning in his heart. He would grieve her, but he would not begrudge her doing what she should.

And she would tell him, before she went through with it, how much she loved *him* too. She would bid him go and make use of this freedom that she knew he did not want. To serve the brethren with his words before the Vicarius, before the Caesar, before the very Augustus if he could.

Where do I go, Lord, to do this?

"Girl. Come here."

Her eyes came open slowly, the fire in her veins not banking. But not twisting into anger, either, as she beheld Yiannis standing in the main room, beckoning to her. She took a few silent steps into the entryway.

He did not bid her any closer. "I need you to go to the markets. We will feast tomorrow, for Saturnalia. I have told the twins they may invite whomever they please—I will tell them tomorrow that it is to be their farewell. We will need candles for every window, fuel for the fireplace, and the food, of course. My men will go with you to carry everything, but they do not know this marketplace. You will see to it."

What is your way, Lord?

She dipped her knees—not mockingly, this time. Much. "Certainly." Then, "I will need money."

"They have it. And spare no expense—I want your sisters to taste of what awaits them with me."

Show me your path, Father. She nodded. "Consider it done. I will return when I can."

Never, even when she thought herself the daughter of a

wealthy man, had she gone to the marketplace with four servants in tow, all of them laden with baskets ready for the filling. It gave her no pleasure, fed no pride to do so now. She hoped it never would have—but certainly not now. Not now. She was no better than they. No higher in standing.

Would not long be free.

Her insides trembled at that thought. She had always been free. Even under her father's rule, she had still been *free.* And she was Greek enough to value that freedom. To have to fight back the thought that if she gave it up, she would be making herself... *less.*

But she had not just been reared with Greek philosophy. And the word of the Lord taught that true freedom was not wrapped up in whether one served man. That it was by serving God that one found freedom.

Something tickled her cheek as she stepped into the busy thoroughfare, and she lifted a hand. For a moment she had to pause and stare when she realized it was a tear. She had not thought she had room for sorrow quite yet, beyond the determination. But there it was.

One of the menservants stepped up beside her, his eyes scanning the busy marketplace rather than her. "Everyone is out and about, it seems. We will be hard-pressed to find all the master wants."

Lead me, Father God. Cyprus smiled and wiped the tear off on the too-fine fabric of her garment. "We will find it all. Do not fear. I know all the best stalls."

And the shopkeepers all pasted on smiles when they saw the coins in the servants' hands. She could see the questions in their eyes—who were these slaves? *Whose* were they? Why were they following around the daughter of Dorus Visibullis? Where did the money come from?

She offered them no answers. Let them wonder.

She led the men from one stall to another, letting the colorful awnings guide her. Blue and red for the chandler who had always been kindest to them, where she loaded up one whole basket with the finest candles for the Festival of Lights. His stall was not the busiest, because he was a Christian and the Hellenists steered clear of him more often than not because of it.

She pressed an extra coin to his palm before he could give her the price for it all—because he was a Christian and the Hellenists steered clear of him. She wished it were *her* money she was being generous with, but this would have to do. As she dropped the silver into his hand, she gripped the swollen joints and whispered, "In the name of our Christ, who we celebrate tomorrow."

The chandler closed his knotted knuckles over the money and whispered back, "God be with you."

"And also with you."

Next was the awning of yellow and purple, where the finest fabric could be found. This was where Mater had bought the green linen Cyprus wore today. This was where she now sought a few lengths of sheerest fabric to drape over the front windows and make the main room look sumptuous and fine.

Ennius—she was fairly sure it was Ennius and not Iovite—nodded his approval at her selection.

She nodded hers at the shopkeeper. He was not a Christian—there were no Christian sellers of cloth in Patara that Mater had ever found. But she murmured a prayer for him as she handed over the coins, that he would see the truth of the Lord this year as he lit his candles to Saturn.

His hand fisted around the coins. "Has your fortune turned again, daughter of Visibullis?"

Her lips felt strange as they curled up. "No, friend. But I will praise the Lord God anyway."

Then came the food stalls. The spice sellers with their fragrant cinnamon and cardamom and cloves. The farmers with their colorful vegetables, cajoled from the winter earth at a slower rate than in the summer, but cajoled still. The herders with their mutton and beef and pork, the fisherman with the day's freshest catches. The millers with their flour from the most fragrant grains. The vintners, casks filled with deepest red wine.

Her last stop was for olive oil—this merchant one of the other Christians. She greeted Cyprus coolly, distrust in her eyes that was far more acute than it would have been had she thought Cyprus simply a Greek, like all her neighbors. It was worse, had always been worse in the eyes of the brethren, that they claimed the faith but did not partake in the fellowship.

Cyprus agreed—it was worse. Much worse to be alone when you should have a family than to simply be alone.

She would soon know that feeling firsthand. For the merchant woman, she withdrew a smile that could not be large, but which she prayed was warm—despite the fact that this was the woman who had accused her of not loving her sisters, who had sent her home in tears. Cyprus motioned forward Iovite, whose basket held the bottle of olive oil from their kitchen. Thanks to Petros, it was nowhere near empty. But she would fill it anyway. "Good day. I need this refilled, and another besides, the same size."

The woman took the bottle without saying a word. Topped it off, and then pulled forward a matching one.

Iovite inspected it, though Cyprus had no idea what he searched for. At least until he said, "This is excellent glass. Is the blower local? My master would like some new glassware for tomorrow's feast."

His master spent money with the speed of a fire on dry fuel. Cyprus pressed her lips together to keep from pointing out as much.

The shopkeeper nodded and pointed down the busy avenue. "The black awning, trimmed in orange. You will find no better in all of Lycia." She shifted, her narrowed eyes more cunning than brown. "And who is your master?"

Cyprus shifted too, under the woman's darting gaze.

Ennius lifted his chin. "Yiannis of Xanthos."

The woman's brows lifted as she settled that slicing gaze on Cyprus. "And is he your master now too, Cyprus Visibullis?"

"No." She took the bottle and tucked it carefully into the basket, between a loaf of sweet-smelling bread and a tin of spices. "But he would make himself so over my sisters, if you wish to gloat over our misfortune. Or you could pray for us." She looked up, met the woman's eyes again.

Surprise had entered into them now, and something shadowed with regret.

Cyprus nodded. "I would prefer the prayers to the gloating. But let your conscience guide you. Good day."

Only silence called out to stop her as she turned away from the booth. Perhaps her small challenge would accomplish nothing, perhaps the merchant would distrust and detest her more than ever. But perhaps...perhaps she would pray. Now and later. Perhaps she would remember them when she went before the Lord.

Cyprus hoped it was the latter. She needed all the prayers she could get.

Now where, Lord? Where am I to go to accomplish this thing in my heart?

"Now where?" Ennius stepped to her side again. "Home? I believe that is all we need."

"Almost. Honey."

"Ah." His eyes lit. "Yes. The master adores honey."

Their baskets, however, were full to bursting. They could carry a jar of honey separately, of course, but she hated the thought of it perhaps slipping from an overburdened arm and smashing. She motioned them down another alley, to the least expensive of the shops. "A small basket first, I think. Nothing large, just for the honey."

Iovite nodded. "Yes. You can carry the honey. It will not be too much for you."

Her lips tugged up. "I should think not."

The basket weaver's stall was near the end of the street. It took Cyprus a moment to find the bent form of the old woman among her wares. But finally she spotted the gray hair, covered with a gray cloth. Her eyes, when she turned them up at their approach, looked watery and weak.

Cyprus abandoned the menservants and came around the table so she could grip the woman's hands. "Old mother, are you unwell?"

The woman shook her head in a lie betrayed by her cough. "It is nothing. Nikolaos has prayed for me. I will be well."

Cyprus smiled and squeezed the warm, wrinkled hands. "I will join my prayers for you to his. They may not be as potent, but the more voices lifted for you, the better."

The bleary eyes sought hers, moving from one of them to the other. "You are the Visibullis girl. The youngest one."

"I am."

"The one that young Petros is so taken with."

At that, Cyprus's smile went soft. "And who is equally taken with him."

"He helped my son—a fisherman. In the courts. Jude could pay him very little, but he helped him anyway."

The smile would not leave her lips. "That is Petros. I am sure he did so with a happy heart."

The old woman smiled too and reached down beside her. "My

daughter, she tans leather. We have been working together on a satchel—her leatherwork, my stitches. It would be a fine thing for him to carry his scrolls around in." She pulled up a leather bag, beautiful and soft.

Cyprus's heart twisted. Her fingers reached out to touch the leather. Buttery and even softer than it looked. "It is lovely. The loveliest I have seen."

"And tomorrow is the day for gifts."

Stroking the leather one more time, Cyprus shook her head. "It is. But I have no money with which to buy such a beautiful bag, old mother. That which these men have in their pockets is not mine. And I would not buy a gift for my beloved with borrowed funds."

The woman grinned and pushed the leather into her hands. "My gift to you. And then your gift to him. Because he is good and deserves it, and my son had little with which to pay. And because you love him, and he you, and he should think of you each time he touches this to draw out his work."

That part of her that was Abbas wanted to refuse—a Visibullis did not need a handout. Better to go without than to accept what she could not pay for.

But the part that was Christ thrummed, and something whispered to Cyprus, *Let her bless you, and it will bless her.*

Her fingers closed around the satchel. "Thank you. I will tell Petros who crafted it, and I am sure he will tell his friends, and your daughter will have more business than she can handle."

The old woman chuckled. "To God's ear, daughter."

Movement caught her eye. She looked up, past the woman, to the alleyway that cut beside her stall and wrapped itself around the building. A man strode through it with a steady pace and unerring confidence, a tall, thin servant scurrying behind.

Timon. Her throat went dry.

The basket weaver noted the direction of her gaze. "He owns the building. His offices are behind, on the upper floor." She shivered—or shuddered. "I would move my stall, if I could afford anything better."

"When your daughter's leather is seen in the acropolis, you will be able to." Cyprus straightened, fingers clutching the satchel. *Timon.* Her heart went still. Her soul settled. And she knew. She turned to the men, met each of their eyes. "Get the basket, and this good matron can direct you to the honey. Then take your burdens home. I will follow within a few minutes, after I run a private errand."

Perhaps, if they knew her—if they cared—they would have objected. They did not.

The old woman grabbed her hand, though. "What are you about, pretty daughter? I feel trouble in my bones."

Cyprus stooped until her mouth was at the woman's ear. "Pray for me, I beg you. And if I do not emerge within half an hour, send word to Petros."

Straightening again before the woman could respond, she strode after Timon.

NINETEEN

"Petros, son of Theophanes!"

It was not unusual to hear his name called when he was near the courts. Not unusual to not recognize the voice. But when Petros turned to seek its owner, his brows knit. It *was* unusual for someone to charge forward wearing a tunic so fine and edged with gold thread.

And even more unusual for Petros's father to be charging in the man's wake, panic on his visage to counteract the broad smile on the stranger's.

Petros gripped his satchel and toyed with the idea of melting into the crowd before the man—and his father—could catch up with him.

But that smacked of cowardice. So instead, he fastened on the vague smile he reserved for strangers that he was unsure he wanted to be friends. The one that was not cold but not warm. The one that said, *Tread carefully. I am not one to be fooled.*

Or he hoped it said that, anyway. It was a smile Father had perfected years ago, and which Petros had practiced incessantly before he appeared before the judge for the first time.

The stranger reached him two strides ahead of Petros's father and stretched out a hand to clasp. "There you are! I have been trying for days to finagle an introduction out of your father, but he has been most sly in keeping you from me."

Petros's fingers curled around the stranger's wrist. Or rather, around the solid gold cuff that had beaten his hand to the honor. His gaze went over the stranger's shoulder to land on Father.

The panic had not disappeared, but it had traveled to his eyes alone and left the rest of his face merely taut. "It was not an attempt at slyness, Vicarius."

Vicarius? Petros's throat went tight as he accepted his own wrist back from the stranger's fingers—no, the governor's. He recognized him now from the bust on display in the courts. Oceanus Servilianus, the vicarius in charge of taxes and justice for all of Lycia.

He had not known he was in Patara. He would not think why he would *be* in Patara now, when taxes were not due and there were no cases before the courts to deserve his attention. The man had been there before, when Petros argued—but he had thankfully not known it until afterward. "At your service, lord."

Oceanus Servilianus smiled. "Glad I am to hear that. Word of you and your charmed tongue has reached me, young Petros. I have come before to hear you, and again two weeks ago, in secret, to be sure it was not a fluke."

His throat would never be anything but dry again. It would never be anything but tight. His lips would never feel natural again as he smiled. "I am honored." Terrified. Bemused. He looked again to Father.

Father widened his eyes, though Petros could not interpret whatever message he meant it to convey.

The governor clapped a hand to Petros's shoulder and steered him away from the court, toward one of the vendors selling skewers of meat. "Come. We will eat and talk. We have much to discuss."

They had? "Excuse me, lord. But I must meet with—"

"I checked with the judge before I intercepted you. Your meeting will be the day after the solstice instead. You do not mind, do you?" Still beaming, Oceanus kept on pushing him away from the proud columns of the court building.

"Of course he does not mind," Father said. *Do not mind*, his eyes said.

Petros shook his head. "Of course not. It is my great honor to pass an hour in your company, Vicarius."

"Call me Oceanus. We are going to be great friends, you and I, Petros. Do you not agree, Theophanes?"

Father cleared his throat—and cleared his eyes of that panic—just as Oceanus looked back at him. His smile was firmly in place. "Of course, lord. My family looks forward to becoming better acquainted with yours."

"Indeed!" The governor steered them to a bench and motioned with his hand. A servant Petros had not noticed trailing them sprang forward and hurried to the food vendor. Oceanus sat, inviting Petros and his father to follow suit.

He sat. And he wanted nothing more than to stand again, and go back to his meeting and his day, so that he could hurry to the Visibullis house as soon as was feasible.

"Now. I want to know your thoughts for my plan, young Petros."

Perhaps, as everyone kept saying, his tongue possessed a certain charm—but it could not provide knowledge where he simply had none. "Forgive me, lord—Oceanus. But I am unaware of what..." His brows creased at the way Father waved a hand.

"Please, Vicarius." Father sat on the very edge of the bench, leaning forward to interject, though Oceanus, in the middle, had been turned toward Petros. "His mother and I have not spoken to him of it yet. This past week he has scarcely been at home, so busy has he been with his latest argument. And it did not seem a topic for a rushed conversation. We thought to discuss it tomorrow. During our time of celebration."

Petros had mentioned his plans for celebrating with Cyprus and her sisters, with Nik and Hero and Kosmas—he knew he had. And his parents had nodded their agreement, exchanging a strange look he had wasted no time trying to decipher.

"But if you do not mention it until tomorrow, then I cannot well invite you all to share the feast at my table, can I?" Oceanus loosed a laugh as thunderous as the surf. "Today is better! Petros, you are going to be my nephew."

"I…beg your pardon?" No other response would come. No reasonable explanation for the bizarre statement would solidify in his mind.

"I have a niece." Oceanus leaned close, his brown-gray eyes twinkling. "Her parents passed away last year, leaving her in my care. She has just turned twelve and promises to grow into a great beauty."

He went still. "I see."

"Now, she is not my daughter, I grant you." The governor straightened again, chest puffed out and shoulders back. "Her parents were not so high of station as I am—my sister married beneath her. But I swore to them I would see to the girl's future, and so I shall. And it is time, of course, to arrange a betrothal."

"Of course." His gaze slid to Father. Father, who sat there like stone, but for the tempest in his eyes. The one that begged him. Pleaded, as eloquently as his lips ever had before a judge, for Petros to react with reason.

But there was no reason. Not for this.

"I have scoured the empire for the perfect match—someone not so high born that he will look down on her own origins.

But someone with limitless potential. Someone clever enough to value the connections I offer and prudent enough to use them wisely."

Someone, he meant, who would be his puppet. Someone he could use, not just the reverse.

"You are that someone, Petros."

Never. Petros smiled. "I am honored that you think so highly of me, Vicarius."

"Oceanus."

"But no doubt my parents have hesitated to bring this up to me because they know I have already offered my hand to a local girl. Our betrothal is unofficial as of yet, but binding to us. I am not free to enter into any other agreement."

The governor did not so much as blink out of turn. "The Visibullis girl—I have heard. A match that would ruin you, son, now that her father has ruined *them*. You are too smart not to know that."

"I am too much in love with her to care." He made sure his smile was the one he gave the jury when he needed to convince them of something that was right, but not quite able to be proven with fact. "I mean no disrespect, lord. Were my heart free, this would be an offer better than any I could have hoped for." Were he a puppet in need of a puppeteer. "But you of all people surely know that a man's word is all he has to trade on—I will not compromise mine."

"A word to one girl, broken of necessity, is no great compromise of your character, young man." The confident light in his eyes shifted slightly, turned to a spark of anger.

That same placating smile remained fastened to his lips. A different tack, then. "True. I trust your niece is a Christian, though?"

Father pressed his lips together, his eyes now asking, *Why? Why can you never do the easy thing?*

Oceanus's brows crashed down. "Of course not."

Now Petros put on surprise—as he did in the courts when a truth was finally revealed that surprised the judge, but which he had known all along. "Oh. You are aware that I *am*?"

Brows still lowered, Oceanus waved that off. "Nonsense I am certain you will forget when living in my palace, son, going in and out before the highest men of the Eastern Empire."

Petros knit his own brows in a semblance of confusion. "So palace life has made you forget *your* gods, lord?"

Oceanus would know he was being treated to a dialectic argument—the knowledge took the place of the anger in his eyes. And paired with amusement.

This man's love for a debate may just prove Petros's salvation, if he could play it right.

Oceanus inclined his head. "You know I have not."

"Why, then, should I?"

Chuckling, the governor wagged a finger at him. "Clever as always. But we both know that the God of the Christians does not pair well with a life of affluence. He is a God for the poor."

Now Petros bowed his head a bit. Respectful in its act...but also a bit condescending in its angle. "I am afraid you have been misinformed, Vicarius. Mine is a God for all men. I daresay this misperception has come solely because we believe God loves rich and poor alike, which is certainly something that appeals to those accustomed to being oppressed for their birth. But my God has been found in the palaces of Egypt. The high chambers of Babylon. The inner courts of Persia. He has filled the halls of his own kings when Israel stood tall and proud, and I fully believe that someday he shall even reign supreme in Rome."

Oceanus snorted a laugh. "Never. Augustus Diocletian has declared Jupiter his high lord, as you well know."

Petros smiled and spread his hands wide. "I did not say it will be in my lifetime, lord, or his. But truth cannot be stamped out, nor can its spread be stopped. It will stand in Rome, and it will speak for itself, and some emperor, some day, will see it and believe, and all the world will follow. That is the power of my God—to shine light into the darkest corners of the world."

Oceanus all but rolled his eyes. "Are we speaking of Rome or of the far-flung reaches?"

"I said darkest, not farthest-flung."

A laugh, big and bright, and Oceanus clapped a hand to his shoulder. "I do enjoy hearing you speak, son. Even of this. You can tell me more about this God of yours when you are my nephew."

Blast it all. Petros tried to make the shake of his head look sad. "I cannot marry anyone who does not follow the Way of Jesus, Governor. It is why my parents have not arranged a match before now."

"Indeed." Father finally spoke up, voice bright and eyes resigned. "We had hoped he would meet a well-born Christian while he was in school at Ephesus, but alas. He fell in love only with the law while in that fine city."

Oceanus ignored Father and kept shrewd eyes trained on Petros. "What if she were to agree to raise any children Christian? Would that suffice?"

Father's eyes went wide. He nodded.

Had they been alone, Petros would have scowled at him and shaken his head. How could he, Theophanes, wisest advocate in all of Lycia, family by marriage to the bishop of Patara, ever think that could be enough? Was his not the voice who had read the Scriptures to Petros most of his life? Was he not the one who had told him so earnestly before Petros left for Ephesus that he must take care not to bind himself to an unbeliever?

He had never known there were any hollow spots in his chest.

But perhaps there had always been, for one filled, now, with something hot and then cold and then as heavy as the rocks that could hide bandits on the mountain roads.

"No." His voice came out soft, in volume. Hard, in tone. "No, I have seen firsthand with the Visibullis family what happens when the parents are not united in such things. It leads to dissent between the parents. And sorrow for the children, who can be fully part of no community. The Christians will never trust them, and the Hellenists will revile them. I will not do that to my own family, Vicarius. I cannot."

The man's servant finally scurried toward them with fists full of skewers, but Oceanus stood. "You will relent. Or perhaps she will convert. You can tell us more about this God of yours—try to convince us of his value—when you come to visit us in Myra. One month's time, son. Think about all you can do from my right hand and come speak with us then." He offered a smile full of pearly teeth. "We look forward to receiving you."

He would be married to Cyprus by then. But for now, he would accept the month's reprieve from this man. "Safe travels home, Vicarius. Are you going by land or sea?"

"Land? Do I look insane to you? I avoid that treacherous road at all costs." Oceanus motioned his full-fisted servant toward them. "Do not stand there like a fool, man. Give them their food and let us be on our way."

Petros accepted the stick with its chunks of roasted meat and vegetables and said a vague farewell to the governor. Only once lord and servant had stridden away did he suck in a deep breath.

He could not bring himself to look at his father. Not when he would just be disappointed with what he saw. "You know this is wrong."

Father exhaled the breath Petros had pulled in. "It is an opportunity we have only dreamed of, Petros. You could be the one to argue for the faith before the emperor—the Augustus himself, or even just one of the Caesars. You could change the world for us all."

"Have I ever once said I felt the Lord calling me to such high honor?" He stepped away, lowering the skewer to his side. He had no appetite. Not now. "If he did, I would follow. But he has not. This is not his path for me."

Father stepped in front of him. "You will entertain the notion before you dismiss it so fully. You will pray about it before you assume you know the mysterious ways of the Lord."

"Yes. I will." He handed the skewer to Father, who took it more from instinct than hunger, he suspected. "And you will promise me that you will too, so that we all know the difference between opportunity the Lord may have given…and ambition that comes from the enemy."

Father's eyes went dark. "You accuse me of listening to—"

"I say what I know. And what I know is that I will not be a puppet for a politician, but that is what Oceanus really wants. A puppet with a smooth tongue to speak the words he wants said."

Father's exhale clanged of frustration as he kept pace with Petros when he strode away. "You do not have to *be* his puppet, even if he does want that."

"Attach the strings, Father, and what choice does a toy have but to dance where his master tells him?" He shook his head and repositioned his satchel when the scrolls inside banged against his leg. "No."

"No, indeed. Stop." Father's fingers gripped his arm, pulling him to a halt. He stepped close. Funny how, until that moment, Petros had not really paused to consider that he was taller than the man he had always looked up to. But Father had to angle his eyes up. And Petros had to angle his down. It had never made a difference before. But now…it did. "This is not about Oceanus at all, and we both know it. It is about Cyprus."

"No." It had been. Had always been. But not now. Not solely. "It is about *me.* It is about being able to live with myself. Being able to stand upright before God. It is about knowing my own failings, my weaknesses, and avoiding what would make me stumble. Father, do not ask me to bathe in wealth and emerge still happy with the filth of the streets. I do not know if I can do it, not without someone by my side to keep me anchored. And that man's niece would never be able to do that—she would have been raised to hate the filth."

He had spent too many hours wishing he had the wealth Nikolaos had been born to. Wishing he looked so desirable to Dorus Visibullis. To be handed it all now, when it could get him nothing but a stranger-wife and power his hands did not know how to grasp... He shook his head. "Please do not ask this of me, not after lecturing me all my life on the importance of choosing a wife who follows the Way. I beg you."

Father now dragged in a long breath. "You do not give yourself enough credit. You are stronger than you think you are."

"Unless I am not. Then what?"

"Then God gives you the strength you lack."

"If I am listening to him. But is that not the point? If I become swayed by the allure of gold, it will deafen my ears to his voice. I need a wife who can whisper his truth in my ear. Who can remind me of who I am before him, of what matters." He met his father's gaze again, held it until he saw the familiar wisdom under the wish for more. "Do you honestly think his niece would do that? Honestly, Father."

"I cannot know. I have never met her, and she is only a child. But she could be swayed to Christianity. Should we not give her that chance?"

Petros looked away again. Turned away—there was no point

in going to the courts, apparently, if his meetings had been changed. But his feet had still been angled to the central buildings in the acropolis. He pointed them the opposite direction instead. Toward the markets. Tomorrow was the solstice, and he had still not found a gift for Cyprus. He had little money left—only what he had earned from his last argument. Not enough for much. But for something.

"You once taught me, right over there"—he pointed to the open school on the corner, where children sat around the feet of their pedagogue—"that every argument we could come up with was not the right one. That every path that looked bright and clear of rubble was not the one we are meant to tread. You taught me that just because a thing *can* be does not mean it *should* be. I will ask God if this is from him. But I need to know that you are asking too."

The flame in Father's eye banked. "I am. We are, your mother and I."

"Then we will arrive at the correct decision together, because he will speak only one truth. And we are all listening."

"We are. And he will." Father reached over, up, and clasped his shoulder. He said nothing more. Just squeezed, then released him and walked away.

Never had Petros felt so alone walking through his city. He wished Nikolaos would appear at his side, or even Hero. That Cyprus would call to him again as he had dreamed of her doing countless times through the years...as she had done only the once, the other day. That someone, some true friend who wanted the best for him whether it included silver and gold and influence or a quiet life in a small-ish town, would walk beside him.

And then he paused, eyes not seeing the familiar streets before him. Because in his heart he heard a whisper that had no words, and yet did. *I walk beside you, every step of the way.*

"Lord." He had prayed every day, trying his best to do so every three hours, as the teachings said he should. He had listened. He had gone where he felt God lead him. But never in his life had he heard—felt?—his voice so clearly. "I know you walk with me. But I want to be sure my feet are on your path. Will you show me your way?"

A few passersby angled annoyed looks at him—he had stopped in the middle of the street, and he stood there murmuring to himself. No doubt they questioned his sanity.

He ignored them, closed his eyes. Thought he would feel no other resonance like that first. And maybe he did not. There was nothing but the echo of it in his chest, his stomach. His eyes opened again, his feet started again on their path toward the marketplace.

The words came again, as light and creeping as fog off the sea, and as undeniable. *My way is love.*

Love. It took so many forms. The kind he felt for his parents, tempered with respect and honor. The kind he felt for his cousin, born of brotherhood and friendship. The kind no one but Cyprus had ever inspired. The kind for the brethren at large, boundless but vague until it had the focus of a brother or sister in need.

But somehow he knew it was none of those of which the Lord spoke. Or, rather, it was all of those, all at once. It was the kind defined by none of the words Greek had for such affection, and yet encompassed all of them. *Agape*, but not just *agape*. Because it contained *eros* and *philos* too. As playful as *ludos*. As long-lasting as *pragma*.

Many-faceted, like the most beautiful jewel. That was the love of the Lord. Because he was all of it and none of it and more than it could ever be.

It made Petros feel small. And it made him feel tall. And it made him feel…sure. That wherever this path upon which he had put his feet went, it would take him where he was meant to be. So long as he walked it with love in his heart.

He imagined himself reaching out his hand, as he had done toward his father when he was a little boy who barely came to his hip. He would reach up as they walked, and he would tuck his fingers into the broad, strong palm that he knew would protect him. That he knew would chasten him. That he knew would always, always be willing to hold on. He imagined himself reaching out his hand, and his own fingers were long, his palm broad. But he put it in a hand bigger, stronger, surer. One that would protect. One that would chasten. One that would always hold on.

He reached out. And it felt, in some strange way, like letting go.

TWENTY

Cyprus finally raised her fist, ready to knock. She had stood outside Timon's door for endless minutes. Questioning. Debating. Asking, over and again, if this was really what the Lord wanted. She knew she tended toward impulsive actions. She knew she did not always think things through. And this...this was too important to treat in the same way she did a walk to the shore.

There would be no turning back once she put her foot on this path.

But for all her questioning, no fear saturated her bones. Her muscles never grew heavy, her limbs never remembered the paralysis that should still be theirs. Tears never burned her eyes. The *why* never returned. She knew. She knew from the red tips of her hair to the brown soles of her shoes that this was the only way to save her sisters.

And she knew she did not have to. She could refuse, and God would make another way. They would be taken away, they would be under the hand of a cruel master, but he would still love them. They would still honor him. He would go with them, if that was the path they took.

As he would go with Cyprus, if she answered this call and gave herself in their stead. She was no Daniel, no Joseph. But she was still his.

And so her knuckles found the wood, and their knock rang through her soul. She felt, as she never had before, as though she floated above herself watching. And yet at the same time, she felt more solidly a part of her body than she ever had.

It made no sense. Nothing did. And yet she was sure.

The door creaked open, and the thin man peered down at her. His eyes, when he saw who was at his master's rooms, snapped to alert. Few women probably dared to approach Timon. "Can I help you, young lady?"

Lady. Not for long. Not outwardly. But the inside…that was up to her and to the Lord. She did not smile. "I need to speak with Timon."

The thin man held wide the door and ushered her in with a bow. "Of course. My master will be happy to speak with the daughter of Dorus Visibullis."

She should not be surprised that he remembered her—he was there the other day when Timon had come, had found her on the street and told her what Petros had done. And Patara was not exactly bursting with young women with red hair. "Thank you."

He closed the door behind her and led her toward a seating area with a low table, surrounded by cushions. Timon was nowhere in sight, but after the servant motioned her to a seat and offered her a drink—which she declined—he hurried down a corridor.

She had a moment's reprieve, nothing more. A moment to wrap a strand of hair around her finger and pray with every revolution that God give her the words. Not her own. His.

His footsteps invaded the silence before he did. They were heavy and sure…and just a bit quicker than she imagined he usually walked. When he emerged from the corridor, he wore a smile on his lips and sharpness in his eyes. "Daughter of Visibullis. Forgive me—I do not know your given name."

"Cyprus." She stood, and her spine obeyed her desire that it be straight. Her shoulders had no trouble staying square. Her chin remained at that angle that bespoke confidence equal to his, but also respect. "Good day, Timon, and good solstice."

"And to you." He held out a hand to the cushion she had just risen from. "Please, be seated. How is your father?"

She would be polite. She sat again and, as he did the same across from her, said, "He is still mired in his grief, I am afraid."

"And Petros, son of Theophanes?" Timon poured himself some wine from the decanter on the table.

"He is well."

"Good." He sipped from his chalice and gave her a smile. To look at him with her eyes alone, she would never have suspected him of being anything but a kind, interested neighbor. Until she looked with her heart, her spirit as well. Then she could feel the rapacious thoughts behind the turn of his lips. "What, then, can I do for the lovely Cyprus Visibullis today?"

She folded her hands in her lap. "All my life I have been warned to tread carefully when I am outside my house. To never go out alone, lest I am stolen away and sold in Rome."

Timon dipped his head in acknowledgment. And kept his gaze steady on her. "Understandable advice for a beautiful redhead."

"I am well aware. I was almost apprehended by two sailors with ill intent four years ago." She paused, drew in a bolstering breath. She could talk around her purpose for an age. Or she could get to it. "But if I am going to be sold into slavery, it will be to benefit my family. How much would you give them, if I were to do so?"

"If you were to..." He jerked forward and set the cup down.

"Are you testing me, young woman? For your friend Petros?"

"Do you really think Petros would send me here alone?"

His eyes were as dark and gleaming as jet. "You have a point. But I cannot fathom—"

"I need dowries for my sisters, to keep *them* from slavery. Better one of us than two being relegated to such a fate."

A long moment slid by, silent and tense. Timon remained completely still, but for the eyes that traveled over her. Assessing her. Determining her value in gold or silver. "Noble of you. To save your sisters."

"I am not interested in discussing nobility. I am interested in discussing money. Five thousand sestertii."

His brows lifted, and a mean chuckle rumbled from his throat. "That is near the highest price ever paid for a slave—and you have no experience as one. If I were to give you that price, I would never recoup my loss."

She stood. "Then I am wasting my time here. If I cannot get the amount I need, I will abandon this plan. Thank you for seeing me, Timon." She spun on her heel, noting that the skinny slave stood by the door. To bar her from leaving or to open it for her?

"Wait a moment!" She heard him stand, take a step after her. "You surely know that haggling is part of any negotiation."

"I have no room to haggle." She turned again but did not sit. "I will get the full amount to pay for their dowries, or I will not do this. I need five thousand sestertii. No more, no less." It still would not provide them the slaves Abbas had promised to be part of the dowries, just the gold. But it would do. That calm inside assured her it would.

Timon pursed his lips and dragged his gaze over her again. "It is an odd thing you ask. I have handled such transactions before, but never with the one being sold. I should discuss this with your father."

"No. My father took himself from this equation when he determined to die rather than protect his daughters. You deal with me alone."

One brow lifted, letting that rapacious gleam shine more clearly. "And how am I to deal with you alone? I will not put money in your hand and then let you go home to deliver it to your sisters—you could vanish with my gold and leave me with nothing. And similarly, I know *you* will not consent to putting yourself into my hands and trusting me to deliver the coins later. You are too smart for that."

She had not thought that far ahead. Making plans for the exchange of money made it so...*real.* She let her eyes slide shut, just for a moment. While she pushed away that tendril of panic that tried to wrap around her throat and squeeze.

The answer surfaced. She did not like it—which was how she knew it was the right one. "If we agree on price...will you give me the solstice to spend with my family? Then the next morning, I will come with Petros. You can give him the money." She trusted no one more to see to her family—though she could not imagine him agreeing easily to this.

She would convince him, somehow. Though that meant that she would have to tell him tomorrow, which would ruin their celebration.

She would wait until the end of the day. She would give him his gift first. He would know something was wrong, he would be able to tell from the moment he looked at her. But they would have a few hours together before they were separated forever. Then she would simply tell him it was what the Lord had led her to do. He could argue, he could insist that he would try to support them all—though he could not, not without the reserve he had already spent on them. But in the end, he would see.

Timon's grunt pulled her eyes open again. His mouth was as

twisted as his profession. "I could just loan you the money for your sisters' dowries."

"I could never pay you back—you would end up taking me anyway."

A sigh to rival the north wind. "Then bring that priest friend of yours instead of Petros."

Cyprus lifted her brows now. "Why?"

"Because Petros will never forgive it if he knows I have helped you in this—and I do not want him for an enemy."

Spreading her hands, she said, "He means to marry me. I cannot just vanish without telling him what I am doing. And do you really think his cousin would keep such a secret from him?"

Timon rubbed his thumb over the tip of his middle finger, his eyes a swirl of thoughts. After a long moment, he snapped upright. "Fine. You can have your five thousand, and you will bring whomever you want the day after the solstice. But promise me this—if you find another way between now and then, you will take it."

She very nearly smiled. He did not *have* to do this deal. But he did not seem aware of it. As if, when he saw the prospect of money on the horizon, he could not say no even when he wanted to. She dipped her knees and inclined her head—she had better practice her shows of humility, if she were to be a slave.

A thought that pierced like a dagger. But she had few choices.

"I appreciate that, Timon. But unless, as my father says, gold rains down from the heavens, I will see you after the solstice."

He grumbled as she made her way to the door. But she did not turn back this time. Simply nodded at the servant, who nodded back. His eyes were blank, any thoughts he had on what had just passed safely tucked away. He opened the door, and she stepped out into the winter sunshine.

One more day of freedom. One more day to be with her family. One more day to show them she loved them.

Nikolaos jerked up in his borrowed bed, chest heaving with the effort to suck in enough air. The dream was still a hazy vision hanging before his eyes. Cyprus, but not as he had ever seen her. In chains. Wearing the tunic of a slave. Cyprus, paraded before a line of buyers with lust in their eyes and money in their purses.

"No." He scrubbed a hand over her face, pressed on his eyes. The image only sharpened. Cyprus, in chains. And behind her... Timon. Nikolaos shuddered. "Just a dream."

But it would not fade. And his chest ached exactly as it had when he had seen that ship tossed by the waves, the sailor lashed to the mast. He heard that frightened cry for help. But it was Cyprus's voice, not the sailor's. And the clinging image shifted, so that it was Cyprus as he knew her, in the green garment she wore frequently, the one edged in gold. Cyprus, walking down a set of steps he would never forget. Timon's.

"No." She would never go to Timon. She would not have to—Petros had already paid their debt and...

Lord, show me. I do not want to make the mistake I did the night of that storm. Please. Show me how to act. What to do.

His vision cleared...or perhaps went dark. The image faded, but then his whole focus was on his ears, so that he was unaware of what might be before his eyes.

"I am sorry, Hero." Mydon's voice, coming from...somewhere. Down the hall? Outside his door? Nikolaos could hear it as clearly as if his host were in this room, sitting at his side. "I am being reasonable—I will not insist on the slaves. But she must come with the twenty-five hundred sestertii. That is the least we can accept."

Twenty-five hundred sestertii. Nikolaos drew in a breath, his senses returning to normal. If Hero answered, his ears did not pick it up. If his eyes had dimmed a moment ago, they were normal now.

Twenty-five hundred sestertii. There was no way the Visibullises could come up with that. No, not just with that. That was just for Rhoda's dowry. Alexandria's would have been the same, so they would need twice that. Three times, if Cyprus were to have a matching one to take with her to Petros's side.

Cyprus.

He shivered, wishing he could blame it on the unlit hearth, the winter air. But the sun was out today, the air barely cool. "Cyprus...what have you done?"

But he knew. He knew what the visions told him, what the voice made clear. He could choose not to believe, if he wanted—to refuse to accept that God could show him such things. But he would not. Not this time.

After pushing to his feet, he slipped out of the door, glancing around for Mydon and Hero. They were nowhere in sight. He had known, really, that they would not be. Which was just as well. He could slip without being noticed down the corridor, to the front door. He let himself out and into the sunshine.

It could not warm him today. Afternoon was already upon Patara, golden and soft. The bankers would be closing or closed already. And they would not open tomorrow—all of Lycia would be celebrating the solstice. The Hellenists, Saturnalia. The Christians, the birth of Christ. No business would be transacted on the holiday. He would have no way to get his gold.

He had some in his room though. He always kept *some* out of the banks, in case of emergency—and this surely qualified. *Lord, let it be enough.* It was not—he knew it was not. He never kept so much out that he would miss it if it were stolen, and seventy-five hundred sestertii was certainly enough to be missed.

But it had to be there. There had to be enough. And so, there would be.

He would gather it. He would go to the Visibullis house. He would ask Cyprus what she had just done and press the gold into her hands to assure her she would not have to go through with it.

No. Uncle's voice resounded in his head with every footfall. *If ever you begin doling out your gold, you will soon find the whole countryside clamoring at your door, claiming desperation.*

He would be happy to help any who needed it. But...but then it would be *him*, not God. Nikolaos, the son of the wealthy Epiphanius, saving the poor with his own bounty. Not Nikolaos, servant of the church, being Christ's hands and feet.

If he put that gold in Cyprus's hand, she would be in his debt. Better his than Timon's, it was true, but...

But better no debt at all. He would not want paid back, but that was hardly the point. *She* would feel the debt. Her sisters. Their husbands. Dorus.

No. No, he could not save them as Nikolaos, their friend. He must act, but not like that.

"Pomegranates! Almonds!"

"Fish! Fresh fish, best the sea has to offer!"

He wandered to a halt at the edge of the markets. Half the booths were already closed, their awnings taken down and the carts gone home for the holiday. But a few stalwart merchants remained, trying to peddle the last of their goods before all the late shoppers went home to prepare tonight's meal and make ready for tomorrow's feast.

To his right, a child whined and pulled at her mother, pointing toward the corner opposite Nikolaos. His gaze followed her finger to where a performer stood, a handful of straggling children watching him. He juggled four brightly-colored vegetables, caught them all, spun. When he faced them again, his hands were empty.

The children whooped in delight, clapping. Nikolaos smiled too. It was, if he were not mistaken, the same performer that had stood on that corner when Nikolaos was a boy. He used to watch him with every bit as much joy as these little ones, trying to focus all his attention on the man's hands, so he could see the trick that made vegetables disappear.

Sleight of hand. Nikolaos had never been able to figure it out as a boy. But now it made his lungs fill with the answer. *But when you do a good deed, do not let your left hand know what your right hand is doing, that your good deed may be done in secret.*

Yes. Yes, that was how he would give—in secret. No one must know. Not his uncle, not his cousin, not the girls.

Spinning away, he hurried toward the church. Neighbors called out their greetings as he passed, and he wished them well with smiles but without slowing his step. Soon, he pushed open the familiar wooden doors, stepped into the familiar cool shadows of the narthex. When he turned for the back hall, he could almost convince himself he still caught the scent of Cyprus, from her nighttime visit yesterday. Still hear her voice whispering through the shadows, calling for him.

He grasped the iron ring of his door. Gripped it but did not tug. Not yet. Not given the way she filled his vision again. In her bridal best, this time. Standing with a smile in this church—a smile aimed at Petros.

She would marry him if Nikolaos did this. Likely before the new year dawned next week. She would be forever lost to him, and he would just be the cousin of her husband.

And that cousin...Petros would not need him anymore, with a wife by his side. Their years of always walking together through life would draw to an end.

But not just Petros. All his friends, all of them, would be married. And he would be here, where he always was. Just Nikolaos and Uncle and the echoes.

Loneliness snaked around him, filling the hall with smoky wisps of future memories. So many hours of quiet. So many faces moving through but never staying. Never caring what he did or where he went or what *he* felt or needed.

Asking, always asking. Always wanting a touch. Begging for a wonder.

But who would care for *his* heart? His soul? Who would...?

"No." He shook himself and pushed into his room, away from those wisps of smoke that would strangle him if they could. "Be gone, foul thoughts, in the name of Jesus." He shut the door with a *whoosh.*

And he watched those wisps—there but not there, sensible but not visible—vanish. He straightened his shoulders and corrected the thoughts that did not belong. Cyprus *should* marry Petros. They would be happy. They had a love that would see them through all the trials of life. And if he did *not* do this, she would certainly not be Nikolaos's anyway. She would belong to some man none of them knew, in a land far from home.

And though their lives were all changing, that was inevitable. It did not mean his cousin would not still be his dearest friend—it did not mean he would have no place among those whose company he enjoyed.

It meant...something more. Because he would *not* be alone, here with Uncle. He would be walking with Christ. He would be stretching out his hand and being Jesus to the flock of people who so needed to feel the Savior's touch. He would be tending those precious sheep with God's love, and it would fill him too.

He would be doing the work of the Lord. And in so doing, he would be refreshed.

"Thank you, Father." He lit the lamp by the bedside and reached under his bed to the loose stone. This he scooted aside until he could reach underneath it, to the cool wooden box that lived its life in secret. His fingers warmed the cedar as he pulled it out, into the light. "And thank you again, Father, for letting this be enough."

He pulled off the lid, spilled out the gold coins, and smiled as they kept coming when they should have stopped.

Even before he counted, he knew exactly how much would be there. And it was enough.

TWENTY-ONE

Rain painted the world in silvers and grays, in misty whites... and in puddles. Petros walked alongside his cousin, Hero and Felix a few steps behind. They were not the only citizens hurrying through the rain. Nor were they the only ones to pause on a street corner and gaze at the sight before them.

The heavens rained gold, as each droplet reflected the light from uncountable candles lit in every window. This was the only time of year when the city donned such beauty, when the early darkness was met with pinpoints of light everywhere one looked. From each window—covered with lattice and cloth and the occasional shutter, but all left open tonight, for the sake of spreading light—came laughter and shouts of joy.

The other citizens out and about all had packages in their arms, smiles on their faces.

Nikolaos's hum was thoughtful. "They worship the wrong god today...but they do it with generous hearts. We could use this to reach them, to help them see that the best gift ever given was given to man nearly three hundred years ago. Given on this very day that they know instinctively is a time for doing just that."

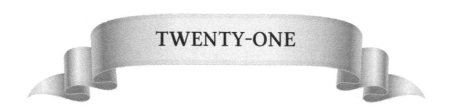

Petros clapped a hand to his cousin's shoulder. "And will that be part of your sermon this evening?"

Nik grinned. "Maybe."

"Maybe? Do you not have it planned?"

Now a shrug. "Uncle only asked me this morning, when the cough settled in. How quickly do you think I can prepare a message?"

Petros laughed and moved forward again. "Well you only have a few more hours to figure it out—and you are on your way to a feast, not sitting quietly in your room, writing."

"I will not stay long. But I gave my word I would be here."

Everyone would have understood him begging off, given that this was the first time the bishop had asked Nikolaos to speak to the gathered brethren. But he appreciated that Nik valued even so small a promise.

Unlike Kosmas, whose absence was loud and heavy.

The Visibullis house—he would always think of it as such, even if Dorus did not own it—stood sentry at the end of the street, as large and impressive as ever. And festive. Someone had festooned its exterior with the same sort of decorations its neighbors boasted—boughs of greenery, brightly colored fabric.

Each candle in each window stood with a halo around it, like a saint painted upon a wall. The utter beauty of it snatched his breath away, leaving him with a strange feeling. As if it were all a dream. As if his family were not at home, angry with him—first at his reaction to Oceanus, and next at his refusal to stay home with them and argue more about it. As if the world were not set to crash down upon the family behind this masking façade.

The door opened as they neared it. Petros entered, stepping quickly out of the way to allow his fellows to find refuge from the rain as well. He shrugged out of his cloak and handed it to the unfamiliar manservant who received them with a gracious bow. Irritation gnawed on him, replacing the awe at the beauty outside. He knew it was Yiannis's house, and that the visitor had every right to act accordingly. Still, it chafed to see the tall man stand to greet them as a host, a film of generosity covering emotions as soft and generous as stone.

The irritation moved into something stronger when he stepped into the main room and saw Dorus, Rhoda, and Alexandria, but not Cyprus. He had a feeling she was in the kitchen again—something that may not have annoyed him had Yiannis not forced her to be and kept her sisters out here rather than letting them help.

Nikolaos stepped even with him and said, voice pitched low, "If you want to slip back to the kitchen to find her, I will keep him occupied."

"You are a jewel of a friend, Nik." He smiled at his cousin and looked behind them, to where Hero and Felix were entering. Hero eyed their too-gracious host with suspicion. Felix stood stiff with something that looked like discomfort but which Petros suspected was closer to fear. No doubt he did not want to be the one to tell Alexandria that Kosmas had left for home at first light, in a litter carried by his father's servants.

No doubt he wanted even less to confess that Kosmas had told Felix to marry her– something Petros would never have believed had he not heard the younger brother grind out his decision when he went to visit last night.

Alexandria scanned their group. Her face gave nothing away—but he saw the way her fingers had woven together, too tightly. She started toward them, ignoring Yiannis, who reached to hold her by his side. Rhoda was abandoning him too, rushing to grip Hero's hands.

Alexandria caught Petros's gaze first, then moved it to Felix. "How fares your brother today, Felix?"

Felix cleared his throat. To his credit, he did not look over for help. He kept his eyes, warm and apologetic, trained on her. "He has gone home to recuperate, at our father's insistence."

No surprise settled on her face. Rather, she lifted her brows. "And? There is more to the message, I presume."

Still Felix did not look away, though Petros would have been hard-pressed to hold her gaze through this next part. His new friend indulged only in a slight clearing of his throat, though. "He would have told you yesterday had you been able to visit—or so he said. He has decided to obey our father's dictates. Claiming he does not dare lose his favor, although..."

"Right. A handy excuse to get out of a commitment he regrets, now that our situation has changed." But Alexandria, being Alexandria, did not crumple into tears. She lifted her chin and straightened her spine. "So be it. Circumstances are trying their hardest to prevent any such alliances, anyway."

The muscle in Felix's jaw ticked. He glanced over her shoulder, to where Dorus had called Yiannis to his side—an actual attempt to grant his daughters a moment without their cousin? Probably something more selfish, knowing Dorus.

Petros took a step toward the kitchen. He needed to see Cyprus...but he could not quite walk away. Felix edged another half-step closer to Alexandria, determination in the angles of his face.

"Alexandria...I know we are strangers. But I would take on my brother's promise and honor it myself, since he has reneged."

"You..." She stared at him. Not looking shocked, not looking offended...just *looking*. "Why? To preserve your family's promise? To save me? To spite your father?"

"All of those. None of those."

"I have nothing. You know that."

"I know." He spread his hands, shrugging. "I cannot explain exactly why, but...I feel the Lord's leading here."

She regarded him for a moment more and then, when Yiannis called her name, angled half away. "I thank you, Felix. We will speak more. But you must know, first and foremost, that I will not abandon my sisters to whatever Yiannis has devised for them."

"I know." His lips tipped up in the corner as he said the words, though she turned away too soon to see it.

Petros fought back a small grin too. Perhaps it was in part Alexandria's beauty that had caught Felix's eye and made him willing to do this thing his brother had asked of him. But he suspected it was admiration for her heart as much as her face.

Petros slipped to the edge of the room so he could follow it out and down the hallway. With every step, the sounds of voices from the chamber behind him faded, and new sounds stole his attention. Pots clanging. A fire crackling. And a blessedly familiar voice raised in a song of praise to God.

He hovered for a moment in the kitchen doorway before she noticed him. Looking, just looking. Memorizing the way the fire caught her hair and the strands echoed it. The way she moved, a symphony of grace even as she bent to stir a pot. The way the candles lit in here, too, caught each curve of her face…and illuminated something new in it.

Peace. The same peace he had felt yesterday as he put his hand in the Lord's. The same peace that reverberated now, yet not with a light touch. It was not the peace of no problems, of tranquility. It was the peace that came of knowing that nothing was right and yet all was in God's able hands.

She caught sight of him and smiled. Perhaps it was the flickering candlelight that made the spark in her eyes look so odd. So determined, so deep, but so sorrowful.

He knew it was not.

She rushed toward him, and he held out his arms, folding her to his chest with more gratitude than he had expected to feel. Holding her close, he memorized this feeling too. How she fit so perfectly against him. How his pulse raced. How the herbal scent from her hair drifted to his nose. "Cyprus."

She tilted her face up. Maybe in acknowledgment. Maybe in invitation. Hopefully in invitation, because he could not resist leaning down and touching his lips to hers. And she kissed him back, an arm around his neck. All sweetness, all love.

It tasted of good-bye. But it would not be. *Could* not be. "Cyprus. What does Yiannis mean to do? You know. I know you know."

She pulled him deeper into the kitchen, to the other side of the hearth, where no one from the door would be able to see them. "To take them. He means to leave me on the streets with Abbas."

He stroked the hair back from her face, tucking it beneath the golden beads that circled her head. So beautiful. "I will never let that happen. You know that."

"I know that." Her fingertips traced his cheek. "But I cannot let him take them. They would be his slaves, and he has a cruel heart."

"We will find a way to stop him." He pressed his lips to her forehead, beneath the green stone that anchored the strands of golden beads into place. "My mother confessed what she said to you, the day you were there learning how to cook."

Her breath shuddered out. Her fingers fell to his chest and tangled in the cloth that his cloak had not kept completely dry. "She is right. You could do great things, and this could be how."

"It is not. It is nothing but ambition on my parents' part, though they refuse to see it. This is not God's path for me."

She said nothing. Just rested her head against his shoulder and held him close. For a moment, he felt only of the joy of it. Then, slowly, he became aware of the way her breath came a bit too fast. Her pulse hammered too hard when he circled her wrist with his fingers. And while he would have been happy to attribute it to his nearness, it was not that. He knew it, even as he hoped it.

His eyes slid shut against the dancing lights of the candles. "What has happened?"

Silence, for a moment more. Then, "Later. For now, I have a gift for you."

His eyes flew open, his brows flew up as she eased away. "A gift? Cyprus, there is no way you could afford—"

"It cost me nothing." And yet she reached into a shadowed corner and drew out a definite *something*.

Something that, as his hands met supple leather, he knew was dear indeed. He ran his fingers over its buttery texture, feeling as much as seeing each part of the satchel in the night-clad kitchen. "How?"

"The basket weaver, on the edges of the market. Her son is a fisherman—you helped him in court. Her daughter made this. The old woman gave it to me, to be a gift to you." She shrugged, her lips curved into a sheepish version of a smile. "It is not exactly from me, I know. It is from them. Would that I could have given you something that I had made with such skill. A gift for which I paid nothing, either in time or money, is not much of a gift."

"And plenty would have refused it, refused to let that old woman give a blessing. You did right. Which makes it from you too, and I cannot express how much I appreciate it." Though he tried with another soft kiss...and then reached into the pocket of his tunic. "My gift to you is not much either. More pretty than precious." It had cost him next to nothing. But it had reminded him of her, as he saw it. Pretty, brightly-colored beads strung on a wire of copper. He fastened it around her wrist.

Her smile was brighter than all the candles in Patara. "It is perfect. Thank you, Petros."

From down the hall came the strum of a lyre, the accompanying tune of a reed whistle. The twins, he knew, bringing a new light into the evening. But it was not one of the usual hymns they played—it was a Greek song. Unoffensive, but not what they usually would have selected on this night of Christ's birth.

Yiannis.

He sighed and stroked his thumb over the pulse in Cyprus's wrist. "We need dowries for them, or he will take them. If I had enough—"

"I know." She touched a finger to his lips to silence him. "I know you would. But you cannot. Not this time. It is not for you to do."

He wished it was. Wished he could just make coins enough appear. Or convince Mydon to accept Rhoda as his son's bride without any gold. But he had tried that last night, when Hero had whispered of the most recent argument with his father. *Twenty-five hundred sestertii*, he had said. Or no wedding.

"I could borrow it."

"Petros." With a shake of her head, Cyprus pulled away and hurried to tend the food when something over the fire popped. "No. It would take you a decade to pay it back with the interest that would accrue, and that is if you stayed at home and kept all your own costs at a minimum."

Hard to accomplish with a wife of whom his parents did not approve and whatever children God may bless them with. He sighed. "A price worth paying, for their freedom. I could borrow it from Timon."

"No!" She spun, eyes as blazing as the fire. "Absolutely not. He would make you his puppet."

The word bit, echoed. She was right. Timon would like to control him every bit as much as Oceanus would. "Then...perhaps Nikolaos has it to spare. He would loan it, if he has. If his uncle has not already had him give it all to the church."

It was worth asking.

Cyprus expelled a long, weary breath. "Can we…can we not talk about it right now? The food is ready, I think. Let us enjoy our meal. All of us together, one last time, before…before the future can bring whatever it will."

She was avoiding something more than just the normal conversation about unpleasant things. He could see it in the way her shoulder hitched, the way her eyes remained glued to the pots when usually they would have sought his gaze to plead with him.

His throat barely worked as he attempted a swallow. Later, she would tell him what had happened. She must.

For now, he nodded. "Nikolaos cannot stay long—he is giving the sermon tonight."

Her lips turned up. "He must be so excited! I know he has long wanted to speak. Perhaps we can all go to hear him. If…"

If Dorus and Yiannis would allow it. Though just now, he did not much care whether they gave their permission or not. "A perfect idea, and a perfect cap to the day. Let us plan on it and tell the others."

"Agreed." She turned to slide something from pot to platter. "Could you help me bring all this out?"

"Of course." He busied himself with helping arrange all the meat and fish, the bread and cheeses, the sauces and fruits and vegetables, on a series of beautiful platters that he knew well had not been in the kitchen a few days ago. Yiannis had spared no expense for this feast, apparently. "Did you make all this yourself?"

Her laugh was an echo of the old Cyprus, clear and sharp. "It would not look nearly as appetizing if I had. No, the twins both managed to help. I think they told him they were napping, so they could see the illumination longer."

"Ah." They were good sisters, all of them. Watching them over the years—frustrations and joys both—he had often wished for siblings. But he had Nikolaos, who was as close as any brother. And when he married Cyprus, he would gain sisters in hers, and more brothers in their husbands.

The *when*, though, felt strangely like an *if* in his thoughts. Which made a warning clang within him.

His every footfall was a prayer as he made his way out of the kitchen, following in her wake.

TWENTY-TWO

Cyprus would let nothing ruin this night. Even if her muscles refused to relax. Even if Petros kept looking at her with that probing, all-seeing glance of his. Even if Yiannis persisted in treating her like she was a slave already.

Perhaps she ought to get used to it...but she just wanted tonight yet to be a daughter. A sister. A friend.

A beloved.

Tomorrow, it would all change. But tonight...tonight she was who she had always been.

She refilled Yiannis's wine and sent him a too-sweet smile that he barely glanced up to see. In her thoughts earlier, she decided she would let herself be just a little smug at foiling his plan.

In reality, she could not waste any energy, any emotion on him at all. He was a Greek, doing what Greeks did. If it had been a Christian brother treating her family so, she would have reason for complaint. But she could not expect a fish to do anything but swim.

He was nothing to her, and would be nothing to her again. Her sisters would be safe from him—that was all that mattered. And tonight she would also be grateful he had not offered the meal to the goddess.

She turned to Abbas with far more emotion. He, too, was a Hellenist in his thoughts. But she could not greet him with the same level of detachment. He had been raised in a Christian family, even if he spurned it. He knew. He *knew* right from wrong and chose wrong anyway. He betrayed the one thing his wife would have wanted him to protect above all—his family. And he sat there now in utter defeat, never considering that he could yet make it all better simply by standing up and using his authority as their father to say, *No. No, my daughters will not live lives of dishonor. Even if I have to become a fisherman, it is better to live an honest life in humility than to sacrifice them for gold.*

But Abbas remained silent. He took a few sips of wine, now and then. Even tasted a bite of the fish sauce—whose recipe Rhoda had wheedled from a neighbor—after Yiannis praised it. But he would not look at any of his daughters.

She focused her gaze away from him too. If she could save him as well...but there was nothing she could think to do to help him. No other way to show her love for him than what she had already done.

Familiar fingers took hold of her hand. She had wandered to Petros's side, but he was certainly not asking for more wine. He tugged on her, just a bit. "Sit," he bade. "Enjoy the meal with me."

Yiannis would scowl at her. But she did not much care. Setting the wine down, she sank to the cushion beside Petros. This would be the last time she ever sat beside him. Her cousin would not take that from her.

Even so, her stomach clenched at the sight of the food Petros put on a plate and passed to her. Nothing looked good, even her favorites. But she thanked him and put a bit of cheese on a slice of bread so she could make a show of eating whenever someone looked at her.

"I would be honored if you would all come," Nikolaos was saying from the cushion beside Petros's. Cyprus had to lean out a bit to see him. He wore an easy, peaceful smile. The kind that came of knowing exactly who he was and what he was meant to do with his life. His gaze swept the collection of friends and interlopers, even including Yiannis and Abbas in its arc.

Felix smiled. "Well, I will certainly be there. I look forward to hearing your insights into the day, Nikolaos. Whenever I pause to think, really think about God sending his son to earth as he did, of Jesus taking on the flesh of man..." Eyes focused on the empty space before him, Felix shook his head. He sat on a cushion near to Alexandria, on the side Yiannis had not claimed, and held his cup before him. He was, Cyprus thought, handsomer than his brother. And certainly of a happier disposition. Alexandria and Rhoda had told her of him, but she had begun to think she would never meet him for herself.

"We will all come." Hero nodded, grinning, obviously knowing well that a few among them would not agree with his claim—and just as obviously not caring what they thought. "And though I am sorry the bishop is not feeling well, I cannot say as I regret that this gets to be your inaugural message, Nik. I can think of no more special an occasion to mark your entrance into the life of a pastor."

Yiannis's glower was darker than midnight. "I am afraid my family will not be going. We do not attend Christian church services."

Alexandria bristled. "Pardon me, cousin. But you own the house—that does not make you head of the family. That role still belongs to our father, and Abbas would not keep us from seeing our friend on such an important night for him. Would you, Abbas?"

Cyprus's every muscle went taut as she looked to their father.

His eyes, at least, were absent that vacant look. He focused upon his eldest daughter with no apparent emotion, but no hardness either.

He had never, never granted them permission to attend a service. Why would he change his mind now?

He sighed. "I see no harm in it, just for tonight."

"Dorus." Yiannis hissed the name, his knuckles going white around the stem of his chalice. "We have discussed this. Christianity will have no part—"

"I find it curious," Nikolaos interrupted. His voice was calm, sure. Easy, despite the fact that Cyprus could not remember him ever interrupting someone mid-sentence. "Curious that you, with your pantheon of gods and goddesses, cannot find room in your tolerance for our one God. Even though you expect us to tolerate your many."

Yiannis narrowed his eyes. "The difference being my pantheon is the state religion—and your one little impotent God is the enemy of the Augustus."

"No. The Augustus may have declared himself an enemy of my God—but the Lord loves *him* as he does all men." Nikolaos took a lazy sip. And smiled. "Petros, why did you study so many philosophies while we were at school?"

Petros apparently had no trouble following his cousin's seeming-digression. He grinned and finished chewing his olive. "Because one cannot argue effectively against a philosophy with which one is unfamiliar. One can only create furious sound that accomplishes nothing."

Felix chuckled. Hero raised his glass in salute.

Yiannis bared his teeth. "I do not need to know much about your ridiculous religion to see its basic weakness—it forbids the worship of my gods. Therefore, it is heresy."

"I apologize. I thought that you, as most of us Greeks, would value truth above all." Petros selected another olive from his plate. "But if you have no interest in discerning whether there is any truth to our teachings, then by all means, continue to hate us all on principle. I can see it makes you a happy man and a gracious host to believe as you do."

Cyprus pressed her lips against a grin. In one fell swoop, he mocked the sneer and insulted a Greek's hospitality—if she had not already been in love with Petros, she likely would have fallen then and there.

Yiannis set his cup down with a *thunk* upon the table. "Have it your way," he ground out between clenched teeth. "You may all go to this meeting tonight. And be assured I will come too, so that when I forbid it all in the future, I can do so with *reason*."

"You will be most welcome." Nikolaos set his plate down, though it was only half-empty. "And now I am afraid I must hurry back to finish preparing my words. You will all follow in an hour?"

"Absolutely." Hero set his plate down too. "But before you go, Nik—my gift to you." He reached into a little bag he had set at his side and pulled out a ridiculously thick scroll. Blank, apparently, as he revealed when he unrolled part of it. "For you to record your thoughts while you are in Jerusalem."

"Jerusalem?" Cyprus frowned. "Are you going on pilgrimage, Nik?"

"Eventually." Grinning, Nikolaos stepped forward to accept the comically long papyrus. "I thank you, Hero. I have small tokens for everyone as well, but I did not want to bring them out in the rain. I will give them to everyone after church tonight—perhaps it will have let up by then."

Cyprus was still stuck on *Jersualem*. She had not heard any talk of a pilgrimage. But it was not the realization that she had missed this particular plan that alarmed her—it was that, when she went through with her plan, her future would be nothing *but* this not-knowing. She would never know the plans and intents of those she loved most in the world. Never know how they fared or what they did.

Would word ever even reach her about her sisters' lives? How many children they had? Whether Abbas improved? Whether... whether Petros eventually married?

Her nose went stuffy and achy, but she blinked before tears could gather.

"How very odd," Yiannis drawled, "that you all give gifts on Saturnalia like we *pagans* do."

"To commemorate the greatest gift of all—Jesus Christ, given by God to man." Nikolaos tucked the scroll into his tunic. Then accepted the cloak that one of Yiannis's lower servants appeared with. He smiled at the assembly at large. "I will see you all soon."

And then never again. Cyprus wanted to surge to her feet and give him a farewell embrace, thank him for all he had done for her these last four years—for healing her, for always speaking faith and hope. For protecting the scrolls and codices that were her heritage.

But it would look strange, so she kept to her seat. Perhaps she could manage some way to thank him at the church.

An unexpected blessing, that—to get to spend this final night with her family *and* go to services. It would be her first time actually sitting through one in those painted walls. Rising with dozens of other believers to praise the Lord. Joining her prayers to theirs. She could think of no better way to spend her last waking hours with her family.

The door closed, and conversation went back to the benign. Everyone ate, asked for refills, laughed and pretended all was right with the world.

Cyprus fiddled with her bread and cheese, rolled an olive

around her plate.

Petros leaned close. "Cyprus—"

"Before we leave, since we are apparently going," Yiannis interrupted in a loud voice. "Gifts! Girl, go out to the garden room and fetch the box I stored in there."

Rhoda leaned toward Yiannis. "But cousin, she would have to go through the garden, and it is pouring rain. Surely your gifts can wait a little while, for the rain to let up."

Odd how he could smile so warmly at her beautiful sister, even as he said, "If rain is going to interrupt our evening, then I suppose we will not be able to go out to this *church* meeting after all."

Rhoda rose halfway, as if to volunteer for the task herself, but of course Yiannis grabbed her wrist and forced her back down.

Cyprus was already on her feet anyway. "I do not mind going into the rain." She hurried from the room before he could find another excuse to ruin the night. In the kitchen, she snatched up her cloak and spun it overtop her.

Paltry armor against the rain that had gone from patter to downpour. Within seconds, she was soaked. But she hardly felt it, hardly noticed the way her shoes squished and sloshed in the mud as she darted across the garden plot, toward the room built into their rear wall. It was where Helena had always kept the little shovels and pots for the garden. It had been years since Cyprus had found any cause to go into it...and she had to wonder at why Yiannis had chosen it as a storage place for his gifts. To keep them secret, perhaps. Or perhaps just to have a reason to send her out in such nasty weather.

She pushed open the door, the squeak of its hinges lost in the drumming of water upon stone. In the dark, she could barely make out the chest that sat in the middle of the floor, but when her fingers closed around its handles, they verified that the surface was far too clean to belong out here.

As for whether it would fare well against the rain...well, that was none of her concern. She hefted it, grunting at the weight, and stepped back into the deluge.

Petros had apparently just reached the kitchen after fetching his cloak. He held the door open for her as she dripped her way inside. "Why did you not wait for me?"

She grinned. "What cause did we both have to get wet?"

Lips pressed, he secured the latch and shrugged back out of his cloak, gaze on the window. "It is monstrous out there. Much as I hate to say it, if it does not let up soon, none of us ought to go out."

"It will let up any moment." It had to. A little rain could not rob her of the chance to finally go to church. She put the chest down in the puddle she was making and took off her dripping cloak. Her garments beneath were not *quite* soaked through, though they were by no means dry.

Petros toed the chest. "What do you suppose he has in there? Vipers ready to jump out and attack us all? Daggers that he will throw with all the precision of an assassin?"

An unexpected laugh tickled her throat. She let it bloom and reached up to press her chilled fingers to his warm cheek. "Nothing could possibly rival my bracelet. Or better still, that smile you give me." It warmed her now, from her toes to the crown of her head.

He rested his forehead on hers. "I love you, Cyprus."

A truth that made her throat go tight. She should have opened her eyes to this long ago—then they would have had more time to bask in it, to understand it. "And I love you."

Footsteps toward the kitchen had them easing apart seconds before Ennius poked his head in. "The master inquires as to what is keeping you."

She had half a notion to drop the chest upon Yiannis's overbearing head. But it was not Ennius's fault his master was a tyrant. "I am coming."

Petros lifted the wet wooden chest before she could. "You scarcely ate, beloved. Sit by the fire when we get back in there—dry out and eat."

The command, spoken with love and coming from Petros, made her smile. "I will."

She followed him back to the room with its bright light and dim laughter, with its divided people and unspoken tension. Her sisters, though seated where Yiannis had instructed them, were both on the edges of their cushions, as far from him as they could get. Rhoda was leaning as close as she could manage to Hero, who was on the edge of his seat as well, bridging the gap. Alexandria was talking to Felix—more space between them than the couple, but obviously intent upon their words.

Petros delivered the chest to Yiannis's feet with a cursory nod and then stepped behind him, to the hearth. He positioned two chairs beside it and motioned for her to join him.

She fetched her plate first and then walked the long way around the edge of the room, avoiding Yiannis. On her way, she paused at Abbas's side. He seemed separate from the gathering, a little island unto himself. She leaned over and pressed a kiss to his forehead. "I love you, Abbas." She always had, even if she had never been sure of what the word meant to him. He was her father. He had sought the best for them, even if they did disagree on what the best thing was.

He looked up at her with mournful eyes. "Where is the gold falling from the heavens, Cyprus? Where is your God tonight, while this cousin plans to steal your sisters away?"

With her free hand, she gripped his. "God is still here, Abbas. It is just that you have never trained your eyes to see him." But *she* looked, and she saw him in Rhoda's smile, so pure and bright.

She saw him in the strength of Alexandria's spine. She saw him in the open welcome of Felix, in the determined bend of Hero's head. She saw him in the patient wisdom of Petros. "But I can. He is here, and he loves us."

"I see only the world fracturing. But I am glad you find hope, even now." He squeezed her fingers and then released them. "Perhaps it will see you through."

It was the closest thing to kind words she had heard from him since Mater's death. She soaked them up, tucked them away, deep inside her heart. And finished her path to Petros and the fire.

Yiannis was opening his chest, but it did not keep him from narrowing his eyes at her. And snapping, "You are trailing mud and water everywhere, girl."

No doubt he meant for her to rush to clean up the mess. And no doubt it would be easier to do so before it dried. But she was not going to lose her few minutes left with Petros. So, with a tight-lipped smile, she merely slipped off her little leather shoes and set them by the fire to dry.

Yiannis turned back to his chest and drew out a length of gold. "Gifts! To my beautiful cousins." Not awaiting permission, he lowered the gold chain over Rhoda's head, then quickly followed it with another, and with a bracelet, and with a circlet for her head. Then a matching set for Alexandria, who looked too stunned to react. Stunned by the audacity and the sheer value of the items, Cyprus knew. But given his smile, Yiannis probably thought it was more in pleasure.

Rhoda had already taken hers off while he was turned to Alexandria. She shook her head. "We cannot accept these, cousin. Your generosity is to your credit, but it is too much, too dear. And not fitting for us to receive as unmarried women betrothed to others."

"And your modesty is to *your* credit, fair one. However..." He glanced over at Abbas, who offered him no help. Yiannis did not seem to want for it. He straightened. "We all know your betrothals are more history than fact. You can never marry without dowries."

"Is that what this is then?" Alexandria had to know it was not—her tone was hard, challenging. "Gold we can use as our dowry?"

"Absolutely not!" A bit of the temper he had shown Cyprus came through, and he turned his scowl on Alexandria. "This, my dear, is my sign to you of my intent. You will both come home with me tomorrow, and I will give you far more than this. Gold, jewels, silks—everything you could ever want."

"No." Voice calm as death, Alexandria took the jewelry off as well. Flung it at his feet. "Keep your gold. I would rather starve than belong to you."

Rhoda put her matching set down with less noise but equal resolution. "We are women of principle, Yiannis. Surely you know that. We would never consent to—"

"Girls." Abbas did not sound angry. Just weary. "There is no immorality here. He would be your master."

Both of the twins stood, and Cyprus stood along with them. It was time. Time to draw in that breath that could never be long enough and say, "No. They will not go with him. I have made a deal with Timon—five thousand sestertii, to cover their dowries."

Her sisters spun on her, horror painting matching expressions on their faces.

Petros gripped her hand. Hard. "In exchange for what?"

She had to close her eyes so she could block out the pain in his. "In exchange for me."

TWENTY-THREE

Nikolaos pulled the hood lower and pressed as tightly as he could to the side of the house. He had originally planned to wait, to sneak back when they should have all been leaving to go to the church. Then he could slip in, leave the gold, and hurry back out through the alleyways, beating them there—they would travel slowly, being so many in number. And no doubt Yiannis would want to stay dry, so he would go in a covered litter, which would guarantee an even slower pace.

But with every step Nikolaos took toward the church, the Lord had whispered louder. He had turned back. Now he pressed himself to the wall of the Visibullis house, beside the open window clothed in light and the fabric that swayed with every breeze. Just in time to hear Cyprus's words.

His eyes slid shut against the darkness.

His hand, chilled, moved into his pocket and the first of the three bags. He had split up the gold, so that he could carry it all without any lumps and bumps to draw attention. In a soft pouch of fabric, so the coins would not jingle overmuch.

He drew the first one out. Gripped it. Whispered, "May it find its aim. May it do its deed. May you bless it, Father, and Alexandria."

He pulled his arm back. Flung the bag past the curtain, into the room full of friends he loved like family. Listened as it burst upon the stone floor, raining coins down. And he ran.

They all jumped at the unexpected noise, Petros making sure his leap up put him in front of Cyprus. It took him a long moment to realize it was no threat that had flown through the window, that spilled upon the floor.

Gold. Gold upon gold, the coins flying upward as their bag hit the ground, rolling, circling.

The twins shrieked and scurried toward it, collecting the errant coins. Alexandria stood, holding up a scrap of parchment still attached to the nondescript black bag. Her eyes were wide. "It…it has my name. *Alexandria's dowry*, it says. It says…oh!" She pressed her hand, still clutching the bag, to her lips.

"No!" Yiannis surged to his feet, charged a step toward them, and met the arm Hero held out to keep him away. Petros could not see what expression his friend wore, but it must have been fearsome, for the other man drew up, fury in his eyes but his lips silent.

Cyprus's fingers dug into Petros's arm. "How could this be? Who would do it?"

He could only shake his head and turn back to watch.

Dorus pushed, wobbling, to his feet. "Gold…raining from the heavens. Do not just sit there, boys—see who is out the window!"

Felix beat Petros there, being closer. They pulled aside the fabric, peered out into the dark and the rain and the mystery. Called out, and got no answer.

Petros clapped a hand to Felix's shoulder. "Whoever did it

must be long gone."

"Twenty-five hundred sestertii." Alexandria's tremulous voice drew them all back around, away from the window, to her quaking, outstretched hands that overflowed with gold. "It is exactly the amount of my dowry. It is...it is a miracle."

Rhoda gripped her sister's shoulders and pulled her close, her own face jubilant. "Praise God! Glory be unto him! You can wed whomever you want, Xan. You will be *free*!"

Free. His gaze sought Cyprus, who watched from a step behind the twins, her eyes just as wide as theirs and shining blue hope. She had traded herself for them. She had made a deal with an evil man to save her sisters from the same fate she would take upon herself. A sacrifice he knew well had been born of the greatest love.

One he prayed would not be necessary. Would this gold be enough to get her out of it? If the twins split it between them?

Felix strode forward and halted before Alexandria. His head inclined in a show of respect. And something more. "You can give it to your sister, Alexandria. I would be honored to wed you with *no* dowry. Let us give it to her so she can marry Hero with his father's blessing."

Her lips still trembled. Her eyes were still damp. But she shoved the gold at her sister with a smile that defied any attempt at describing it. "Yes. Yes, Rhoda, it should be yours. Take it. You need it more."

Petros's gaze caught Cyprus's, tangled with it. Silently he asked, *Is that enough?*

Her lips parted.

Nikolaos crawled under the window, wishing there were a second one for this room. Wishing Hero would rush to Rhoda. But when Nikolaos peeked into the room, he saw that his friend had taken only a few steps toward her, away from the fuming Yiannis. He still fully faced the window.

Nikolaos ducked back down, safely out of sight.

"Would that I could say you did not need it, Rhoda. You know that I would wed you with nothing, were the choice solely mine." Shame colored Hero's tone. Guilt no doubt bent his shoulders.

Rhoda spoke his name in a voice fragrant with love.

Nikolaos peeked up again, over the window ledge. Hero was finally moving toward her.

Dorus, however, still stared at the center of the window. Glad he was to the side, behind the sheer fabric that would aid the night in protecting his identity, Nikolaos drew out the second pouch. Lifted it to his lips and whispered, "May it find its aim. May it do its deed. May you bless it, Father, and Rhoda."

He drew back and threw.

The second bag did not burst—likely because it struck Hero on the shoulder, and he softened its landing. He cried out and spun as if to face down his attacker before he seemed to realize what it was.

But Cyprus knew. She finally unstuck her feet from the floor and ran forward, scooping up the bag before anyone else could. "Rhoda! This one is for Rhoda!" She loosened the drawstring and poured the gold out into Petros's waiting palms, cupped to receive it.

She could not see for the tears. But she could still count. Or perhaps did not have to count. Another twenty-five hundred sestertii.

Yiannis cursed, shoved aside the servant trying to soothe him, and stormed from the room.

The air Cyprus drew in tasted of relief. She would not have to go to Timon tomorrow. Five thousand sestertii worth of gold had just flown through their window. Had rained down from heaven.

She jerked her head toward Abbas's chair. *Gold rained down from heaven.* But he was not there. He was lunging for the window, sticking his head far out into the night and letting in the rain.

"Who is out there?" he called. "Who? Show yourself!"

Cyprus pressed the now-empty bag into Rhoda's middle, kissed each of her sisters on the cheek, and dashed after Abbas. He leaned so far over the sill that he could well fall, being as weak as he was. She clutched at his shoulders and pulled him back in. "Easy, Abbas! Whoever it was, he is obviously a friend, not an enemy. Do not hurt yourself for trying to discover his identity."

"No." His eyes were bright. So bright they looked unnatural, feverish. He shrugged off her hands and gripped the window's ledge. "No, I must know. I must know who knew to make gold rain down."

Cyprus peered out into the night. There were lights everywhere—but they were pinpricks, like stars come down from heaven to light the city. They only made the shadows deeper, and the rain distorted everything, making solid what was vapor. And vapor what was solid. "Whoever it was is gone."

"No. No, he came back with a second. He will come back with a third."

She shook her head and, failing to tug Abbas away, at least tugged the fabric back into place to protect him from the rain. "I have no need of a dowry, Abbas. Timon will release me from my promise, he said he would—and Petros will marry me with nothing."

For the first time in weeks, he looked at her. Really looked at her, deep into her eyes. And he reached out a hand and touched hers where it rested nearby. "I have three daughters, Cyprus, not just two. You are every bit as deserving of gold as they. That you would do what you did for them..." He blinked, too rapidly to speak of anything but tears, and shook his head. "You shame me. And you make me so, so very proud. As your mother would be, if she could see what you would sacrifice for your family while I lay there as if already dead."

The sob choked her. And propelled her over, up, until she could wrap her arms around Abbas's neck.

Nikolaos had not dared run this time, lest they hear his steps. He had instead edged toward the corner of the house as silently as he could. Not so fast that any eyes would note one of the shadows moving. Not so fast that he failed to hear the exchange between Cyprus and Dorus.

Thank you, God. He was listening. He was seeing. All these years living in a home surrounded by faithful women, having come from a home of the most devout Christians—and this was the first Nikolaos had ever heard genuine love in his voice. Genuine seeking.

Dorus's heart had broken when Artemis succumbed to the sea—but now his pride finally had too, thanks to his daughter's willing humility.

Nikolaos rested a hand on the third bag of gold, where it rested against his stomach. The window would not work a third time, not with Dorus and Cyprus stationed there. *How then, Lord?*

A wisp of smoke teased his nose, and his eyes followed its

imagined path upward, to where it curled out of a neighbor's chimney, a darker shadow against the cloud-ridden sky. The rain was easing up, though it had not stopped entirely. Every home would have a fire lit tonight.

Fire. The hearth—the chimney. His pulse quickened. He could drop it down the chimney, if he could climb up onto the roof without being heard. Though if it landed on the fire, the bag could catch and burn, making it difficult for them to retrieve. He could send the coins down without the bag though. They would fall to the ground beneath the metal cradle that held the logs out of the ashes. It may be a chase for them to catch them all, but better a laughter-filled game than burned fingers.

He wasted no time on second thoughts. Instead he circled the house on silent feet, until he reached the wall that met it at the rear. Onto this he climbed, and then it was a matter of hooking his fingers into the crevices between each stone and pulling himself up.

The roof tiles were cold and slippery beneath his feet. And all of Patara spread out before him, a sea of twinkling lights in a world of darkness. His breath stuck in his throat as he stood and just watched each flame dance. Singing their silent praises to the One who had set each star in place.

He padded without a sound over the roof, back toward the front of the house. Smoke rose from the nearest chimney, the one belonging to the kitchen. The others were dormant, but for one—the one in the main chamber. He headed for it, each step careful.

How had Cyprus ever had the courage to fly from rooftop to rooftop, jumping between?

He drew the third bag out, unlooped it from around his neck. His hood was stiff with the oil he had coated it with, not wanting to let him take it off.

He won the argument. Lifted the bag. Closed his eyes against the smoke. And against emotion that he would not name. "May it find its aim. May it do its deed. May you bless it, Father, and Cyprus. And Petros. Bless them with all the joy they deserve."

He held the bag out over the chimney's opening. Tilted it over the hole. And let the gold rain down.

Gold rained again, its tinkling like a thousand bells, filling the room with a music Cyprus's ears had never known. She spun, and Abbas too, trying to figure out where the sound came from.

Petros pointed to the fireplace as the first coins landed with little puffs of ash. Then more, and more, and more still, the fire licking up around them and only making them shine. Some of them bouncing up, away from the fire, and landing in the shoes Cyprus had left there to dry.

Something caught in her throat. Maybe it was another cry. Maybe it was a laugh. She could hardly tell the difference. "You were right, Abbas."

His hands gripped her shoulders, stronger than they should have been, given how little he had eaten lately. "And I will find our benefactor. I must. Stay here."

She pivoted as he leaped—leaped!—out of the window. But she made no move to follow. She did not care, just now, who had given the gifts. It only mattered that God had heard and had chosen, this time, to spare them. He had met that most unreasonable demand of her father's...and he had provided a way for them all. A way that did not require her sacrificing herself.

Her eyes met Petros's. He should be angry with her. And he should be relieved. And he should be joyous and furious and exhausted from it all. He should need time to sort through it before he faced her.

He ran for her, pushing Yiannis aside when he dared to step into his path. Then his arms encircled her, and he was holding her flush against him and his voice was in her ear. "You beautiful, foolish girl. I love you."

Or maybe he should just say that, and no more. And hold her close while the last of the gold rained down into her shoes and her sisters clapped at seeing her in Petros's arms.

Nikolaos heard Dorus's shout as he loosed the last of the coins—and wondered if that little show had been his own will and not the Lord's. How would he get away unseen now? He tossed the bag down and headed away from Dorus's voice, weaving around the bedchambers' chimneys, no longer caring about making his footsteps silent.

For a moment, he saw Cyprus in his mind's eye, soaring overhead. But the houses in this part of town were not built so close together, even if he were crazed enough to want to fly as she had. No, he instead simply opted for the wall opposite the one he had climbed up, opposite where Dorus had run. He dropped down onto it, then onto the ground.

"Stop! I beg you!"

Too close—how had the old man moved so quickly after not eating for weeks? He should have been easy to outrun. Not even looking over his shoulder to see, Nikolaos took off.

His leather boots slipped on the wet stones with every other step, it seemed, his arms wheeling out by instinct whenever he turned a corner. And he turned them every chance he could get. He knew the city too well to get lost, but not well enough, apparently, to find a happy hole to duck into.

And all the while, Dorus pounded inexplicably behind him.

He must be drawing on reserves of energy Nikolaos could not fathom.

He took another turn, realizing too late his error—what had once been an open alley had recently had a building constructed at its end, closing it in. He was trapped. Unless he could scale another wall, scramble across another roof—

A hand closed over his shoulder, panting breath in his ear. "Stop this—take pity on an old man and *stop*."

Sighing, Nikolaos turned.

Dorus's eyes did not go wide. His face showed no surprise, just...elation. "Nikolaos. Why?"

His chest was too full to let in any discomfort. He spread his arms. "Because God loves you. And he did not want your daughters to pay this price."

Dorus's silver hair was onyx in the night and the rain. He nodded, once. "He loves *them*."

"You. All of you. The father as well as the daughters."

Every other time he had said anything like this, Dorus had turned away, deaf to the truth. This time, he soaked it in with the rain. "I do not deserve it."

"No. But he gives it anyway. As he gave his Son, first as a babe on this night nearly three hundred years ago. And then on a cross, to take your punishment for you."

"As my girls were willing to do for each other." He focused on the wall beside them. But saw, Nikolaos guessed, his daughters. "I never understood. I never...I loved Artemis. I loved my daughters. But not like that. How do you love like that?"

Nikolaos's lips pulled up. "By letting him love through you."

Nostrils flaring, Dorus nodded a slow, contemplative nod. "Perhaps." Then his eyes went sharp again. "Why the mystery, if you wished to do this for them?"

A mystery he had thought it absolutely necessary to preserve—but then, who would have had this conversation with Dorus? Even so. "They cannot know, Dorus. They will feel indebted to me. They will try for the rest of their lives to pay me back—or else they will shout of my generosity far and wide, and this will become about *me* rather than about God. And that is not what a gift should be. Not about the giver. A gift, a true gift given from nothing but love, should be done in secret. So that God alone sees. So that the giver's only reward is what the Lord decides to bestow. Not even the joy of seeing their joy. Just the joy of knowing one did what one ought."

Dorus lifted a brow. But it was not question in the expression. It was understanding. "You are a good man. I would have been proud to call you son, had God not laid his claim on you first."

Nikolaos smiled. And he felt down to his bones the truth of that—he was God's. Above all else. Above all others. "But he did. And Petros will be a far better son to you, and a husband to Cyprus. He loves her with that same love that baffles you."

"I know." Dorus stepped aside. "You had better hurry to the church. You have little time to get there and dry enough to fool your cousin."

Nikolaos nodded, repositioned the oiled hood, and took a step past Dorus, toward the street. He paused when even with him. "You promise me you will tell no one? As long as I live, no one can know."

"As long as I live, my lips will be sealed."

It would have to do. With another nod, he slid back out to the street and flew toward home. The church.

TWENTY-FOUR

Petros jiggled the gold out of Cyprus's shoes, smiling with every plink of every coin into his palm. Each one a blessing. Each one a token of God's great love for them.

Dorus sloughed his way back in, dripping and squishing with every step. And smiling like never before.

Cyprus turned to him, though she did not release Petros's arm. "Did you find him?"

Dorus shook his head. And peace shone from his eyes. "It does not matter though. I see now." He said no more, and he did not need to. His eyes said it for him.

Hero gripped Rhoda's hand. "To the church?"

Alexandria tucked hers into the crook of Felix's arm. "To the church."

"Give me a few minutes to change into dry clothes first." Dorus raised one finger. "I will be but a moment."

An adorable little sound like the mew of a kitten came from Cyprus's throat. "You will come with us, Abbas?"

His *smile*. "I will. Tonight and every other time you go. If you will have me by your side after all this."

The girls all shouted their agreement, sending Dorus out with a chuckle to get changed.

Petros slid the gold onto the table. It would probably not appease his parents—not when they were still dreaming of their son gaining the ear of the Augustus himself. But it would provide a house for him and Cyprus, out from under their roof. But close enough by that, when they saw that God had not wanted that for him, they could visit daily. Play with the children that would hopefully soon fill its rooms. Mother could teach Cyprus how to cook and keep a house until they could afford hands to help them. Father could walk with Petros to the courts every day.

Cyprus rested her cheek against the side of his arm. "Who was it, do you think?"

"I have my guess." For now though, he just kissed the top of her head and let the issue rest. "I will go with you tomorrow to tell Timon you do not need his gold."

Her chuckle rumbled against him. "He will be glad to hear it. He did not want you for an enemy."

Petros's lips quirked up. "He may be without scruples, but he is not without brains."

"I am ready!" Dorus hurried back into the room, clothing dry and arms carrying a load of stiff cloaks. "Something you girls missed when you were purging the house—the slicks I always took with me on my ships. They will keep us dry."

He handed them out, his eyes straying to the gold. He met Petros's gaze. "I would recommend not leaving that lying about for Yiannis or his men to find. He is put out enough that I doubt he would be above stealing what we could never prove was ours."

"Excellent point." Hero swept all three stacks into a bowl that had, earlier, had bread in it. "We will take it to my house, until after the service. If that is all right with everyone?"

When no one disagreed, they all headed out into the night. The rain had stopped, but it still splashed beneath their feet as they walked. Music to match the twinkling candles.

Petros kept Cyprus's hand tucked in his all the way there, through the brief stop to deposit gold and collect Mydon and his wife, to the church. He only let go once he had led Cyprus inside and situated her on one of the hard benches, nestled between a sister on one side and her father on the other.

"I will be right back," he said in a whisper. The room was full of whispers as the brethren filled it, packing in shoulder to shoulder. Everyone wanting to join in the worship on this holiest of nights. "I want to see Nikolaos."

She nodded, eyes bright with knowing.

He stole a long breath and slipped out of the crowded narthex, down the hall, into his cousin's familiar bedchamber.

Nikolaos was bent over his desk, an oil lamp spilling golden light on a tablet filled with writing. His hair was dry. So was his tunic.

Petros's was not, even given that the rain had been only mist on the way here and the oiled cape had covered him. Surely Nikolaos's hair should have been soaking wet if he were out in the downpour. It would not have had time to dry.

But he could think of no one else who had the means—and the desire—to save the Visibullises. "Did you do it?"

Nikolaos made one more letter before looking up, his smile vague and his eyes that particular kind of distant that bespoke great ideas simmering behind them. "Write my sermon? I did. I was just adding a few finishing touches. I think it will be a good one, Pet."

Petros shifted from one foot to the other. "That is not what I meant. The gold, Nikolaos. Was it you?"

His cousin's face was as blank as the scroll Hero had given him. "Gold?"

Could it *not* have been him? Suddenly Petros was none too

sure. "Someone tossed gold through the window and down the chimney. For the girls' dowries."

Now Nikolaos's eyes lit, and his lips smiled. "Praise God! It must have been someone from the church."

"Perhaps." Perhaps. And perhaps it did not matter *who*. Just *that*. "I would thank whoever did it."

Nikolaos chuckled, shuffled all his notes together, and stood. "Of course. But unless someone steps forward, I suppose we must give our thanks simply to the Lord."

"Indeed." Petros smiled and stepped aside so Nik could come through the door.

He paused before he did. "So when is the wedding?"

Petros's smile could only grow. "Soon."

EPILOGUE

Seventy Years Later

Artemis touched the flaming wood to the last of the candles and stepped back. They lit the whole room, the whole house. The very night.

One of the babies clapped. His older sister came up and slipped her hand into Artemis's wrinkled palm. "Why do we light the candles tonight, Grandmother?"

Artemis scooped up the little one and held her close. Breathed her in. Her little Mary was all freshness and life and love. "To remind us of the light God sent into the world on this night, my sweet. For us. Because he loves us so much."

Mary giggled at the kisses Artemis pressed to her neck, pushing away and clinging close all at once. Her eyes, as blue as Mater's had been, snagged on the hearth. "And why do we put out our shoes? It is a strange place to leave presents."

Artemis laughed, full and deep, and put little Mary back on her feet. "Have I not told you this story before?"

Mary's plump cheeks nearly covered her eyes as she screwed her face up in thought. "Have you?"

"I have. But...you may have fallen asleep during the telling last year."

"Not this year! I am four now. I will stay up *aaaaaaall* night. Until I see Saint Nikolaos come."

In the corner of the room, Mary's mother laughed. "You think so, sweetness? I think you should come sit here with me and listen to Grandmother's story."

Mary made no objection. She snuggled in between Korinna and her husband. And all the eyes in the room turned to Artemis.

She drew in a long breath and fingered a lock of silver hair that had slid over her shoulder. It had once been brown, as deep and dark as Korinna's was. As Abbas's had been. But it was Mater's hair she saw when she blinked—as red as a flame. As red as young Mary's.

"It happened many years ago. Before the Great Persecution of Diocletian that sent us all into hiding when I was a babe. Well before Constantine became emperor and made Christianity the faith of the empire. When Nikolaos was just training to be a priest in Patara, not yet a bishop in Myra. When it seemed all was lost."

She told the story of how her mother and aunts lost everything. Of how her grandfather had given up hope. She told the story of how no one would help them. Of how her mother would have been sold into slavery to save her sisters.

Of how Saint Nikolaos had tossed the gold down the chimney, into Mater's shoes, and set the world to rights. "And my grandfather chased him down, caught him, thanked him profusely—but Nikolaos made him swear he would never tell who it was. Because a gift should be given in secret, as Christ instructed. He did not want any praise for it."

Mary's eyes were wide...and sleepy. "How do we know, then? How do we know it was him?"

Artemis's lips turned up. "Because my grandfather confessed it to Abbas on his deathbed. But my father kept the secret. For years upon years, until his cousin died. But then...then *all* the stories came out. Of all the ways Nikolaos had helped people over the years. All the gifts he had given and never claimed. All the ways he had shown love to his flock. How he had stood up for justice. Fought for the brethren, protected them during the Persecution. And even appeared to people where he could not possibly be. Sometimes in dreams. Sometimes just *there.* Even after his death he would appear. Calming storms. Inspiring people to choose the right path."

Mary bounced. "But how, Grandmother? *How?*"

Artemis stood and walked over to the line of shoes waiting to be filled with almonds and fruit...and a single gold coin in the toes. Hers was not the only house that set them out, these days. Her aunts and their families had all started the tradition together, and Aunt Alexandria and Uncle Felix had taken it with them to Rome when they eventually settled there. All their neighbors in both East and West Empires had taken up the tradition too.

And those who had moved had no doubt shared the story where they went, and other children would wake up tomorrow to a surprise that would remind them of how God loved them. Everywhere, all through the empire, when people wanted to give a gift anonymously, they would sign *Saint Nikolaos* rather than their own name.

The giver. The wonder worker. A servant of God.

How?

She had asked Abbas that same question as she stood by his side at his cousin's funeral and listened to the grateful stories of a flock that would never forget him.

His answer found its place on her tongue now. And it was the only answer she would ever need. "Because he believed."

Turn the Page to Find . . .

Author's Note

What inspired the writing of this book and some interesting historical details on the real Nikolaos of Patara and Myra.

The Didache

Before the Bible was canonized,
when few families would have had the Scriptures,
they all had this—a pamphlet of The Teachings
of the Twelve Disciples,
which is basically a handbook on how to be a Christian.
It is believed to have been written
as early as 50 A.D.

Discussion Questions

For book clubs and reading groups,
or for you to ponder after reading.

AUTHOR'S NOTE

In December of 2014, I was getting frustrated with Christmas. The commercialism, the materialism, and all this *Santa* stuff. I wanted it all to mean something more...and I was ready to pull the plug on anything that didn't have to do with Jesus. But before I did, I decided to look up the history of who in the world Santa Claus really was, and what he had to do with my savior's birth.

What I discovered was not a jolly old elf full of magic. What I discovered was a man who loved God with his whole heart, who gave generously and in secret. What I discovered was a man who performed miracles, not magic. A true servant of the Lord—and I hated how his image had been perverted over the years.

As I read the stories that led to our Christmas traditions of stockings and gifts coming down chimneys, I knew I wanted to tell this tale in the context of my Visibullis family. And so, I did.

While there is much information on the man we know as Saint Nicholas, most of it clamors of exaggeration and lore. But there are kernels of truth to be found in it, and most sources agree on the basic facts—Nicholas (or Nikolaos, as it would have been said in Greek, his native tongue), was born and raised in Patara, Lycia (present day Turkey), which was Greek at the time. He would have been schooled there in his early years, gone to a larger city for high education, and then returned. We know he served as a priest in Patara, likely went to Jerusalem on pilgrimage, and ended up a priest and then a bishop in Myra, fifty kilometers from Patara. He protected his flock during what is known as the Great Persecution under the Roman Augustus, Diocletian. He quite possibly attended the Council of Nicaea in 325 during the reign of Constantine, where he is said to have slapped a false-theologian named Arius, who claimed that Christ was not divine.

The stories of his miracles are wide and bountiful, ranging from the healings he performed as a child, all the way up through visions people had of him after his death, in which he was said to have calmed angry seas and saved dozens of lives. A ruler even claimed, during Nikolaos's lifetime, that the saint appeared in his bedchamber one night to advise him against a decision that would harm the people. We cannot know where fact ends in these stories, but we *can* know that God is capable of using his servants in these miraculous ways if he so chooses.

In Europe, you would be hard pressed to find a town without a church dedicated to Saint Nicholas. And for centuries, children would put their shoes by the fireplace on December 6, the Feast Day of Saint Nicholas (the day he died) and receive small treats—and something golden, be it a coin or an orange—in the toe. For centuries, when someone wanted to give a gift anonymously, they would sign Nicholas's name instead of their own—their way of saying, "This is a gift from God, not from me."

Eventually, the celebrations of Nicholas and of Christmas merged together, though that would not really have been the case so soon after his death—my epilogue is pure poetic license. Saint Nicholas became the symbol of the one who gave gifts to remind us of the Christ child. Different cultures began adding his stories to their own histories, calling him by their own version of his name. It was the Dutch whose name for him (*Santa* meaning *saint* and *Claus* being a nickname for Nicholas) eventually stuck with Americans.

My prayer is that as you read this interpretation of who Nikolaos may have been as a young man, you come to appreciate that he was so much more than our traditions today give him credit for being. My prayer is that we can all take a few cues from him... that our gifts become less about us. And more about Him.

THE DIDACHE

TEACHING of the TWELVE APOSTLES

The Teaching of the Lord by the Twelve Apostles to the Gentiles.

Chap. I.

[1] There are two Ways, one of Life and one of Death; but there is a great difference between the two Ways.

[2] Now the Way of Life is this: First, you shall love God who made you; secondly, your neighbor as yourself; and all things whatsoever that you would not have done to you, neither do to another.

[3] Now the teaching of these words is this: Bless those who curse you, and pray for your enemies, and fast for those who persecute you; for what reward is there if you love those who love you? Do not even Gentiles the same? But love those who hate you, and you shall not have an enemy.

[4] Abstain from fleshly and bodily lusts. If anyone gives you a blow on the right cheek, turn to him the other also, and you shall be perfect. If anyone presses you to go with him one mile, go with him two; if any one takes away your cloak, give him also your tunic; if any one takes from you what is yours, ask it not back, as indeed you cannot. [5] Give to everyone that asks you, and ask not back, for the Father wills that from our own blessings we should give to all. Blessed is he who gives according to the com-

mandment, for he is guiltless. Woe to him who receives; for if any one receives, having need, he shall be guiltless, but he that has not need shall give account, why he received and for what purpose, and coming into distress he shall be strictly examined concerning his deeds, and he shall not come out from there till he has paid the last farthing.

6 But concerning this also it has been said, "Let your alms sweat into your hands till you know to whom you should give."

Chap. II.

1 And the second commandment of the Teaching is:

2 Do not kill. Do not commit adultery; do not corrupt boys; do not commit fornication. Do not steal. Do not use witchcraft; do not practice sorcery. Do not procure abortion, nor kill the newborn child. Do not covet your neighbor's goods.

3 Do not forswear yourself (swear falsely). Do not bear false witness. Do not speak evil; do not bear malice.

4 Do not be double-minded nor double-tongued; for duplicity of tongue is a snare of death.

5 Your speech shall not be false, nor vain, but fulfilled by deed.

6 Do not be covetous, nor rapacious, nor a hypocrite, nor malignant, nor haughty. Do not take evil counsel against your neighbor.

7 Do not hate anyone, but some do rebuke and for some do pray, and some do love above your own soul (or, life).

Chap. III.

1 My child, flee from every evil, and from everything that is like unto it.

2 Be not prone to anger, for anger leads to murder; nor given to party spirit, nor contentious, nor quick-tempered (or, passionate); for from all these things murders are generated.

[3] My child, be not lustful, for lust leads to fornication; neither be a filthy talker, nor an eager gazer, for from all these are generated adulteries.
[4] My child, be not an observer of birds [for divination] for it leads to idolatry; nor a charmer (enchanter), nor an astrologer, nor a purifier (a user of purifications or expiations), nor be willing to look on those things; for from all these is generated idolatry.
[5] My child, be not a liar, for lying leads to theft; nor avaricious, nor vainglorious, for from all these things are generated thefts.
[6] My child, be not a murmurer, for it leads to blasphemy; neither self-willed (presumptuous), nor evil-minded, for from all these things are generated blasphemies.
[7] But be meek, for the meek shall inherit the earth.
[8] Be long-suffering, and merciful, and harmless, and quiet, and good, and trembling continually at the words which you have heard.
[9] Do not exalt yourself, nor give audacity (presumption) to your soul. Your soul shall not be joined to the lofty, but with the just and lowly shall you converse.
[10] The events that befall you accept as good, knowing that nothing happens without God.

Chap. IV.

[1] My child, remember night and day him that speaks to you the word of God, and honor him as the Lord, for where the Lordship is spoken of, there is the Lord.
[2] And seek out day by day the faces of the saints, that you may rest upon their words.
[3] Do not desire (make) division, but make peace between those at strife. Judge justly; do not respect a person (or, show partiality) in rebuking for transgressions.
[4] Do not be double-minded (doubtful in your mind) whether it

shall be or not.
[5] Be not one that stretches out his hands for receiving, but draws them in for giving.
[6] If you have [anything], give with your hands a ransom for your sins.
[7] Do not hesitate to give, nor in giving should you murmur, knowing who is the good recompenser of the reward.
[8] Do not turn away him that needs, but share all things with your brother, and do not say that they are your own; for if you are fellow-sharers in that which is imperishable (immortal), how much more in perishable (mortal) things?
[9] Do not take away your hand from your son or from your daughter, but from [their] youth up teach [them] the fear of God.
[10] Do not in your bitterness lay commands on your man-servant (bondman), or your maid-servant (bondwoman), who hope in the same God, lest they should not fear Him who is God over [you] both; for He comes not to call [men] according to the outward appearance, but on those whom the Spirit has prepared.
[11] But you, bondmen, shall be subject to our masters as to the image of God in reverence and fear.
[12] Hate all hypocrisy, and everything that is not pleasing to the Lord.
[13] Do not forsake the commandments of the Lord, but keep what you have received, neither adding nor taking away.
[14] In the congregation confess your transgressions, and do not come to your prayer with an evil conscience.
This is the way of life.

Chap. V.

[1] But the way of death is this. First of all it is evil and full of curse; murders, adulteries, lusts, fornications, thefts, idolatries, witchcrafts, sorceries, robberies, false-witnessings, hypocrisies, dou-

ble-heartedness, deceit, pride, wickedness, self-will, covetousness, filthy-talking, jealousy, presumption, haughtiness, boastfulness.

[2] Persecutors of the good, hating truth, loving a lie, not knowing the reward of righteousness, not cleaving to that which is good nor to righteous judgment, watchful not for that which is good but for that which is evil; far from whom is meekness and endurance, loving vanity, seeking after reward, not pitying the poor, not toiling with him who is vexed with toil, not knowing Him that made them, murderers of children, destroyers of the handiwork of God, turning away from the needy, vexing the afflicted, advocates of the rich, lawless judges of the poor, wholly sinful. May you, children, be delivered from all these.

Chap. VI.

[1] Take heed that no one lead you astray from this way of teaching, since he teaches you apart from God.

[2] For if indeed you are able to bear the whole yoke of the Lord, you are perfect; but if you are not able, do what you can.

[3] And as regards food, bear what you can, but against idol-offerings be exceedingly on your guard, for it is a service of dead gods.

Chap. VII.

[1] Now concerning baptism, baptize thus: Having first taught all these things, baptize into the name of the Father, and of the Son, and of the Holy Spirit, in living water.

[2] And if you have not living water, baptize into other water; and if you cannot in cold, then in warm.

[3] But if you have neither, pour thrice upon the head in the name of the Father, and of the Son, and of the Holy Spirit.

[4] But before Baptism let the baptizer and the baptized fast, and any others who can; but do command the baptized to fast for one

or two days before.

Chap. VIII.

[1] Let not your fasts be with the hypocrites, for they fast on the second and fifth day of the week; but you shall fast on the fourth day, and the preparation day (Friday).

[2] Neither pray you as the hypocrites, but as the Lord commanded in His Gospel, so pray you: "Our Father, who is in heaven, hallowed be Your Name. Your Kingdom come. Your will be done, as in heaven, so on earth. Give us this day our daily bread. And forgive us our debt as we also forgive our debtors. And bring us not into temptation, but deliver us from the evil one. For Yours is the power and the glory forever."

[3] Pray thus thrice a day.

Chap. IX.

[1] Now as regards the Eucharist (the Thank-offering), give thanks after this manner:

[2] First for the cup: "We give thanks to You, our Father, for the holy vine of David Your servant, which You have made known to us through Jesus, Your servant: to You be the glory forever."

[3] And for the broken bread: "We give thanks to You, our Father, for the life and knowledge which You have made known to us through Jesus, Your servant: to You be the glory forever.

[4] "As this broken bread was scattered upon the mountains and gathered together became one, so let Your church be gathered together from the ends of the earth into Your kingdom, for Yours is the glory and the power through Jesus Christ forever."

[5] But let no one eat or drink of your Eucharist, except those baptized into the name of the Lord; for as regards this also the Lord has said: "Give not that which is holy to the dogs."

Chap. X.

1 Now after being filled, give thanks after this manner:
2 "We thank You, Holy Father, for Your Holy Name, which You
have caused to dwell in our hearts, and for the knowledge and
faith and immortality which You have made known to us through
Jesus Your Servant, to You be the glory forever.
3 "You, O, Almighty Sovereign, did make all things for Your
Name's sake; You gave food and drink to men for enjoyment
that they might give thanks to You; but to us You did freely give
spiritual food and drink and eternal life through Your Servant.
4 "Before all things we give thanks to You that You are mighty;
to You be the glory forever.
5 "Remember, O Lord, Your Church to deliver her from all evil
and to perfect her in Your love; and gather her together from the
four winds, sanctified for Your kingdom which You did prepare
for her; for Yours is the power and the glory forever.
6 "Let grace come, and let this world pass away. Hosanna to the
God of David. If anyone is holy let him come, if anyone is not
holy let him repent. Maranatha. Amen."
7 But permit the Prophets to give thanks as much as they wish.

Chap. XI.

1 Whoever then comes and teaches you all the things aforesaid,
receive him.
2 But if the teacher himself being perverted teaches another
teaching to the destruction [of this], hear him not, but if to the
increase of righteousness and the knowledge of the Lord, receive
him as the Lord.
3 Now with regard to the Apostles and Prophets, according to the
decree of the gospel, so do.
4 Let every Apostle that comes to you be received as the Lord.
5 But he shall not remain [longer than] one day; and, if need be,

another also; but if he remains three he is a false prophet.
[6] And when the Apostle departs, let him take nothing except bread till he reaches his lodging. But if he asks for money, he is a false prophet.
[7] And every prophet who speaks in the spirit you shall not try or prove; for every sin shall be forgiven, but this sin shall not be forgiven.
[8] Not everyone that speaks in the spirit is a Prophet, but only if he has the behavior of the Lord. By their behavior then shall the false prophet and the [true] Prophet be known.
[9] And no Prophet that orders a table in the spirit eats of it [himself], unless he is a false prophet.
[10] And every Prophet who teaches the truth if he does not practice what he teaches, is a false prophet.
[11] And every approved, genuine Prophet, who makes assemblies for a worldly mystery, but does not teach [others] to do what he himself does, shall not be judged by you; for he has his judgment with God; for so did also the ancient Prophets.
[12] But whosoever says in the spirit: Give me money or any other thing, you shall not listen to him; but if he bid you to give for others that lack, let no one judge him.

Chap. XII.

[1] Let everyone that comes in the name of the Lord be received, and then proving him you shall know him; for you shall have understanding right and left.
[2] If indeed he who comes is a wayfarer, help him as much as you can; but he shall not remain with you longer than two or three days, unless there be necessity.
[3] If he wishes to settle among you, being a craftsman, let him work and eat.
[4] But if he has not handicraft, provide according to your

understanding that no Christian shall live idle among you.
[5] And if he will not act thus he is a Christ-trafficker. Beware of such.

Chap. XIII.

[1] But every true Prophet who wishes to settle among you is worthy of his food.
[2] Likewise a true Teacher is himself worthy, like the workman, of his food.
[3] Therefore do take and give all the first-fruit of the produce of the wine-press and threshing-floor, of oxen and sheep, to the Prophets; for they are your chief-priests.
[4] But if you have no Prophet, give to the poor.
[5] If you prepare bread, take the first fruit and give according to the commandment.
[6] Likewise when you open a jar of wine or of oil, take the first-fruit and give to the Prophets.
[7] And of silver, and raiment, and every possession, take the first-fruit, as may seem good to you, and give according to the commandment.

Chap. XIV.

[1] And on the Lord's of the Lord come together, and break bread, and give thanks, having before confessed your transgressions, that your sacrifice may be pure.
[2] Let no one who has a dispute with his fellow come together with you until they are reconciled, that your sacrifice may not be defiled.
[3] For this is that which was spoken by the Lord: "In every place and time offer me a pure sacrifice, for I am a great King, says the Lord, and my name is wonderful among the Gentiles."

Chap. XV.

[1] Elect therefore for yourselves Bishops and Deacons worthy of the Lord, men meek, and not lovers of money, and truthful, and approved; for they too minister to you the ministry of the Prophets and Teachers.

[2] Therefore despise them not, for they are those that are the honored among you with the Prophets and Teachers.

[3] And reprove one another not in wrath, but in peace, as you have in the gospel; and with every one that transgresses against another let no one speak, nor let him hear from you until he repents.

[4] But so do your prayers and alms and all your actions as you have in the gospel of our Lord.

Chap. XVI.

[1] Watch over your life; let not your lamps be quenched and let not your loins be unloosed, but be ready; for you know not the hour in which our Lord comes.

[2] But be frequently gathered together, seeking the things that are profitable for your souls; for the whole time of your faith shall not profit you except that in the last season you be found perfect.

[3] For in the last days the false prophets and destroyers shall be multiplied, and the sheep shall be turned into wolves, and love shall be turned into hate.

[4] For when lawlessness increases, they shall hate and persecute, and deliver up one another; and then shall appear the world-deceiver as Son of God, and shall do signs and wonders, and the earth shall be delivered into his hands, and he shall commit iniquities which have never yet come to pass from the beginning of the world.

[5] And then shall the race of men come into the fire of trial, and many shall be offended and shall perish; but they who endure in

their faith shall be saved from under the curse itself.
[6] And then shall appear the signs of the truth: first the sign of opening in heaven; then the sign of the voice of the trumpet; and the third, the resurrection of the dead.
[7] Not, however, of all, but as was said, "The Lord shall come, and all the saints with him."
[8] Then shall the world see the Lord coming upon the clouds of heaven.

DISCUSSION QUESTIONS

1. What were your thoughts on gift-giving and Christmas traditions before reading this novel? Did the story make you think of anything differently? Were you surprised to learn about who the original Santa Claus really was?

2. In the first chapter, when Cyprus has her accident, we get a glimpse into the Greek thinking about children and their worth. Were you surprised by it? Angered? What would you have told your parents about the miracle if you were in Cyprus's shoes?

3. When we meet Nikolaos, he is performing a miracle for the first time in years; yet through the book, we see even him struggle to reconcile his doubt with his faith, his feelings with his knowledge. Do you ever struggle against what you know is God's plan for you? Or question whether He can use you? Did his story change your perspective at all on the miraculous? On the men who make decisions to follow God rather than raise a family?

4. What would you have done in the sisters' position after the ship went down? Would you have remained by Dorus's side or risked the dangers of the world to get away from him?

5. What did you think of Petros's decisions through the book—in how he dealt with his feelings for Cyprus, for Nikolaos, and what he did for the Visibullises?

6. Were you surprised by Cyprus's decision to save her sisters? Did you agree with it?

7. Yiannis represents the prevailing Greek/Roman mindset during the time. What were your thoughts when he came on the scene? How would you have reacted to his presence and demands?

8. Petros's mother thinks she's acting for the good of her son and the entire church. Do you think she had a valid point? How do you think she would have reacted to Petros's decisions at the end of the book?

9. At the end, we see the story of why we get gifts in our stockings that have come down the chimney. Did you know this story already? Was it surprising? Fun? Odd?

10. In the Epilogue, our main characters' descendants are musing on how Nikolaos managed to do all he'd done: because he believed. How is this still carried out in your Christmas traditions today? Do you have any traditions you feel embody the true spirit of Saint Nicholas? The Christ child? Any you'd like to change or add?

YOU MAY ALSO ENJOY...

Austen in Austin
Eight Texas-set novellas based on Jane Austen's novels

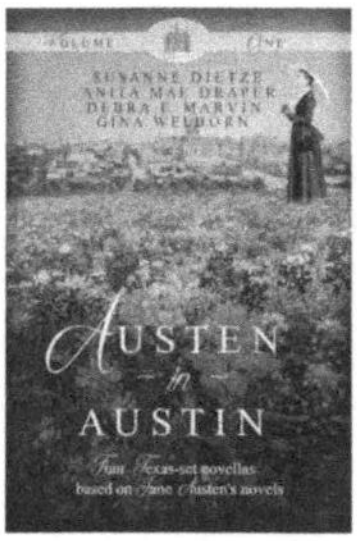

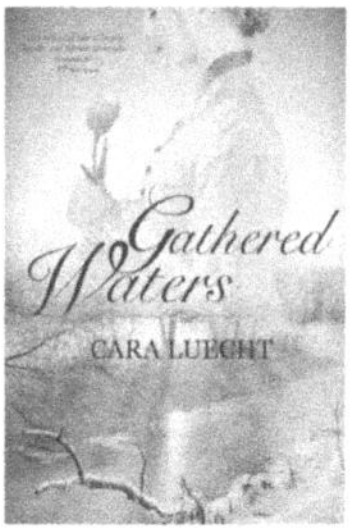

Gathered Waters
By Cara Luecht

They want to worship as their hearts demand...
but can they sacrifice everything for it?

CPSIA information can be obtained
at www.ICGtesting.com
Printed in the USA
LVHW091254101119
636878LV00001B/84/P

9 781939 023834